Second Edition
ISBN: 978-1-7388676-3-9 (Special Edition Paperback)
ISBN: 978-1-7388676-1-5 (eBook)

Content warnings include descriptions of violence, death, blood, and violence towards women and children.

# C. H. FOLAN

# THE QUEEN IS DEAD

*For every woman who has had her story stolen from her
and those who have fought to take it back.*

# PRONUNCIATION GUIDE

**Alane:** AH-Lane
**Bodhe:** Bo-DEE
**Eimear:** EE-Mur
**Fiadh:** FEE-ah
**Findlaech:** Fin-LAYCH
**Gille:** Gill-YAH
**Gruoch:** GREW-ahch
**Laoise:** LEE-sha
**Mael:** MAY-il
**Eldr:** EL-durr
**Mo lasair:** Mu-LAH-sir
**Mormaer:** MOR-mur

# MAP OF THE AREA AS REIMAGINED FOR THE STORY

*The queen, my lord, is dead*

*-Act 5, Macbeth*

# PART ONE
## -A GIRL-

# ONE
# ELDR

*I must tell you that most of what you know of me is a lie.*

*True, some of this fabrication is of my own doing, my blood and sweat bringing together the threads that were woven into the tapestry of my life. Nevertheless, I have allowed my deeds and choices to become narrative and evolve into lore.*

*It is the natural progression of any story.*

*However, I object to how my tale has been usurped by the men who appeared in it. I suppose it is a woman's lot to be first a father's daughter, then her husband's wife, and finally, possibly, her son's mother. In the world into which I had been born, a woman was most easily character-ized by the men who owned her. I am sure that the kingdoms of Moray and Alba, those territories that would later be known as Scotland, were not alone in their predisposition to mistake being indentured for having an identity.*

*The world that created me was a broken one, composed of scarred territories and bitter men playing at kings. Moray, my home, had laid in dominion to Alba for generations, taxed heavily and used as the first line of defence against marauding Norsemen and other mysterious enemies that spilled forth from the northern sea. Mac Bethad tried, as did we all, to bring Moray the freedom and the peace it deserved. It has been said in* the years since that the road to hell is paved with the best of intentions. The dead that haunt me still have assured me that my eventual passage toward the eternal shall be one bathed in the shadows of old blood.

It is a fate I have long since accepted, and though my death may not be restful, I can only hope that it will bring me once more to the sides of those I have loved and lost. For yes, even I, history's most fiendish queen, have loved and been loved in return. And like many women before me, love was an insufficient shield against the full rage of a world thrown off its delicate balance.

Here am I sure that I have lost some of you. I hear your angry words, your bitter protest. You were a queen, I hear you say. You were first a lord's wife and then a king's. What could you possibly know of hardship? Of toil?

I have known the back of a husband's hand, have been subject to his drunken whims, and have toiled to bring forth his heir. There is no woman, no matter how common or how highly born, who has not been in some way subject to the desires and ordinances of a man.

I will, however, grant one concession.

I was never a victim.

I was always exactly what I needed to be.

Those who knew me called me murderess, witch, hag, and crone. Others called me My Lady and Your Majesty.

One called me Mother.

One called me mo lasair—my fire.

I carry all of these names with me. I have collected them and made from them an armour that no arrow nor sword can pierce. This armour is made of the strongest metal and forged in the heat of my lust and anger. I know every chink in its mail and its every weakness.

Leave the tapestries to my sisters.

Bring me my sword.

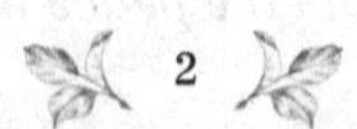

Her first husband's name was Gille Coemgáin mac Maíl Brigti, and their earliest meeting took place when Gruoch was fifteen years old. When the ravages of time had left her an old woman, and she found herself turning in her bed in the deep quiet of the night, unable to sleep, Gruoch would sometimes allow herself to think back upon that first meeting.

Gille had been tall and thin and walked with a particular hunch, leaning much like a tree will when subjected too long to harsh winds. Or like one that has learned to bend to save from snapping at the trunk or lifting at the root.

There had been a flurry of excitement when he had entered the fortress and into Gruoch's life. He and a handful of his men had ridden past the gates and into the main yard, their black and bay horses slick with sweat, mouths foaming around their filthy bits. Gille had been at the head, calling out in a loud voice for the King's son to show himself. Gruoch had been worried at first upon hearing the harshness of his tone but had felt considerably better as she heard her father's hearty laugh respond to the stranger's call.

"Gille, have you lost your way on my mountain? Or have you finally taken me up on my offer of hospitality?"

Bodhe's head appeared, following shortly after the sound of his voice as it boomed through the hall's main doors. The heavy wood creaked as he made his way through, his powerful hands pushing them open as though they weighed nothing. Gruoch knew that each door carried a considerable heft since they were a practical defence against both the cold winter winds and any marauding tribes or soldiers.

Though her father was shorter than Gille by at least two hands, his broad shoulders and ruddy face made for an imposing figure. If Gille was the bending birch tree, Bodhe was a stout pine, made to outlive and outlast its gentler, deciduous cousin. The sturdy logs of such pines had built their fortress and the walls that surrounded it, and Bodhe loved to recount how he and his men had felled those trees and built their homes themselves.

Crinan, the mysterious great-grandfather Gruoch had never met, had been blessed with an abundance of heirs. This blessing had meant an assurance of the line and guaranteed the younger children a liberty not afforded to their elder siblings. Some had been presented with an escape from the tediousness and constraints of court, and when Bodhe, a languishing middle son, had asked for this freedom, it had been gladly granted. Crinan had been pleased that his son would want to live so far north, further still than Inverness, the closest settlement of its size nearby. As Bodhe was fond of reminding his daughter, it was important that a leader lived out among his people and that he was seen often and everywhere. A man who could not live among his men was not a leader, and one who hid himself away in a castle could never hope to be the kind of man who inspired true love and confidence.

Her father had claimed these things, and as she did with most everything Bodhe told her, Gruoch held the advice close to her heart.

Gille's smile was genial as he held out a waiting hand at Bodhe's approach. Bodhe clasped it soundly and grinned, taking a step back as Gille slid down from his mount. He held out the reins without looking, and a young boy, who received a swift swat from his father as motivation, quickly grabbed for them.

Gruoch looked on at the travelling party and counted eight astride and twelve more on foot. Their stables were solid and well built and would probably house the additional horses along with Bodhe's own, but it would be a tight fit should the twelve men a-ground be expecting to share the stable tonight.

Bodhe's voice did not carry as he spoke to his friend. After a moment, the tall man clapped his host's back and guided him toward the other riders, who were quickly dismounting. The men were dressed against the April chill, and Gruoch noticed that a few wore mantles of fur over their belted tunics, whose ornately trimmed sleeve cuffs and necklines denounced them as nobility. One of these, a man whose dark, coppery brown hair fell about his eyes, caught the girl's stare as he pushed back the stray strands. He grinned openly at her and nudged a man to his right while he nodded in her direction. His companion, a black-haired man with an impressive beard, snorted in response and shoved his friend away from their horses and towards the main hall.

"And what do you think you'll spy, little eldr? A king?"

Gruoch felt Hertha's hand clamp onto her shoulder. The pinch of strong fingers and a rough whisper sent a fright through her body. A gasp flew from her mouth, and Gruoch clasped a hand to it as she was spun around, coming face to face with her guardian.

"A king, Hertha?" Gruoch's voice was muffled by the fingers that still hid her grin. "Do you think so?"

"Hardly a king, little flame. A man pretending at kingship is more like." Her tone was gruff, curt. Hertha looked past Gruoch and toward Gille, who was making his way into the hall, its heavy door held open by one of Bodhe's men.

"I knew he was not a king," came Gruoch's tart reply. "He is not wearing a crown, and his tunic is made of too coarse a wool."

Hertha swatted at her charge's head. Though she attempted to duck quickly, Gruoch's movements were too slow to escape Hertha's deft palms. While Gruoch felt a hand smack at the back of her head, the touch was gentle and failed to live up to the ferocious airs Hertha allowed her voice to adopt when she spoke to her charge.

It amused Gruoch that this voice was never so daring when it was addressed to her father.

The Norse woman had once travelled with the North Men who had sailed across the narrow seas from their pagan countries in swift longboats, armed with cruel axes and crueller intentions. Hertha sometimes told stories of her country, with its rocky shores and flat lands. She said it was a land that had existed before time and that her gods were even older than the Christian God and the Christ, his son, an idea that scandalized Gruoch while also filling her with a secret thrill. Hertha had been a healer in her home country as well as a warrior, and it was her skill with medicine that had kept her alive when Bodhe and his father had beaten the heathen northerners back to their ships and into the sea.

She claimed to have been shaped by the wind and toughened against the rocks. Whenever Gruoch took in Hertha's pale blue eyes and ashen blonde hair, she found such a story easy to believe. There were deepset lines at the corners of Hertha's mouth and eyes, as though the years of scowling had etched them there permanently. She boasted that her knowledge of plants and ability to read the skies had come from the gods themselves, given over the centuries to humans who knew how to listen to them. Her knowledge of herb lore and healing was astounding, and her reputation had spread across her master's territories.

She had been lady's maid and protector to Gruoch since the death of Bodhe's wife during his daughter's sixth winter.

And Gruoch loved her.

"Aye, you're a wise one yet, *eldr*," Hertha said, grabbing at a red braid and tugging it gently.

Gruoch pushed the hand away, smoothing the ginger plait back and away from her shoulder, letting it fall against her back. Such auburn locks were a trait in her family and in many of the families who lived across Moray. When she had still been a small child, enraptured with the wild woman's magical potential, Gruoch had been told that she was eldr, which meant flame in the tongue of the Norsemen. Hertha had sworn that if the fire in Gruoch's heart could but one day match the fire in her hair, she would be unstoppable.

Hertha had regaled Gruoch with stories of women in her native country who fought like demons alongside their men, riding their horses and carrying shields and blades. Gruoch didn't much care for the idea of having to ride into battle and had told her guardian as much, reminding Hertha that Bodhe had been a more cunning warrior than she and her family of marauders. Under her father's protection, the people of Moray could build their homes and raise their families, knowing that their lord would keep them safe whenever the heathen would-be conquerors chose to cross the bitter sea.

"Leave at my hair, Hertha," Gruoch said, trying to sound cross and authoritative. "I'm not a child."

"No, in this, you are right, little flame. I know this, you know this, and I suspect your father may have recently remembered it as well."

Gruoch narrowed her green eyes as she drew her shoulders back, trying and failing to appear imposing. "What do you know, Hertha?"

"I know nothing, girl," Hertha replied, turning away suddenly." But I know enough to know the things of which I know nothing about." Then, she paused and looked back at Gruoch, smiling as the girl worked to decipher what she had heard.

The moment of levity was short-lived, and Hertha motioned impatiently to Gruoch that she should follow. Gruoch turned to cast one quick look back at the visitors. She caught a glimpse of the black-bearded man making his way into the hall, closely followed by the man with the rich brown hair, the one who had smiled at her. She felt a girlish flutter in her chest, though she resigned herself to tear her gaze away and follow Hertha away from the hall and towards the main house.

"Does my father mean for me to marry?" Gruoch called her question ahead to Hertha, whose brisk pace kept her a few feet away. *Oh please, God*, Gruoch thought to herself as she felt her cheeks burn. *Let it be the one with the hair in his eyes, the one who smiled at me. I think I should die to love so handsome a husband.*

Hertha snorted derisively. The sound irritated Gruoch and shattered her hopeful mood. The girl bristled as she picked her way carefully through the yard. Hertha had never married, never borne children, and would ever be a slave in Bodhe's house. Even though in her secret heart, Gruoch loved her foster mother dearly, Hertha's response to her question had set Gruoch's blood afire and quickened her temper. She forced herself to breathe, knowing that Hertha would take satisfaction from riling her.

"Oh yes, marriage. What else in this world could you hope for or expect, girl? If you're so anxious to wed, why not ask him directly? Do you have a suitor in mind? Could it be the rider I caught you staring at like a lovesick farmer's daughter?"

"I am a farmer's daughter," Gruoch shot back.

"You are a lord's daughter, a prince's daughter, and you ken it well." Though the tone remained casual, Gruoch understood that Hertha had no intention of humouring any girlish fantasies. "Your father might own these lands, might ride through them and may have the final say in what lives or dies here, but don't make the mistake of thinking he is of the land and for the land in the way his tenants are." Hertha walked up to the front door of their home and turned, waiting for Gruoch to catch up to her. "You aren't one of them, *eldr*. You mustn't ever forget that. They won't."

"And you mustn't forget yourself, Hertha," Gruoch told her as she walked past and through the open door. "I am the lady of this house, and you will speak to me thus."

This time Hertha's slap was true, and as Gruoch stepped through the threshold, she did so rubbing the back of her tousled head.

# TWO
# THE BRAZEN AUDACITY

Hertha forced Gruoch to change her tunic and handed over one of delicate white linen whose cuffs had been carefully embroidered with decorative trim. She took out Gruoch's windswept plait and combed thoroughly through the long, red hair, taking the time to smooth the locks and tame the tangles that inevitably found their way there. She smoothed the hair as best she could, using her spit-laden palm more than once in an effort to calm it. Once the waves had been somewhat smoothed, they left it hanging loose and flowing down Gruoch's back.

The girl had been warned of the dangers of vanity and the virtues of modesty by the holy men who had travelled the road South, stopping to rest and preach in Bodhe's hall. Still, she felt a secret thrill when the silk of her hair brushed against her neck or when she caught sight of it in a polished surface or still pool. She was sinfully proud of it and knew it was becoming, and Gruoch was pleased that Hertha had left it loose rather than braiding it back and away from the face in the crowned style of the Norse people.

When Hertha went to pin the folds of fabric at Gruoch's shoulder, the girl was surprised to see her mother's brooch in the older woman's hand. Hertha handled it gently and pinned it to the mantle, securing two corners tightly. The thick fabric had been dyed a light purple, and Bodhe had purchased it from a travelling peddler a few seasons ago. It was another of Gruoch's silly and secret pleasures, as she knew the purple favoured her colouring. Such fine things rarely saw the world outside their home, and her mother's brooch never left the small hide bag that housed it. Gruoch watched breathlessly as Hertha passed the corners of the mantle through the circular ring, which she carefully pierced with the pin. The polished silver gleamed in the soft light.

"Will we be dining in the hall with the men, the travellers?" Gruoch asked, trying and failing to keep an easy and casual tone.

Hertha looked at Gruoch sharply before busying herself with the folds of the mantle, making sure that they hung just right against the young girl's back. Gruoch stood quietly and allowed Hertha to preen and tidy her charge as she saw fit. For all her grumblings and sharp words, Gruoch knew Hertha loved her almost as much as she herself loved the older woman. Though she was, in all reality, their prisoner, Hertha was a valued and trusted member of the household. Bodhe often listened to her stories of battle and went to her for healing. He had even built their hall, a long, low building made of wooden poles and mud, in the style of her countrymen. He had adorned it with tables for his tenants and any visiting dignitaries to use, and many meals had been served there during his tenure.

"Remember that even an enemy is a source of knowledge and an opportunity to grow," her father had often said while Gruoch sat adoringly at his knee, his rough hands petting her wild and burnished hair. He had claimed that the Romans had also adopted ideas and styles from the peoples they had conquered and that this habit had made them all the stronger. He valued the wisdom and opinions that Hertha brought to his home. He treated her accordingly: he had granted her stewardship over his only legitimate heir after the death of his wife, the only woman he would ever wed.

"Am I beautiful, Hertha?" Gruoch's voice was timid and low. The older woman paused in her work to look up, eyes harrowed by hard lines. Still, within them shone a light that was soft and sorrowful.

"Eldr, you burn brighter than many, and many a man will you draw to your light." Here she paused, reaching up to tuck a stray strand of red silk behind Gruoch's ear. "But remember that fire is a temporary thing: it can only burn while there is something to consume. So don't let this concern with beauty be what consumes you. Instead, kindle your flame and nurture your spirit. Use your beauty if you will and remember that a woman must become adept at whatever weapons she has."

"Why must everything be about fighting? Why can you not simply give me an answer? Speak plainly!"

Hertha's hands came to Gruoch's face, and she held the head squarely and pulled the girl slightly closer. Her pale blue eyes looked deeply into the green ones that shone in the younger face.

"Tread carefully tonight, Gruoch," she said quietly. "You are not your own. Protect your heart, and don't be so quick to give it away."

The two women stood there for a moment with their gazes locked until Gruoch felt her neck begin to ache with the effort of leaning towards Hertha, and she gently pulled away. Hertha's hands released their hold, and she stepped back quickly. Whatever softness had been in the troubled eyes was quickly smothered by the cool detachment that usually hung there.

Gruoch smoothed the front of her tunic and gently touched her mother's brooch. She smiled at Hertha and nervously grabbed at a long lock of red hair, bringing it over her shoulder as she ran her fingers through the ends.

"Your face holds every secret you hide in your heart, girl. You think you can mask your thoughts, but you are not as talented as you may think." Hertha turned from her charge as she spoke and made her way toward the door. "If you mean to survive, you will have to learn to lie."

The noise of the men in her father's hall reached Gruoch before she and Hertha had stepped through the door. The raucous echoes of riotous laughter and booming voices carried through the longhouse, filling the space up into its rafters. The sound was only as strong as the smell of bodies, warm and unwashed after a long and muddy ride. Gruoch supposed that the riders had likely come from further North and were likely journeying South, as did most who passed through Bodhe's lands and supped at his hall. These men were hungry and weary from their journey, and the hall, with its warm fires and crisp ales, offered a welcome respite from the hard road.

Hertha guided Gruoch towards the first table, where her father sat next to the tall man who had ridden at the company's head. Bodhe's balding head was bent near his guest's, whose own light brown hair was speckled with slight hints of grey. The latter seemed to be regaling his host with some humorous tale not meant for a lady's ear since he faltered in his words as he caught sight of their approach. Bodhe slapped his companion soundly on the back and urged him to continue, much to the apparent embarrassment of his guest. Gruoch turned her face away as she sat, as much to avoid whatever unsavoury topic was being chewed as to alleviate some of the speaker's discomforts.

Hertha stood close behind as she often did when they had guests. She would sometimes dare to sit next to Gruoch at the table when the hall was quiet, but she kept her distance now, a mask of placid servitude sitting neatly over her usually fearsome features.

A serving girl brought over a plate of roasted rabbit, and Gruoch allowed another to fill her cup with ale, although she had never really developed a taste for the drink. Hertha would bring a cup of water when she could, but now with the eyes of her father's guests upon her, Gruoch could hardly refuse to partake in what Bodhe had offered them as refreshment.

Her stomach was twisted into knots, such that the idea of eating any of the fragrant meal placed before her seemed unlikely and possibly treacherous. She concentrated on tearing tiny pieces of the meat and bringing small bites to her mouth, which she chewed nimbly and minutely. The rabbit had been young and prepared beautifully, and usually, Gruoch's mouth would have watered at the smell of rosemary. Still, the many strange eyes that continuously caught her own when she looked up from her plate had killed whatever appetite the inviting odours had managed to conjure.

"Daughter," came Bodhe's voice from her left. "Gruoch."

She quickly dropped the small morsel she held in her fingers and wiped them on a small piece of linen on her lap. She turned to face Bodhe, making sure to garnish her face with a smile as radiant as she could muster through her nerves. As Gruoch looked, she met her father's ruddy face and beaming expression and the quiet and equally nervous-looking face of his guest.

"Yes, Father?"

Again, Bodhe's strong hand clapped soundly against the shoulders of the man to his right, sending the slighter man dangerously closer to his plate.

"May I have the honour of introducing you to a friend of mine? Here sits Gille Coemgáin, nephew to the Mormaer." Her father's eyes danced in the light of the fires that burned nearby, and the twinkle that Gruoch found there could not have solely been blamed on an abundance of ale.

Gruoch understood then the cause for such feasting and merriment. The Mormaer acted as Steward for the King, keeping the territory safe and acting in the monarch's stead. As the Mormaer's kin, Gille was an important guest indeed.

"My lord," she said demurely, casting her eyes down and bowing her head respectfully. "We have great respect for your uncle in this family. The Mormaer of Moray has kept our lands safe and free from Norse aggression for the better part of my life, and I am humbled to meet his kinsman."

"Your words are kind, my lady," Gille responded. His voice was low, much deeper than Gruoch would have credited to a man of his build. It was a smooth voice, temperate. It was the voice of someone used to speaking and having whatever he said obeyed. As he responded, their eyes met briefly, and Gruoch was shocked to see a hint of colour rise in his cheeks. She smiled gently and turned her attention quickly back to her meal. That a grown man who looked to be at least fifteen years her senior should blush at her words gave Gruoch a secret thrill. She could feel the burn of Hertha's stare in the back of her head and ignored it. She decided to press the advantage.

"There is kindness in what I say, but I hope foremost that you hear the truth in it. Our tenants have benefited from your uncle's benevolence and leadership, and I am truly grateful to have had the chance to welcome you into my father's hall." Gruoch kept her voice sweet and light and tilted her head to look up at Gille through sweeping lashes. She dared a subtle look towards Bodhe, who, although possibly displeased at his daughter's coquettish behaviour, still smiled warmly, his hand resting firmly between Gille's shoulders. Gruoch knew it for a hand that held two meanings. The first was a touch for welcoming, an assurance that Gille was sacred and would be offered every protection as her father's guest. The second meaning in that touch was that of a father who had warned another man of what awaited should he err in his step.

Gille appeared to have gleaned the double weight his host was conveying in the simple weight of his hand, and he turned in Bodhe's direction, breaking his gaze away from Gruoch. She smiled to herself as he did so. Then, turning her attention back to her plate, Gruoch was pleased to find her appetite suddenly returned. She took a bite of the tender rabbit and drank from her cup, allowing the ale to wash away the smoky taste of animal flesh. She felt pleasantly drunk, her belly warmed by the knowledge that she had had such a noticeable effect on Gille. She knew that she had made a significant impression and succeeded in affecting him more strongly than she herself had been. She shifted slightly in her seat, darting her head discreetly to look back over one shoulder. Hertha stood but a few paces back, but her expression remained unreadable. Whatever Hertha may think of such behaviour, Gruoch was pleased with herself.

She allowed herself another smug taste of the bitter ale, but the glow of her self-satisfaction had her forgetting herself, and Gruoch drank greedily, causing a sharp cough to work its way from her throat. She hacked unpleasantly, sputtering into her drink and bringing a hand quickly to her lips in an effort to contain the cough. Gruoch was sure that her cheeks were now flaming as red as her hair. Any feeling of power and strength dissipated along with her pride. Had Gille seen?

She dared to look up from her plate in his direction, but the visiting lord was still turned away, heavy in some discussion with Bodhe about what Gruoch gathered to be unrest to the north in Orkney. Thank the heavens for small blessings, she thought, berating herself for such an unladylike act. Gruoch's hands reached for her hair, smoothing it back and away from her face in a gesture made easy from habit. However, she felt her fingers freeze in their tracks as she happened to look out and catch the glance of a man who sat a few paces away at a nearby table.

The rider with the dark copper hair stared openly at Gruoch from his seat beside the man with the black beard, who was speaking in a fiercely animated fashion with the lord of Ross, who sat to his other side. Ross, a quiet yet intelligent man who had often worked closely with Bodhe, seemed more heated than usual and jabbed vigorously into the air with a hand as he explained some point to the black-haired visitor.

Blue eyes bored into hers, and Gruoch felt her cheeks warm suddenly with the heat of her returning blush. Her breath caught in her throat at the intensity of the man's gaze, and she knew that she should turn away and cast her eyes somewhere else before someone noticed the immodest and blatant stare cast in her direction. Still, Gruoch found herself unable to look away. She could not tear her eyes from his for the sake of propriety nor for the fact that Hertha had surely noticed this man looking at Gruoch and would have harsh words for her later. Then, almost imperceptibly, the man nodded his head slightly in the direction of the door; his silent invitation made all the more evident by the rakish grin that suddenly adorned his face.

The brazen audacity of such a suggestion was enough to break the spell, and Gruoch tore her eyes away quickly, lowering her shoulders to square them sharply. She tilted back her face just enough to allow a regal look to return to her features. She turned her attention back to her father and Gille. As though feeling new eyes upon him, the latter turned back slightly in Gruoch's direction and offered a small smile. She returned it shyly, letting her eyes drop down and away. Gruoch glanced towards the cup of ale and swiftly decided against risking another taste. She sat back into her chair, keeping her eyes cast down at the hands which lay clasped primly in her lap.

"My lord mac Cináed, I wish to thank you for this gracious welcome and feast. My men and I are thankful for it."

"The honour is mine in hosting the son of the Mormaer of this great territory. Please, Mac Bethad, tell me: how does your father, the lord Findlaech?"

Startled at the sound of a new voice so close to her, Gruoch allowed her gaze to rise. She felt a sudden and swift heaviness in her heart as she looked upon the copper-haired man who stood suddenly within a few feet of her from his place before Bodhe.

"He is well, your highness, and ever grateful for the continued peace with Alba and your just brother. I know Findlaech looks upon Duncan as a friend and ally to us brigands here in the North. Such grace makes it easy to pretend that the southern lords truly do view us as equals." The man's tone was light, and his face merry. He stood straight before his host with no sign of a dip to his head or shoulders. Although Bodhe considered himself a man of his people and more casual than most royals, he was still a prince and the brother of the reigning king of Alba to the south. Since Bodhe hailed from a kingdom to which the territory of Moray swore and paid fealty, it was bold of this stranger to speak so casually with her father.

"Tread easy, cousin," came Gille's deep voice, whose assonance hinted at a slight warning. "Remember in whose hall you have recently supped and whose ale you have been so generously partaking."

The man roared, throwing his head back and sending out a cacophonous sound of mirth. The laugh was loud but brief, and he smiled and nodded as its echoes quieted. He bowed his head slightly to Bodhe before winking openly in Gruoch's direction as he caught her looking on. Shocked, she quickly busied herself by waving a serving girl over in search of a cup of fresh water.

"My apologies to you and to your daughter, whom I seem to have most grievously offended."

Gruoch refused to look back in the stranger's direction, choosing instead to keep a careful eye on the ministrations of the serving girl and the steadily rising level of water at her hand.

Bodhe laughed in response, a genuine sound of merriment and mischief.

"Mac Bethad, only a warrior such as you could be so brave as to throw your weight around and flirt with my only child." Her father's voice was easy, and Gruoch heard no warning of menace or insult. "But you seem to have turned Gruoch's nose up higher than I have ever seen it go."

Gruoch ignored her father's words and took a slow and careful drink from her cup. She took her time and allowed all three men to watch and wait for her response. Such a dance gave her precious time to think and allowed Gruoch to cast an illusion of grace back over her embarrassed features.

"Not offended, Father," she said finally. "I believe it is the duty of any well-born lady and hostess to model for all who may benefit from a proper exhibition of behaviour and decorum. But, for my lord, I can only suggest a cool cloth to wet and take to his eye. He seems to have something caught in it which causes him discomfort."

Her words sent Bodhe into a fresh peal of laughter, and Gruoch was intrigued when Mac Bethad's raucous voice joined in. Only Gille remained tight-lipped and silent.

"Aye, my lady, it pains me greatly. The light cast in this hall is much too bright, and my eyes are finding it difficult to adjust to such a glow." Mac Bethad was looking at her again now, catching her eye and smiling in a way that was different from before. There was still a hint of teasing, but something else left its traces in the way he looked on. Something much more open and sincere.

He was noticeably younger than Gille, perhaps even fewer than ten years older than her. His face was smoother and lacked the weary lines of a veteran soldier or even a man exposed too long to hardship, though fine wrinkles from laughter edged the corners of his eyes and mouth. Mac Bethad looked in every respect a lord's son, one used to finding his pleasure in life without having had to sacrifice much in its pursuits.

Gruoch scoffed and pushed back her chair. Hertha was at her side immediately and helped Gruoch with her mantle as she rose from her seat. As she stood to her full height, Gruoch made sure to keep her face firm and her shoulders square. However, when she looked back at Mac Bethad and his shining blue eyes partially hidden by a strand of hair that had fallen into his face, she felt far from stately or strong. She felt like a child suddenly playing at things she had no business getting involved in. The room was stifling, and she needed air.

"If you will excuse me, my lords, Father," Gruoch said, coming round the table and curtsying gracefully before them. "The hall grows rather raucous for my ears. My handmaid and I shall take in the air."

Bodhe waved his hand at them quickly, dismissing his daughter and allowing her to retreat. Gille rose quickly to his feet, his long body and legs unfolding somewhat awkwardly as he stood. Once standing, Gille bowed slightly before her, his face respectfully neutral. Only Mac Bethad seemed somewhat disappointed, although his smile never left his face. He bowed his head slightly in Gruoch's direction and then to Bodhe before turning on his heel and heading back to his companion, who seemed to have been watching his friend with a mixture of humour and embarrassment.

Gruoch waited for him to be seated before nodding to Hertha and signalling that she should lead them from the hall. As Gruoch broached the door, she refused to heed the millions of voices in her head that screamed for her to turn back for a final look. Instead, she went forward, keeping her gaze ahead, and she stepped out into the evening air that held frost and a smell of snow in its grip.

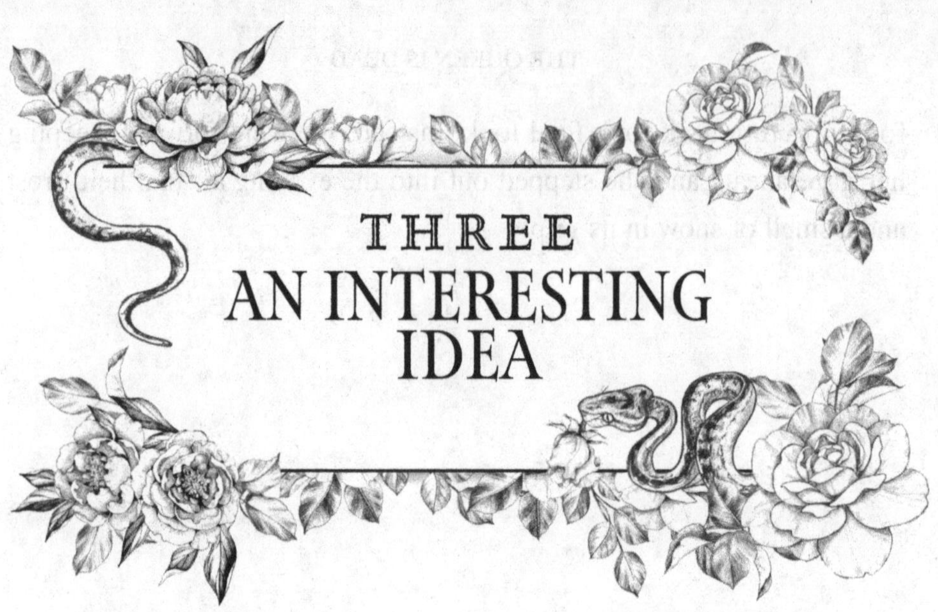

# THREE
# AN INTERESTING IDEA

Although Bodhe was the legitimate son of a king and was a prince in his own right, he had never really developed a taste for the politics and intrigues of court. His father, Cináed mac Duib, had been a fierce warrior and an even stronger politician. When Bodhe told his only child stories of her grandsire, he spoke of a man who had been stronger than the mountains and older than the boulders that made up their base. Cináed had achieved the status of a mythological hero in the eyes of his kin in the years since he had fallen in battle near Strathearn on the banks of Loch Earn. To believe Bodhe was to think that upon the king's death, the heavens had opened up and wept a deluge that lasted three days and three nights. He claimed the wind had become a veritable tempest as it knocked against towers and trees, lifting stones into the air and making of the night a fit of terror.

According to the laws and customs of their people, the Tanistry had convened after Cináed's death and the Tànaiste, the heir chosen by this council of nobles, had been named as king. Bodhe's father had long before voiced his desire that his son, Duncan, be his heir, as he was the first-born son and a man of great charisma who had been leading and inspiring soldiers. The council had agreed.

At the time, Bodhe was still fresh-faced and untested. Rather than begrudge his eldest brother his title or remain in the southern reaches of Alba where his father's stronghold had been built some generations before, Bodhe had asked leave of his brother. His leave had been granted, and Duncan had tasked his younger brother with regency over the small northern hamlet, as well as the lands that surrounded it, where Bodhe had agreed to build his home. Duncan had been pleased by his brother's desire to live among the people he governed, and permission was granted without hesitation. The boon to this decision was the protection that Bodhe's sword and troops would grant the long-suffering people who inhabited the northern reaches of Moray, those who had too often been subjected to the spears and axes of invading Norsemen.

Because he had spent most of his life free from the expectation of ever having to rule as king, Bodhe had received a sophisticated education in regard to kingcraft. He was a fierce warrior and a man beloved by many. However, this blunt and frank honesty kept him from becoming as coldly an effective strategist in terms of courtly duties and expectations as he might otherwise have been.

The morning after their feast, as Gruoch sat by the hearth sewing and mending her father's tunics, she heard his heavy footsteps just outside their door. As she put down her sewing to greet him, she found his expression contained a mixture of amusement and dread, like a young boy with a secret he was struggling to keep.

He had been up surprisingly early, considering the amount of ale that had been ingested the night before and had left their house before dawn. Gruoch had been awoken by the sound of father's great bulk moving through the darkness, and she had heard the careful catch of the door as he left. Hertha, her sleeping companion, had heard the noise as well, and both had lain in silence after Bodhe's departure. Surely, Hertha would have her opinions and theories about this unexpected excursion of her master's, but Gruoch didn't want to hear them yet. Rather, she contented herself with remaining mute and going over the events of the previous night in her mind. She thought of Gille with his easy manners and quiet strength. She thought of Mac Bethad and his dark hair. And his wink. And his grin. And his insufferable airs.

And his handsome face.

Gruoch had continued to revisit her reverie as she made repairs to the clothes in her sewing pile. Hertha had gone to walk the fields and replenish some of her stores. She maintained an impressive collection of herbs and made sure to keep her supplies as stocked as possible should the need for them suddenly arise. Her absence had given Gruoch leave to work with the ease of one who knows they are not observed, and the girl allowed her mind to wander and reflect on what had transpired during the feast.

When Bodhe returned home before Hertha did, Gruoch was startled from her daydreaming and pricked a finger on the tip of the bone needle she had been using. A small drop of scarlet blood beaded on the end of her finger, and she brought it quickly to her mouth lest the red liquid fall and stain one of the few cleaner tunics that her father owned.

Bodhe's face was one of secret mischief and hesitant delight. Gruoch smiled at the sight of him like this and set the sewing aside. She remained seated silently in her chair as she watched him come closer and take a seat for himself on one of the wooden benches. He kept his tongue as well, choosing instead to stoke the fire that Hertha had made before leaving. He gently tossed another small log into the flames, sending crackling sparks into the air. The dark smoke billowed and curled, finding its way into the nooks and crannies of the thatch walls, darkening the mud and peat that coated and held them firm. Father and daughter sat watching the fire consume the new kindling for a moment before Bodhe drew in an audible breath and spoke, not lifting his gaze from the hearth.

"I've spoken to Gille. He has brought forth an interesting idea."

"Oh?"

"I've come then," her father continued, "to hear your thoughts on the matter."

Gruoch remained still as she watched Bodhe speak to the fire. She took a small breath, collected herself and forced her body to regain its calm composure even as mystery and intrigue coursed through her very blood.

"I would gladly give them to you, *athair*, but I will need some clue or more information before I can do so to the best of my ability. What idea has been brought forth?" Gruoch was pleased with the steady tone of her words.

Bodhe finally managed to wrest his gaze from the fire before them and found his child's eye. She smiled at him to encourage him, surprised at seeing her boisterous and jolly father so quiet and hesitant. Gruoch could not have dreamed of the internal struggle that jostled and shoved along the corners of Bodhe's mind as he regarded his only child, struck by the resemblance she bore to his beloved wife.

"He has asked for you," came the quiet response. "For your hand."

"Oh."

She had never felt so eloquent.

"What say you then, my girl? It would be a fine match. You are a princess in your own right, daughter of a prince and niece to the reigning king of Alba. Gille has been named successor to the Mormaer of Moray. Your marriage would align the two houses, the two regions."

This was an unexpected addition to the conversation. Gruoch had assumed that Mac Bethad, son to the current Mormaer, would have been named as his heir. However, now was not the moment to discuss elections and the decisions of ruling men.

It was time to discuss a possible decision of her own.

"I am deeply honoured to be considered at all and to have been asked for," she began. "I am even more touched that you would come to me, *athair*, and ask me for my opinion."

"You are precious to me, Gruoch," her father continued, still staring into the fire, though a noticeable creep of scarlet blossomed in his ruddy cheeks. "You are my only living child and the only part of your mother I have left. I would never force you to marry against your will. But I do ask that you give it serious consideration, if only for the sake of our people. It would give the southern kingdom a stronger foothold in the North, and Alba could reinforce its dominion over Moray."

"Has it ever been otherwise?" Gruoch asked. "We have never heard whispers of rebellion or dissatisfaction from our tenants and countrymen. Why should they resent Alba? They have benefited from its protection and its trade. Is a conjugal alliance so sorely needed?"

"Not sorely, no," Bodhe reassured her. "But there are those who would see Moray independent of Alba. You will learn, daughter, that sometimes peaceful times give way to false impressions of security. The people grow bored and bored men are dangerous beasts."

Gruoch said nothing, choosing instead to ruminate on these ideas. There was no doubt that a marriage between herself and Gille would solidify ties between the two territories and make them stronger against foreign powers and invasion. It could also help to maintain the tenuous peace that had been so hard fought for.

She allowed herself to bring forth Gille's face into the forefront of her mind. She pictured his heavy eyebrows and the steady brown eyes beneath them. She saw his strong jaw and calm smile and played with the image of him standing tall before her, reaching out a hand for one of hers. The picture her mind brought forth was not a terrible one. It was even somewhat tempting. She had come of age and would soon be expected to marry. At least this option promised advancement and escape from her small home, as well as the thrill of an adventure.

"When must you have your answer, Father?" she asked cautiously. Tempering her excitement, Gruoch knew that such a decision should not be made in haste. She hoped she would be given some time before Gille needed confirmation either way.

"Take the day and consider it, Gruoch," her father said, exhaling audibly, a sudden burden very obviously lifted from his shoulders. "Gille and his men will not leave before breaking their fast tomorrow morning. Reflect and consider your options. Do remember, however, that such an opportunity and such a match would likely never come your way again."

Gruoch nodded at his words and smiled reassuringly at him as he rose to his feet.

"I will think of this. You have my word." She hoped that her voice sounded more collected than she felt. "I will give you my answer soon."

"Aye," was all Bodhe said as he made his way to the door, collecting his mantle against himself a little as he walked out into the brisk April morning.

Gruoch took up her cloak from the foot of the bed and pinned it quickly. She knew Hertha's usual collection spots and knew that she would be unable to make any decision this big without first hearing what her foster mother would have to say.

She checked the fire in the hearth, stoking it slightly, and walked hurriedly out of their home in search of Hertha, the only woman who could give her the kind of advice she desperately needed.

Gruoch found Hertha about a mile east of the settlement. She was kneeling in a field of heather, and one woven sac that had been placed down next to her was already bulging with the fragrant cuttings of gathered plants. As she approached Hertha, Gruoch watched as the woman gently took hold of one stem at a time, turning and inspecting the plant before either choosing to free it from her hand or to make short work of cutting it with her small blade. The wicked silver knife was always on Hertha's person and ready to be used should she happen upon a plant or herb she could use. It was working now, quickly severing branches of purple heather from their bases and placing them delicately into a second bag as Hertha whispered old words into the wind. She would bring these branches home and hang them to dry until the flowers were harvested.

It was only once she had grown old and been stripped of freedom herself that Gruoch would recognize that love had been what caged Hertha and kept her from fleeing. In her naive youth, Gruoch had been convinced it was the might of her father's armies that discouraged the Norse woman from trying to escape.

Hertha's freedom had been impeded by a different kind of force altogether.

"An infusion of heather can stop a cold or clear a head of rheumatism," she had told Gruoch as the girl had watched, fascinated, as Hertha brewed a tea from the plant when her charge had suffered from a terrible cough the previous winter. "It can also help you if your waters burn upon release." Gruoch had been too curious to be embarrassed or mortified that Hertha should speak so casually of such water. Hertha had looked at her and been pleased with what she saw: An apt pupil and an engaged mind.

Gruoch didn't bother to announce herself to Hertha as she stepped closer. She was sure that Hertha had become aware of her presence before sight or hearing had announced her approach. Magic was a black art, and Christ the Lord protected all good men and women from witches and their craft. The priests were always so fond of shouting and groaning such things when they beheld the freedom that Hertha was granted. Still, Gruoch knew that her maid could not be an evil creature of Satan while at the same time providing her charge with a parental love that Gruoch cherished. She could, however, see how it might be unsettling to a person who was not loved so by Hertha to have the Norse woman greet them without first having looked in their direction.

"Which one is it, *eldr*? The eagle or the falcon?"

Gruoch stopped a few feet from where Hertha worked and considered the question. She did as Hertha had taught her, listening both to the question and to the silent words that carried them along. Hertha called it listening deeply.

Gruoch sometimes struggled with the patience necessary for such a task.

"The eagle," she answered after a moment. She had heard the silent words behind the question. "My father thinks it would be a good match."

Hertha finished her work without answering, and Gruoch contented herself by standing nearby, maintaining the quiet. She relished the feel of the weak spring sunlight that warmed her face and turned her head to the east in order to soak it in. The perfume wafting from the heather only added to the serenity offered by the open field, and the distant scream of a goshawk danced on the breeze.

Hertha grunted, bringing her hands to her knees and pushing herself up. She dusted the front of her tunic for loose dirt and pushed back some strands of greying brown hair that had strayed from her braided crown. Gruoch did not offer to help Hertha as she rose. The older woman's pride would never allow it. However, the light glinting in the grey hairs woven through the braided hair allowed a terrible thought to push its way to the forefront of Gruoch's mind. For how much longer would she have her fierce warrior mother? If Gruoch were to marry, would her father and husband allow Hertha to accompany her?

"You knew what I meant? Which man was which?" Hertha's voice was tart and teasing.

*I listened deeply, just like you said*, Gruoch thought. "I assume you meant Gille for the eagle because of his size and regal nature, though I cannot think of whom you meant for the other."

Hertha glared with annoyance as she settled the two bags of heather to the saddle of her horse which stood nearby. There was no hobble to keep the horse from wandering, and the beast nickered softly at Hertha as she worked to fasten the load. Hertha spoke to the horse as she did to the rest of the world around her: in quiet and foreign whispers that carried some unknown quality. The horse's ears flickered towards Hertha, and its liquid eyes were calm. Once the plants were secured, Hertha turned to glare at Gruoch, irritated by the false play at innocence.

"Don't play the fool, Gruoch; you aren't beautiful enough for it to be a truly effective defence," Hertha said harshly. "The falcon, girl, the falcon! The one who sweeps by too quickly to be noticed and snatches the prey. The one that is cast into the eagle's shadow but can never be kept there long."

"Mac Bethad."

"Aye, Mac Bethad."

"He is a buffoon," Gruoch replied hotly, thinking again, embarrassed, of the crude wink. "Honestly, Hertha, the way he behaved last night during the feast… He is too brazen and too bold for my father to consider him a good match, and besides, Gille will soon surpass him in rank and power."

"An outranked buffoon, is he?"

"Yes. Gille is to be Mormaer, and my father thinks it could seal a more permanent and secure alliance between Moray and Alba."

Hertha nodded, contemplating the words. Listening deeply. She clucked to her horse, who plodded gently in the direction she guided. Gruoch turned and walked to Hertha's right, silently taking her hand. Hertha allowed it, although Gruoch was sure she had surprised her companion with the gesture. They had often walked hand in hand when Gruoch was a girl, but the habit had escaped them of late. Gruoch felt Hertha's cool fingers, rough and calloused from work, and was reassured. She looked down at their entwined fingers as they walked.

A small cut on Hertha's thumb had begun to bleed, and the warm liquid had trickled down, staining a path from digit into her palm. Gruoch took her hand away quickly and pointed to the cut.

"Hertha, your hand. The blood."

Hertha looked at her hand without pausing in her step.

"There is power in blood," she said quietly. "Yet a sprinkling of water will wash this hand clean, little flame. No need to falter. I've some figwort in my stores that can help close it up nicely."

Gruoch hurried to catch up but didn't risk retaking the bleeding hand. The sight of blood had always made her feel weak, and the crimson streak that stained Hertha's palm sent a quiet shudder of revulsion through Gruoch as she followed the older woman back home.

# FOUR
# THINK OF ODIN

After trekking home with Hertha, Gruoch greeted her father warmly. She was pleased to see how delighted Bodhe had been to hear that she would accept Gille's proposition of marriage. He had lifted Gruoch into the air, holding her in an embrace that nearly shook her bones loose, and she had wrapped her arms around his neck in as strong a grip as her young body could manage. As Bodhe gazed happily into his daughter's eyes, Gruoch had seen trapped within his eyes all of the words that were forbidden to the prince, the warrior, and the man. Instead, he had to satisfy the overwhelming emotion he felt by allowing his love as a father to shine through.

She knew such a moment was all the more precious for its rarity.

"You are sure?" he asked as he placed Gruoch gently back onto her feet.

"I am," she replied, voice strong. "I want to do this."

"You do not need to do this for me."

"I am not doing this for you, *athair*," she assured him. "I am doing this for me."

Her father nodded his understanding, and a rough palm came to cup her cheek gently. They stood there a moment longer in an easy silence before the palm fell away from her face, and Bodhe made his way from their home, going out to seek his friend and soon-to-be son-in-law.

"Be true, Gruoch," came Hertha's voice from somewhere in the shadows. "Are you sure this is what you want?"

Gruoch turned to face the older woman- the only mother she had ever known and smiled. She lifted her face towards Hertha's, pulling back her shoulders and allowing herself to stand tall and strong.

"I am sure, Hertha."

Hertha's head dipped once, her face turning down and away from the girl's proud gaze, and her knee gave a subtle and almost invisible bend.

"Then I am for you, my lady." Although uttered in Hertha's all too familiar voice, the words seemed foreign and odd to Gruoch's ears.

When Gruoch would think of this moment later in her life, she would curse her inexperience and the lack of wit that kept her from recognizing the moment for what it was. When she had become old, when she had survived the trials that were to come, she would look back at this seemingly innocent moment and see what she had missed then in her joyous and youthful excitement. She had willingly and happily ended her childhood by taking the first of many steps that would lead her from a place of joy and innocence, guiding her toward the dark corridors of blood that she was destined to tread.

Life was not a sure thing nor an easy one, and Bodhe had never been one for unnecessary pomp or frivolity. In his mind, there was no reason why the marriage could not take place before the lords were meant to leave and complete their examination of the surrounding lands. He had allowed Gruoch to accompany him while he discussed the plans for the wedding with Gille. Gruoch had sat meekly by, hands clasped in her lap, as the two men in her life discussed the next steps to be taken.

"I am overjoyed that you have responded so to my suit, my lady," Gille had said softly, his expression seeming to denounce sincere happiness at her acceptance of his proposal. "I will admit, though, that I was not prepared to make you a wife quite as quickly as your father seems to intend."

"Seems no point in delaying things," came her father's gruff response. "We have a holy man to say the words. We've witnesses for the sealing of the bonds."

Gille considered the words carefully, making sure to think about what Bodhe had said and to avoid the appearance of a rushed decision or a closed mind.

"I am set to return to the Hill after seeing a few other settlements, perhaps in a fortnight. I very much doubt the lady would be comfortable joining me on such a rough journey. We have considered none of the fineries that she would expect."

"I assure you, my lord," Gruoch said. "I have little use for such things."

She could feel Hertha's smirk burning into the back of her head, but Gruoch ignored the feeling in favour of the proud look in her father's eye. The answer had pleased him.

Gille looked happy as well.

"That may be so, Lady," he replied. "But it would grieve me for our first days as man and wife to be spent in the company of my soldiers and men."

A thought came to her mind, unbidden and unwelcome, of Mac Bethad's blue eyes and rich, brown hair. Gruoch tucked a red curl behind her ear, brushing it from her face just as she brushed the thought of the Mormaer's son from the forefront of her mind.

"I shall ride quickly," Gille promised, reaching for her hand under the careful watch of his future father-in-law. After a glance at Bodhe, whose calm expression encouraged her, Gruoch allowed Gille to take her hand into his own. The touch was proper and platonic, almost fatherly, but it still gave her a secret thrill. Her hand was clasped in the hand of her betrothed. The idea was not an unwelcome one, although she still felt the weight of her nerves hanging about painfully in the pits of her gut.

"We shall prepare during your absence," Bodhe agreed. "But you must cut this ride short. Your tenants can wait. Your wedding will give them cheer and hold them off until another opportunity to travel presents itself."

"Give me five days," Gille asked, gently releasing her hand and rising to his feet. Gruoch remained in her seat as Bodhe took to his legs and once again clasped Gille's arm in fellowship.

"Five days," Bodhe repeated solemnly.

*Five days*, Gruoch whispered into the echoing depths of her somersaulting mind.

And so, after a final bow in her direction and one last firm handshake with her father, Gille rose from his seat and walked out of the family home. Bodhe smiled and nodded to his daughter once more and left swiftly, following his guest out the door. Gruoch was certain that Bodhe and his men would accompany their guests to the gates to see them off if only to close the heavy wooden doors again once the visitors had gone.

The short period that had been granted before the wedding allowed the household to quickly prepare for a simple feast and dance. It also allowed for Hertha and Gruoch to pack a modest chest with some linens and a few tunics, including the beautiful purple mantle that she had worn the night of her meeting with Gille. Gruoch made sure to include a few other combs and adornments that she would need. It pleased her that Bodhe had asked that she wear her mother's brooch during the wedding and told her it would be hers to keep thereafter. Gruoch took it gratefully.

Bodhe had two sheep slaughtered in preparation for the wedding feast, and servants brought forth eggs, fish, and a few other simple foods that the early season could provide. Late April in the highlands did not often offer occasion for bountiful harvests, but the lord was pleased with the meal his household could put together.

On the fourth night, the day before Gille was set to return, Hertha and Gruoch sat by candlelight, absentmindedly repairing a few torn tunics and leggings. The girl would not have dared to suggest aloud that Hertha's attention was distracted, though her own certainly was. Now that the wedding was mere hours away, the anxiety and nerves were becoming unbearable, and Gruoch could not keep herself from second-guessing her decision. When would she see her father again? Would Gille accept that she bring Hertha along with them? Would he be a brute once they were away from her home and tucked away within the walls of Crown Hill? Would the ladies of the court sneer or look down at her? Could she be happy away from the wild hills and moors where she had been raised?

"If you don't say at least one of your thoughts aloud, I fear they will strike you dumb for all the knocking they are doing against your skull." Gruoch looked up at Hertha as she spoke, but the stoic older woman never lifted her eyes from her sewing.

"How do I choose the one that concerns me the most?" Gruoch replied almost bitterly. "Have I made a mistake, Hertha? Is it too late to go back to how it was before Gille and his men ever arrived at our gates?"

Hertha's needle paused midair, and she slowly lowered her hands into her lap. She breathed in deeply and exhaled the breath slowly, closing her eyes. When she finally opened them again, Gruoch was surprised that they seemed to glisten in the soft firelight.

"There is no going back now, little flame," Hertha said finally. "You have made a choice, and whether you like the path you're on or not, to go back on your word now would be as perilous a journey as it would to simply go forward."

"I know you're right, Hertha," Gruoch began, "Only...."

"You're not the first woman to be afraid of her future the night before she weds," Hertha said, not unkindly.

"I am not afraid."

"You are a liar, Gruoch. And still a lousy one at that."

Gruoch mimicked her guardian then, taking a moment to breathe in through her nose, holding the breath deep in her lungs until they began to burn with a pleasant ache. She slowly released the air through her mouth, closing her eyes as she controlled her breath. Gruoch pictured her own face in her mind's eye and imagined a hand wiping away every worried line, each invisible tear stain, any dark circles under the eyes. She imagined wiping the cheeks smooth and dry, watching as the corners of her lips rose to meet this cleansing palm. When Gruoch opened her eyes once more, Hertha nodded mutely to her.

"Good, girl. Good. That is the face you must remember to wear. It is the face of a warrior, the face of a queen."

Gruoch cracked then, and a smile burst its way through her stoic facade.

"I am no queen Hertha," she chided lightly. "Gille will be Mormaer, but that is a long way from being king, like my grandfather."

"The face of a queen," was all the Norse woman would say.

Gille had made an effort for her.

He had scrubbed in what must have been frigid water, for his face, though noticeably free of grime, presented red cheeks that appeared slightly ruddy from the cold. His hair, a light hue of sandy brown, had been neatly brushed back from his face and bound in a leather knot. He didn't have the chance to fetch anything from home in the time he had been gone, and so the tunic he wore was the same Gruoch had seen him arrive in the week before, although it too had undergone a serious cleansing. However, the mantle around his shoulders, a dark forest green, shone in its silken folds. The material was as rich and luxurious as befitted his station. The pin at the shoulder was a simple twist, though the gilded copper had been recently polished.

Gruoch, too, wore the clothes her groom had first seen her in, although this time, Hertha had gone to great pains to embroider small purple heather blossoms into the complex weave of plaits that gathered the red hair. She had watched silently as Hertha twisted and braided the hair away from her face and into winding coils that crowned her head with crimson plaits. Gruoch had pinched her cheeks and been instructed to bite down on her lips for them to gain a little colour. She was pleased and more than a little satisfied at the looks of awe that her servants wore as they looked upon her, and although she knew that vanity was a sin, she secretly delighted in this wicked, prideful feeling. Hertha, whose beliefs harboured no love for Christ and kept her free of such feelings of shame, smiled at her charge. She knew without having to be told that Gruoch was quietly exulting in her own beauty.

"You burn true, my girl. This is no little flame that stands before me."

"Thank you, Hertha. For everything. You've meant so much to me for so long now, and I...."

"Hush now," the older woman said briskly, quickly sweeping away a few fallen stems of heather from Gruoch's skirts. "Do not soften on me yet. You have work yet to do that will require strength. Believe me."

Gruoch blushed at the words, for she had gleaned their honest meaning. Truly, she had been thinking of her wedding night with increasing worry as the day progressed. She hadn't had a moment alone with Hertha all day, and although there were a few other maids about, she could no longer keep from asking the questions that had been burning in her mind.

"What will he expect?" Gruoch asked quietly, embarrassed. "What will I have to do?"

Hertha did not laugh, for she knew the girl to be a secretly sensitive thing and that asking such a question would not have been easily done. For that reason alone, Hertha kept her face still and refrained from her usual brusque demeanour. She considered the question quietly before giving her solemn answer.

"Close your eyes and think of Odin."

Crown Hill put Bodhe's home to shame.

Nestled, as its name suggested, into the bosom of a generous hill that sat on the banks of a swift river, Castle Hill was the seat of the Mormaer. From there, he could rule the vast counties and hamlets of Moray. It was there that Gruoch would go with Gille the morning after they were married.

It had a stone foundation and three stories, a rarity in Moray. Though ambitious builders had begun constructing more sophisticated homes and buildings in Alba to the south, lumber, mud, and peat were still the most popular and accessible in the northern reaches. Crown Hill was a unique feat of patience and shared labour first undertaken two generations before.

Gille claimed that there were at least fifteen rooms throughout the tower and that the surrounding walls protected another half dozen or so smaller outbuildings. Bodhe's home was much more modest, built in the typical style of Morayan blackhouses, which were buildings made from peat, earth and thatch, so-called because the lack of chimneys caused the smoke from fires to darken the walls. Gruoch had long believed that their Norse meeting hall was the most impressive thing to have been constructed in all of the northern reaches, and her first sight of the tower at Crown Hill was the first of many times over the course of the following years that she would realize how small her conception of the world had been.

Findlaech, though he was Mac Bethad's father, had officially declared Gille to be his successor shortly before the latter had come to visit Bodhe. Bodhe entertained his daughter's questions only so far as the answers could potentially serve her as the future wife of a Mormaer, and he refused to get into the intricate and delicate details that had motivated such a decision. It was Ross who filled her in on the salacious gossip years later, once everything had begun to unravel and Norway was once again a real and tangible threat to their shores. Ross had said that Mac Bethad had been passed over due to his passion and hot-hotheadedness, that the Tanistry and even his father had thought him too mercurial and inconstant to lead. In their words, Mac Bethad could be trusted to lead men only so long as the weight and responsibility of a crown never posed itself on his head. He would be a loyal and devoted general and would have to satisfy himself as such.

And so Mac Bethad would be absent from Crown Hill when Gruoch and her husband arrived there as newlyweds. Gille mentioned in passing that Mac Bethad had been sent even further north along with other nobles to monitor the ever-encroaching Norse powers. Gruoch was not surprised that he should be absent from his father's home. What occurred the night of Gruoch's wedding had been made clear to her that Mac Bethad would do everything within his power to avoid being in her presence for the foreseeable future.

She could not blame him for this.

# FIVE
# THE LADY GRUOCH

The wedding itself was quick and was over before Gruoch truly became aware that it had even begun.

The ceremony was held in the great hall since the tiny chapel that had been built on their lands scarcely held more than five occupants, and the newlyweds had managed to accrue a rather impressive guest list. Most of the tenants who lived within the fort or close by came with offerings of early flowers, lambs, or whatever could be spared. Besides these modest farmers were Gille's most loyal soldiers and men. This meant that some of the riders who had arrived with him had already left for their homes and would not be in attendance. It bothered Gruoch that she should feel anything when she learned that Mac Bethad had bothered to return and would be a surprise addition at the wedding.

The rings that were exchanged were simple bands of silver since there had been no time to collect gold ones. The ring that now adorned her right hand had belonged to her mother, and Bodhe had given it to Gille with his blessing and love. The girl was touched that her father would be willing to part with it after keeping it, albeit secretly, for these past nine years.

Gruoch's fingers had trembled as she fought to slip Gille's ring past the second knuckle, and she had heard a small laugh come from somewhere amongst the congregants. She felt a blush rise from her neck and chest and stain her cheeks, but she resolved to keep her face calm as she twisted the ring furiously. Finally, Gille helped her adjust the ring and managed to wedge it onto her finger himself. This brought another chuckle, and this time it was shared among a few of the onlookers.

Her ears buzzed, and Gruoch's vision seemed to blur as the priest spoke out in Latin, blessing their union and bestowing God's love and commandments down onto those who had gathered there. She had a simple grasp of the tongue, but her nerves didn't allow her to concentrate and make out the solemn phrases that were being chanted. Finally, after a pause, Gille stepped awkwardly towards her and gently grasped her shoulders. Gruoch looked up in a kind of numb confusion as Gille leaned into her and kissed her briefly and succinctly on the mouth. His lips were gone before Gruoch had fully registered their touch. As the guests cheered and cavorted, Gille took one of her hands in his own and raised them above their heads. Gruoch brought her free hand slowly to her mouth, where she touched the strange stinging in her lips.

Bodhe was the first to come forward. He swept her into his strong embrace, and his kiss landed soundly upon her cheek. He released her, reaching for Gille's shoulder, which he clapped firmly with an open palm. Gruoch's eyes sought Hertha, who stood mutely and away to the right, the distance between them befitting a lady and her waiting-woman.

It shamed Gruoch to realize how badly she wanted to grasp Hertha's hand and have her foster mother take her away from the noise and the explosion of feeling that had grappled her. Hertha's eyes spoke volumes, telling Gruoch what she needed to hear without uttering a sound.

*Your face. Your every feeling is shown upon your face.*

Gruoch breathed deeply and forced her cheeks up in a strained smile as she grinned maniacally at her father and her husband. If Gille could read the fear or anxiety on his bride's face, he said nothing to that effect. He smiled pleasantly at her and even raised a small hand to his lips, kissing her skin gently. Again, the touch of his mouth left a cold and stinging sensation upon her flesh that was nothing like the spreading warmth that Gruoch had heard the older girls had whispered about in moments of stolen gossip.

When supper was served, the clergyman was given a place of honour at the head table a few places from where Bodhe sat. The feast itself was impressive, and Gruoch knew that her father was proud of what his household had put together with such short notice. The meats were fragrant, and the ale flowed freely. The guests roared with laughter, and the hall echoed with song and cheer. Men and women sat alongside one another on the long benches, and as the evening progressed, more than one maid was swept up into the lap of an inebriated visitor, forced to slap and gasp with mock displeasure and shock.

Once again, Gruoch ate very little but allowed herself a little more of the ale than she would typically have done. She had only the most rudimentary of ideas as to what awaited her once she was alone with her new husband. She knew that the ale would help by, if nothing else, allowing her to deepen the incredible numbness that had enveloped her since the ceremony itself.

"I have words that I would like to say," came a slurred voice above the cacophony.

"Quiet, you mongrels!"

"Ross has words he would like to say!"

"And I have a word for Ross' mother!"

More laughter, followed by the heavy thump of a fist against wood.

"Let him speak," came Bodhe's booming voice, cutting through the din like a hot blade through flesh. "I would hear what my friend would say on this day of celebration."

Ross, who stood at his table with a stance that suggested he had partaken quite generously of the ale himself, steadied himself by laying a palm against the wooden surface. He raised his tankard into the air before him, pointing in the direction of the head table. He bowed his head to Gille and Bodhe before prostrating himself into a ridiculous bow in her direction. A foot slid out from behind and placed itself firmly into Ross' backside, sending the man sprawling forward. A strong hand shot out, catching Ross's arm and helping the man to steady himself. Ross straightened himself and looked down, smiling in gratitude at Mac Bethad, who returned the smile as he pulled his hand away. The bright blue eyes found Gruoch's once again, and there was something hidden behind them, some word or feeling that she could not decipher. Rather than allow herself to become lost in this unwelcome and confusing gaze, she stared once more at Ross, who seemed to have found his feet.

"As I was saying," he began, running a hand through his dark blonde hair, pushing the sweaty locks back from his round face. "I would like to raise a glass and a toast to the happy couple. My lord Gille Coemgáin, there is no man tonight that I would follow more happily into the bloody jaws of death, and my lady Gruoch, if you will permit such flattery, there is no woman here whose beauty can hold a candle to your flame. You are a golden couple, and we toast to a joyous and fruitful union. To the future Mormaer and his lady!"

"To the Mormaer!"

"To the lady Gruoch!"

Gruoch took a small drink from her cup in response to Ross's words, and the speaker sank back onto his bench with little grace, catching himself on Mac Bethad's shoulder as he went down. She turned to face Gille and smiled. He returned it warmly before turning his attention back towards the men and lifting his cup for another drink.

The hall was immediately filled once again with loud voices and laughter, and Gruoch's head began to ache from the pounding of the noise against her temples. She was sure that the ale was not helping matters either. Her blood felt hot as it rushed through her body, burning away the comforting and cool feeling of pleasant numbness that had occupied it thus far. She wiped at her brow, which glistened with sweat despite the chilly evening outside the walls of the banquet hall.

She looked over her shoulder to Hertha, who stood at the accustomed place by the back wall. She stepped forward, bending towards the girl in order to be easily heard.

"You are well?"

"My head is spinning," Gruoch confessed. "I am in need of air. I think I will take a short walk before my husband retires."

Hertha looked quickly and subtly in Gille's direction, and Gruoch followed the gaze. Bodhe and Gille were almost head to head in conversation, and the host's arm flew as he recounted some story or other.

"I think you will have time to gather your wits," Hertha said drily.

She helped Gruoch to pull back her stool and to rise from the seat. The two women walked quickly and nimbly in the direction of the door, nodding thanks to the revellers who raised their cups in their direction as they passed.

The guard at the entrance opened the heavy wooden door for them, and the two men who stood just outside helped him close it quickly lest too much of the cold April wind made its way into the hall. Hertha offered Gruoch her arm, who took it gladly; her pride was willingly sacrificed in favour of the sense of familiarity and comfort that the other woman offered. They walked slowly as Gruoch's head cleared. Their steps were unhurried, and as they walked leisurely along their way under the immense canopy of indigo and stars, she found her breath steady, and her pulse calmed and found an easy pace.

"Toasting to the Mormaer and his bride, as though my father were not well and alive in Crown Hill."

Hertha and Gruoch stopped quickly as the sound of an angry man's voice carried on the evening breeze from somewhere close by.

"The toast was a gesture of loyalty and goodwill. You do wrong to find insult in a thing that is said with good intent."

Another voice. This time calmer, rational, and almost pleading. Gruoch looked at Hertha, who peered into the darkness in the direction from which the voices seemed to have come. She considered a second more before coughing somewhat obnoxiously in order to alert the speakers to their presence.

The voices were silent, and Gruoch shrugged to Hertha, who continued to look out and in the direction from which the sound had originated. After a brief moment, the sound of scuffling boots was heard, and the dark silhouettes of two men appeared, a regal backdrop of mountains and stars behind them as they approached. One of these men held a small torch that helped to illuminate the features that the bright moon had failed to reveal sufficiently.

Banquo's bearded face was alight in a gentle smile, and he bowed his head respectfully to Gruoch as he and his companion approached. She was not surprised to see Mac Bethad, his features marred by a deep scowl. His face was lined in irritation, and it was a striking change from the laughing and charismatic man he had shown himself to be before while in her presence. He did not look at Gruoch. Rather, he kept his eyes trained on Banquo and gave a quick jerk of his head as though to suggest that they continue to walk and find a more private place to continue their argument.

Banquo tactfully ignored this not-so-subtle invitation to move on.

"You look beautiful, my lady," he told Gruoch, his tone kind. "Gille is a lucky man."

"In more ways than one," came Mac Bethad's surly voice. "Is there anything given to that man that he rightly deserves?"

Gruoch's mouth dropped open of its own accord, and she felt anger flush through her at the words. Although Hertha braced a knowing and anticipatory hand on the girl's upper arm, she could do nothing to dampen the sting in Gruoch's voice as she barked back at Mac Bethad.

"Perhaps he is lucky to have been given such a loyal soldier and general in you, my lord Mac Bethad. And perhaps I am lucky to have chosen for myself a man who can inspire such loyalty and love amongst the men who cheer him in my father's hall."

Banquo's hand mirrored Hertha's, gripping his friend firmly as Mac Bethad took a step towards their host's daughter. Hertha, whose bloodsong still held the faint melody of ancient battle cries, pulled Gruoch back towards her, shoulders squaring in response to Mac Bethad's threatening steps.

Gruoch stood her ground and fought against Hertha's grip and the attempts to pull her back as Mac Bethad stepped nearer. He was not as tall as Gille, but this did not stop the warrior from staring down at Gruoch with blue eyes made almost black by the inky darkness. She refused to shy from him and recognized his show of brute strength for the empty gesture that it was. Gruoch had seen birds and rams puff themselves so in order to seem more impressive. This man was behaving no differently, and he would not dare lay a hand on her in anger while he was a guest on her father's lands. Certainly not on the night she became her husband's wife.

They stood for a moment, and the air between them seemed to crackle with his furious energy and her prideful stubbornness. Neither seemed willing to be the first to relent, and Hertha caught a glimpse of Banquo shaking his head slightly.

It seemed they were both responsible for difficult children.

Gruoch was surprised when she saw Mac Bethad's cheek twitch with a sudden dimple, and the lazy and crooked smile returned suddenly to his face. His shoulders dropped their defiance, and his body was suddenly relaxed; the tension melted away. Banquo's relieved sigh was exaggerated. Hertha's maintained silence was equally audible.

"I am right, my lady, even if you may not agree," Mac Bethad said softly. "He does not deserve you."

"No man does," Gruoch responded before thinking, her nose rising characteristically into the air.

This time, the smile that split Mac Bethad's face was luminous.

"If the gods were kind, my lady, perhaps they would have found me worthy of such a challenge." His voice was light and teasing as it had been that day in the hall when he had teased her in the dining hall.

"Your gods are not my God, sir," Gruoch responded tartly. "And to my God, marriage is a holy sacrament, not some light promise to be jested at."

"All the gods are one god, and their blessings are fickle," came his casual answer, "though a man would truly be blessed through a union with you."

The words cut her indignant fire and the response Gruoch had been preparing sputtered and died in her throat. He was too sure and too at ease; she could not match him if he ignored all rules of decorum and played so callously.

"We will say goodnight, my lords, and the goodwill of all gods go with you." Hertha stepped firmly towards Gruoch, linking their arms firmly once again. The tone in her voice and the strength in her body left no room for argument or discussion. She took a step, making as though to lead her charge from the inappropriate debate they had stumbled upon.

"There are stars in your eyes, lady," Mac Bethad continued, though his gaze had slipped from the women and seemed to trail off and into the distance. "They leave fire and gold in their trails. They are cascading in your hair. Why do you dance so? You would burn me with such hands."

Banquo was at his friend's side before Gruoch had even been aware of his movement. He stood before his friend, grabbing him by one shoulder and waving his free hand in Mac Bethad's face, though the latter didn't acknowledge the movement. His distant stare was unfettered by his friend's increasingly frantic waves.

"She is the moon, and the moon is her. See how she reaches her hand towards my hand?"

"You, Norsewoman, I need your help." Banquo's voice was clipped and rushed, and a faint hint of panic flecked his words. "He will fall. We must catch him and lay him on his side. Gruoch, is the way clear?"

Hertha hesitated for only a moment before her arm fell away from Gruoch's. She stepped quickly towards Mac Bethad, whose mouth had quieted in response to a sudden drooping of the muscles in his face. The urgent tone of Banquo's voice effectively shattered any outrage Gruoch may have felt at his use of her Christian name. It was clear that formalities had become an impossible luxury.

Mac Bethad's jaw was slack, and he seemed weak on his right side. Suddenly, his body jerked and tightened before it was overtaken by a series of convulsions. Banquo seemed familiar with such a sight, and Hertha allowed no shock to show on her features as she helped the bearded man to lay his friend gently upon the ground before attempting to hold the thrashing arms and legs still with his own body. Hertha assisted quickly and efficiently, keeping Mac Bethad propped on his side as the wild tremors rocked his body. As he strained, it was clear that the effort to keep the flailing limbs of his friend under some semblance of control took every ounce of Banquo's strength.

Gruoch quickly looked out to see if the noise had attracted any other wanderers searching for cool air and a chance to clear their heads, but the yard seemed empty. They were lucky to have found themselves near enough to the stables for the wooden walls to partially block them from the view of the main hall.

"His head, Gruoch." Hertha's voice was collected, but the urgency of the situation was still evident in the clipped tone of her words. "Support his head."

Gruoch dropped quickly to her knees, putting out of mind for the moment the fact that her skirts would likely be soiled and stained by the marshy soil in which she knelt. She did her best to push such trivial matters from her mind as she took in Mac Bethad's form that still struggled against the grips of his friend.

As gently as she could amidst the jerking and sharp movements it made, Gruoch placed her hands on either side of the sweating face and gingerly lifted it into her lap. She held his head there, trying to cradle it, all the while being careful not to allow her hold to bring him to harm. The flesh was pallid and slick with perspiration, even in the cool evening air. The dark hair was being plastered down to the sides of his face, and the proud mouth was still slack and tense, the body's movements and spasms causing even its host to move in contradictory ways.

Gruoch could not tell if Mac Bethad was aware of himself or what surrounded him, but she sought out his eyes all the same. The dark blue gaze swept past her face, peering off into an unfocused distance. Still, there were moments in the frantic and quiet panic where she could have sworn that his eyes found hers and that some desperate message was trying and failing to make itself known.

After what could have only been minutes, it became clear that the movements had slowed and were becoming less violent. Still, Banquo and Hertha held on. Gruoch caught the look of deep and sincere gratitude that Banquo gave Hertha as Mac Bethad's body finally slowed and stilled.

Gruoch watched as they slowly released their holds on Mac Bethad, who lay panting and gasping on the cold ground. As they allowed their arms to free themselves of their cargo, she allowed herself only a few light strokes of his dark hair once before gently lifting Mac Bethad's head from her lap and placing it softly down onto the soft soil. Before the dark head had touched the earth, Banquo quickly removed his outer mantle, using it to create a barrier between his friend and the dampness. Gruoch lay her charge upon the rough wool, and no one spoke.

Banquo rubbed a hand through his beard roughly and then pushed back the black hair that had fallen into his face. He turned and spat, trying to catch his own racing breath. Hertha, as always, was cool and seemingly unaffected, though Gruoch noticed the way the older woman studied Mac Bethad's prostrate form.

"Injury or birth?" Hertha asked.

"He fell from a horse as a child," Banquo replied honestly, fatigue clear in his voice. "He has suffered the fits since then. My lady," he turned in Gruoch's direction, and his face and voice were pleading. Gruoch did not miss that the familiarity of her given name had been abandoned and that Banquo had slipped back into formal terms. "No one save his own father, and I know of this condition. I believe it to be the main reason why his father did not fight for Mac Bethad to succeed him. The others, the men, especially Gille… no one must know of this."

"But surely no one can fault him if he has been injured-" Gruoch began.

"Swear it, girl." Banquo's calm voice was gone, and in its place came a desperate hiss. "Please, I beg this of you. You must not tell a soul."

She looked back at Banquo and then once more at Mac Bethad, whose eyes remained closed and whose slack mouth was beginning right itself.

"I swear," she stammered. She paused and forced herself to draw breath. "I swear," Gruoch repeated, this time the timbre in her voice sure and strong.

Banquo nodded, and Gruoch felt Hertha rise from the dirt. She placed a hand on Gruoch's shoulder, who lifted herself from her crouch.

"He will be fine now." Hertha's words seemed more factual than inquisitive.

"He will," Banquo replied. He fussed at Mac Bethad's mantle, pulling at the ends and then tucking it around his friend as though he were a child in his bed. "He will awaken soon. I will tell him what you have done, both of you. He will not know how to say it, but he will be grateful."

"Gruoch, we must return," Hertha said, her voice expressionless and cool. "You will be missed."

As she led them both away, Gruoch stole one last look behind her, taking in the shadowed shapes of Banquo and Mac Bethad as they rested on the cold ground. She watched their breath escape into the night, becoming billowing clouds of silver mist and ice.

# SIX
# PROPERLY MARRIED

At first, Gruoch found Gille to be a good and patient husband. He never yelled or scolded her, and his touch was always kind and gentle. Indeed, his patience was made obvious to her on their very first night as husband and wife when he bowed over her hand and kissed it chastely, refusing Bodhe's offer of their home and insisting that he sleep by the fires outside with his men. As he had told Gruoch's father, things could be made real and true upon their arrival at Crown Hill, and she had blushed at his meaning. Bodhe had nodded, his face unexpectedly grateful, and Gruoch was allowed one more night in her childhood home and in her bed. Still, she had tossed and turned that night, mind racing over quiet images of Gille's face approaching hers and the frightening thrashing of Mac Bethad in the arms of his unexpected benefactors.

Although Gruoch knew that the sun was bound to rise as it did every other morning, still, the first rays of dawn seemed to come too quickly. Gruoch wrestled with the deep and instinctive feeling that this was no ordinary morning. Something within her was brewing, and she felt herself shedding away her youth as though it were a mantle that could be dropped from her shoulders. Her belongings were simple, few, and had already been packed away. In little time, everything was gathered and made ready to leave.

As Gruoch gathered her things and prepared to step over the threshold and into her first adventure, her father placed a heavy hand on her shoulder, forcing her to pause in her gait. His face shone with pride, and his smile was bright, though unfamiliar moisture tinted his eyes as he beamed down at his only child. His embrace was strong and engulfing as he took her to him, and Gruoch breathed in deeply the familiar smell of his sweat. She felt the sting of tears prickle in the corners of her eyes, and she shut them fiercely as she buried her head into the broad shoulder. She wiped them quickly as Bodhe pulled away, and Gruoch kissed his ruddy cheek before he could stop her, the red beard tickling her skin.

Bodhe gifted his daughter the sturdy brown pony that she loved and often rode, as well as a treasure that Gruoch had secretly and desperately hoped for. As she watched Hertha approach with her own modest sack of belongings, Gruoch could tell that her guardian was pleased as well as she that they would be travelling together to Crown Hill. Hertha would be a noticeable loss from Bodhe's home, and Gruoch recognized and appreciated the generosity of such a gift. Her father had laughed at the joy that had taken his daughter at the sight of Hertha approaching the party of riders with her bags and travelling clothes.

Gruoch rode with Gille as the party left, sitting behind him on his large bay mare with her arms circling his waist. Her own pony had been laden with her things, leaving little room for a rider. Although she knew him for her husband, Gruoch found that she was unnerved by the closeness of Gille's body, and she fought to keep her limbs from trembling with the nervousness that she felt.

Bodhe and his men stood at the large open doors as the daughter of his heart rode away over the moors, and his bright hair and waving arm held her gaze until both slipped under the horizon.

As though some part of her already knew that she would never again see her father, Gruoch burned the image of the first man she had loved into the wells of her heart in the way that only children can.

Gruoch knew that her inexperience and youth sometimes frustrated Gille, for she carried with her a naivete that he could not help but find tiresome. She did not understand how to run or manage the affairs of a home such as the one she found at Crown Hill, and she was thankful to learn that she was not expected to manage the servants and people who lived there. This responsibility fell to its formidable housekeeper, Alane, who oversaw the daily operations and kept everything running smoothly.

Hertha had little to do with Alane, thinking the kindly and grandmotherly woman to be too mousy and pathetic to be given much credence. Although Gruoch debated that her successful handling of the estate should be reason alone for their respect, Hertha was unconvinced. Gille had told Gruoch before their arrival that the kindly housekeeper was treasured by Findlaech, who counted on her to keep things running smoothly.

The thought that Gruoch would be living under the same roof as Mac Bethad's father, in the halls and rooms he had grown up in, alongside her new husband, was a strange and confusing ache in the back of her mind. She could not help but be curious. Would Findlaech resemble his son in appearance? She had been able to piece together that their personalities lacked any familial resemblance, although the two men were said to have been close. Would the Mormaer take one look at her and read in her eyes that she knew his son's deepest secret? Would Gruoch blush to look upon the Mormear after stroking his son's hair from his brow as he lay pallid and weak upon her lap?

Thankfully the bustle that greeted them upon their arrival at Crown Hill helped to distract Gruoch's racing mind from such concerns. As they rode into the courtyard, Gruoch was left speechless at the sight of the tall, stone tower that stood, domineering, in the centre of the fortress, sending its shadow out to blot the smaller wooden buildings and huts that lay at its foot. The tower had been built into the eastern side of a hill, using the very foundation of the earth to solidify and strengthen the structure.

More people than Gruoch had ever seen walked through the muddy yard, speaking loudly with one another, leading livestock, and looking up to greet the riders at the gate. Children rushed forward as they made their way in, rushing dangerously about the horses' legs until a few harsh words from one of Gille's men scared them away.

"What do you think, my lady?"

Gille's voice was kind as it reached her ear through the din that surrounded them. He twisted slightly in his saddle, and Gruoch looked up in order to catch his right eye as it peered back at her over his shoulder.

"I have never seen anything like this," came an honest reply that would have benefited from some more serious mediation. "I mean," the words stumbled now as Gruoch scrambled to make up for seeming so inexperienced and young in the world. "I just mean that I have never seen such a stone tower so close. It is truly remarkable."

Gille nodded and turned in the saddle once more, bringing out his right forearm and signalling that she should grasp it and dismount. Gruoch did so, forcing her legs to cooperate even after the long ride and hoping that her feet would find the dirt beneath them with at least the semblance of grace. Gruoch could hear Hertha's voice in the back of her mind without even having to search her out.

You will get one chance at a first impression, Gruoch, the voice said. Make it a strong one.

Whatever her concerns were, it seemed as though few of the people around them were paying Gruoch any attention. A few women, whispering to friends or sisters, pointed at her subtly with chins and eyes. Gruoch drew up her face, smoothing back her mantle and shaking back her hair. She made sure to meet as many curious eyes as possible. They would know her for their lady in more than name.

She would make sure of it.

Alane had broken through the gathering mobs and made her way to where Gruoch stood by Gille, who dismounted as well before handing off his reins to an eager groom. Alane's arms shot out, and a smile broke open her face in a dazzle of teeth. She came to Gille and held him by his arms as she beamed up at him, clearly pleased at his return.

"You did take your time after allowing the news to reach us," she scolded, her voice unable to hold a note of crossness. "But here you are." Now the bright eyes found Gruoch, and Alane's hands left their warm grip on Gille's arms and found his wife's cheeks.

Alane's face was open and welcoming, her brown eyes firmly entrenched in deep wrinkles. The skin was worn and loose around her mouth, but Gruoch saw in Alane a handsome woman, one who had been beautiful in youth and who carried vestiges of that beauty in her smile and the shine of her gaze. Gruoch smiled back. It was difficult not to.

"And look at what you've brought us," Alane gasped, turning the face in her hands slightly as though to better take it in. "You are a lucky man, my lord."

"I know it without you having to tell me, Alane," Gille chuckled. His arm sought Gruoch's shoulders, and he pulled her slightly against him and out of the woman's reach. Her hands, roughed by work and weather, fell away and came to clasp together at her stomach.

"Well," she continued, her voice bustling. "I shall have your things brought up to my lord's chambers, and we shall set you right. Poor dear, you'll be needing to bathe after your journey?"

"That would be lovely, I thank you," Gruoch replied, taking a step towards her. "My woman can help me get settled if you would be so kind as to show us the way."

In her usual and quiet way, Hertha had appeared at Gruoch's back, keeping a respectable distance from where she stood. Still, her presence was a welcome fire at Gruoch's back. The girl turned slightly and caught Hertha's eye, seeing there the beginnings of what would surely be many comments about Alane's clasping hands and big smile.

Gille's hand was still loosely perched behind her shoulder, and Gruoch turned to face him. He still wore the soft and quiet smile that usually adorned his expression when he looked at her, and she returned it easily. Their eyes held, and although Gruoch did not want to be the one to fold, she was unable to keep the heat from rising in her cheeks, and she finally looked away as she felt a blush overcome her.

"Come dear," Alane said again. She nodded to Hertha in acknowledgement and motioned that she should follow. "You'll want to be presentable when you meet the Mormaer when he returns tomorrow. And I wager your new husband would not begrudge you a bath." And with one last quick look to her husband, Gruoch followed the older woman away from the yard and towards the tower.

Gille's rooms were modest in comparison to what Gruoch would later learn made up the Mormaer's apartments, but they were still more than she had ever experienced in her father's house. A small fireplace adorned the room, around which were nestled two wooden chairs and a small sheepskin rug. A strong table sat by the window, and a small stone bowl that had been recently filled with flowers sat on the smooth pine surface. There were a few chests and shelves and the typical clutter that came with comfortable and extended living. A bed, larger than the one she had slept in back home, was nestled towards the back of the room. Blankets and furs had been heaped upon it, and it, too, had the appearance of being well-used. Gruoch's eyes shifted away quickly and found Alane, who was carefully filling a wooden tub with water by the fireplace.

"Thank you," Gruoch said again, unable to think of anything else to mention. Her thoughts and mind were racing, and her tongue felt thick and stupid in her mouth. She was overwhelmed, though she was doing everything in her power to appear completely at ease and calm. Gruoch rubbed her palms against her skirts to wipe away the cold sweat that gave away her agitation.

"There," Alane said as the tub appeared to be filled to her satisfaction. "Will you require any help, my lady?"

Gruoch shook her head and returned the kind smile.

"That will be all, Alane," she replied. "Hertha will assist me from here."

"Of course." The jolly woman's smile remained plastered to her face, but it seemed to Gruoch that the corners dipped ever so slightly as Alane's eyes sought out the unfriendly figure of the Norse woman who still stood quietly by. Alane nodded briskly and wiped her own wet hands on her tunic. "Of course," she said again.

As Gruoch heard the door close behind the housekeeper, she exhaled sharply and allowed her shoulders to slump. She ran her hands through her hair and stretched them into the air. Her every muscle ached from the long ride, and she was stiffer than she had anticipated. The water would feel heavenly after the muck and mist of the past few days.

"That woman smiles more than she has reason to," Hertha said gruffly.

"Only you would take offence at someone being too friendly," Gruoch replied, although she was too weary for her words to carry any real reprimand. "Could you please take a moment from your offence and help me with my bath?"

Hertha's movements were silent as she made her way to her charge and began to help with removing Gruoch's mantle and tunic. The clothes were dirty and soiled from the ride and would have to be cleaned soon if anything was going to be done to save them.

"You will not find me beating the mud from your clothes," Hertha said, reading Gruoch's mind as was her usual trick. "Your new friend can likely convince the stains to up and leave the cloth with nothing but the power of her smile."

"Now who is the child," Gruoch chided as she stepped into the lukewarm water. She sank gratefully into it and allowed the water to rise above her shoulders as she sat. Hertha's response was muffled by the water as Gruoch took a breath and allowed herself to sink below the surface, blissfully welcoming the dark and silence.

The two women ate a small supper at Gille's table. Gruoch had asked to be excused from supper in the main hall, and Alane had been gracious in her understanding of their desire to eat privately. She was exhausted, and the thought of having to sit and eat while tens of dozens of strangers looked upon her was more than Gruoch was willing to bear. She had asked Gille's forgiveness for her rude behaviour when he had come briefly to check that she was settling in. He had not so effectively hidden his disappointment at her preference to eat in their rooms, and Gruoch sensed that he had wanted her in the dining hall with him. Still, he kissed her hand softly and granted his permission. He had assured Gruoch that he would have food sent to her and that he would inquire as to where Alane had decided to quarter Hertha. His reminder that her guardian would sleep away from her that night brought back the threat of a blush as the second meaning of his words took root in Gruoch's mind. Hertha would not sleep with her, but Gille would.

Gruoch pushed a small piece of bread against her plate, playing with some of the savoury juices from the roast meat that lay untouched. The thought of eating sent her already tremulous stomach into tighter fits, and she was unable to muster much of an appetite. Hertha watched the girl play with her food, allowing it to get cold, before reaching over and grabbing the meat for herself. She ate with obnoxious ease, licking her fingers clean after swallowing every last morsel of the rabbit from Gruoch's plate.

"I suppose you think I've no reason nor right to be nervous," Gruoch said irritably. "And that you see nothing wrong with stuffing yourself while I sit here and turn myself inside out."

"You've reason, I suppose," Hertha said with little circumstance. "You Christians do have a way of allowing shame and guilt to taint the sight of a naked body. I will never understand how there are so many of you when you are all so damned afraid of that lies under the clothes of another."

"I am not ashamed!" Gruoch shot back. "There is no reason for shame or guilt. Gille is my husband before God, and I am pleased to be his wife."

"I hope you will still say so in the morning. That you are pleased, I mean."

Gruoch threw the bread deftly at her companion's head, and Hertha snatched it from the air before bringing it to her mouth, where it suffered the same fate as the rest of Gruoch's meal. Hertha smiled a little then, and Gruoch was angered upon seeing the pity in her eyes. She didn't want or need Hertha's sympathy. Gruoch stoked the anger in her belly, feeding it her every worry and anxious thought. It was a welcome change from fear and nerves. The heat of her rage was melting away some of the uncertainty out of a primal desire to be right and to prove to Hertha, as it seemed Gruoch was always trying to do, that she was stronger than the Norsewoman thought.

"You have taken steps that I never have, eldr," came Hertha's unexpected words. "You are a wife now. You are the wife of the man who will one day lead these people and rule this place." Her voice dropped slightly, becoming uncharacteristically soft. "I can not protect you from the world as I have before. I can only hope, my *eldr*, that I have given you what you will need when the moment comes to protect yourself when the time comes that I am no longer there to do so."

"Hertha," Gruoch began and reached for her friend's hand. Small fingertips found Hertha's strong wrist and touched it gently. As their hands came together, Gruoch imagined Hertha not only as a foster mother but as a birth mother as well. She took everything she still remembered about her father's wife and the woman who had born her, and she imbued the fluid memories into Hertha's grey eyes, into her high cheeks, and her tense forehead.

Any further words were forgotten as they both heard the sound of the door latch and the scrape of the wood against the rough floor as Gille made his way into the room. He stood for a moment without speaking, and the three of them sat in an uneasy silence. Finally, Hertha pulled her hand from Gruoch's and pushed back her chair. Quickly and without circumstance, she walked from the room without looking back at the girl whose gaze followed her desperately. Gille closed the door behind her when she left.

"Have you eaten?" His words were slightly slurred and loose in his mouth as Gille took a step into the room, pulling at the pin that gathered his mantle at the shoulder.

"I have," Gruoch lied quickly. "Thank you for arranging it."

Gille nodded and pulled the mantle away before bundling the cloth and tossing it away to the floor at the foot of the bed. Quickly, as though her presence changed nothing in his routine, he lifted the tunic from his body and threw it to rest next to his mantle.

Gruoch still sat at the table, frozen and shocked at the sight of her husband in nothing but his leggings. Was she expected to undress with such casual disregard? Would he be disappointed by what he saw when all was revealed?

Would she?

"Come here, Gruoch," he said firmly, one hand outstretched. "Come here."

She pushed back her chair and forced herself to stand, struggling to put one foot before the other in order to make her way to him. As Gruoch came within arm's reach, one of her husband's hands grabbed her shoulder and pulled her close. Gruoch stood before him, hands hanging dumbly at her sides, completely unsure of how to proceed and exactly what was expected of her. Not for the first time, Gruoch regretted her father's insistence that she be kept away from boys as a child and young woman. She suddenly felt so very stupid and unsure, and she was convinced that Gille would become frustrated at having such a hesitant wife, one who could not even bring herself to lay a hand on his bare chest.

Gille did not seem to be bothered by Gruoch's lack of initiative and perhaps had even rightfully expected it. He removed her mantle with as little care as he had shown his own, and her bare skin shivered as it came in contact with the air when her tunic was pulled free and over her head. She quickly clasped her arms across her chest as Gille knelt and pulled her hose away.

"Get into the bed."

His voice was not unkind.

Gruoch did as he asked and stared fervently at the ceiling after catching the first sight of him removing his own leggings. The bed dipped and groaned as he slipped in beside her, and the feel of Gille's hand on her stomach nearly caused Gruoch to leap from beneath the covers in shock. She closed her eyes tightly and forced her breath from her lungs, convincing them to take in a little air so as to keep her from fainting away.

Gille pulled away the blankets, and Gruoch screwed her eyes even tighter, refusing to let the tears that welled there spill and betray her fears before Gille. He lay still, and Gruoch could feel his gaze on her even without needing to look.

"You are beautiful," he said as his hand stroked along her hip. "My wife. My lady."

There was an awkward fumbling of limbs and a sharp pain that made her gasp. It was, however, mercifully brief, and after exerting himself, Gille turned to his side and fell asleep, his deep breaths soon turning to gentle snores. Gruoch lay awake next to him, afraid to move lest he should awaken and fumble on her again. Her eyes found the dying embers in the fireplace, and she shivered even though the bed was heaped with furs and even though the naked body of her husband emitted a heat that Gruoch would have otherwise found suffocating.

She was a woman, a properly married woman.

And no part of her was truly convinced of it.

Gruoch reached for her leggings. She sat daintily on the edge of the bed and began to pull them on. Hertha moved quietly into the room, making her way to the fireplace in order to stoke the embers that lay there. Neither one spoke, both too stubborn to be the first to acknowledge the invisible changes that had taken place. Hertha gathered the plates that lay unclaimed from the night before and made her way back to the door, making it clear she would leave and bring the dishes to the kitchen if there was nothing to be said.

"I did not think there would be so much grunting," Gruoch said to Hertha's back and was delighted in the sudden break of the older woman's stride. "Or that he would snore after."

Hertha's shoulders gave the smallest of shakes, and she turned back to face Gruoch.

"I suppose I should have told you about the noises they make," she said, a wry smile giving her words a teasing edge. "Although I don't know much about Morayan techniques. But I suppose a man is a man, be he from Odin's lands or Christ's."

Gruoch returned the smile, and a fleeting understanding passed then between them. Their relationship had shifted. Evolved. There was something else there now, a friendship that could only have been born at the death of another kind of relationship. Hertha would always be a mother to Gruoch, but perhaps now she could also be a friend.

"I have to get ready and find Gille," Gruoch said briskly. She rose in order to slip the tunic over her head. She smoothed the linen against her body and straightened the sleeves. "Findlaech is due to arrive today, and we must be there to greet him upon his arrival."

"Can you manage your mantle?"

Gruoch waved a hand at Hertha, playing the dismissive lady.

"Get rid of those dishes and make yourself useful. I can manage to finish dressing."

By some sheer force of luck, Gruoch managed to dodge the small rabbit bone that was suddenly launched in her direction. When she turned back to scold the offender, Hertha had already left the room.

Alane was wringing her hands in expectation as Hertha and Gruoch left the tower and made their way toward the generous crowd that was gathering in the yard. It appeared as though the people who stood assembled in wait consisted of farmers, merchants, and soldiers, as well as their wives and children. The faces on display seemed to show eagerness and sincere excitement at the prospect of their lord's return. It pleased Gruoch to see how beloved Findlaech was by his people, and she hoped that she and Gille would manage to inspire such loyalty and devotion when their time came to ascend the throne of Moray as stewards for Alba.

When she noticed Hertha and Gruoch approach, Alane made her way quickly to them before giving Gruoch a quick and slight curtsy which brought a smile to the recipient's face and a quiet snort of derision from her companion. Alane either did not hear Hertha or made the choice to ignore her and instead focused her attention on Gruoch, taking her lady gently by the elbow and leading her through the crowd, which parted respectfully before them. Gruoch noticed once again how some of the women leaned their heads close to one another and whispered. The men bowed their heads respectfully, each careful not to look her directly in the eye.

Alane led her to Gille, who stood apart from the crowd and closest to the gates, which had been opened in anticipation. He smiled warmly at their approach and reached a hand for Gruoch, who took it somewhat reluctantly. It seemed to Gruoch that since her arrival at Crown Hill, she was constantly in the arms or hands of one person or another. She found herself to be suddenly irritated by the constant feeling of fingers leading, guiding, and pushing her along. She smothered the irritation behind a warm smile of her own and allowed her hand to drape upon Gille's as she stepped to him. He kissed the knuckles politely and allowed Gruoch to take back her hand.

The time spent waiting for the Mormear allowed Gruoch to better take in her surroundings, and she allowed her eyes to travel as best they could without being too obvious about her distraction. The walls that surrounded the fortress were higher than those her father had built to protect his home, and the logs that formed it seemed larger as well. It would have taken many men years to build and improve upon such a defence. The courtyard itself contained a large stable, several stalls for trade, and a large stone well. There were other smaller buildings that Gruoch guessed were private dwellings for the inhabitants of Crown's Hill or perhaps even barracks for the soldiers and guards. She craned her neck slightly, allowing her gaze to travel the three stories of the tower. She noticed what she thought might be the window to her room. The chamber benefited from an eastern exposure, which meant that mornings flooded the room with light. Gruoch had been pleased to wake to such a thing and found pleasure in watching the drenched golden light send dancing beams of swirling dust.

Suddenly, there was a rise in the noise of excited voices as thundering waves of hooves became pronounced. The earth seemed to tremble under the legs of so many beasts, and the joy and expectation the watchers felt became palpable in the air. Gille's hand found the small of Gruoch's back, and he carefully led her aside a few feet and away from the entrance. Gruoch was grateful for the consideration he gave her, knowing that should the riders arrive too quickly, she could be trampled under the mount of an overeager soldier, happy to be home.

The noise and rumble of the horses lessened somewhat as they crested a small hill outside the gates, and Gruoch was finally able to spy the company as it approached. It seemed at least forty strong, and the horses' muzzles were flecked with sweat and foam, clear indications of a long and hard ride. The soldiers astride them seemed just as tired, but many wore the long smiles of a weary traveller returning home. As Gille and Gruoch watched, the riders filed by through the open gates and into the yard.

After only a few men had made their way in, Gille suddenly bent a knee and bowed, and his hand on her back reminded Gruoch to do the same. She curtsied deeply, keeping her head bowed, and her eyes turned down until she felt Gille rise to his feet at her side.

"Gille! You've returned and brought something back from your travels, I see."

Gruoch raised her gaze and found the portly figure of a grizzled man standing before her. His clothes were dusty and dirty from the ride and they seemed no finer than any of the men who rode with him. His face was deeply lined, and his cheeks bore the stubble of more than a few days free from a knife. His eyes seemed to jump out from behind the crow's feet that framed them, and Gruoch realized that the rich blue was immediately familiar.

Findlaech's son had the same eyes.

"My lord Mormaer," Gille said, taking the offered arm and clasping it around the wrist in greeting. The older man thumped Gille upon his shoulder, reaching up slightly to do so, and his boyish mannerisms and easy way reminded Gruoch suddenly of her own father. "May I present to you the lady Gruoch?"

Findlaech bowed his head slightly in her direction.

"I ken your father well, lass," he said with a certain gruffness and familiarity. "I don't think I could have held these lands against the heathen Norsemen without his help."

"A good and true friend is a treasure indeed," Gruoch replied. "I only hope to prove my loyalty to you as well, for my father's sake and my own."

Findlaech nodded at her words and winked at Gille. Gruoch was shocked by the simple gesture, as it was all too easy to imagine a younger set of blue eyes winking in very much the same way.

"You've chosen well, Gille," Findlaech said. "I can understand now," he continued in a louder voice, "why my son has proven to be so jealous of your good fortune."

Gruoch's eyes shot away before she could help herself and danced precariously over the company of riders before she had even become aware of it. Her gaze found him still astride his horse. Banquo, ever faithful and constant, was in the expected place at Mac Bethad's side. He seemed relieved to have arrived, and the black beard looked wilder than when Gruoch had seen him last.

She took a breath as a set of familiar blue eyes found her own, and Gruoch tore her gaze away quickly, looking down instead at her feet in the mud.

"Are you telling stories again, Father?" Mac Bethad's voice carried easily over the noise that lessened as more soldiers found wives and families, and horses were taken away to be groomed and watered. "It would seem so. Look how you've made the poor lady blush with your unkind words. To say nothing of what her poor husband must think."

Findlaech reached for one of Gruoch's hands, and she let him clasp it. As he held it gently, Gruoch raised her face to better meet his eye.

"My apologies, dear lady, Gille." Findlaech's voice was still easy, clearly one used to speaking with little fear of repercussion. Still, it was not unkind. " I meant only that my son has spoken of your beauty and virtue since meeting you in your father's home. The joke was meant to be at his sake, not yours."

"There is no need to apologise, my lord," Gille said for the both of them. His tone, although formal, was noticeably more clipped.

"You will be pleased to hear, no doubt, that Banquo and I shall not burden upon your hospitality for long, my lady." Mac Bethad spoke without looking at them as he dismounted his horse. Banquo, ever the quiet witness, followed suit, though the exasperation at his friend's words found its easy place in his eyes and around his tense mouth. "Someone has to keep the northern shores safe, and it can't be done from the comforts of a tower."

The insult lingered in the air, and none dared to recognize it for what it was. Finally, it was Findlaech who sighed in exaggerated weariness and clapped Gille once again on the shoulder, guiding him toward the tower. Gille allowed himself to be guided along, and Gruoch fell into a dutiful step behind him. Hertha appeared from thin air next to Gruoch, suddenly stepping into Gille's vacated place. Gruoch was grateful for the familiar presence as the two women walked together. She could not be sure that could have been trusted not to hesitate in her step or linger back in hopes of another sharp word with a blue-eyed man whose unexpected appearances into her life were becoming less and less unwelcome.

But Hertha was there, and their steps were in sync as the two left the company of the riders and followed Gruoch's husband into their new home.

# SEVEN

# EIMEAR

rown Hill bustled with life and business on even the most ordinary of days. Its tenants and resident merchants kept the
public spaces bustling with movement, colours, and goods,
and there was always something to be done, to be mended, to be purchased or traded. Even the ladies who resided in the small outbuildings,
and Gruoch in her tower, were kept busy with social engagements and
other wifely occupations. By the time June had arrived, Findlaech's do-
main was alive with activity.

Guests and travellers were often coming and going from the Hill, and
these visits meant more preparation and planning for Gruoch, aided in no
small way by Alane and the other household staff. One frequent visitor
was Mael, the younger brother Gille had spoken of. He was tall and thin
like Gille but lacked his easy manner and graceful movements. Hertha
had commented on the slickness of him, saying that he was as sly as a
fox creeping through long grass. Where Gille was open and inviting to
those with whom he spoke, Mael seemed to paint every word and every
expression with some other purpose. Gruoch had noticed early on that
his smile never truly seemed to reach his eyes, which remained clear and
ever calculating. Though younger than Gille, it was impossible to miss

the influence Mael seemed to weave upon his sibling, and it was clear to anyone with eyes that Gille listened to Mael and considered his advice solemnly.

Gruoch did not care for her brother-in-law.

At their first meeting, he had looked her up and down with a kind of familiarity Gruoch had not cared for, as though his brother's wife was by proxy his own property or somehow under his authority. She managed to curtsy appropriately, but there had been pungent bile under her tongue as she had smiled falsely at his smirks and snide comments about her country manner.

Bodhe's country manner would knock him onto his ass, Gruoch had thought to herself in secret and wicked delight after a particularly taxing encounter.

Gille continued to be kind to her and patient whenever she made a mistake. Mael seemed to use this to his advantage, making himself a confidant and adviser for his brother in the wake of his silly wife's inexperience. Gruoch often walked in on them huddled in close conversation by a fire or over a pint of ale, their furious whispers and wild gesturing suddenly muting themselves somewhat until she had passed by. It was Hertha, with her silent feet and her ability to melt into shadow, who first pieced together what the men spoke of.

"That man speaks of death," she had told Gruoch quietly one afternoon as the two walked together in the courtyard.

"Of whom do you speak?"

"You know of whom I speak. Mael, your husband's brother. He is a firebrand. He is a crow and a bringer of bad omens." Hertha's voice, although hushed, was heavy with a dread that did not often embellish her words.

"Death?" Gruoch asked, making sure to keep her voice low. "What are you talking about Hertha? Whose death?"

"His own," she replied. "Though he does not yet realize as much. He is trying to inspire rebellion in your man."

Gruoch smiled at a merchant, pausing to finger a collection of pelts he had displayed. She paused, allowing him to think she was considering his wares as she considered the news Hertha had shared. Gruoch said nothing, merely nodding once to him and then moving on. Hertha stayed in step at her side.

"There is peace in the North, Hertha, and the South for that matter," Gruoch responded carefully, keeping any sign of concern from her face as they walked. "Against what should he rebel? What could Mael gain from inciting my husband to treason and war?"

"The old ways still hold sway in these reaches," came Hertha's frustrating answer. "Your father may have been naive to believe that his family's hold in Moray was as strong as he claimed it to be. It would seem as though Findlaech is not the subservient steward most would see him as."

Gruoch continued to smile and nod to those who walked past, feigning interest in the stalls or the dresses of the women they met, halting Hertha in her troubling speech and allowing herself the time to process the implication of what had been said.

"These men are much like your father in the sense that it is easy to forget when a woman is present and easier still to forget that she has a mind to think and ears to hear." Hertha's tone took on a more familiar bitterness, one it had worn often before. "The crow caws to his brother that his power in the North depends on the loyalty of a Mormaer who seems dissatisfied with an allegiance that is too heavy to hold. Gille is being poisoned with the very real idea that Findlaech will sever ties with Alba and make Moray autonomous once more. Should this happen, Gille's power and hold in the area are gone, and he would be left with no other option than to slink south."

"Findlaech would never risk open rebellion against Alba," Gruoch said, half-convinced. "Duncan would make a powerful enemy, and his many allies make him even more so. Findlaech has peace, his people prosper, and he is a king in his own right. Why would he ever want or need more?"

"I have told you what I think and what I have heard, eldr," Hertha said stonily, her words clipped, making it clear the conversation was at an end. "Make of this information what you will, but never say you were not forewarned."

Gruoch considered Hertha's warnings long after they had spoken, and the echoes of fear she had felt upon hearing them the first time would twinge against the back of her mind whenever she saw Mael and Gille walking together, their heads bent in deep conversation. Or still, when their hushed voices filtered under closed doors in her apartments. Gruoch weighed the information, trying to determine whether it shifted her in one way more than another. It would not be easy to ignore and dismiss Hertha's words as her guardian had never lied or exaggerated a truth before. Gruoch could not understand why she would choose to do so now.

And so Gruoch waited, allowing the implications of such treasonous ideas to ferment themselves in her consciousness, giving her mind the time to process the importance and risk of such things so that when the moment presented itself, she could press Gille for some kind of impression without the handicap of fear and concern pressing on her. She needed to feel her worries now in order to speak with her husband without the burden of feeling when the opportunity presented itself.

Gruoch forced herself to be patient and even tried to be even more attentive to her husband while Mael kept residence at the tower. She smiled adoringly at Gille, served him his ale herself, and even sat at his knee when they were alone in their rooms, stroking his thigh as she asked him to tell her stories of his youth and adventures.

Her patience was rewarded, and an opportunity for honest discourse presented itself late one night when summer had come to the highlands. Gille and Gruoch lay in their marriage bed, blankets pushed back in the warm night air, the breeze cool against their bare skin. Gruoch lay her head on Gille's chest, stroking it gently, as Gille played with the long strands of her hair, combing it softly with his fingers.

"Gille," she began, using his Christian name, which was something she still rarely did. "My love, my courses have not come these past two months."

The fingers stilled for a moment, and Gruoch felt Gille's sharp chin come to rest atop her head.

"What are you saying, Gruoch?

She lifted her head from his chest, finding his eyes and smiling.

"Hertha tells me that I am with child."

Gille's eyes shone brilliantly at this, and his arms swept her up, holding her even tighter against him. He kissed Gruoch's hair fervently before gently pushing her away once more in order to better look at his wife.

"You are happy then, I take it?" Gruoch asked him, her voice softly teasing.

"I am happier than I can say." His words were heavy with emotion, and his joy seemed to radiate from a smile that stretched across his face. The glow of the candles cast dancing shadows through his eyes as they shone at her. "You have brought such blessing into my life, Gruoch. I love you, my wild girl. Words cannot properly say, cannot express…"

Gruoch cut off his words, bringing her fingertips gently to his mouth. She smiled at him, ecstatic herself at his apparent joy and excitement. She had been nervous and somewhat anxious at sharing the news of her pregnancy with him, and his reaction was more than reassuring.

"You will always protect us, will you not? As you swore to when we exchanged vows in the presence of my father and God?" Gruoch tried to keep her voice light as she eased into murkier waters. "You would never do anything to put us, the bairn and I, in danger?"

Gille looked at her, concern and confusion darkening his features. He took one of her hands in his own and lay it against his heart. Gruoch felt the steady thump under her palm, somewhat reassured by the heady and visceral realness of the beating.

"Gruoch, you are the most precious thing in my life," Gille said, his eyes boring into hers. "And our child could not be more wanted. I would protect you both with my life."

"I am afraid," Gruoch ventured, daring another risky step. "I am afraid that you may mean such words now but act against them in the future."

"Never." Gille's tone was firm, and it sent another wave of reassurance through her troubled thoughts, smoothing them away and eroding the sharp corners of the stress she had been carrying in her mind.

"You are happy here, Findlaech is good to you, and you shall be Mormaer. I want to know if these things shall always be so."

Gille's eyes narrowed slightly, the brows heavy over them.

"Why would you ask me such a thing, Gruoch? Where do these words come from?"

She considered her next words carefully. She lowered her head and allowed her cheek to find purchase once again on her husband's chest. Gruoch made her voice small as she replied.

"A woman feels things," she began, "She senses things. Sometimes, when you speak with Mael, you seem worried or concerned or angry and frustrated, and you come to me yet are miles away. I do not like to see you so distracted and so distanced. I fear what his influence may lead you to do."

Too far.

Gruoch felt Gille retreat in some way, even though his body didn't move. He breathed deeply and stroked her hair once more, but Gruoch knew that she had lost him.

"I will not listen to you speak against my brother, Gruoch." He spoke calmly, but the warning there was as clear and as vicious as ice. "You are my wife, and you have my heart, but my brother knows my mind and my every thought. We have shared much, and I will not have you slander him. You do not know of what you speak."

"You are right," she attempted, trying to smooth him back to a restful calm. "I should not have spoken of such things. I could not possibly understand the help and relief that his council surely brings you."

Her words did not work as she needed them to. Gruoch had taken her chance and pushed it too far. She had betrayed too much of what she had been carrying since Hertha had first shared her concerns. It would not be easy to get past this.

"I am tired, and you will need to rest." Gille's voice left no room for discussion as he blew out the candle on the table near their bed. "Go to sleep, wife. Let no more ugly thoughts poison your mind. Think of our child and fill your heart with love. A child takes in such things from his mother. Do not fill my son with bile and suspicion."

It was dark, and Gille rolled away from her. Gruoch lay in their bed, more troubled than ever.

It was made immediately clear to Gruoch that Gille had spoken of her suspicions in some way with his brother, for soon Mael was shooting her with expressions of sneering victory whenever he could.

You will not turn him from me. He comes to me for help and guidance, not you.

His face spoke the words clearly even though he could not say them aloud. Gruoch kept her face void of feeling or expression, as Hertha had often tried to teach her to do, rather than engage in his petulant show of dominance and challenge. Gruoch smiled back at him sweetly, asked after him, and pretended not to notice the ease with which he slithered into her husband's every decision.

As her baby and her belly grew, it became easier for Gruoch to distract herself from whatever Mael and Gille were or were not plotting. She took quiet moments to rejoice in the swell of her stomach and was delighted when she first began to feel the child moving inside her. Hertha hovered even closer now, a protective shadow that was forever cast upon her charge. She made no appearance at deference when she forced Gruoch to eat a second helping at meals or when she forced the girl to sit and rest steadily swelling ankles.

Hertha scolded her for eating too much or for eating too little, for walking too far or not enough, and this behaviour soon belied the truth behind Hertha's motivations. Gruoch had walked alone into territory that was unknown to Hertha. The path that Gruoch now walked on was one that Hertha had walked alongside but one she had never journeyed herself. All she could do was try to clear the way for Gruoch's heavy steps.

The next few months found a steady rhythm, and Gruoch allowed herself to feel the bliss of impending motherhood wash over her. There was a feeling of satisfaction in knowing she would bear Gille his first child, and although the women of the Hill sometimes whispered and gossiped of Gille's illegitimate brood spread through the area, Gruoch paid such words no mind. Her husband had never struck her as anything but a God-fearing man, one for whom a vow held importance and meaning. Whatever he had done before joining himself to her through their marriage was of little importance. Gille may have other children, but hers would be the first legitimate one. Their children would fill the Hill with laughter and joy, and Gille and Gruoch would grow old, surrounded by their family.

It was easy to lose herself in such fantasies, and Gille was often a too-willing participant. They would lay together in the warmth of their blankets, and he would gently stroke her belly and would laugh in delight when he felt the child move under his hands. Although he could never have paid such attention in public, Gruoch treasured these quiet moments with her husband and thrived under his undivided attention.

The winter solstice came and went, and Christmas mass was celebrated in a small stone chapel on the grounds. Gruoch was allowed a short reprieve from her confinement in order to attend, and she was heaped with blankets and mantles to protect her from the cold and to hide her swollen body, a sight considered unbecoming of a noblewoman. Although the building was rudimentary and modest in both decor and size, the occupants of the Hill filled it to bursting, and the beautiful Latin hymns and prayers filled the night. It was her first Christmas away from her home, and while Gruoch missed her father terribly, she also thought of the joy she would feel when she would get to introduce Bodhe to his first grandchild. She had been told to expect the child before the ides of February were upon them.

Gille had been so attentive and loving to Gruoch in the first months of her pregnancy that it troubled her when such moments became rarer. His absences were longer and more frequent, and as the child in her belly began to lower itself after Christmas, Gruoch struggled to move as easily as she had in the early months.

Hertha had spoken with some of the women at Crown Hill and had been told of Eimear, a cunning woman who came highly recommended. When she had broached the topic with Findlaech one evening as they ate in the hall, the Mormear assured Gruoch that she could trust Eimear.

"She delivered my own son," Findlaech had said kindly, gently patting Gruoch's hand in assurance.

Although her praises were sung by all who had benefited from her services, Eimear was not painted as someone particularly kind or patient. At their first meeting, Gruoch found the woman to be brusque and almost rude as she prodded and touched Gruoch's stomach without first asking permission. Hertha had smirked as she stood standing by, nodding her approval at the way Eimear went about her business with the cool and confident detachment gained only through the course of many years of experience.

"The birth is imminent," Eimear had said as she spanned Gruoch's belly with her hands. "You must rest as much as you can before this babe makes its way into the world."

"All will be well?" Gruoch's question had been posed in a small voice, and Eimear had sighed, stopping to cross her arms and look Gruoch squarely in the eye.

"If you are nervous, pray to the Mother that she watch over you both."

"I often pray to the Virgin," Gruoch replied sincerely.

"Her too, then, if it comforts you," Eimear had said flatly. "I will return in a few days." After a few more touches of Gruoch's stomach, Eimear had gathered her things and left. Although Hertha seemed reassured by the cunning woman's experience and willingness to assist in the birth, Gruoch was still uneasy. There was a strange familiarity in the way Eimear had looked into Gruoch's eyes, as though some secret communication had been passed between them. Taking Eimear's warning to heart,

Gruoch suppressed her anxiety as best she could and forced herself to rest more often than she had been, though she found it difficult to be still for very long.

True to her word, Eimear returned three days after their first meeting. Gruoch had retired to her bed, Hertha standing by her bedside, and Eimear entered the room with a small basket of supplies. She nodded permission to Hertha's silent inquiry before the Norse woman opened the basket gently in order to shift through its contents.

"I've brought the herbs we'll need should she bleed too much," Eimear said, speaking to Hertha after hearing a few approving grunts as the latter considered the supply of medicinal plants.

Eimear had no patience for the girl's fear or uncertainties. When she spoke to Gruoch, Eimear expected to be obeyed immediately, and her hands were not always gentle as she handled her charge. It was difficult to place her age. Her face was wrinkled, and yet her eyes were alert and bright. Her gnarled hands shook as she sipped her water from its tankard but felt sure and strong when they felt along Gruoch's stomach and taking in the baby's form and feeling. As she worked, Eimear explained to the mother-to-be that she was trying to ensure the baby's head was in the correct position.

"The bairn is stubborn," Eimear grumbled as she pushed uncomfortably against Gruoch. "It insists on moving against its own self-interest."

The girl tried to raise herself to her elbows, only to feel the heel of Hertha's palm gently but firmly push her back to the mattress. Gruoch sighed, frustrated, as her back became prone once more.

"What do you mean, Eimear?" She asked, hating the small sound of her voice. She cleared her throat, allowing her lungs a deep breath. "Explain. Please."

Eimear grunted as her hands kneaded and pushed on her patient's swollen stomach. Gruoch ground her teeth as a small whimper climbed into her mouth, determined to keep the traitorous noise from escaping.

"I will have to turn it," Eimear said simply, in a tone that almost suggested the baby had done this deliberately to keep her from things she would much rather be doing. "It will hurt. You," she said to Hertha, "hold her. Do not let her squirm away."

Hertha's right hand clamped down on Gruoch's left shoulder, effectively pinning her to the mattress. The left hand, however, came to grip Gruoch's own hand, and she clasped it firmly, entwining their fingers. Hertha offered Gruoch a brief and fleeting smile. Hertha nodded to the girl who lay trembling on the bed and watched as Gruoch closed her eyes and took a shaking breath.

Eimear had not lied.

Gruoch's body raged against the pressure that was suddenly mounted upon it, and her muscles screamed. She bit down unto her lower lip, her teeth relentlessly pushing against the soft flesh until the salty taste of her blood filtered unto her tongue. Still, she made no scream, and Hertha's strong grip on her hand was an anchor to which Gruoch could tie her attention and focus.

Eimear's hands finally let up their ceaseless pushing, and Gruoch allowed herself to slowly open her eyes. The old woman was wiping a thin sheen of sweat from her brow with the back of one twisted hand, but she wore an expression of pleased satisfaction.

"It must be a boy," Eimear said. "Another boy without the sense to know what's good for him."

Gruoch exhaled, the tension and pain slowly fading from her consciousness, and Hertha's fingers squeezed hers one final time before the two women stepped away, allowing Gruoch to slip into a dreamless sleep.

"What would you have him think of you?"

The harsh whisper of words pulled at Gruoch in her sleep, tearing her away from the beautiful numbness of empty dreams and back into the discomfort and aches of her body. She lay on her side, piled high with blankets against the chill of the evening air that came in through the window. The flames in the fireplace sent out a warm glow, and Gruoch felt the heat licking at her back, cutting away the cold January air. She lay still, closing her eyes and trying to lull herself back to the sweet embrace of sleep.

"I would have him think his father a loyal nobleman. One who is honourable and does not bend meekly to the will of younger brothers."

Gille's voice now joined the second, and as sleep fell away, awareness set it. She realized the first, angry whisper belonged to Mael, though what he was doing in her husband's private apartments, Gruoch could only guess. She kept herself immobile, eyes shut, forcing her body to continue to breathe slowly and deeply as though she were still deeply in the thralls of slumber.

"Everything is in place," Mael replied, his words echoing like a veritable hiss in the darkness of her mind. "You have the girl to tie you to Duncan, and the king would only see in you an honest and valuable lord if you should be the one to reveal Findlaech's treachery."

"You have no proof!"

"His son travels the coast and the moors, gathering support against you! The men of the North are desperate under Duncan's taxes. You must think strategically, brother." Mael's voice managed to slice through the air with the same deftness as a blade cutting through flesh, but it still flowed with the same grace as a hand that gently cupped a cheek. The double-edge to her husband troubled her. Gruoch forced her breath to remain calm, worried that Gille would notice she was awake.

"Keep your voice down," Gille whispered furiously, as though reading her mind and sending a chill down her spine. "If you wake Gruoch, I will kill you myself."

A pause.

"Besides," Gille continued, "Moray benefits from the support of Alba's soldiers in defending its borders."

"The men would say differently, should you ever open your ears and listen," Mael shot back. "They say that forces are too few and far between and that Morayan blood stains the earth that Alba claims to protect."

"It is in Alba's interest to protect Moray. The people know this."

"Duncan is her uncle. You have aligned yourself with the South. You are a loyal subject of Alba and would ensure that Moray remains safe and prosperous. Findlaech wants to tear it away and has already sent his son to pull at the seams."

Another silence.

"Everything is in place," Mael continued softly. "And I am here, brother. We can do this together. I will not leave you to shoulder the burden alone."

The cramp that sent her back into spasms came upon Gruoch suddenly and with little warning. It had crawled out of the constant pressure in her womb and hips and nestled itself firmly in the small of her back. Caught off guard, she was unable to help the small gasp that escaped her as the vice in her bones suddenly tightened itself. Knowing that she had given herself away, Gruoch made a show of slowly stretching her body and rubbing at her eyes. She rolled onto her back and sent her hands to her hips, gripping them. She pretended for a moment to think she was alone before allowing her eyes to open and settle on the pair of men by the fireplace, standing in mirrored expressions of shock and concern. Her husband quickly stepped to her and sat beside Gruoch on the bed. Mael's expression, one Gruoch could only study for the cruellest of brief moments, displayed a more selfish version of concern. Did he suspect she had been listening?

"Gruoch, what is it? Is it the bairn?" Gille's voice still held the whispered cadence of his previous conversation, as though his mind were still pulled in twain.

She struggled to sit up, Mael falling steadily from her thoughts.

"It's too early," she said, panicked. "There are still a few weeks to go."

"Brother, fetch my lady's handmaid." Gille's voice lost the subterfuge it had been carrying and found the timbre of a lord and leader accustomed to obedience. "Have her send for the cunning woman and tell her to come here once she has done so."

Mael looked on for a moment before resigning himself to the task and sweeping quickly from the room.

In the years to come, whenever she allowed herself to look back on the night her child was born, Gruoch was always frustrated by the fog that seemed to hand over it. Everything seemed to be coated in some kind of dreamlike stance, as though her mind had devised some way of keeping her from reliving it in full. She would think on it later, sure in her belief that no woman would ever willingly bring to life a child after having already born one if she could not find some way of forgetting the previous experience.

As she recalled the events of that night through an outsider's lens, a witness to the events unfurling around her, she remembered interminable hours. She remembered her throat, hoarse and dry from screaming. She remembered Hertha's steady presence at her side and the feel of her palm smoothing away the hair from Gruoch's sweaty forehead. She remembered Eimear's voice, gentle and encouraging early in the birth, becoming more demanding and urgent as Gruoch struggled through her labour. She could look back and watch herself writhe in the bed that was soaked with perspiration and blood. She saw herself cry out for her mother and sob like a child.

Gruoch would come to understand later in her life that at that moment, drenched in her own blood and grasping at Hertha's hands, she had been just a child.

When her son was finally delivered from her, Gruoch became aware enough to realize that he made no noise. The concern she felt was mercifully brief, for she lost consciousness shortly after the babe left her. Eimear had been forced to cut her with a small and clever blade, and the loss of blood had pushed Gruoch from herself.

When she did finally wake, her son had been alive for hours and, according to Eimear, would likely continue to be. The old woman had bound him tightly in wrapping clothes and laid him in a wooden cradle by the fireplace. As Gruoch struggled to open her eyes, the first thing to assail itself to her senses was the soft sound of the baby snoring and cooing gently in his sleep.

As she woke, Gruoch felt Hertha tense beside her, perking herself up from her own exhaustion. She knew without asking that Hertha had not once left her side. When Gruoch was able to rouse herself and look at her guardian properly, the fatigue and worry were clearly etched into the shadows around Hertha's metallic eyes. Gruoch had never before seen the love Hertha bore displayed so openly and honestly. Her hands were as gentle and kind as a mother's as she stroked Gruoch's cheek and harsh and quick as they brushed away a stray tear that escaped the confines of her own proud eyes.

"*Eldr*," was all Hertha said.

"Your bairn lives," Eimear called from the fireplace, placing her hands on her knees in order to help lift herself from her chair. "And it seems you will as well. You are lucky you are young. Your body will recover this time."

Gruoch's body ached in ways she had never dreamed possible, and it screamed at her when she attempted to raise herself and sit. Hertha's hands held her down gently, keeping her still.

"You must rest now, Gruoch," she admonished gently. "You fought bravely, little warrior. And so did your son. But you must both allow yourselves to heal and to build up your strengths."

Eimear watched this exchange, pleased, and nodded her head.

"Listen to your Norse woman, my lady," she said as she made her way towards the door. "I think she would take a blade to Death himself should he try and come for you now."

"I want to hold him," Gruoch said weakly, looking back to Hertha.

"He sleeps," Hertha assured her. "I will bring him when he wakes."

"Has Gille come? What has he said?"

There was a moment of silence as the woman seemed to consider their next words. Their hesitation threw a chill of fear through her. Was Gille displeased?

"He is a man and, therefore, cannot be expected to know what to say in these situations," Eimear said finally. "The babe is early, so the babe is small. Your husband seems to have expected a fully formed soldier to spring from your womb."

"Will he be alright?" Gruoch asked. "The babe, I mean. Will he thrive?"

"Though he may be small, he is fierce," Hertha assured her. "He has sprung from living flame. And he has me to watch over him while you sleep."

"I will bring the herbs we spoke of," Eimear said pointedly to Hertha. "Keep him from her bed for at least two moons, and if that man has any sense, he will listen."

Hertha nodded. Before Gruoch could ask them what they meant, her body betrayed her and cast her back into the sweeping black of exhausted sleep.

# PART TWO
## -A MOTHER-

# EIGHT
# BEGINNING TO SEE

True to her word, Hertha had not left Gruoch's side while she slept through that first night of her son's life. Indeed, for the next few months, she was never very far at all, never leaving Gruoch out of earshot should she or the boy need for anything.

It still amazed Gruoch to see how soft and gentle Hertha was as she held the boy to her, stroking her cheek against his downy one and smelling the sweet scent of his hair. She was a vision far removed from the fierce warrior and protector she had always been when it came to his mother. Although her hand had often found Gruoch's in moments of fear or concern, Hertha had never been the openly affectionate creature she became when she held the babe in her arms. It was clear that Lulach had woven some spell over his guardian.

Even Gille had finally come around in regard to his son. The first few interactions between father and son had been awkward for them all and secretly painful for Gruoch. It hurt her to see the disappointment plain on her husband's face as he took in the baby's frail body and the annoyance that crossed his features when Lulach fussed.

"Are all bairns so scrawny?" he asked, holding the boy in his strong forearm and gazing down at him, his look a mixture of pity and something darker. "He doesn't seem to grow. There is no fat to him."

Gruoch held her arms out for the baby, and her husband relented him to her. She wrapped Lulach more securely in his swaddling clothes, bundling him against the winter chill.

"What do you expect, my lord," she asked, her tone moderate. Gruoch refused to allow the stream of venom that washed through her mind to filter into her words and betray how she felt. "He will grow. Give him time and remember that he did come early."

Gille nodded, still unconvinced, and rose from his chair. Gruoch stayed in her seat by the fireplace but nodded demurely in farewell as her husband looked on. More words were hanging behind his eyes, other concerns she knew he wanted to broach with her. Although Gruoch knew these conversations were inevitable and should not be ignored, she dreaded them.

At Eimear's insistence and Hertha's not-so-subtle reminding, Gille had been an inactive bedfellow. He slept at his wife's side most nights as the tower afforded few rooms as comfortable as their own, save Findlaech's, but he often came in late at night, smelling of other women. Gruoch was surprised to find that she didn't mind and at how relieved she was to avoid whatever conjugal obligations Gille might expect. Eimear had been clear; her body would not survive another childbirth.

Gruoch was not fool enough to believe that things could not continue in this way. For all his faults, she knew that Gille considered himself a God-fearing man, and he had sworn marriage vows in front of a holy man and the eyes of their Church. The ire of Christ might have been an insufficient discouragement from visiting the beds of a few serving maids. Still, it seemed as though some ingrained religious guilt made it impossible for Gille to neglect his wife entirely.

"We will have more children," Gille had told her as he made his way to the door. "You are young yet, and Lulach will be the first of many."

"It will be as God wills," Gruoch said demurely to his back as he left the chamber, the wooden door closing loudly behind him.

The sound of the door coming to rest in its frame caused Lulach to squirm in her embrace and to emit a mewl of displeasure in his sleep. Gruoch rocked him gently, sweeping a finger down his brow and along the ridge of his nose.

"Your god will have no say in the matter," Hertha said quietly from her seat nearer to the window where she sat, badly pretending to fold blankets. "Not if you do as Eimear has instructed."

Gruoch did not take her eyes away from her son's sleeping face as she considered Hertha's words. The midwife had not spared Gruoch's feelings as she had outlined for them the reality of the situation and the consequences of Lulach's difficult birth. In the simplest of terms, Eimear had explained that Gruoch's body would not suffer another pregnancy and certainly not another labour. Giving birth to another child would surely mean the end of her own life.

The herbs that Eimear had given to Hertha were brewed into a tea that Gruoch drank every evening. The girl did not ask Hertha to explain the different properties of the herbs that were used or even the names of such plants. She was heartbroken to think she would have no more children, but the idea of leaving Lulach alone with his father should she die in childbirth was enough for Gruoch to forgo the idea of a large family and drink back the bitter potion Eimear supplied.

Of course, Gille could never know of such an arrangement. It would mean death for Eimear and Hertha and dishonour and shame upon her family and father.

Out of respect for Eimear's advice and concern for Gruoch's health and that of their son, Gille left his wife to herself for the first six months of their son's life. Gruoch spent this time doing her best to strengthen her baby and help him grow, and it caused her no measure of joy to see him thrive and become alert to the world around him.

Gruoch found a dark kind of humour in the situation when, as an old woman, she would allow herself to look back on those times, to think of how little she knew of the world and yet how satisfied she'd been to believe that she held it in her arms.

She should have held on tighter.

During the first year of Lulach's life, Mael was a constant visitor, and his visits left Gille mercurial and unsteady. No sooner had Gruoch managed to turn her husband's moods sunny or light than Mael would return, with his pointed words and his toxic whispers, setting Gille's blood to a frenzy with blazes of loyalty, duty, and what it truly meant to be a man. Gruoch watched, exasperated, as this man, this younger brother, managed so easily to spin the lies that wound Gille up so tightly. It was almost pathetic to see to what extent her husband allowed himself to be spun up by such a spider's ministrations.

Gruoch knew that Mael was aware of her scrutiny and active dislike, and she was sure that Mael did whatever he deemed necessary to ensure that he armed himself against it. This presence of mind was all too obvious to Gruoch when she considered the looks Mael would give her in the presence of her husband, his face a perfect mask of respect and civility while his eyes gleamed and danced with the knowledge that it was he, and not Gruoch, who held Gille's ear.

She also saw how Mael looked at Lulach with a strange distance in his eyes. He never held the babe save for those terse moments when Gille forced his brother to acknowledge the boy. Mael acted as though Lulach were simply an extension of Gruoch herself and not Gille's first legitimate son, a potential Mormaer and an heir more likely than himself.

"I like not the way he slithers at your husband's heel," Hertha had breathed to Gruoch, taking Lulach and bringing him to her chest, where she nestled to the baby as he cuddled into her shoulder, his pink face full and sweet.

Gruoch chucked Lulach gently under his chin and stuck out her tongue. Lulach was growing ever more aware of the world around him and of those with whom he spent most of his time. It still shocked his mother to think of a time before him, a time when his deep eyes had not been there to look back at her as she held him close. As Lulach grew, she learned to be content with wrapping herself up in his small world and ignoring her husband and his brother. Gruoch decided that she would let them scheme and talk amongst themselves. She could no longer bring herself to care.

Life was a strange blend of blissful moments of peace, love, and an antic agitation regarding a growing sense of threat among the northern shores. Word had reached Moray, and even the King in Alba, that the Norsemen were slowly gathering forces once more. The fear of a fresh assault and even war was tangible and tasted sour on the damp and misty spring air, which should have brought with it a refreshing cleanse from the stale winds of winter.

Findlaech had often been gone, travelling through the villages and hamlets of Moray, gathering soldiers and helping to reinforce walls and fences. There was also the question of taxation, of taking from the people what Duncan and Alba claimed as their sovereign due. Gruoch had grown up watching her father's tenants bring their tithes to their home before these payments made their annual trip south toward Edinburgh. Her father had claimed that the people were happy for the protection of Alba's extended reach. Still, as Gruoch took in the toil and never-ending work of those over whose lives she now held a particular responsibility, she could not help but wonder if Alba asked for more than Moray's people could stomach.

Such thoughts were complicated and confusing, and Gruoch put them out of her mind, spending her energies and time memorizing the dimple in her son's cheek and the soft velvet skin at the nape of his neck.

Since rumours of war in the north had reached them, Gruoch had observed a steady and growing bustle in her new home. Crown Hill was alive and crawling with visitors as ever, but now a greater number of these carried weapons and provisions. Moreover, stores were stocked and rationed more strictly than they had been upon her arrival in anticipation and preparation for sieges or a lack of access to crops.

As the spring melted away, taking with it the constant wet and rain of April, the warm and sunnier days of May found her welcoming a guest Gruoch had not seen at Crown Hill since first arriving there.

Hertha found Gruoch in her apartments, laughing as Lulach stumbled after a delicate wooden horse his mother had found for him at a vendor's stall. He clutched at the figurine in his chubby hand, wobbling with the dangerous and tottering speed of toddlers as he made his horse gallop over fur rugs and jump over other discarded playthings.

Gruoch looked away from her son briefly as Hertha entered the room, smiling at her friend before turning her attention back to the gleeful child. Hertha made her way in quietly, coming to sit in the wooden chair next to Gruoch. For a moment, neither woman spoke, Lulach's imaginings providing them with the excuse to sit in silence and merely watch.

"The Mormaer's son has returned," Hertha said finally. "The falcon."

Gruoch looked away from Lulach's play and found Hertha's gaze fixed on her.

"Mac Bethad?"

"The same."

Gruoch turned her attention back to her son. "It is a shame Findlaech is not here to greet him. I know he would have liked to see his son. We spoke shortly before the Mormaer's departure, and he mentioned that he thought of Mac Bethad often now that he saw Gille and I with Lulach."

"He asked after you," Hertha continued as though Gruoch had not spoken. "I told him I would pass along his greeting."

Gruoch rose from her chair, smoothing down the front of her skirt. She held out a hand to Lulach, who accepted it sullenly, still grasping his horse tightly.

"As he should and as I am sure he did for Gille," Gruoch responded. "I am the lady here. It is only fitting that he should inquire as to my health. I shall seek him out and make sure that Alane has prepared suitable quarters."

"Surely an unnecessary task," Hertha said dryly. "I am sure Alane felt a tremor on the wind the second a guest of such import had turned his horse in the direction of the Hill."

Gruoch chuckled to herself at Hertha's stubborn resistance to Alane's charms and bent to pick up Lulach, whose small steps would not allow him to keep up with them. She kissed his cheek and handed him to Hertha, who accepted the boy into her arms with little ceremony. She nodded to him solemnly and whispered a few guttural words under her breath.

"Do not let Gille hear you speaking to him in your northern tongue, Hertha," Gruoch reminded her yet again. "You take your life in your hands when you disregard me."

As stoic as ever, Hertha replied by crossing her eyes at the bridge of her nose and inciting a fresh wave of giggles from the boy.

They made their way to the main hall, where a number of tired and weary men sat at wooden tables with tankards of ale in their hands, their boots still muddy from the road. A large stone fireplace crowned the northern end of the room, and though there was no need to light it on such a mild and balmy day, it was, as ever, a rallying point for the more senior men to gather. Such a group stood there now, a few seated on some stone benches while a few stood before the empty hearth, speaking and gesturing wildly.

Gruoch recognized Banquo from his shock of black hair and his beard, which had grown thicker and longer since the last time she had laid eyes on him. He sat on a bench, his back hunched forward and his forearms resting on his thighs as he looked before him at the men who stood there in what appeared to be a heated argument.

There she saw Ross, his face rough from the wind and his cheeks heavy with stubble. He paused in his speech as he saw Gruoch approach, taking a moment to nod and bend his knees gently in her direction. It was more formal than necessary, as her husband was not yet Mormaer, but she had come to expect such overt politeness from the man her father had always considered to be a friend.

Although the man to whom Ross spoke was turned away from her, Gruoch recognized him just as easily as she had the others. One broad shoulder dipped slightly as Ross averted his gaze, and a tanned cheek appeared over it. Mac Bethad's chestnut hair had grown longer as well since his last visit to the Hill, and strands of it fell in the piercing blue of his gaze. Gruoch found her body finding a strange stillness as both stood for a moment, their eyes finding the other's, neither one willing to offer the first dip of the head or bending of the knee. Finally, it took a small punch to the arm from Ross to send Mac Bethad into an obviously be-grudging and ever so slight genuflect. Gruoch nodded in return, allowing herself to dip into the slightest curtsy.

"My lords," she called to them as she approached, holding Mac Bethad's gaze. Gruoch purposefully ignored the strange fire she saw kindling there behind the humour he always seemed to bring to the forefront. "Welcome home. If you will forgive me, you seem still weary and tired from your travels. Are preparations underway for accommodations? I see you've ale. Would you prefer the chance to bathe?"

"It takes a brazen woman to tell a man he needs bathing while he is in his own father's home." Mac Bethad's tone was easy, his words clipped with that undercurrent of wit that usually peppered them.

"No, my lord," Gruoch replied, grinning. "Only one who fears the scent of the prodigal son will likewise return to stay in the room where my husband takes his meals."

Mac Bethad's smile crept easily to his face and found its way to his eyes. He shook his head slightly and held up his hands in mock defeat.

"Of course, my lady," he said, turning to Banquo and winking. "I should have remembered the sharpness of your wit and the delights of your tongue."

This time, Ross's punch landed harder against Mac Bethad's arm, making the latter wince in a mock grimace of pain. Gruoch felt herself blush in embarrassment at Mac Bethad's words, exasperated that he could say such glib and sly things to her, and even angrier with herself for reacting like a naive and shocked maiden. Her cheeks warm and undoubtedly red, Gruoch ignored the last comment and smiled at Banquo, who returned it apologetically.

"We have been looked after, my lady," came his soft and easy voice, the timbre steady and sure. "I thank you, and again, apologize for my idiot friend."

"And now my own chosen brother attacks me!" Mac Bethad took on an injured tone, dramatically rubbing the arm that had suffered Ross' assail. "What lessons to teach the little one."

Gruoch turned over her shoulder and saw Hertha standing a few paces behind, still holding Lulach, whose horse was still being made to frolic one some invisible heath. Lulach chortled happily, undeterred by the strangers that surrounded him. Gruoch knew only too well the feeling of safety that immediate proximity to Hertha could provide.

"He has all the teachers he needs," Gruoch told Mac Bethad, turning back to him once she felt the rushing of her blood slow and cool. "But I thank you for your concern."

The men who sat nearby, bored with the discourse and ready to return to their drinks and stories, diverted their attention. Banquo pushed back from his knees and allowed his back to come up. He shook his head quietly to himself and reached for his ale.

"You are well then, my lady?" Ross asked. His tone was courteous, and his expression seemed sincere.

"I am, thank you. My husband…"

"Yes, where is he?" Mac Bethad interrupted, making a sudden show of looking around the hall. "I have been busy defending his borders and seem to have mistakenly assumed he would want a report."

"He and a small party of men left on patrol two days ago," Gruoch responded, refusing to rise to the occasion.

"He must be either a very trusting man or a stupid one to leave you here," Mac Bethad continued, turning away completely from Ross and taking a step towards her. "Alone, where any brutish man might come along and say rude and suggestive things."

"Hardly alone, my lord," Gruoch said, standing her ground and lifting her chin to look him more squarely in the eye. "You have your friends, and I," she nodded over her shoulder towards Hertha, who was undoubtedly watching the exchange, "Have mine."

Mac Bethad looked over Gruoch's shoulder, and a sudden shift in his smile told her he must have spotted a rather unimpressed Norsewoman. Gruoch made no effort to move as Mac Bethad approached and walked past her in the direction of her son, though she turned slightly as he did so. She watched as Findlaech's son knelt before her own, who held out his small wooden horse in a solemn show of pride. Mac Bethad nodded appreciatively to Lulach and said something too low for Gruoch to hear, though Lulach's face broke into a glorious smile. After clapping the boy soundly on the shoulder, Mac Bethad rose to his feet and turned to face her once more.

"A shield-maiden and a strapping young man to protect you? I suppose you are not so helpless as all that."

"Not so helpless at all, my lord," Gruoch said, tilting her head slightly to the side and allowing her eyes to look down once, demurely, before rising back to meet his own. This time, she was pleased to see a shiver of shock dance over Mac Bethad's features, his Adam's apple dipping quickly as he swallowed before the effect was lost and the carefree expression once more adorned his face.

"So I am beginning to see," he replied.

The summer was a long and difficult one. The northern raiders were relentless, and wave after wave of their longboats breached the beaches of Moray, spilling hordes of violent and bloodthirsty warriors onto the sand and rocks. Villages were destroyed and fields burned, sending the few survivors racing from their homes and scrambling over the hills in search of shelter. Findlaech had ordered more patrols and had requested that neighbouring villages and settlements send able-bodied men to Crown Hill for training. He was still hesitant, however, about asking for Southern support.

"He is making a mistake in waiting so long to ask Duncan for help," Gille ranted to Gruoch one evening as they ate in their apartment. "We need reinforcements and weapons, and we need soldiers who know how to wield them if we ever plan on ridding ourselves of these barbarians."

The room was quiet and mostly bare of Lulach's toys and things, as he had taken to sleeping in a chamber with some of the other boys. At the cusp of three, he was already running around after the older children and imitating the games he watched them play. Gruoch allowed her eyes to wander to a few forgotten items and to the wooden horse that had so captured his attention a few months ago. A cold feeling of dread threatened to push up from the pits of her stomach and stop the air in her chest. What if the worst were to happen, and the Norseman made their way to Inverness? Would they slaughter her son on their way to killing her father?

"Findlaech is stubborn, and his pride will cost him men's lives," Gille continued, undeterred by his wife's silence. "Sweyn Forkbeard will call on troops in Hibernia to supplement his legions of pagan axe men. We are sure of it."

"I am sure you will know what to do, Gille," Gruoch told him softly, attempting to calm the rage that set the muscles in his arms to twitching. "You will find the solution, and you will help Findlaech to see it as well."

Gille sighed, running his hand impatiently over his chin as he considered her words. Gruoch watched as he took them in, turning them in his mind and weighing their worth.

"I will send for Mael," he said as Gruoch's heart thudded dully in her chest. "He will know what to do."

# NINE
# SHE, TOO, BECOMES A GHOST

In the short years of Lulach's life, time passed for Gruoch in that slow and steady way that it did for all parents of small children. In those blissful early days, she could spend hours doting upon her child and marvel at each tiny toe, each delicate finger, and her heart would melt at each coo and sigh. Then, only too soon, those feet and hands became sturdier, thinner, and moved with more confidence and strength. Lulach went from a babe in arms to an inquisitive and curious boy before Gruoch could truly grasp how much her son had grown.

The boy allowed his mother to escape the world in which she had suddenly found herself since the Norse menace had grown ever stronger. It seemed as though stories and rumours of raids and pillaged villages and homes were reaching them with steady and alarming regularity. As a result, Gille had become even more withdrawn from his family and more harried. He spent his days and nights in the companies of other lords, pouring over maps of the area and plotting how best to push the northern invaders back into their longboats and back into the seas.

This increased stress, and urgency, meant that Mael became a constant presence at Crown Hill. Gruoch could not miss the look of utter triumph on his face when they crossed paths every so often in the yard or one of the winding halls of the tower. *I am here*, the expression said, his eyes smug and his smile the absolute pinnacle of brotherly love. *I am here, and he needs me. You are not required. You haven't the answers he seeks.*

Gruoch worried about Mael's deep and lingering anger towards her, as well as his desire to push her aside to gain further access to Gille. Hertha and Gruoch both knew that this unfiltered access would allow Mael more than ample opportunity to bend his brother's ear, all the more with talk of revolt and rebellion against Findlaech to secure their power in the North through a show of loyalty for Duncan in the South.

"He must still believe that Findlaech is planning to take Moray out of the grips of the Alban king," Hertha whispered to Gruoch fervently as they watched Lulach practising with a small wooden sword. "Your husband and his brother will act quickly to keep that from happening, for such an act would leave Gille with no power and no title to inherit."

The two women strolled through the open air of the yard, taking in the sweet and gentle air of a pleasant September day. Gruoch held her tongue as she considered Hertha's words. Gruoch still did not want to believe that her husband, a man her father had deemed worthy of his only child, could fall so low as to betray the Mormaer. And yet her every nerve was alight with the fear and trepidation that lay in the realization that Hertha was most likely right. Gruoch knew it was only a matter of time before the poison Mael had been steadily feeding her husband took root in his guts and sharpened his ambitions into pricking spurs.

Lulach tripped on a loose stone and sprawled into the dirt. His mother rushed to him, eager to leave Hertha and her words a few steps behind. Gruoch helped the child to his feet and brushed the dust and dirt from his tunic. His solemn eyes considered hers for a moment before he leaned in and placed a feathery soft kiss upon her cheek. With that, his sword was back in his hand, and he had returned to sparring with some imaginary opponent.

The boy had already seen two full summers. Gruoch had matured and grown as well, a woman of eighteen and ripe childbearing age. She knew that the other ladies whispered about her flat belly and the lack of heirs she had provided for her husband, other than the small son with whom he seemed quietly unsatisfied. She had taken every precaution at both Hertha and Eimear's urging and reminding, carefully drinking daily tonics made from the herbs the midwife had provided since Lulach's difficult birth. Any longing that Gruoch might have felt for more children was swiftly and efficiently crushed under the love she felt for the child she already had and by the fear that any siblings she tried to bear would mean the end of her life and the beginning of a lonely one for her son.

Gille had expressed his frustrations over Gruoch's apparent barrenness in subtle yet cruel ways. He would often speak within range of his wife's hearing with his soldiers, friends, or worse, his brother, about his desire to fill his home with many strong children. He commented on the beauty and fertility of other women and the God-given duties of a wife. The man she had fallen in love with at the age of fifteen had become a stranger to Gruoch. Their quiet and intimate conversations and lovemaking were replaced with the ravings of a boorish and insecure man who seemed in a constant need to measure his successes and accomplishments against those of other men and who seemed destined to fall short of his own expectations each time.

It seemed as though all of the inhabitants of Crown Hill walked a tentative line, and Gruoch treasured every small step, for it seemed inevitable that wind should blow in and sweep her from her course and far from the path she had been treading.

The day her son died became a strange and hazy recollection of random events in Gruoch's mind. For example, she would later remember that he ate precisely one egg that morning with a piece of bread and that he insisted on putting his tunic on himself. On the other hand, she would not remember if the day was bright, cold, cloudy, or warm. She could not remember what she had done that morning to fill her time. Instead, her memory was a strange cacophony of seemingly unimportant details that clamoured over one another for her attention. Each one screamed that if she had simply paid attention, looked more closely, and seen the things she was meant to have seen, her son could have lived.

Would have lived.

Gruoch had allowed herself to become too much of a silent witness, a complacent bystander. She had permitted the pieces of her life to move without her approbation until the rules had changed without her even being aware.

Gruoch did not remember what she was doing before hearing Alane screaming for her and Gille. She did not remember who she was with or to whom she was speaking at the time. Gruoch could only remember the uneven feeling of the stones beneath her feet as she ran in the direction of the frantic screeches and the thought that she must find Lulach, for surely the child would have been frightened by so much screaming.

A kitchen maid held Lulach against her body, cradled like a bride in her arms. The boy's face was pallid and blue, the lovely dark eyes staring vacantly ahead. Gruoch stopped short, confusing, settling over her limbs and slowing them down, making her feel as though she were walking along the bottom of a loch with her clothes weighing her down. She held out her hands for her son, even as others rushed forward and past where she knelt.

Alane's screams were still piercing through the noise of those who approached the scene in horror, and Gruoch was unable to make a sound loud enough to be heard over the older woman's wails. So she stood, mute and dumb, with her arms outstretched, waiting for the maid to give her the child so that his mother might calm the others and explain that it was a mistake, a simple misunderstanding.

Gruoch stood there, arms empty and waiting, as Hertha appeared from the crowd and stepped briskly towards the maid, forcefully taking Lulach from her and turning towards Gruoch, kneeling to lay the boy on the rushes that covered the floor.

"Step back, damn you!" Hertha's usually collected voice was a snarl, a warning given by a wild animal before it bites. "Give us some air."

Gruoch watched as Hertha wiped some thick foam and spittle from the corners of Lulach's mouth, opening his lips to sweep a finger inside. Hertha brought an ear to his mouth and stayed that way a moment before bringing her head to the boy's chest and laying her ear there. Gruoch watched the ministrations, still silent, still standing with her arms held out in front of her. Later, she would recall how her limbs had begun to tremble with the effort, and she had worried they would ache too much for her to hold Lulach when she could finally comfort him. Surely after so much confusion, he would need to be settled.

Hertha slowly raised her head from the boy's small chest, and Gruoch watched as she brought a hand gently to his face, her fingers sweeping closed the lids that covered those beautiful eyes. Once freed of the spit that had coated them, the garish hue of grey and purple of Lulach's lips was revealed. Gruoch would remember the shade. It was the colour the sun makes as it releases its final breath, the violent remains of light melting into a dark death, surrendering to twilight.

There would come a time in Gruoch's story when she would rage and scream, fighting against the powers that held her back or opposed her wishes. There would come a time when she would be the most dangerous and powerful thing in a room. However, in the hours and days that followed Lulach's death, that fiery rage and passion were yet unknown to her. Gruoch passed them in dejected silence, watching in confusion from a fog of pain that kept her gasping for air. She had no breath for words. It was enough work to force herself to draw breath.

Gille had forced Gruoch to return to their rooms, pushing her harshly into a chair by the fire. He had taken her by the shoulders and shaken her roughly. Her teeth clashed against each other and bit into her tongue, filling Gruoch's mouth with the sudden and sharp taste of iron and rust. She allowed her husband to attack, hoping that his rough hands would snap her out of the fog she had stumbled in and would help her mind to awaken itself, to thaw. Even then, in her stupor, Gruoch searched for Hertha.

Why hadn't she followed? Did she still have Lulach?

Gruoch did not know where they had put her son, and the thought that he could wake up at any moment, confused and frightened, sent waves of nausea coursing through her.

"He was given something," Gille was saying, spitting his words and running his hands through his beard. "My son was poisoned, Gruoch. This is a clear and direct affront and attack on me."

"Poison?"

"But this will not stand. Those responsible will be punished harshly. My enemies will see what befalls those who would try and cross me, those who would try to weaken me."

"If he has eaten something to make him sick," Gruoch tried again, "We must fetch Hertha. She will know what to do. She will…"

The sting of Gille's palm against her cheek was a fire in the sudden cold numbness that racked her skull. Gruoch's jaw ached, and she saw bright spots of light before her eyes as her head reeled from Gille's assault. Then, tenderly, she brought a hand to her flesh, the skin warm under her probing fingers.

"That bitch!" Gille was furious now, chewing his words through a mouthful of spit that flew from his gnashing teeth and twisted lips. "Who else would know how to dose him so quickly, so effectively? Who else would manipulate things to ensure that no one else could reach him in order to administer an antidote?"

"You think," Gruoch swallowed painfully. Her cheek had filled again with blood. "You think Hertha poisoned him? You think Hertha would hurt Lulach?"

Gille's eyes blazed in their sockets, two dark flames that sent a shiver through Gruoch's body and made her recoil in her seat. He strode quickly back to his wife, reaching out and grasping her firmly by both shoulders. Gruoch winced and hated herself for flinching, for looking away from him.

"I know what she has been whispering about me, about Mael!" Although quieter than his earlier bellowing, Gille's voice was tainted by a frantic bitterness that Gruoch could not recognize as belonging to her husband. "She means to weaken me, to make me appear vulnerable. Mael had tried to warn me about your heathen pet, but I would not listen. I forgot that even the most domesticated of dogs can bite."

Gruoch took a shaky breath and forced herself to look her husband in the eye, searching desperately for any sign that the man she had married could still be found, that any vestige of him still existed.

"Gille, please. Let me speak to Hertha. Let me see Lulach. I want to see my son!"

"If there is any justice in the world, Mael will have dealt with her already."

Gruoch's stomach dropped, and her teeth chattered in her mouth, even though her body felt as though it had been set on fire.

"Gille, take me to them. Please."

Gruoch knew that could not have been gone for long. Still, it seemed as though the world around her had suddenly rushed by in a swirl of sweat, confusion, and ice. No more than half an hour could have passed from the moment Lulach's body had been discovered to when Gille escorted Gruoch back down the long stairs and into the courtyard. However, the time that had passed her by had been sufficient for Mael, and a contingency of soldiers, no doubt, to take hold of Hertha and make true Gille's threats.

Hertha's head, her bloated face already rigid and twisted in its final grimace, had been placed upon a spike on one of the outer walls. Flies danced around the distended tongue and lit upon it before taking flight once more to inspect the open and staring eyes and the gaping and ragged wound that had separated the neck from her shoulders. Gruoch would later learn that the body had been taken away and burned in a refusal to grant proper Christian burial. Gruoch did not tell them that Hertha would have preferred to burn, that she would have laughed at their feeble attempts to humiliate her, and that whatever curses they had feared her capable of would surely follow each of them now. The stench of her blood on their hands was fragrant and would remain so for the remainder of their days, drawing close the crows and spirits who would undoubtedly haunt the battlements of Crown Hill until the final stone had crumbled from its ruins.

Gruoch, too, had become a ghost.

She wandered the yards and halls of Crown Hill silently, eyes cast down at her feet. She stumbled along blindly, her steps tumbling along the stones. Her clothes became dusty and soiled with wear, and she slept sporadically in quiet and dark corners without stripping herself of them first. Once a source of vanity and pride, her hair had grown lacklustre and dull, twisting together into greasy and tangled knots. There was no need and no reason to clean herself or care about how she presented herself to others. Gruoch had become a husk of her former self, and whatever fire she had carried in her body before, whatever flame Hertha had seen and named her for, had been extinguished when Lulach had been killed. Hertha's death had firmly crushed the glowing embers that had been left to smoulder within Gruoch's heart.

*I am eldr no more*, she thought. *There is nothing left of me to burn.*

At first, Alane had tried to keep Gruoch somewhat presentable. Her ministrations had varied, and she had tried to have her lady bedridden and given herbal teas before forcing the servants to dunk Gruoch in a cold bath to shock her senses. Alane had maids pin down Gruoch's flailing arms as the older woman attempted to drag a comb through the red hair and wash the grime from Gruoch's face.

Gruoch had bitten Alane's hand, her teeth tearing through the papery flesh of the housekeeper's palm and drawing blood.

Alane had since kept a wise distance, though Gruoch knew she still hovered nearby, safely keeping herself out of the way.

Gille moved through his days as though he had lost his wife as well as his only son. Gruoch saw their friends move to comfort him, men clapping him soundly on the back, women reaching out gently to touch his arms, his shoulder. She sometimes watched in a bitter kind of amusement as her husband played at mourning and allowed pretty and vapid girls to bat their eyes at him and exclaim their sympathies. A strange twist pulsed in Gruoch's stomach when she recalled herself at fifteen and the way she had looked up at Gille through her lashes.

It was an interesting and frustrating stalemate for them both. Gille, his mind filled with paranoia and whispers of treasonous rebellion, would no doubt be relieved if his mad wife should throw herself from the tower or else poison herself to join the child she had lost. It would free him from any moral or legal obligation towards her since to put Gruoch aside now would be an affront to God and leave him appearing cold and unsympathetic in the eyes of these sycophants that surrounded him.

Gruoch, on the other hand, was just as trapped. She had often stood at the windows in the tower, looking down at the cobbled yard below. Though the opening was not overly large, it would be possible to slide a body through. She could easily imagine the sudden rush of cold wind and the welcome crushing end that awaited her should she decide to take her suffering into her own hands. Indeed, her heart welcomed the thought. Her body, aching and crying out for the soft weight of her son, an extension of herself that had been so cruelly ripped away, would have been relieved to sleep.

To rest.

The existence that Gruoch had begun to lead, this mind-numbing day after day after day, would, however, have to continue. But, more than anything, Gruoch feared the risk of losing her son in the afterlife if God saw fit to punish her for ending the one she still possessed. So, she rattled on as the ghost of Crown Hill, pondering which punishment she could suffer more easily.

Gruoch barely ate, noticing over time with strange amusement that her tunic and leggings had become looser on her body. The bones in her hands appeared sharper, and the veins there protruded like ropes beneath the taut flesh. Perhaps prompted by her appearance and the misgivings of their parents, the children of the Hill avoided Gruoch and ran from her path when they saw her stumbling in their direction. Truthfully, she avoided them as fervently as they did her. The sound of their laughter was ice in her heart.

Let them think me some kind of wraith, some undead thing come to haunt them and steal them away, Gruoch thought to herself. No good can come from being close to me.

In the passive way of all prisoners whose sentences are for life and who have given up marking the days into the stone walls of their cells, she was aware that time was passing and that the world around her had not stopped. The searing pain that rested behind her eyes and throbbed in her skull did not keep the sun from rising. The nausea that Gruoch felt when she walked by the wall that had housed Hertha's rotting skull did not keep others from communing there and enjoying the sunshine after the bones had been removed.

She knew that Findlaech came and went. She was conscious of a tense fragility in the air, and Gruoch watched from dark corners as her husband walked the yards with Mael, their heads bent close conspiratorially as they spoke in hushed tones. A line was being drawn, and none of the Hill's inhabitants, whether a spectre, a living being, or somewhere between, could close their eyes to it.

Gruoch considered the ramifications of Findlaech learning of her husband's conspiracies. At the least, the Mormaer would disown his heir and, at most, have him killed. Perhaps she, the wife of the plotting traitor, would be put to death as well. Gruoch convinced herself, with little effort, that Fate owed her at least this one small kindness. She could not risk taking her own life if it meant eternal separation from her good and innocent child, but the stroke of another's blade could very well reunite them. Could she convince Findlaech that Gille plotted against him? Could she be the one to tip the scales and push this constant and irritating waiting game into action?

There were nights, just before drifting off to join Hertha and Lulach in her nightmares, when Gruoch would think of her father and ache to feel Bodhe's strong arms envelop her.

Gruoch was walking alone one cold and clear November evening when the trembling sound of hooves upon the earth suddenly reached her ears. She had been walking outside along the perimeter walls, running a hand along the rough wooden poles, relishing the sharp sting of each sliver that pushed its way into her skin. She watched in detached amusement as men quickly opened the gates, allowing entry to a company of a dozen or so riders. Whatever interest Gruoch had held in the arrival was quickly lost, and she returned her attention to her walk. She brought her injured hand away from the wall and studied it in the flickering light of the torches.

Her palms were filthy and caked with dust and grime, but she was able to make out a thick piercing of wood in the soft pad below her thumb. A sliver had embedded itself deep in the thick of the flesh. Gruoch brought the fingers of her uninjured hand up to touch the shard. A shiver of pain jolted through her body at the contact, and she felt a sudden thrill as her nerves screamed, reminding her with sudden and delicious certainty that she was still alive. Gruoch had almost forgotten that pain could exist outside of her heart, of her stomach.

She brought an index to her injured palm, catching the sliver of wood beneath the jagged nail and tearing at it slowly. Gruoch watched as the blood pooled as she tore at the skin, and the sight of it didn't turn her stomach as it once had. Instead, she found it fascinating, and Gruoch was immersed in the shadow of her blood as it began to slowly ebb and weave its way along the lines of her palm. The hand had become a crimson spider web, and it had ensnared her every sense. So enthralled was she in the sight of her bloodied hand that Gruoch was deaf to the sound of approaching feet.

She jumped as a hand came down gently upon her right shoulder.

Had Alane gathered her courage and decided to try again at taming her shameful mistress? Had Gille, tired of the embarrassment she must present, decided to take matters into his own hands and rid himself of her?

Had the ghost of Lulach or that of Hertha, wavering shades that sometimes stepped forward from obscure corners, finally managed to reach out from the veil and touch her?

The corners of Gruoch's mouth rose in a gentle smile, but her teeth clamped together tightly behind her lips, jaw clenched. She spun around, jerking her body away from the unexpected and unwanted contact.

Mac Bethad's hand lingered in the air between them for a moment before he lowered it to his side as he took her in. The moon shone brightly in the sky above, and the numerous torches affixed to the walls around them revealed him to her, although his brown hair appeared almost black in the shadows that were cast. Gruoch easily recognized the piercing gaze of the eyes that beheld her, even if the crisp blue of them was lost to the night.

"My father has told me what happened to your son."

Gruoch winced at his words before she could help herself. She did not want to speak of Lulach, and she certainly did not want to speak of her son with the boastful man before her.

She wanted to be left alone.

Gruoch allowed her eyes to hold Mac Bethad's gaze a moment longer before turning them away and taking a step back. She studied the path before her, eager to find a means of slipping away.

"He told me that they blamed your shield maiden and that she was killed for it."

The pounding was back, and the sound of blood rushing in her ears was deafening. Gruoch's breath became laboured as her body reacted to the words he spoke, every muscle cinching itself tightly. The stabbing pain behind her eyes became acute, and bile rose in her throat. She needed to go, and she needed to go now.

"Gruoch, look at me!"

A recent snowfall had left the courtyard slick and somewhat treacher-ous. She would take her chances and dash away and pray that if a stone did cause her to stumble and fall, her skull would crack and burst upon the path and the soil would soak up her blood and mix itself with Her-tha's.

As Gruoch made a wild and sudden leap for freedom, a hand like a vice clamped itself around her forearm and grounded her. She shrieked, and another hand affixed itself to her mouth and smothered the sound. Gruoch struggled against her captor, striking at him with her hands, one already slick with blood, and trying to tear at the face with her nails. She was spun around, the hand around her forearm releasing her only to pin both arms down. She was pulled back and held tightly against a broad chest. Gruoch could feel the startled pounding of Mac Bethad's heart against her spine as his arm locked her against him, his other hand still covering her mouth. She tried to tear at his fingers with her teeth, but the strong hand did not allow the slightest movement.

"I am here, *mo lasair*."

The voice at her ear was low and the tone soothing, but something wavered. Gruoch tried to raise herself against her captor to kick out, to twist, anything, but his firm grip was unyielding, and the warmth of Mac Bethad's breath stayed on her neck and at her ear.

"Stop fighting me, woman!"

Gruoch struggled harder, hoping to feel the displacement of a bone, wondering if he could snap her neck if she managed to turn sharply enough in his embrace.

"Please, let me help you!"

She screamed a muffled roar into the palm that still covered her mouth.

"You helped me once! For God's sake, let me help you now!"

The memory, unbidden and unwelcome, of Mac Bethad's pale and sweaty face in her lap was visceral. It was as though Gruoch could still smell the snow in the air of the cold April night from years ago, and she could hear Hertha's clipped and effective orders telling her to hold his head. Gruoch heard Banquo's pleas for secrecy. Mac Bethad had looked into her eyes as he thrashed on the ground, incapacitated and vulnerable. Yet, despite the violence of his fitful movements, she had held him.

Now, it was Mac Bethad who held her as the pain rendered itself into her every limb, sending wave after wave of tremor and vibration through Gruoch's exhausted body. It was he who held her as her knees finally buckled and who caught her to him as she fell. He brought Gruoch to his lap as they came to the earth, keeping her out of reach of the snow-covered stones. Mac Bethad pulled her against him, rocking her like a child while Gruoch gripped the collar of his tunic in her hands. He smoothed back her filthy hair while she sobbed into his neck, the tears she had not been able to release coming as a sudden and welcome deluge.

His cheek lay against the top of Gruoch's head as they rocked, and he whispered soft words as her sobs turned to shaking breaths and gentle hiccups. Exhaustion overcame her. It was as though finally finding her tears had released Gruoch of her manic energy and had granted her body a momentary catharsis.

Even once the tears had subsided and stopped, they held one another upon the stone path. Gruoch had chosen her haunts well, and she and Mac Bethad were well hidden from the view of any curious night owl who may have happened to look from a window or through the yard. So, they sat in silence, bodies sore and unsure whether to give up their tenuous struggles.

"She didn't kill him," was all Gruoch could say.

"Don't speak of it now," Mac Bethad whispered, his breath tickling her hair. "We will speak of it, but not now."

Slowly and gently, Gruoch pushed herself away from the sodden and damp front of Mac Bethad's tunic. She wiped at her eyes, feeling the swollen and tender skin there.

"I should go," she said, trying to steady her voice. "It would do you no good for anyone to find us here."

Mac Bethad made no move to stop her as Gruoch extracted herself from him. Instead, he rose to his knees and held a hand, allowing her to put her weight on him as she rose unsteadily upon shaking legs. He got to his feet swiftly, hands still reaching out as though to catch Gruoch should her balance fail her.

They stood there for a moment, suddenly unsure of what to say. The strange spell of intimacy that had lain over them as Gruoch cried onto Mac Bethad's chest had been lifted, and the reality of the world around them had come crashing back.

She had kept his secret, and Gruoch knew he would keep this one for her.

She told him as much.

"Gruoch," Mac Bethad said quietly. "We have never… I have never properly thanked you for what you did and for what you continue to do by keeping my secret. It grieves me now to see you suffer so alone when you and Hertha succeeded in helping me that night."

"There is only one way to end my suffering now," Gruoch whispered. "But I am too afraid to do what needs to be done."

"We are but poor players in all of this," Mac Bethad replied, stepping closer in sudden urgency. "Playthings. Fools pretending at kings. But I can tell you now that I will not allow for your pain, for your suffering, to be in vain."

Gruoch smiled morosely at his words and his attempt at comfort.

"My suffering is all that I have."

"It doesn't need to be this way, Gruoch," he pressed, stepping even closer to her, eliminating what little distance remained between the two of them. "I know you will carry this for the rest of your days, but all I ask is that you let me help you bear the weight of it."

Gruoch brought a hand to Mac Bethad's cheek and touched the stubble there. If he was bothered by the smell or the sight of her filthy hand, he made no sign. Rather, he sighed slightly at the touch and leaned his cheek into it.

"There are no more words, Mac Bethad."

It was true. She was spent.

His lips were on hers before Gruoch could properly register what he had done. They were rough and dry from the road, but the pressure of his mouth on hers was soft and light. Gruoch made no move, no motion, and after a brief moment of stillness, he pulled away from her.

"Things will not always be this way," he said as she took her hand away from his face. "I will not allow them to remain so."

Gruoch stepped back as she sighed and turned from him, holding out an arm for balance as she walked away. She did not know how long Mac Bethad stood there in the light of the torches, for she did not turn back to see.

# TEN
# A LACK OF BETTER IDEAS

The next few weeks progressed very much in the same way as those that had come before. Gruoch kept up her silent and constant patrol of Crown Hill, unkempt and dishevelled, but the fierce pain that had previously driven her steps had been doused, leaving in its place a steady numbness. She did not speak again with Mac Bethad after that night, even though he and his company of riders remained at the Hill for another few weeks. She did her best to avoid him, and he did not seek her out. When their paths did cross in some kind of limited capacity, Gruoch did not miss the strength of his stare as blue eyes found green. There were unspoken words there, lingering and dangerous. But Gruoch had had her fill of danger, and she had resigned herself to patience. She knew that Death would come for her, and she could wait until it did, knowing that she would greet it as an old friend.

Alane, perhaps encouraged by Gruoch's apparent docility, took it upon herself once more to look after her lady's grooming and appearance. One morning, Gruoch allowed Alane to lead her to her room, where a tub of cold water waited. Carefully, as though at any moment Gruoch might once again become violent, Alane helped her to remove her leggings and soiled tunic. The chill of the water sent a shock through her body as

Gruoch lowered herself slowly into the tub, and the fierceness of her shivers was not entirely unwelcome. It felt like a strange, tingling short of waking.

At first, the women did not speak, and the only sound in the room came from the gentle splashing and flowing of the water as Alane poured it over Gruoch's head and down her back. Gruoch closed her eyes, and images of Lulach came to her unbidden. The sound of the bath reminded her of bathing her son before the fire, of his smile and the look of love in his expression. She was surprised to feel the hot prickle of tears behind her closed eyes. Gruoch had not thought herself capable of more tears.

"My lady, may I speak openly?"

Gruoch did not open her eyes at Alane's cautious words, choosing instead to keep them closed and to protect the vision of her child. Instead, she nodded in response to the question.

Alane hesitated. "I know that your woman, that Hertha was not overly fond of me, and I will not lie to you now and say that I was not sometimes afraid of her heathen godlessness. However," her words trailed off, becoming weaker before finally dying on the tip of her tongue.

No one save Mac Bethad had mentioned Hertha to Gruoch since her friend's murder. Gruoch was surprised that the first to do so would be Alane, who had spoken honestly when she described the lack of love between herself and Hertha.

*My friend. Did I have another in this place? Any place?*

Her thoughts were at war with the simple peace that accompanied images of Lulach, and Gruoch forced herself to breathe and to give her strength and attention to the vision.

It was too late, and Lulach stepped out of her mind's eye and back beyond the veil.

"What is it, Alane," Gruoch asked, eyes closed and voice steady, the pain at losing sight of her son kept out of her tone.

There was another trickle of water down Gruoch's neck before Alane spoke. "Well, I just wanted to say that I can't and won't believe it, my lady. She may have been a heathen, but I know she loved you and your little boy."

"She did."

Alane's fingers worked at the tangles in Gruoch's hair, separating the sodden locks carefully to comb through the worst of the snarls.

"I told lord Mael as much when he first told my lord Coemgáin that she had poisoned the boy. I told them that she would do no such thing."

Gruoch's breath caught in her throat. Gille's words came back to her, ringing through her mind.

Mael had tried to warn me about your heathen pet, but I would not listen.

Gille and Mael had spoken of Hertha and likely of Gruoch as well, just as the women had spoken of the brothers and the likelihood of revolt. Had Mael, whom they had suspected of filling Gille's mind with poisonous thoughts of treachery, begun by first turning him from his family and those who were close to him? Could the snake have known that by taking Hertha from Gruoch, he would also be stripping her of any remaining strength or courage?

A thought came to her then, one so full of terror and so dark that Gruoch felt it in her flesh as it rose and pimpled.

Had Mael something to do with Lulach's death?

"Did my husband's brother ever speak to you about Hertha, Alane? Did he mention Lulach?"

Alane sighed from behind Gruoch as she searched for an answer.

"I do not want you to think that our discourse was regular, my lady, or in any way significant. He made some comments in passing to the staff, and I overheard him speaking with your husband on more than one occasion as I brought them a meal or a fresh ale. Men like that have a tendency to speak unguarded before the likes of me. Of course," and here was the attempt to smooth over any rude words. "I mean no disrespect in saying so."

Gruoch placed her hands on the sides of the tub and rose slowly to her feet. The water dripped from her hair and down her back as she stood, and the fire was not sufficient to keep the cold air from sending a chill through her as Gruoch rose from the water. She turned slowly towards Alane, knowing full well that she must resemble some drowned creature as she stood shin-deep in dirty water before the older woman.

Alane's eyes widened slightly as she took in the sight of Gruoch rising like some avenging ghoul from the murky bath, but she stood and nodded at her lady's next words, taking Gruoch's arm and helping her to step out of the tub.

"You will tell me all that you heard. You will keep nothing back. And you will tell me now."

Alane did as Gruoch asked.

Gille was startled when he came into their rooms late that night. He was not expecting to walk in and find his wife sitting like a statue before a dying fire. He had probably not expected to find her awake. They had barely spoken in weeks, a mutual avoidance making itself manifest between them.

"I would speak with you, husband." Gruoch's words met Gille as he stepped in, slicing through the stillness.

Gille made his way into the room with feigned leisure that grated at her. He removed his tunic and stood bare-chested in his leggings as though preparing for bed.

"So, you've decided to speak and be civil?" He made his way towards the bed, pulling back the covers and furs. "You've come back to yourself, is that it? Well, if you've come to ask my forgiveness, you needn't waste your time. You were grieving, and so was I. You are a woman and cannot be expected to face such things rationally. Your hysterics are but a part of your gentler nature. No apologies are necessary."

A vice twisted itself in Gruoch's stomach, and she winced as she took in his words. The fury there was twofold. The first that he should think for a moment that she had come to apologize, that he should expect it brought bile to her mouth. The second aspect of Gruoch's anger, and perhaps the bitterest of the two, was the fact that not long ago, she would have agreed with him.

"I assure you, husband," Gruoch said, pushing down her revulsion and keeping her voice light. "I have no apology for you tonight."

Gille paused, looking at her, before sighing and lowering himself into the bed.

"Do as you please then, Gruoch," he said sharply. "It seems you will even without my blessing. I should thank you, however, for bothering to change your clothes and cleaning yourself. At least you can look like the proper lady, even if you refuse to behave like one."

"Did Mael tell you that Hertha poisoned Lulach? That she was somehow responsible for his death?"

"I shall not speak of such ugly things. There is nothing to be said. It is done."

"It is not done!"

Gruoch rose from her seat, fists clenched into the sides of her tunic. She stepped toward the bed where her husband lay, and she found a delicious sense of satisfaction when she noticed his eyes widen slightly at her approach. He had not expected this from her.

"You will answer my question," Gruoch said then, stopping at the foot of the bed and looking down at him, knowing that the faltering flames of the hearth would throw her shadow over Gille and cast him into a darkness of her own making.

She relished the thought.

"Your words serve no purpose, Gruoch, other than to upset you and to tire me. Our son is dead and should be mourned. So, we mourn. Men who are more knowledgeable in such things than I tell me he was poisoned, and I believe them. Who other than Hertha knew of such secret and terrible poisons, of such heathen trickery?"

"What proof is there to be found in a lack of better ideas?!"

"You will lower your voice," Gille said, his words low. "If you can, look and judge your own behaviour. Not only did she poison our son to fuel me into a mistake, but she has also been poisoning you against me."

Gruoch stared at him in silence, trying to digest the things he said and to decipher them for any semblance of sense.

"You know that Hertha raised me, protected me. She was the only mother I have ever known. She knew I would marry you before I did!"

"Her influence ran deep," Gille agreed, twisting Gruoch's words to suit his purpose. "I do not doubt you loved her. It was this very love that kept you from seeing her true nature and ambitions."

"Ambitions?!"

"Mael knew her for a snake and did his duty by his lord and brother. He told me of her spying and eavesdropping, her constant listening around corners. He saw the two of you whispering."

Her head had begun to ache, and Gruoch forced herself to breathe. She would not become the ranting and hysterical creature he had made her up to be in his mind.

"My lord, if we whispered, it was out of concern! Hertha feared Mael would try and lead you into rebellion against Findlaech, and I am beginning to fear she was only too right."

Gille had swept his legs out from the bed so swiftly that Gruoch had barely registered that he had gotten to his feet before he stood before her. His hands came and gripped her upper arms below the shoulder, his fingers digging themselves painfully into the flesh there. He shook her once, hard enough to make her teeth rattle against one another and split the soft inside of her cheek. Warm blood leaked into Gruoch's mouth, and she spat, darkening the front of Gille's chest with droplets of scarlet.

His right hand left her shoulder and rose of its own accord, and Gruoch flinched, screaming internally at herself at the show of weakness. Gille's hand hovered in the air, and she saw his shoulders heave as he struggled to calm himself. The hand finally lowered and came to rest gently against her cheek. Gruoch stood still, bloody spittle wetting her chin.

Gille bent towards her, lowering himself so they might look each other in the eye without forcing her to look up at him. She was surprised that he would humble himself in such a way.

His eyes shone as he looked at her, and Gruoch saw the pain that was etched in the lines around his mouth and brow.

"I loved our son Gruoch, and I love him still."

A sob broke through, surprising Gruoch and sending her hand to cover her mouth in hopes of stifling any more.

Gille brought his other hand to her face, effectively cradling it in his palms.

"This grief consumes you, Gruoch, and causes you to see evil where there is none, to cast into the shadow that which belongs in the light. Our child is dead, but we will have more. We will rise from this stronger than before."

Gruoch said nothing. She realized that in the weeks since Hertha's death, she had neglected the potion Eimear insisted that Gruoch take daily to keep her from conceiving. She knew in the pits of what remained of her soul that even if she could bear more children safely, she would die before she allowed herself to bear another child of Gille's.

He looked at her a moment longer before sighing slightly and straightening his back, bringing his face above Gruoch's once more.

"You are no fool, my wife, and I should not presume to speak to you as though you were. You misunderstand me, and you misunderstand my brother. All that we do is in the interest of Alba, of Moray, and our family."

There it was. Although the confession was weak and far from whole, it was enough to assure Gruoch that Hertha had not been wrong and that Mael must have seen in Lulach's death an opportunity to rid himself of a potential complication and threat.

But how would such an opportunity come to present itself? The voice in the back of her mind was not lulled to peace by her husband's gentle touch and comforting tone. It would keep Gruoch awake that night as she lay next to her husband's sleeping form, one arm thrown over her hip after he had made love to a still and complacent partner. It was not quieted as she plotted the easiest way to escape the next day to Eimear's hut in the nearby woods to beg for something to ensure that her womb remained empty. The voice did not die or wither, even as the coals in the hearth crumbled into ash, and the room was cast into familiar darkness.

Gruoch was ever aware of the rising tensions in Moray even though she did her best to keep herself sheltered from the world and numb to its turning. She ate, dressed and kept herself clean, but she kept her own life at arm's length. She passed the hours by walking through the courtyard and along the perimeter wall, allowing her mind to wander as she passed the secluded corner where Mac Bethad had held her one impossible night and had kissed her despite a thousand reasons that forbade such things. As Gruoch walked there, her hand would sometimes find her lips and trace them gently. More often, it stayed at her side, hidden and clenched as she walked.

Gille and Gruoch had found a comfortable stalemate. She gave him no reason to be angry or ashamed of his wife, and in return, he left her alone in every way that mattered. He often slept away from their apartment, preferring to spend his time with his brother or in the arms of more amenable women. Gille's visits to Gruoch's bed were rare and perfunctory, his desire for more legitimate children the only thing that tied him to her. Of course, he had no way of knowing that Gruoch would bear him no more children. She took great satisfaction from the fact that Hertha had played such an important role in assuring that Gruoch would not get pregnant by helping to procure her Eimear's remedy and by bringing Gruoch to the cunning woman in the first place.

Still, even as she kept her distance, it was impossible for Gruoch to ignore the preparations that were taking place at Crown Hill. Findlaech, still the true lord of Moray, often travelled amongst his villagers, tenants, and loyal men, amassing support for the inevitable conflict. Like his son, he travelled with a small and select handful of men he trusted above all others. Angus, a gruff and taciturn soldier who often walked at Findlaech's side, was a particular favourite of Gruoch's. She appreciated that he showed no fear or disgust when he saw her, recognizing in her a deep desire to be ignored, which he obliged.

Gille, though he was the appointed heir, only accompanied him on certain trips and was often left at the Hill to organize incoming supplies and the men that had travelled to the Hill in order to join Findlaech.

Gruoch knew that Mael was not unaware of her suspicion and contempt for him. He often caught her eye as she skulked silently down the halls. Where the servants and nobles of the Hill now went out of their way to avoid her gaze and to keep from her path, Mael seemed to delight in smiling with fraternal familiarity to Gruoch when he saw her approach and to bow his head in acknowledgement of her.

Gruoch also noticed that when Gille left the Hill, Mael made it his business to follow her and shadow her steps. He usually had the wherewithal to keep his distance from her and to feign disinterest or surprise at their meetings, but his saccharine acting made Gruoch's blood boil. *He may have twisted Gille's mind and ear*, she thought desperately to herself, *but he will never have mine*.

Gruoch was standing with her back to a window in the great room of the tower, watching women as they sewed together woollen tunics in quantities that far outnumbered the men of the Hill, and she did not notice Mael approach quickly enough to avoid him. He stood at her side, a respectable distance away, and when Gruoch turned from him in order to look from the window, he mirrored her movements. Gruoch stood there, uncomfortable and frozen for the space of a moment, before making up her mind. She refused to acknowledge Mael's presence and decided instead to step away from the window and take her leave of him.

"You are lucky to have such a brave husband and lord, my sister," he said suddenly under his breath, causing Gruoch to stop mid-step.

"I am aware of what I have and of what I should know, brother."

"To leave such a beautiful wife and make his way towards Hibernia to fight off the heathen Norsemen will be no easy feat. The shores of Clontarf are far from welcoming," he continued, as though Gruoch had not spoken.

She hated to learn about her husband's impending departure from Mael, and Gruoch forced herself to feign indifference. She had not realized that Gille would be sailing to the green isle to the West of the Morayan coast. She knew the Norsemen had long held certain territories along the eastern coast of Hibernia and that the inhabitants of the isle had still not succeeded in fighting off the invaders, who had, in turn, begun to build more permanent settlements further inland. Supported by the Norse kings who ruled on the islands of Orkney, these armies were encroaching ever further onto lands held by allies of Moray and Alba. The ever-present fear of a Norse stronghold so close to their own shores and a subsequent invasion was a real one. While Moray had been keeping an eye on its enemy to the north, they had allowed the one to the southwest to gain power and strength.

It was obvious now why Findlaech had been so restless and often out amongst his men and why preparations were being made. He would lead them overland and across the narrow sea to Hibernia, undertaking the long and dangerous voyage to ensure the continued freedom of his people.

"Gille is brave and knows what is right," Gruoch said as she stepped from the window and away from Mael, "Even though evil and its influence can filter in anywhere. He is strong enough, I hope, to keep his ear closed and his heart true."

She looked at him then, and Mael smiled to himself before turning to catch her eye.

"Influence is indeed a powerful thing," Mael said, his voice full of agreement. "That is why I thank the Lord and God above that he and you, my sister, are free from the sway of your own treacherous handmaiden."

Gruoch's breath caught in her throat, and she felt as though she might launch herself at him to tear at his eyes. Instead, Gruoch forced herself to be still and to keep her expression blank. Although she thought it would kill her to do so, she bowed her head to her brother-in-law in parting. As she allowed her gaze to rise, Gruoch's attention was caught by movement at the window. People were bustling out of the way of a group of riders that were entering the gates. Surely, these men were but another set of reinforcements for what she now realized would be an assault as deadly and as dangerous as any her people and her family had faced in many years.

The riders were welcomed to the Hill and made comfortable that evening in the hall. Although the number of occupants rose steadily, the kitchens did their best to supply the visitors with meat and ale, even if some meals consisted mostly of bread and porridge.

Gruoch had perfected the air of detachment and of cold countenance that cloaked her from the attentions of others and allowed her to move relatively unmolested throughout the halls and rooms of the Hill. However, the increasingly cramped quarters were becoming harder to navigate, and her restless soul was unable to sit quietly in her room. There were too many memories of Lulach there, and her anger could not be appeased by merely sitting or sewing. Gruoch needed to move to keep the poisonous fury in her blood from boiling over. She was afraid that if she sat quietly or still for too long, a scream as loud and as long as any ever heard before would burst unending from her mouth.

So that night, Gruoch sought the relative freedom of the grounds once more. Most of the newcomers were drinking in the Great Hall, their boisterous voices and raucous laughter filtering into the stillness of the night.

She turned her face towards the sky, breathing deeply and enjoying the cool and calming brush of the wind across her face. The early days of spring were upon them now, and the warm weather meant easier sailing conditions. Moray would have to strike soon before their enemies had the chance.

This particular night was warm and clear, the ebony skies perforated and adorned by millions of shining stars. It felt oddly cleansing to stand in their light and to allow it to wash over her, as though the celestial torches could in some way burn away the darkness that was slowly and steadily creeping through her body and hiding in the corners of her fractured mind.

Gruoch heard his feet approach her before she had even heard him speak. Still, she kept her face turned towards the heavens, desperate to take in as much of the light as she could, feeling even then some impending sense of dread looming nearby.

"Is it rude of me to say I am glad to see you looking more yourself, my lady?"

"I haven't the energy to stay and debate manners with you, my lord."

Mac Bethad stepped towards her then, and the pair stood shoulder to shoulder. Gruoch felt rather than saw as Mac Bethad lifted his own face and took in the stars.

"I have thought of you often," Mac Bethad said softly.

"I wish you had not," she told him, not quite honestly, as the wind carried away the whispers of her voice.

Gruoch felt Mac Bethad's fingers touch hers as they hung limply at her side, seeking purchase before his palm slipped to cover hers, taking her hand gently and firmly into his own. He moved slowly as though she would startle and run. Indeed, Gruoch knew she very much should have.

They were in no private corner now, and anyone bothering to look would see Mac Bethad standing alone with the future Mormaer's wife, their hands clasped.

Still, his hand stayed entwined with hers even as they kept their attention diverted elsewhere.

"I am glad to see you before I leave."

"You are headed to Hibernia?" Gruoch's fingers flexed as they tightened their grip.

"I am." A pause. "I have seen your father. He will be leading his own men over the sea to push back the Norsemen."

Bodhe.

Gruoch had not seen her father in years. The last time she had beheld him was as she rode away with Gille after their wedding. She remembered the sight of her father's bulk as it waved back to her, becoming smaller and smaller before being swallowed by the horizon.

Gruoch's voice caught. "Please tell him," she began before swallowing a lump in her throat and taking a deep breath. "Please tell him that I long to see him and that I miss him terribly." She thought for a moment. "I do not know if he knows of Lulach's passing. Or Hertha's."

Mac Bethad stayed silent at her side, seeming to understand that she did not require him to respond. Only his fingers spoke, brushing her own softly, becoming more daring as they explored her palm. Gruoch shuddered as she felt the back of her hand brush his upper thigh as he brought it closer to him.

"I will keep him in my sight," he said as he brazenly brought her hand to his chest. "My father will be on the field of battle as well. I shall charge myself with the safety of them both."

Gruoch sighed and pulled her hand away. Mac Bethad did not fight to keep it.

"Thank you."

"Will you think of me, Gruoch? Will you send up prayers that I, too, may return safely?"

At this, she broke her gaze and allowed it to travel to the man next to her. It was hard to see him properly, even with the glow of the stars, but she recognized the sharp line of his jaw and the curling dark hair that fell about his eyes. As though feeling her eyes on him, Mac Bethad turned his own face from the sky and found her gaze.

"I did not think you put much stock in God and prayer. What would my prayers matter to you?" Gruoch smiled as she spoke, though her face belied no trace of happiness.

"It will matter that you are the one praying for me."

Gruoch cast a quick look around them. It did not seem as though any people were paying them any heed or particular attention. Some women walked nearby with folds of wool or linen, some carrying plates or buckets. Patrolmen walked easily along the wall, talking quietly amongst themselves. The war was still far away and had not permeated the ease with which the people of Crown Hill had grown used to living.

Still, Mac Bethad was leading her down a path that was dangerous in its own right.

"I am still my husband's wife."

"I have not forgotten."

"Haven't you?" Gruoch heard the edge in her voice and wondered at it. Why was she angry? She did not care to protect Gille's feelings, and not so very long ago, she had longed for death. Why did she tread with such caution now?

It would not be until much later in her life that Gruoch would recognize that silent but steady feeling that steered her then as the desire for revenge and the need to be alive and able to see it delivered.

Mac Bethad shifted his weight and sighed. Gruoch could hear the exasperation creeping into the sound.

"Will you always seek to be contrary with me, Gruoch?"

Once again, he had used her Christian name. Gruoch was surprised to realize that she was smiling. She looked at him one last time, and she felt the strength of his eyes as they bored into her. She bowed her head and took a step back and away from him.

"You will have to return and find out, my lord."

# ELEVEN
# THE MORMAER

Gille left shortly after Mac Bethad's arrival, accompanied by a battalion of men. Gruoch watched as the soldiers, most of them mere farmers and unaccustomed to a real battle, hugged and kissed their families before making their way into their ranks. Women clasped their men tightly, and children grabbed on to their legs. Gruoch noticed the alarming number of fresh faces amongst the ranks of soldiers, boys too young to have yet grown a proper beard. She could see Lulach among them, appearing as he would have at that age, and forced herself to look away.

Gille found her before his departure and bowed over her hand before giving Gruoch a perfunctory kiss on her cheek. His movements seemed automatic yet calculated, as though he thought it his duty to put on their performance for his men as they left behind their own families.

She had worried that Mael would be left behind, that he would be left in charge over Crown Hill and that she would be left subject to his whims. However, it was made obvious very quickly that Gille would be bringing his brother along and that Mael would act as a general for Findlaech, along with Gille, Mac Bethad, and her own father. It was the veteran soldier Angus, Findlaech's man, who would be staying behind to watch the fortress. He had already proven his mettle in battle, and an old injury to his leg left him incapable of fighting as he once had. Gruoch knew it bothered him to be left behind when so many young and untried boys were being told to go. Still, she was glad for Angus' presence. He was a rational, if not somewhat gruff, mind in a sea of fear and turmoil. Should word reach them that the men had failed, and the Norsemen would be pushing further south, Angus would orchestrate their flight to Dunsinane to the southeast and finally to Fife, where Duncan's men would give them shelter.

So it was that the next few days melted into weeks, and still, they had received no word concerning the success of the troops. Gruoch found a quiet ally in Angus, and they spent many silent hours together in the Great Hall, Angus studying maps while Gruoch studied Angus. His body had not grown fat and soft as did the bodies of so many men as they reached middle age, and his brown hair was speckled throughout with grey. Scars and old wounds tattooed patterns across his arms, and a few marred his neck, telling the story of his past exploits. Although his loyalty to Findlaech was apparent and obvious to anyone, she realized during their forced companionship that his first loyalty was to Moray itself and, by extension, its Mormaer.

The first messenger arrived nearly three weeks after Gille had followed Findlaech from Crown Hill. The pony he rode frothed horribly; the black muzzle painted in bloody foam. Its sides heaved with effort, and the messenger slid, exhausted, from its back.

Angus and Gruoch had noticed the approaching rider while he was still at a distance since so much of their days revolved around the observation of the world around them, desperate for any sign that things would soon move on in one way or another. Gruoch had run into the courtyard and rushed to the gates, desperate for any kind of news. Angus met her there and gave the sign that the gates should be opened to welcome the approaching rider.

Angus grabbed the pony's reins as the messenger dismounted, handing them off to one of the old men who had stayed behind to care for the livestock. Gruoch watched the grooms leave, hoping that the poor beast would not fall dead before being given some water and rest. The messenger had ridden far and hard to deliver his news.

The messenger was young, barely a man, although his face already bore the wicked scar of a wound only recently closed, trailing from his left eyebrow to his cheekbone.

"What news?"

The question escaped Gruoch without her consent, slipping past her lips and past due regard for decorum. As the resident lady of the Hill, she should have welcomed the man and had servants bring forth ale or at least a stool. However, Angus said nothing, and no one else would have dared reproach Gruoch for her lapse in manners. They were all as starved as she for whatever words the messenger might have to say.

"The battle goes in our favour," he said, still panting slightly from the exertion of his ride. "We met them on the fields of Clontarf, and now most of the Norsemen have fled Hibernia, thanks to the efforts mustered by our own troops and those of the king of Munster, who was only too happy to see the heathen run from his shores."

"There is work left to do then," Angus asked.

The messenger took another deep breath and nodded. "He that they call Sigurd has fled back to Orkney, and so have the other Norse lords."

"Jarls," Angus said suddenly. "They are called jarls."

"Jarls then," continued the messenger. "There remain a few Hibernian kings who have shown themselves disloyal to the high king there, but the armies should make short work of such insurrections."

"And our brothers and sons? How fare the men of Moray?" Gruoch was glad for Angus's questions. She had many herself, and yet she struggled to formulate them.

For which man's well-being should she ask first?

About whom did she most want to ask?

Was the desire greater to learn that Mac Bethad and her father were both well, or did Gruoch yearn to hear, in the deepest and foulest pits of her soul, that Mael, or even Gille, had fallen in battle?

"I was sent along by the lord Coemgáin when the battle turned in our favour to keep his family and subjects abreast of their success. Unfortunately, I have no other news for you."

Angus nodded and clapped the young man familiarly on the back.

"And we thank you for your message," he said. "Come. You must rest and eat. I apologize that we pressed you so before allowing you to pause and breathe."

"I would be most grateful for your hospitality," the messenger admitted, allowing himself to be led away.

Angus looked over his shoulder at Gruoch as he departed, his expression clear even though he spoke no words.

*Patience.*

The patience that Angus had counselled was a difficult proposition and yet one that Gruoch had no choice but to accept. Thankfully, she was not tested long, as a second rider appeared less than a fortnight after the first.

This rider approached Crown Hill more cautiously, his horse moving at a steady walk but no faster. It seemed that whatever message this rider bore with him weighed him down and slowed his steps.

Gruoch had been in her apartment, sitting by the fire and fruitlessly attempting at embroidery to keep her mind occupied, when she heard the sudden rushing of feet in the hall outside her door and the rising of voices in the yard. She made her way to the window quickly and observed the quiet rider as he approached the gates, which were swung open in order to permit him.

Angus had beaten her to the yard and to the messenger, who Gruoch recognized quickly as the lord of Ross. His joyful face had become harder since she had last beheld him, and the dusty gold of his blonde hair was darkened and matted by sweat in the warm June air. His face made every attempt at neutrality, but the absence of relief or joy on his face was even more telling than a scowl could have been.

Angus suddenly turned away from Ross, and as Gruoch approached, the older soldier spat angrily into the dirt at his feet. He did not look at her as Gruoch made her way to them, but Ross bowed his head in acknowledgement, bending his knee more than was necessary.

"Ross," Gruoch said calmly, finding her voice. "You come bearing news? What have you told Angus that he should keep from looking at me? We received word not long ago that things were progressing in our favour. Is that no longer the case?"

The neutral expression slipped quickly from Ross' face, replaced with a bitter and jaded grimace.

"The battle is ours, my lady," he said tersely. "But it has come at a cost."

She steeled herself for the worst and forced the flutter in her stomach down in order to keep her voice from wavering, either from fear or excitement.

"My lord Coemgáin?"

Ross shook his head. "He is well, my lady. Your husband and his brother are alive and have fought bravely against the insurrectionists and invaders. The Battle of Clontarf is ours."

"Then…" Gruoch found she no longer had words or the breath to speak them.

"The lord Findlaech has fallen," Ross said as Angus spat once more into the dirt. "Killed by the Norse as the battle drew to a close. The cowards ran him through, piercing his back and severing the spine. My lord Mac Bethad found him on the field. He has sworn vengeance on those responsible."

Findlaech.

Gruoch pictured the smiling face, the eyes so similar to Mac Bethad's. She could hear his booming voice, and the joyful boisterousness that had so reminded her of her own father. Gruoch's mind then slipped to Mac Bethad, and she pictured him cradling the body of his father as he died in the dirt and mud. Would the trauma be enough to bring on another fit? If so, would Banquo succeed in keeping it from the attention of the others?

"There is more to say," Ross said quietly, his eyes darting around the yard. "However, I would prefer our counsel continue somewhere private. Angus?"

Angus looked at Gruoch then, his eyes afire.

"The lady Gruoch will accompany us," he said to Ross as he nodded in the direction of the tower.

"I am not sure. I mean, such things should likely not be spoken in the presence of a lady."

Gruoch bristled, and Angus spoke for her.

"If what I suspect is indeed what you have left to say, I should think the lady Gruoch deserves to hear it."

Ross nodded unhappily and followed Angus into the tower. Gruoch stepped silently behind them, closing the door as they went.

In the mysterious way of most rumours, news and stories had arrived at Crown Hill before their subject had. Gille and Mael rode home, along with the remainder of their men, roughly five days after Ross had delivered the news of Findlaech's death. In the short interim, shows of mourning had already begun at the Tower. Findlaech had been beloved by the people of Moray, and their grief at his death was apparent.

It was Alane who reminded Gruoch of a fact that had escaped her notice as she paced the halls of Crown Hill, awaiting her husband's return.

"Your husband shall return as the Mormaer," Alane told her one morning as she brushed out Gruoch's hair. "You are now truly the lady of Crown Hill."

Gruoch allowed Alane to continue combing her hair as she considered the housekeeper's words. Gille had been named Findlaech's heir before he and Gruoch had even married, and he would now be expected to fulfill the role he had inherited. She thought of Mac Bethad once more and pictured him on the field next to his father's broken body and the rage he had quietly expressed at being looked over by Findlaech. Banquo had claimed his friend's mercurial temperament had turned the Mormaer off from proposing to the Tanistry that Mac Bethad be his successor. However, those who lived at the Hill and had left to defend it had all been witness to the way Findlaech consulted Mac Bethad and considered his advice, how he seemed to give preference to what his son had to say over what Gille, the heir named, would contribute.

Gille's return, along with Mael and the men of Crown Hill, was met with a tired kind of relief. Wives and children rushed to welcome home their husbands and fathers. The greetings were desperate in a way they had not been at the men's departure, for it seemed as though something, some essential sense of hope and future, had died back in Hibernia. What was more, Gruoch could immediately see that her husband was not immune to this pall and that it angered him to arrive at a less than jubilant celebration of welcome.

Alane, Angus, and Gruoch stood to greet them as Gille and Mael entered the yard and dismounted from their horses. Angus and Alane knelt deeply before Gille, who stepped to his wife, placing a stiff arm around her waist.

"I am glad to see you are all well," he said. "I have missed my home and those who kept it safe for me."

"We are glad to see you safely returned," Gruoch managed. Gille's arm was a dead weight around her, and her body seemed painfully aware of it. Her skin felt as though it had been pricked by a thousand blistering needle points.

"Many happy returns," Angus added in his deep and raspy timbre. His eyes darted quickly to Mael, who had dismounted as well and made his way over to where his brother stood.

"Is this meagre welcome all you could conjure for your lord and master?" Mael directed his question at Alane, who blanched visibly at the reproach. She curtsied again, wringing her hands before her chest.

"Provisions have been rationed quite strictly, my lord," she explained quickly. "We have all gone without in order to send what we could North towards those who fought."

"Findlaech was proud of what the Hill provided," Gille said solemnly, leaving Gruoch's side and clasping a hand firmly on Angus' shoulder. "I know he was proud to know you were here, keeping his home safe."

"I would give anything to have been there when he fell," Angus said, keeping his eyes fixed on Mael's smirking face. "If only to have gutted and thrown down he who slew the greatest lord to have ever resided at the Hill."

The silence was pregnant and tense, broken only by a last hurried bow from Alane, who rushed away to see that the soldiers and lords were given a proper welcome.

"You have a new lord now," Mael said, meeting Angus' hostile glare with a cool and collected air before he turned his attention to Gruoch. "Many blessings on you as well, my lady and my sister."

He leaned into her before Gruoch could step away, grasping her upper arms firmly and planting a chaste kiss on her cheek. Her lungs froze of their own accord, and Gruoch's body allowed no breath to enter it as the sweaty smell of him stung at her nose. She fought against the urge to wipe the faintly wet sensation away from her cheek, clenching her hand into a fist while hiding it behind her back.

"Brother," Gruoch managed as he stepped away from her, and the tainted air was blown away by a merciful breeze.

Gille took his leave of her then, gesturing both to Mael and Angus that they should walk with him. It seemed he was eager to begin his new role in earnest and was quick to question Angus on the remaining food stores, the number of peasants who had been taken in, and other matters that Findlaech could no longer oversee.

As Gruoch watched the three of them walk towards the Tower itself, she was surprised by the sudden and violent feeling that began wrenching its way through her every nerve and vein. It was as though her skin had been sliced open, only to have hot oil poured into it, one that followed every sinew and bone until it filled her with vitriol. Having grown so used to numbness, Gruoch was not able at first to recognize this feeling and to call it by its proper name.

For the first time since the deaths of her son and her surrogate mother, Gruoch's heart beat something other than cold and despair through her veins. She relished the surge of heat, the sudden rushing in her ears, and the angry and vengeful pounding of her heart.

It was rage.

It was wonderful.

Created with Sketch.

Gruoch would never be sure how the people of Crown Hill first came to know of the stories that hung about Gille and Mael in the days after their return or even precisely when her husband and brother-in-law became aware of them. At first, Gille pretended not to notice the increasingly daring and accusatory glances that were shot his way as he strolled through the compound. Mael had no such decorum, and Gruoch had seen him push a man and draw his dagger at some perceived slight. The people had grown accustomed to her spectral presence, her quiet and passive existence among them, and indeed, since so many thought her to be mad, they often forgot themselves when in earshot of Gruoch. She heard them repeat the foul stories and gossip that Ross had first shared with them before Gille's return.

*They say he was there when the Mormaer was killed.*

*They are saying it was him.*

*I heard it was the brother.*

Ross had been visibly uncomfortable, struggling to say his piece and seemingly made all the tenser by Gruoch's presence. He had avoided her eyes, locking his attention instead on Angus, who took in his friend's words quietly and without reacting.

"You are sure?" Angus had waited for Ross to be delivered of every painful detail before posing to him the question Gruoch was burning with as well.

"I have no real proof," Ross replied. "It was one of Findlaech's own guards who was said to have seen it. He was run through as well but still had breath when Mac Bethad came across him in the field as he searched for his father."

Angus considered this, one hand running itself over stubbled cheeks.

"But Mac Bethad believed him?"

"Aye," Ross continued. "He'd have no reason to doubt the guard's word. He'd been a loyal subject for years. He had tried to step in and defend Findlaech but said that the vile serpent cut his legs out from under him as he made his way." Ross's agitation broke through his efforts at composure. "What kind of coward kills a man from behind?"

Angus had looked away then, staring into the fires of a hearth that lay nearby.

"The same kind that whispers in his brother's ear in order to rule through him," Gruoch told them.

Ross had stayed the night at Gruoch's insistence and had left early the next morning to head south towards Alba and Duncan. At her urging, he had promised to stop along his way and pay a visit to Bodhe and bring him news of his daughter and to bring Bodhe's own message back to his daughter when Ross would return to Moray.

"Tell him I long to see him," Gruoch had asked Ross as he mounted the fresh mare she gave him despite his reticence. "Please. Ask him to come and spend time at the Tower with me."

Ross had nodded to her and then to Angus, who had also come to see him off.

"I will do as you ask, my lady." As quickly as he had burst in, Ross made his way from the Tower and towards the King of Alba, who would have to be notified not only of his steward's death but of the suspicion surrounding it.

Ross had left almost a fortnight before, and still, Duncan did not come. Nor did Bodhe, whom Gruoch missed more than she had realized when she had asked Ross to stop and pass along her messages. In the meantime, Gille wandered his home in an apparent effort to ignore the heaviness that lay there while Mael confronted any manifestation of what he considered to be an affront.

Late one evening, Mael came upon Gruoch as she walked along the perimeter of the yard. She had grown so used to being ignored that she had allowed herself to lose concentration, to turn away any thoughts or attention to her surroundings. It was at such a moment that Gruoch felt a hand as strong as stone grab her wrist and wrench her back mid-step. She stumbled and felt herself being pulled back until her spine was flush with the chest of a man not much taller than she.

Mael's vile breath gave him away before he had even uttered a word, and the hand that did not grip Gruoch's wrist grabbed at her waist, holding her against him with a crushing and suffocating force. She made no sound, even though the sharp pain that shot through her wrist was enough to make the bone ache.

Gruoch felt his mouth, hot and rank, as it moved against her ear, and she shuddered at the whisperings he poured there.

"You could tell him what I have done, what I still may do, and he would not believe you."

Mael was right. Even if Gruoch were to tell Gille that his brother had attacked her, her husband would storm and rage against Gruoch and her seemingly inexplicable hatred and agenda against his flesh and blood. The frantic words were still at her ear, and the breath that expelled them lay as moist and toxic droplets on the skin of Gruoch's neck.

"I know what you've tried to say against me already, little sister. When your boy died, when that bitch killed him. I know you blamed me in the deepest and darkest parts of this body."

The hand that held her waist slid slowly across Gruoch's abdomen, and it took everything in her power to keep from retching as it made its way along her body in a show of dominance.

"The worst part," and now the breath was closely followed by a ghost of lips dancing at her earlobe, "is that you were right. You are a stone around his neck. Your weak boy was a blight on our family line, and that heathen cow got what was coming to her."

Tears stung Gruoch's eyes in her quiet rage, threatening to spill. She blinked rapidly, refusing to allow Mael the satisfaction of a response to his words. It was torture to remain frozen, to keep herself from tearing at his eyes and his hair at his words, at the confession that she had longed for.

At that moment, it was just as difficult to keep the bile from erupting from her stomach as it was to keep her fingernails from plucking the orbs from Mael's cankerous face.

*Things will not always be this way.*

Gruoch heard Mac Bethad's words from the night he had found her, wild and broken, wandering alongside the very walls where she found herself now.

*I will not allow them to remain so.*

And as though he had been conjured by the memory of his words, Mac Bethad rode once again through the gates of Crown Hill and into her life.

Mael broke away from Gruoch as they heard the sound of the guard rushing to open the gates for the party of riders, some fifty men strong. He moved back quickly, smoothing a hand over his stringy hair and straightening his tunic. Gruoch suppressed a lingering shudder and stepped from the shadow and into the dancing light of the torches.

She caught his eye as Mac Bethad rode past and saw as he took in Mael from where he stood, scowling openly a few feet away from her. Mac Bethad's face was cloaked by the inky darkness, but the steady fire that lit his eyes was unmistakable. Gruoch realized quickly that things had been set into motion that would tear her from her home and her path, setting her on a journey whose destination was still unknown.

Still.

She would welcome it with open arms.

# TWELVE
# THE DEEPEST SHADOWS

Her first husband's name was Gille Coemgáin mac Maíl Brigti, and he died when Gruoch was twenty years old.

The riders that arrived at Crown Hill that evening appeared tired but relieved to be within the gates of the compound, and there seemed to hang over them a pall that could not be ignored. Horses, weary from a long trek, sweated and steamed as grooms hurried forward to lead them away to be stabled and fed. Curious merchants, villagers, and other visitors to the Hill crowded at a respectable distance, some clearly eager to cast their eyes upon the son of their beloved former master.

Although they were obviously fatigued, the riders did not tarry in the yard. They moved with purpose and premeditation as though each had some pressing concern to attend to. People moved quickly out of their way, and in a matter of mere moments, most of the riders had dispersed further into the yard, into outbuildings, and into the tower itself.

Gruoch watched the goings-on, ever aware of Mael standing nearby. Mac Bethad seemed intent on avoiding her and made no effort to come to Gruoch or even to look her way. Banquo, his ever-present companion, stood to the right of his lord, nodding solemnly at some quietly spoken request. He listened intently to Mac Bethad before finally looking in her direction.

Gruoch felt uneasy.

Gille appeared at the door of the tower's base, accompanied by a few of his personal guards, as well as half a dozen of Mac Bethad's riders. Her husband walked with his head high; his arms extended in greeting and welcome. A few servants stood by with their torches held high. Gille's guards, she noticed, kept a hand hovering at the handles of swords still hidden in sheaths.

As he noticed Gille's arrival, Mac Bethad stopped speaking to Banquo and turned to face his approaching host. Gruoch stood still as Mael brushed suddenly by, striding past her to walk alongside his brother. She felt a chill rip down her back as though her spine had been coated in ice, and the unease in her stomach rolled over on itself.

"Welcome, Mac Bethad," Gille called out jovially. "A warm greeting for the hero of Clontarf."

"Many thanks, cousin," Mac Bethad responded, the tautness of his features betraying the lightness in his voice. "It is good to be *home*."

There was the briefest of pause as Gille searched for a diplomatic response to Mac Bethad's pregnant words.

"We are glad to have you, *cousin*," Mael offered.

Mac Bethad allowed his gaze to drift to Mael, and it seemed to any of those with eyes that the former looked upon the latter as though he were a maggot discovered in spoiled meat, unpleasant but unsurprising. If Mael found insult in how his kinsman looked down at him, he had the sense to pretend otherwise.

"I am glad you are still here, Mael," Mac Bethad continued. "The coming festivities would be incomplete without you."

"Festivities, cousin?" Gille's voice had returned to him.

The sudden vice around her arm made Gruoch gasp, and the sharp point in her lower back came without warning. One of Mac Bethad's riders stood suddenly behind her, holding her tightly. Gruoch did not struggle and forced herself to remain calm. Whatever was about to happen would unfold, as so many moments did, whether or not she interceded. In this, as in many things, Gruoch was a powerless witness in her own life.

She felt a strange flutter as Gille's head spun suddenly as he became aware of the circle of riders that had enfolded him and his guards. His eyes found her own, and as he took in the stranger holding his dagger to his wife's back, Gruoch saw an old passion flame in his gaze that she had not seen in many months.

Gille looked at her as he had when they had first been wed and when she had carried Lulach in her belly. He looked as though he could kill anything or anyone that would threaten or cause her harm. Gruoch had almost forgotten that Gille had loved her once. Perhaps, as the look of anger and horror on his face suggested, in a way, he still did.

"What is the meaning of this," he growled softly. "Why do your brigands surround their lord with naked weapons? Why does that man threaten my lady with his blade?"

"It is over for you," Banquo responded. "The people have turned against you and all that you stand for. They will not follow a traitor."

"On whose authority do you brand me thus?"

"We have been sent by Malcolm, son to your high king."

Gille's eyes widened in shock before his teeth settled into a grotesque snarl as he laughed bitterly.

"You have but fifty men," he said. "You think you can take Crown Hill from me?"

"The men of the Hill do not stand with you," called a voice from the crowd.

Gille turned sharply at the sound of the latest voice, and Angus stepped out from behind a group of Mac Bethad's riders. He stood as erect as his damaged body would allow; his scarred hand steady as it gripped the hilt of his broadsword.

"Angus, you filth," Mael spat. "You would betray your lord? The one Findlaech himself chose as his successor?"

"Don't you dare speak his name," Mac Bethad said quietly. "Keep it from your foul mouth."

"Gille Coemgáin mac Maíl Brigti, we see you for the treasonous dog that you are," Banquo said, his low voice carrying easily through the still night, and it echoed in the yard. "We know that you and your brother slew the lord Findlaech, the true Mormaer, on the battlefield of Clontarf."

"This is madness!" Spittle flew from Gille's mouth as he spoke, and he spun quickly as though seeking support from those who stood around him.

"We have been made aware of those loyal to Findlaech, those who would kneel now before his son, Mac Bethad." Banquo continued as though Gille had not spoken. "All others will be struck down for Moray to heal and prosper once more. The rot in the wound must be cut out."

It was as Ross had warned. The people had heard the whispers and the rumours fueled by Findlaech's slain servant, and the tide of anger had swept along, becoming a wave that would eventually crash against the shore, washing away what was found in its wake. Gruoch realized that, as Gille's wife, the wave would come for her as well. She would be washed away in this murderous current.

She would be with Lulach and Hertha.

She could rest.

The nod from Mac Bethad was almost imperceptible, but it swept a current through his men that sent them into a movement that seemed almost rehearsed, as though they were suddenly immersed in the steps of some familiar dance. The few guards that had accompanied Gille were struck down quickly, with clever daggers making short work of exposed throats. Gruoch closed her eyes too late to miss the first body thrown from the upper levels of the tower, and she heard the wet thump it made as it landed on the stones and dirt below. When Gruoch dared to open her eyes, her stomach turned violently upon itself at the sight of a boy not much older than her whose skull had burst upon hitting the ground. The dirt and stones upon which he now lay were littered with the gory remains of brain matter and blood pooled beneath him. As Gruoch stared into his vacant eyes, another body crashed to the earth behind him, spattering what clean space was left with a fresh torrent of scarlet.

She watched, unable to look away, as those who survived the fall were quickly extinguished by the soldiers at whose feet they fell. The night that had been so quiet and peaceful not moments before was split suddenly with the groans and screams of dying men. Gruoch stood through it all, struck dumb by the sudden stench of copper and the sight of men she knew, men she recognized, dying terribly before her.

Gille and Mael were grabbed quickly, and their arms were bound in rope and tied behind their backs. Gruoch watched in some strange and detached trance as villagers and merchants, women and men, rushed forward to spit on her husband and his brother. Some were even bold enough to throw stones at them as they were brusquely taken away. Mac Bethad's riders marched the two prisoners towards the small stone chapel where they celebrated Mass and had christened her son, and Gruoch looked on as the small building became an improvised prison. Gille and Mael were pushed inside with little ceremony, their hands still bound, and were followed by three soldiers, as another two stood guard at the door.

Gruoch was knocked back to her senses by the sting of a stone against her brow. Mutely, she lifted a hand to the place, and she felt the skin throb where the stone had hit. As she wiped her fingers across the wound, Gruoch felt the unmistakably warm trickle of blood as it made its way slowly down the side of her face. It was the sight of her own blood, dark against the white of her cold hands, that suddenly prompted a hysterical laugh to burst from her mouth. The sound was piercing, but it was short, lasting only as long as the ragged and stale breath that remained in her stagnant lungs. It was at that moment, at the sound of her hysteria, that Mac Bethad finally allowed himself to look at Gruoch.

It was as though the sight of her blood finally tore apart his cold composure. A flicker of some indecipherable emotion brushed across his features, and he seemed to come undone. Whatever restraint he still grappled with was forgotten, and he strode toward her, pulling his broadsword free. Gruoch saw then the emotion for what it was.

Rage.

She understood that it would be Mac Bethad who would release her from this hell and send her back to her child.

Happy that of all men, he should be her executioner, Gruoch closed her eyes and waited for the cold metal to find her.

Instead, she felt the arm of her captor release her, and the point of his dagger left her back. At the dizzying rush of sudden liberty, Gruoch's eyes flew open, and she struggled to comprehend what she now saw. Mac Bethad stood there, his broad back turned to her, as he faced out into the brazen crowd.

"The lady is guiltless in this," he roared. "You will not touch her. Any man or woman foolish enough to cross me in this will not breathe long enough to err again."

Those who still stood by, their hands gripping what rocks they had gathered, turned glaring faces away, making their way towards the dead. Gruoch shivered at the open hate and hostility that she was regarded with. She had walked amongst these people mere moments before and had lived at their side for years. Had they always hated her so? Or had their anger at Findlaech's death at Gille's hands bled over onto her as well? Gruoch looked down, dumb, at her hands where the evidence of her cut had stained them. She was the wife of the traitor they had now openly revolted against. How long would it be until her body also lay broken among those of Gille's men?

Mac Bethad had spoken in her defence. Could Gruoch dare allow herself to think that whatever feelings he harboured for her would be enough to keep her alive? The bodies of Gille's men were thrown unceremoniously into a pile, their weapons and armour stripped from their broken bodies. This was the consequence of treason, and it was clear that the people of Moray thirsted for justice. Gruoch doubted that her husband's blood would suffice in quenching it.

Speaking over his shoulder, Mac Bethad addressed her in a hoarse voice, startling Gruoch from her thoughts.

"You are not hurt badly?"

She shook her head. "I am fine," she croaked,

Mac Bethad nodded then and strode away quickly, making his way towards the chapel. Gruoch watched as the space between them grew, and his angry strides made short work of the distance he covered. As he reached the chapel, he threw open the door, slamming it behind him as he entered. At this, Banquo sent a wordless order to Angus, who bowed his head slightly before making his way to Gruoch.

"My lady?" He spoke gently to her as he approached, as though she were some frightened mare that could lash out or run. "My lady, would you allow me to accompany you to your rooms?"

Gruoch searched Angus's face for some answers to questions she was not yet able to form. The cheeks darkened with stubble, and the deep-set eyes had become familiar to her in the long weeks since Gille and Mael had left for Hibernia, and she found no malice or threat in his face. He offered his hand to her, and Gruoch took it gratefully. He wound her arm through his own, holding her up and guiding her steps towards the door to the tower. She stumbled once, tripping over an outstretched limb, and Angus held her up, steadying her as Gruoch regained her footing.

"Keep your eyes on your feet, my lady," he said gently. "Do not look."

Although she did not watch as they set the bodies aflame, the stench of roasting flesh and hair found her anyway, and Gruoch knew it would linger and foul the air for days. By the time Angus had led her back to her room, the light that was thrown off by the blaze streaked through the window, illuminating the chamber with fierce and whirling dervishes, making even the deepest of shadows dance.

Gruoch lay upon her bed when she heard the creak of her opening door.

She was on her back, looking up at the shadows being cast onto the ceiling by the bonfire outside, finding in the winding shapes the scenes of a faraway battle she had only heard of. She saw men strike against men, saw them fall and be torn apart. She saw a strong silhouette cut down and watched as the other shadows danced and threw themselves on the ground and into the air in a horrible dance of mourning and anger. It was hypnotic.

Gruoch did not look away from the ceiling as the sound of shuffling feet made its way closer to her. The sound eased once it was firmly in her room, and whoever had entered paused only a few feet past the threshold.

She heard the bedroom door close and the latch catch.

Her body felt no sense of urgency as her head fell slowly to the side, allowing Gruoch to catch a glimpse of the one who had come into her private space. She said nothing to Mac Bethad as he stood there, leaning against a wall. He was preoccupied, furiously washing away at his gruesome hands and tunic with a damp piece of cloth. Gruoch wondered if her husband's blood also figured among the spots that stained the grey wool.

"Your tunic is ruined," she said to him softly. At the sound of her voice, Mac Bethad ceased the frantic scrubbing of the cloth.

"I did not want to come before you like this," he said demurely.

Gruoch sighed at his words and turned her attention back to the ceiling. "It seems to me that it is entirely within your power to do whatever you like." Here, in the confines of her room, with the smell of burning flesh crashing upon her, Gruoch found a certain kind of apathetic bravery. What more could be taken from her? If Mac Bethad wanted her virtue, her life, or both, she would not fight to keep them. Her soul was still her own, the only thing untouched in the ruin of her life, the only thing Gruoch still possessed.

"Gruoch, please. I am sorry for what you saw, but I make no apologies for the act itself. Your husband or his toad brother murdered my father, their sworn lord. Findlaech's ghost has haunted me every night since, reminding me of my filial obligation to him."

Gruoch said nothing. She knew only too well the power and sway of ghosts.

"May I speak with you?" Mac Bethad kept his voice neutral, almost eerily polite. She was not used to this uncertain and clumsy persona. The vision of his winking face in her father's hall came unbidden and unexpectedly to the forefront of her mind. It no longer felt like a memory but like some strange act of voyeurism. Gruoch was no longer that scandalized and proud girl, and he was no longer the mysterious and rakish rogue. She was of the undead, and he was a bloodied sword.

"You have already made your way into my chambers," Gruoch responded, pushing away the vision of his playful eyes. "It seems a strange time to stop and ask permission."

She heard the exasperation in his sigh and looked over once more, watching as Mac Bethad pushed off from the wall and ran a dirty hand through his dark hair. He took one step toward her and seemed to remember himself, halting in his movement and standing still once more.

"I meant what I said to those outside. I will not allow harm to come to you. They are swept up in their anger, but none of the men loyal to me truly believe that you were complicit in your husband's plots."

"The stone that struck me would suggest otherwise."

A pause. "The offender has been dealt with."

"You should not have done so. These people know nothing of me, only that I am a mad and dishonourable wife. That my husband killed their lord."

"Alane has spoken on your behalf, and it was clear that her testimony and vows of honour held more weight even than my own."

So, Alane had defended her during some secret meeting or trial, and judgment had fallen without Gruoch even needing to be present. Feelings of gratitude towards the older woman warred with irritation until, once more, the cold numbness overtook her and settled her soul.

Better to feel nothing than to break her heart over understanding what it was trying to feel.

"Gruoch, I want you to know that I have seen your father. We went to his hall before making our way here."

"Is my father regretting his choice of a son-in-law?"

"Your father is dead."

Gruoch sat up then, quickly and with jerking movements. Mac Bethad kept his gaze steady and unflinching as she threw her legs over the side of the bed and ran to him. He steadied her as Gruoch grabbed angrily at the front of his tunic and wrenched at it with her hands. His large hands came to cover her own, but he did not try and stop the assault. Gruoch kicked at his legs, tore one hand away and brought it to his face in a desperate attempt to shred the skin there. He caught her wrist easily, still saying nothing.

"Was it not enough that you've avenged your own father?" Her words were little more than shrieks, the hysteria behind them casting them into an octave more animal than human. "What has mine done? Why would you kill him too?!"

Mac Bethad held her wrist firmly in one hand and grasped the back of Gruoch's head with the other. He pulled her face to his own and pressed his brow to hers before speaking. Her neck ached with the effort to wrench herself away, yet Mac Bethad's grip held firm, keeping her flesh against his.

"He was killed as a traitor, Gruoch, but he was not slain by me or mine." Gruoch felt Mac Bethad's breath on her face as he spoke. "This, I swear to you."

She brought up a knee then, in a hard and purposeful movement, catching him in the place of vulnerability all men shared. He uttered a guttural sound of pain as he released her, doubling over and falling to one knee before her. One hand was clenched over his stomach, and the second kept up a frail attempt at blocking the blows that Gruoch rained down upon him.

"What are your words? Nothing! You have no honour! You are incapable of it!"

Her pain fueled her and gave Gruoch an unexpected strength, but Mac Bethad forced himself back to his feet, groaning as he did so. His hand left his stomach and caught her arm mid-flight, interrupting her blows. He wrenched Gruoch closer to him, his eyes blazing as he looked down at her, his face covered in a fresh sheen of sweat.

"There are those who say he was in league with your husband to overthrow Duncan's hold in Moray."

"It's not true!"

"Of course it isn't true," Mac rasped, his voice a desperate growl in the stifling air of the chamber. "Your father had nothing to do with the plans to overthrow Duncan."

Gruoch's hand went limp in his grasp, and she sobbed loudly, the violent strength that had filled her moments before abandoning her just as aptly. Her mind was drunk on Mac Bethad's confession and the gravity of such words. Her knees gave way, and Mac Bethad thrust an arm around her waist, supporting her and holding her against him. Gruoch's face was cradled into the crook of his neck, where the cold smell of sweat and blood assailed her.

"Who?" The sobs that wracked her left little breath for speech. "Why?"

"Malcolm," he said. "The same man who has condemned your husband."

This could not be. Malcolm was her father's nephew. Duncan was Bodhe's older brother. Why would such a thing have taken place?

"They are saying it was a failed coup," Mac Bethad continued, his voice quiet but steady, and the words pounded forward with little attempt at comfort. "They are saying that Gille and Bodhe worked as one to plot and assassinate my father in order for Gille to take control and maintain order in the North. They would have then aligned their forces to march south and take Alba from your uncle. Malcolm has decreed them both traitors."

Her throat was hoarse and felt as though some clawed demon had torn it to shreds, and the sound of her blood still pounded in Gruoch's ears. She forced herself to take deep breaths, kneeling on the ground on all fours, seeking purchase in the steady presence of the stones beneath her. Mac Bethad knelt at her side and removed his hands, leaving patches of flesh made suddenly colder by their absence.

"It is senseless," Gruoch finally managed. A wave of nausea overtook her, and she breathed again to keep herself from retching. "My father has never wanted Alba. He has ever been a faithful steward in the North."

"There are strange and wicked seeds being sown in Moray," Mac Bethad responded. "There is a poison here, and I mean to find those responsible for the decay of my country." He paused for a moment as he waited for Gruoch to catch her breath. "Will you help me, *mo lasair*?"

"I long to die."

Mac Bethad said nothing while they sat in silence, contemplating what Gruoch had said. They both knew it to be true, but she was still surprised to discover in the darkest parts of herself how sincere the words were.

"Gruoch, please do not leave me."

She laughed then, bitterly, bringing up a hand to wipe furiously at the tears on her face. She looked at him, kneeling by her on the floor, hands on his knees as though he were a child. There was pain on his face, one that Gruoch recognized and could understand. Her torment had demanded to be felt in solitude, whereas Mac Bethad's seemed to cry out for companionship.

"What would you have that I can give, Mac Bethad?" She was tired then, so deeply tired. "I am hollow, empty."

"I would have you come to me, willingly and completely. I would marry you, Gruoch."

She smiled a twisted and angry alignment of lips. "I have told you once before. My husband is still alive."

"He will not live long." The words were said with no cruelty or anger, just an exhausted confirmation of what they both knew to be true.

Gruoch was struck by a sudden feeling of boldness. " I wish to speak with him. I wish to ask him about my father."

Mac Bethad nodded. He rose to his feet and held out a hand to Gruoch so that she might do the same. She ignored it, wrestling with aching limbs until she stood before him. He said nothing as he watched her struggle to her feet and merely pulled away his hand. They stood for a moment in the chamber, suddenly unable to find anything more to say.

It was he who broke the silence first.

"I will never force you, Gruoch. I would give you all of myself and protect you with the very breath of my body, and I would worship you so long as you lived. But—" at this, he crossed the invisible line between them, stepping towards her but keeping his hands at his sides. "I will never force you."

"I know," she said simply. She knew as well as he that he meant what he said.

"Please," he whispered, taking one small step closer. "Let me hold you."

In response, Gruoch brought her hands to cup his face, pulling it down to her. If her lips tasted of salt and tears, such things were quickly mended by the need that overcame him as they embraced. Mac Bethad's hands came to her shoulders, pulling her tightly against him, only to make their way to her hair and twist within the strands. She gasped again, her body burning for air and for some other more basic need as Gruoch allowed her hands to stray from his face. They travelled over the hard muscles of his shoulders and chest, pushing aside the woollen tunic until they found flesh.

Mac Bethad groaned then, pulling himself away gently. He stroked her face softly and kissed her brow with chaste lips, even though his chest rose and fell swiftly in a mirror image of her own.

"Marry me," he asked again, his lips against her forehead. "Choose me."

"You know as well as I that there is no choice," Gruoch said quietly. "The fates have made fools of us both."

He pulled back slightly to look her in the eye and seemed satisfied by what he saw there. He kissed her softly once more on the mouth and let her go.

"Come," he said. "I will take you to Gille so that you might get your answers."

# TWELVE
# THE DEEPEST SHADOWS

Gruoch and Mac Bethad walked hand in hand through the corridors of his home, and Gruoch quickly became aware that there was something in the way Mac Bethad held himself that made it clear to those who saw them that he would tolerate no discourteous look or word. There were many glances cast in their direction as they passed, but most of these seemed more curious than hostile. People took in the sight of their tightly clasped hands and the way Mac Bethad slowed his gait so that he would not drag her behind him. They walked in tandem, with Gruoch's shoulder brushing his arm.

"The fire is still burning," Mac Bethad said to her as they came to the main door. His voice held a note of apology.

She nodded. "I can still smell it."

"It can't be helped now. Can you stomach it? We will have to pass somewhat close by as we make our way to the chapel."

"I'll be fine." If he doubted her resolve, Mac Bethad seemed to know better than to voice such concerns. Then, Gruoch was struck by a sudden thought. "Wait."

"What is it?"

"Is Mael with him? Are they together?"

It was now Mac Bethad's turn to nod.

"Aye," he said. "They are. Would you have me remove him so you might speak to Gille alone?"

"Please," she answered. Gruoch wanted to speak with the man who had been her husband these past five years, the father of her only child. She wanted to speak with him without the souring influence of his cursed brother.

"I will see it done." He paused a moment, looking at their conjoined hands. "Will you walk with me like this?"

"If it does not bother you to be seen holding the hand of the disgraced and unfaithful daughter of a condemned traitor."

His fingers squeezed hers in response, and suddenly he was pushing open the door into the chilled night.

There were streaks of red bleeding over the eastern horizon. The dark purple and blues of the firmament were being infected with the soft, golden streaks of dawn. No wonder her body felt such fatigue and weariness. It had been hours since Mac Bethad had arrived at Crown Hill.

The light of the bonfire was harsh as they stepped into the yard, and Gruoch squinted, trying to get her eyes to adjust to the brightness. The lit yard threw into sharp relief the number of people still lingering there who now looked upon her and Mac Bethad as they stepped out. Somewhere, in the beating chambers of her heart, Gruoch felt Hertha's strength course through her. She kept her chin high and met the eyes of those who stared at her, some in wonder, others in anger. Many of these people had stood by as Hertha had been killed and had ignored Gruoch as she had sunk into her depression. She would not hide her eyes from them now. She would make them feel as insignificant as they were. She was the flame, and it was they who should fear being burned.

Mac Bethad nodded to his men as he passed with Gruoch and called out abrupt and simple orders to some of them. These men jumped at his voice and moved quickly to obey. It was clear that Mac Bethad had more than the obedience of his soldiers. He had their reverence and their respect. He was his own kind of flame.

Finally, they came before the chapel, where two soldiers stood watch outside the door. They stepped away without a word as Mac Bethad approached them so that he might enter with Gruoch. Before they did, he turned to her once more.

"He will have been beaten. It may be hard to see."

"I have seen worse things than a beaten man," Gruoch said, though the thought of seeing Gille broken and injured sent a revolted hesitation through her. "I will be fine."

"I will have Mael taken out." With these words, Mac Bethad pushed open the door.

It was quiet in the chapel. As the pair made their way in, Gruoch spied Gille immediately. He was sitting on the stone floor, his arms tied tightly behind his back, his ankles bound in rough rope. A few feet away, Mael lay on his side, arms and feet also bound. As Mac Bethad and Gruoch approached, Mael let out a bark of laughter.

"She moves quickly, the sloven bitch."

The guard who stood by Mael kicked him in the stomach, making the prisoner double up on his side in agony. Mael retched and spat crimson. Still, his malicious and mocking eyes never left Gruoch's face.

Mac Bethad gently let go of the hand he had not released since their walk had first begun in the confines of the tower. He pointed to Mael and addressed the guard who had kicked him.

"Take him out. Keep him bound and bring him outside. If he cannot hold his tongue, beat it back into his head."

The guard bent at once to wrench Mael to a sitting position and, a second, stepped up quickly to grab his legs. With no gentleness or care, they lifted the prisoner and bore him swiftly out of the chapel. Mac Bethad watched them leave before turning to Gruoch once more.

"I will wait for you outside."

"I will come soon."

His eyes drifted once to Gille, who had still not lifted his face to them. Mac Bethad gestured to the remaining guard, and the two men walked out, leaving Gruoch alone with her husband.

There were so many questions she wanted to ask him, so many things Gruoch needed him to confirm. Yet as she looked down at him, his tall and lanky build looking impossibly small, all Gruoch could think of was the man who had cradled her swollen stomach, who had been so gentle with her in the early days, and who had looked at her with such pride. Where was that man now? Was he still there, hidden away within this shell that stood bound before her? Had Mael's poison withered away all that Gruoch had loved about her husband?

"He has claimed you as well, then, along with my title?" Gille's voice was tired but seemed without malice.

"There was no claim," she corrected him gently. "It was a choice freely given."

Gille contemplated these words for a moment before finally lifting his face to look at her. His right eye was swollen almost completely shut, and the face Gruoch had looked on in love and anger was almost unrecognizable. He had been beaten more severely than she had allowed herself to consider. His lips were split, and his teeth blackened with rich blood.

"I am glad you are alright," he said with a slight wheeze as though his ribs pained him. "I am glad you were not hurt."

"But you have hurt me," Gruoch said, remembering herself and her mission. "You have colluded with Mael, and because of your treachery, my father is dead."

"I have made mistakes, Gruoch. I have trusted the wrong people, people I thought had only love and the best intentions for me. Be wary that you do not err as I have."

"Why?" The question seemed simple enough, even though it had lain so heavy on her heart and tongue. "Why does the King believe you conspired with Bodhe? Why kill Findlaech? You were his successor. Could you not be content to wait?"

"None of that matters to me now, Gruoch."

"It matters to me!"

Gruoch wanted to grab him then, to slap him and shake him and inflict upon his already bruised body as much pain as she could. She wanted to take the torment and suffering that had weighed on her since their son had died, and she wanted to crush him with it until the breath was finally snuffed from his lungs.

Instead, Gruoch knelt before Gille and used her sleeve to wipe away as much of the blood and grime from his face as she could. He closed his eyes at her touch, and a shining trace of moisture made its way down one cheek.

"I loved you when I saw you in your father's house," he said gently. Gruoch allowed her fingers to rest gently against his cheek as he spoke. "I was so proud to be able to bring you to my own."

"What happened, Gille?" Her voice wavered. "Why did you push me away after Lulach was born? Why did you let Mael kill Hertha?"

"There is no answer I can give which will satisfy you and none that I can give whose honesty I can be sure of. I know nothing anymore. I no longer even know myself."

"You were a good man," she reminded him, their knees touching. "And we loved each other."

He closed the eye that was not already swollen shut, and a shudder wracked him.

"They will kill me, Gruoch," he began. "And they are right to do so. I was weak, and I allowed myself to be played."

"Tell me what Mael did," she begged him. Gruoch cupped Gille's face gently, trying to support the weight of his head. "Gille, I know you loved me once. Tell me what he did."

Gille kept his eyes screwed firmly shut. "He planted doubt in me. Mael said that a boy as small as Lulach could never be my son, that you had been untrue. He told me you conspired with Hertha against me, and that Bodhe had intended to worm his influence into my house through the guise of a daughter."

"Tell me," she demanded. "Gille, tell me all of it!"

But her husband's lips were closed as tightly as his eyes, and he wrenched his face from Gruoch's hands as though they had suddenly burned him.

A flare of rage burned through her with a suddenness that scared her. "Did Mael murder our son?"

"Get her out of here!" His voice burst out of him as though it would rip itself loose. "Get the whore out! I cannot stand to look at her!"

Gruoch shook his shoulders. "Gille, stop! Speak to me! You owe me this, at least!"

She heard the door behind them open, followed by the sound of men rushing towards her. One of the guards came forward and sent Gille sprawling to the floor with a blow to his head. It cracked sickeningly against the stones, and Gruoch held her breath for a moment until she heard Gille groan and wheeze weakly as he lay.

"Do not kill him." Mac Bethad strode quickly to her and looked down at Gille's pathetic form. "Not yet."

Gruoch turned from them and ran to the door, hoping she had not lost her chance. She burst outside and spun wildly, eyes darting around wildly until finally, they found purchase on that which she sought. Not far from the chapel, Mael knelt at the feet of a guard who held his sword out towards him. Mael's body was strung tightly, his muscles contracting violently at the sound of Gille's screams. In his mouth, someone had thrust a dirty rag. Gruoch ran to him and pulled the gag free. The soldier looked on, bewildered and shaken, unsure how best to proceed. She knew his reticence to touch that which he considered as belonging to his lord would not last forever and that she must be swift.

"Why did you conspire against my father and my son?"

Mael grinned at her, licking his cracked lips. "Did your charms fail to disarm my brother? How does it feel to know that you lost him so utterly in the end and that it was I to whom he listened? I to whom he felt most bound?"

"Why is my father dead?"

Mael's smile betrayed his eagerness and the enthusiasm that he felt at the idea of delivering unto her another mortal blow. "Because he colluded with Findlaech! Because they would free Moray from Alba's clutches together! Are you so foolish to think there was no love lost between your father and his elder brother?"

"This lie is lazy storytelling, and I grow weary of hearing it!"

"Findlaech named Gille his successor because he knew it would please Duncan. He meant to lead the people into rebellion, and your father would have helped him to do it! Duncan has always been wary of Bodhe ever since he agreed to send your father away."

"Lies."

"He knew that Findlaech could not be trusted. He had Malcolm explain all this to Gille. You cannot conceive of the rewards they promised your husband should he kill the Mormaer."

"These tales you spin are too convenient to be believable."

Mael looked at her with the same cool and smug expression that had so enraged Gruoch in the past. "If you do nothing else, be wary of Malcolm. He is an adder waiting to strike."

"Gruoch?" Mac Bethad's voice pierced the night, and the guard finally made his move. Rather than risk touching her, he pulled Mael away and threw him onto his back. He then stepped firmly between them.

"God be with you, sister," Mael growled as Mac Bethad stepped up behind her. Gruoch felt his arm at her elbow as he tugged her firmly to her feet.

"That is enough, Gruoch," he said as she rose. "The morning is breaking, and justice must be delivered swiftly."

She allowed herself to be led away and heard Mael's insane cackling as she walked. Gruoch looked at Mac Bethad as he placed a hand at the small of her back, guiding her forward. Gruoch searched his face for some meaning she could not grasp. Was it true? Had their fathers planned an uprising? Had Mac Bethad known of it?

"Please," she began, "Do not kill them yet. I need only a little more time...."

Mac Bethad stopped suddenly, and he held her arms firmly, turning Gruoch to face him head-on.

"You must not ask this of me, Gruoch. Do not ask me to be merciful or for clemency on behalf of your husband. You must know that there are those who would see you killed alongside him, and you must give them no further weapon to use against you."

"Something has been plotted," she tried again. "There is something else at work."

"Gille and Mael will be beheaded as traitors in the yard. I will wield the blows myself. You will watch."

Her eyes closed of their own accord, bowing to the pressure that piled behind them.

"No, you cannot ask this of me."

"Gruoch…"

"I will watch gladly as you take Mael's head from his shoulders. I will lead the cheer myself! But do not ask me to watch as you slaughter my son's father."

"You must, my love. You must show the others that you condemn his traitorous actions and that you have no part in them."

At this, Mac Bethad released her shoulders. He stepped back and offered his hand once more to Gruoch. She looked at the upturned palm for a moment, and she felt the earth tilting beneath her feet. She watched as though from a distance as her hand rose of its own accord and settled against the one outstretched. She did not allow herself to return to her body as it was made to stand next to Alane in the yard next to the dying bonfire, her arm wound tightly around Gruoch's shoulders. She did not return even when Mael's head was knocked cleanly into the dirt by a smooth arc of Mac Bethad's sword. It was not Gruoch that trained her eyes on Gille's face and who held his gaze even when the eyes themselves were made suddenly vacant by a whirl of iron and a rupturing of the soul.

When finally, both men were dead, Gruoch rejoined her body and was permitted to return to her chamber, where exhaustion cast her down into a dark and dreamless sleep, freeing her from the obligations of thought.

# PART THREE
## -A QUEEN-

# FOURTEEN
# PEACE FOR THEM ALL, PERHAPS

Gruoch's second husband was Mac Bethad mac Findlaech, and they were married five years after their first meeting.

The ceremony was small and humble, the lack of circumstance a response to both the deaths that had occurred at the Hill so shortly before and the ever-present rumblings amongst Mac Bethad's supporters at his choice of bride. Gruoch was the widow of a man killed as a traitor. She had born a child who had died and had not been pregnant since. She was far from a lord's ideal candidate in the eyes of any sane or logical man.

"Nothing about us is sane or logical," Mac Bethad had told her when Gruoch had shared her concerns. "And I care little for the opinions of other men."

This, she knew, was not true. Gruoch saw how Mac Bethad shone under the attention of his men. He blazed through as though he were a star falling from the skies, illuminating those around him as he passed. Their love and devotion to him were clear, and he thrived when they came to him with questions or to slap his shoulder with a rough jest. He led easily, and his charisma set him apart from Gille, who had been an efficient chief but had never been a natural or charming one.

At Banquo's insistence, Mael and Gille's bodies were burned rather than be left to the elements and scavenging animals. Gruoch was quietly grateful to him for this small mercy. It was not the Christian burial that Gille would have desired, but it was still a welcome alternative to what the men had clamoured for. She was glad for Banquo, for his calm and steady presence at Mac Bethad's side. Where Mael had been a poisonous ichor, infecting Gille with doubt and paranoia, Banquo was the stone in the bed of a rushing river, unmoving but providing a foothold for anyone struggling with the current.

He stood behind Mac Bethad in the small stone chapel on the day of his friend's wedding. Alane had insisted on helping Gruoch to prepare, and the quick work of her hands through her charge's hair brought to Gruoch's skin the ghostly touch of another mother who had braided Gruoch's hair for her first marriage. She felt Hertha's eyes on her from beyond the pale as Gruoch readied herself to wed Mac Bethad and thought of what Hertha would say if she were there. Would she understand what Gruoch did? Would Hertha find her weak?

Such thoughts and concerns were stronger than Gruoch's ability to ward them off. It seemed as though the ghosts and spirits of her previous life had found renewed force in haunting her new one. Even Lulach still followed her, and Gruoch often heard his laughter around a corner or glimpsed him darting into a room, never able to catch up with him. She kept such things to herself, knowing in some deep or primal place that she couldn't speak of visions with anyone, even the man she loved.

Even Gille managed to creep into her thoughts as Mac Bethad took Gruoch's hands in his before the priest. She stood with Mac Bethad before the altar where Gille had been bound only days before, where Gruoch and her first husband had spoken their final words. It was strange to stand in such a place, thinking of her dead husband as Gruoch married a new one.

She was not the frightened and excited girl who had married Gille with naive hopes. She had tasted life outside her father's home, which opened Gruoch's eyes to the suffering of men and women in a way she had not experienced before. She had not seen much of the world, but the parts she had seen had affected her in ways she knew she still did not completely understand. Mac Bethad was not taking a bright-eyed girl to wife; he was taking a revenant; she was a woman who had gone to the brink only to return as something different. She had become one of those who still kept a foot in the land of shadow amongst her dead.

Gruoch and Mac Bethad spoke the words, and the priest blessed their union and those who had gathered. Banquo smiled broadly at the words, and Gruoch heard Alane's happy sob as Mac Bethad ignored the solemnity of the place and grasped his wife firmly, hands clasping behind her back as he pulled Gruoch towards him. His mouth met hers in a hungry crush, and she allowed herself the blissful quiet of sinking into his embrace, his fire burning away the cold thoughts that slunk through her mind. With her eyes closed, it was all the easier to ignore the look of reproach from the priest, along with any shades that might appear in the dark corners of the chapel, to stare at her with the kind of judgment only the dead possessed.

For all of his boisterous energy and passionate excitement during the wedding, Mac Bethad was surprisingly subdued as the two of them made their way upstairs after the wedding feast. He held Gruoch's hand firmly as they ascended the winding steps, with a band of raucous followers at their heels, guests prepared to see the wedded couple put to bed. She looked at him from the corner of her eye and smiled. He caught the glance and returned the grin. They walked leisurely, much to the displeasure of those who teased them boisterously as they followed behind the couple.

"Precious lamb, look how his knee trembles like an untried boy's!"

"Mac, where is the lusty warrior?"

"Perhaps if she held a Norse axe in her hand, he would pay her quicker attention."

"There is to be nothing quick about it," Mac Bethad finally called over his shoulder to a roar of laughter and cheers. "Now be off. You follow and gossip worse than old women. We can find our way without you."

The laughter mixed with groans and objections, and as Gruoch dared to glance behind her, she saw that Ross finally stopped the small mob from following and directed the others back the way they had come. Banquo had not joined the fray nor the women who usually served her. Rather, it seemed as though Mac Bethad's loyal soldiers and men in arms had formed most of the crowd.

As they slipped up and away from the boisterous crowd below, Mac Bethad apologized to Gruoch quietly on behalf of his friends.

"It is a harmless joy, although I am sorry it comes somewhat at your expense. My men have had little reason to laugh of late."

"It is good to have laughter once more in this house," Gruoch replied, surprised at how true the words were.

She had asked Mac Bethad for little when she had accepted his proposal, but one of Gruoch's more pressing concerns was a vehement need to avoid Gille's old rooms. She could not begin her new life in the space where an old one had ended. It was too much to imagine laying with Mac Bethad in the bed where she had lain with Gille. In the place where she had struggled so to bring Lulach into the world.

"We will use my father's quarters," Mac Bethad had told her when Gruoch had shared some of her concerns. "The Tanistry has not named me Mormaer, but my father would not begrudge us the use of his space."

The room was bigger than Gille's, with two tall windows instead of one. A large fireplace and hearth filled one of the northern corners, and an oaken table and chairs sat close by, as they had in her previous chambers. However, this room was also filled with shelves that held more books than Gruoch had ever seen. She entered the room and made her way there, picking up one of the fragile volumes and gently touching the vellum pages.

"Where did they come from?" Gruoch's voice betrayed the awe she felt. Books were rare in their part of the world, and she knew few who could read and write.

"My father bought some from monasteries while he travelled. We had a monk stay with us for a few years in my childhood, and he made my father a few copies of the texts he carried with him."

"The holy stories?"

Mac Bethad took the book from her hand and turned the pages softly, his fingers resting easily on the pages as one accustomed to doing so. "Scripture, yes, but also texts about the heavenly bodies, plants, and the natural world. Numbers." He turned more pages. "There are a rare few in Greek, but most of my father's books are written in Latin."

Gruoch looked at Mac Bethad, her eyes growing wide. "Can you make sense of them?"

He closed the book and set it gently on the shelf. "A little. I was tutored as a lad, but I admit I was more predisposed towards holding a sword than a quill."

"Predispositions do not limit who we are or what we can do," Gruoch said quietly. "I was predisposed to think you arrogant and rude."

Mac Bethad smiled broadly, showing his teeth. He threw his head back and laughed. "I am those things," he said as he raised a hand to cup her face.

"You have been arrogant, and you have been rude, but such things are not who you are."

He quieted then, though the smile did not leave his lips.

"Who am I then, Gruoch?"

She brought her hand to his, where it rested against her cheek.

"Mine," Gruoch said, again surprised at the truth in her words.

Mac Bethad brought his face closer and rested his brow against hers. Gruoch's eyes closed, and she felt a surge of warmth spread through her cheeks. His free hand found the small of her back, holding her gently. The touch was sure but not possessive. The pressure there brought reassurance rather than restraint.

"I am," he whispered. "I have always been yours."

Gruoch brought her face away from his gently and forced him to look her in the eye.

"I have not always been yours," she said. "I have known a man and born him a child. This man killed your father and has thus been put to death. I am sure there is no lack of well-bred ladies of loyal families you could have chosen from."

Mac Bethad sighed, closing his eyes.

"Look at me," Gruoch whispered roughly. "Don't hide from my words. Answer my question."

"You have not asked it."

"Why me?"

The blue eyes opened at that moment, and there shone in them a light that illuminated the fire within, the absolute certainty in the face of her hesitations.

"There could be none other for me," came Mac Bethad's rough whisper as he brought his lips against Gruoch's ear, the hand at her back suddenly more demanding. "You are the strength in which I might finally rest and a home to which I might finally return. I have been looking for you my entire life. You are yourself, not anything before or after. You are Gruoch, and you are here."

She believed his words with every quake and shiver of her body.

It was different with Mac Bethad, as she had known it would be. Gille had never been brutish or forceful with her but laying with him had been almost methodical in its clear purpose. Gille had other women with whom to waste his time in pleasure, but his time in her bed had meant to get Gruoch with child.

Mac Bethad was slow in his explorations. He kept candles shining so as to, in his own words, better take her in. He kissed and caressed and encouraged her own affectionate gestures, groaning in pleasure under her touch. There was no need for modesty or restraint, and Gruoch knew that Mac Bethad had more on his mind than potential heirs. His gaze was insistent and piercing as he locked his eyes with her, and he brought forth from within her such terrible pleasures as to make her gasp for breath.

It was different with Mac Bethad in so many ways.

When he spoke to her or asked her questions, he truly cared and listened to her response. He never rushed Gruoch to answer and considered her words carefully. Mael had held Gille's ear, but Mac Bethad seemed to have many counsellors and was the wiser for it. Ross brought him diplomacy, Angus brought loyalty and history, and Banquo brought steadiness in the face of passion. Gruoch, according to her husband, brought peace.

"That is something I will never truly bring you," she had told him one night as he held her against his bare chest. "There will be no peace with me, my love."

His fingers played lazy circles in her hair, and she felt the thump of his heartbeat beneath her cheek.

"Why should you think such things, Gruoch?"

"Because I do not have it in myself enough to give to another." She did not parse her words with him as she had with Gille. There was no calculation needed, no wary stepping around the point. "You brought me happiness when I thought my heart had turned to stone, but my mind still rages."

Mac Bethad considered her words before answering.

"Your father?"

"And my son," she replied. Her hand found his forearm and traced an old scar that wound its way through the flesh there. "You have had your revenge, and your father's ghost rests easily. I cannot say the same for those that I have lost."

"But their killers have been put to death."

"I am not so sure."

Mac Bethad brought his fingers to his wife's chin, pulling up gently so that she might look him in the eye. He held her stare a moment before kissing her gently between her brows.

"Then we will have to make you sure," he said before pulling her to him once more and leading her into bliss.

Gruoch had Mac Bethad to herself for a few weeks before he was called away.

Angus, with his finger ever on the pulse of the ransacked North, reminded Mac Bethad that although the Norse threat from Hibernia had been momentarily extinguished, the source of the danger lingered still.

Raiding parties, though fewer, still managed to land north of Moray, in Caithness, whose people had already adopted Norse traditions and customs. Gruoch sat quietly in the great hall as her husband, and his advisors poured over a rough sketch of the province and the northern territories.

"Thorfinn calls for aide," Angus insisted. "Sweno, his traitorous uncle, would see him unseated in Caithness and a pagan ruler seated in his stead."

"It cannot come to pass." Ross now, with his strained voice. Gruoch raised her eyes to the men who stood by, unafraid of being caught watching. Her second husband did not possess the same qualms as her first when it came to her participation in matters of state. She was not shielded from such talk nor made to think it was not her place to hear it. "Moray has held a tenuous relationship with Sigurdsson since his boyhood. It is an alliance we cannot bear to lose."

"Thorfinn Sigurdsson was a friend of my father's and a friend to my home." Her husband's voice already betrayed the fire igniting within him. "And so it shall remain."

"The men are tired," Banquo reminded him. "You must not ask this of them yet."

"The men will fight if asked," Mac Bethad insisted. "There is an honour to be gained in this, and men hungry for the chance to prove themselves loyal to me and not to my predecessor."

"Duncan could send troops," Ross added. "We have acted on his behalf, unseating a traitorous plot. You would not be unfounded in asking for his aide."

At his words, Gruoch felt her heart quicken its pace. Her uncle had held a particular place in her thoughts since she had spoken to Mael before he died. The things he had said had eaten away at her and crawled deep within the dark and twisted recesses of her mind, where they waited anxiously. If Gruoch was to believe his final words to her, Mael's revelations of a secret plot with Malcolm, Duncan's son, would explain her father's unjust murder in the name of duty. But Mael could not be trusted, even in death.

She would need to hear it from Malcolm himself.

"Duncan is my uncle. Remind him of his orphaned niece, who was true to him even when wed to the false Mormaer."

The men fell silent at her words, and Ross frowned at the intercession. Banquo looked on, his face as impassive as always, as Angus's grin broke over his face. He clapped Mac Bethad on the shoulder as Gruoch's husband sought her eye. There was something there that she could not read.

"The peace you spoke of?" His voice was cool and betrayed nothing.

"Peace for us all, perhaps. Finally," she replied.

He nodded to Ross, who exhaled audibly before turning on his foot and walking briskly from the table. Angus clapped Mac Bethad a final time before taking his leave as well, trying his best to disguise the limp in his stride. Gruoch watched as they passed and answered Angus's parting smile with one of her own.

"Can I count on you both, then?" Mac Bethad looked at her a moment longer before turning his gaze to Banquo, who nodded.

"Always."

"And you, Gruoch," Mac Bethad continued. "You will manage here until I return? I do not think I will convince Angus to stay behind this time, though would you still be far from unguarded."

" We must keep what bonds of loyalty remain to us," Gruoch said, rising quietly from her seat. She made her way to them, reminding herself to keep her eyes raised, that she need not play at submission as she had before. There was no longer a need. "True friends are rare and must be protected at all costs."

"Your wife is wise, my friend. I had wondered since she debased her-self in accepting you." Banquo's words lilted slightly as he spoke, as though the ghost of a laugh hung behind his lips.

Mac Bethad's face split into a bright smile, and he took her hand before bringing it to his lips.

"Do not remind her, my friend," he said. "Lest she changes her mind in my absence. Can I count on you as well then, my lady?"

"Always," Gruoch replied, her words a mirror of Banquo's, as the three of them stood united in the bright hall, the map and its foreign concerns forgotten for a moment in the echoes of Mac Bethad's deep laughter.

As Mac Bethad's wife, Gruoch enjoyed greater freedom than she had as Gille's. Though the eyes of her guards were ever-present, she did not feel their suffocating weight as she had when Gille had been alive. Though mostly ignored her during her madness, she had still been forbidden from leaving the courtyard or wandering the fields and heath beyond the great walls. With Mac Bethad's blessing, Gruoch was free to wander what the men of Crown Hill had determined a safe distance, which allowed her to seek out Eimear in her cottage, which stood only an hour's walk from the main gates.

Her small home, a neat construction of stone and mud, sat nestled in a small wood. A fresh and quick brook bustled nearby, and an impressive garden of herbs and wildflowers surrounded the quaint cottage. Gruoch had seen little of Eimear since Lulach's birth and rarely alone, as she was only granted permission to the Hill when called upon to heal someone of importance. During her ghostly wanderings, when sadness and grief had turned Gruoch into a lost thing to be pitied and ignored, she had heard the townsfolk and peasants speak of Eimear when they forgot to care that Gruoch was there. They called her *cunning woman*, a term Gruoch knew could slip easily on a tongue and sound rather like *witch*.

Still, she longed to speak with Eimear again, if only to keep up her private stores of herbs and ensure enough tincture to keep her from conceiving.

Some feeling she could not name had kept Gruoch from revealing to Mac Bethad the special remedy she took that kept her barren. She could not explain why she kept this truth from her husband, and it was simply easier to ignore the gnaw of dishonesty and continue as she always had. Gruoch could almost hear Hertha's words and could imagine her tone as she said them.

*Your Christian men are too highly concerned with the bodies of their women. And you are still too highly concerned with the thoughts of Christian men.*

But Hertha had not known Christ, and she was not alive now to chide Gruoch. As she often did, Gruoch reminded herself that she should not give Hertha's ghost such power over her life and allow her foster mother's memory to rest.

Ghosts, Gruoch was learning, could be ignored when provided with enough distraction.

Mac Bethad had been gone a fortnight already, and she was surprised at how hungrily she missed him, how acutely she felt his absence. Gruoch had become used to being wanted, consulted and *lived* with, and her sudden isolation seemed unending. Not so very long ago, she had been accustomed to being alone and had relished in her solitude. The nights were the longest, and the large bed she shared with her husband was cold and empty. Her hands would stroke his pillow and search under the blankets and furs for the heat of his body. Deep within herself, Gruoch felt an ache and hunger that kept his blue eyes etched into her mind and the rough feel of his skin on her palms.

Eimear was a welcome distraction.

"You are enamoured," she said to Gruoch during one such visit.

Gruoch didn't deny it. She felt at ease with Eimear, and the need to be coy or proper didn't seem relevant or important. She could be honest, and what was even more welcome, she could be silent if she so chose. There were no expectations.

"And yet," Eimear continued, "you are here again today for more of my tonic. I am glad to see that love has not so rattled your wits that you would disregard my warnings. No matter how much you love the man, you will die before bringing forth any of his children."

Gruoch fingered a bundle of rosemary that hung from a ceiling beam, the dusty smell wafting down in gentle, sunlit waves. Still, she said nothing, relishing the quiet reprieve of Eimear's cabin.

"He does not know, does he?"

"I felt no need to burden him with such a truth," Gruoch replied. "I told him I would make an unsuitable wife and that he should take another. He has made his choice."

She glanced at Eimear and saw the cunning nod at her words, the blank face as close to approving as Gruoch could expect. Eimear worked quickly, her pestle working against the wooden sides of her mortar as she ground together the ingredients for her client's tea. The sounds of the scraping were comforting and calm in the stillness of her quaint home.

"Do you not worry that God will punish you for stopping any more children?" Eimear's voice was casual, but Gruoch understood the implications behind her words. Eimear made no secret of the fact that she was not a Christian woman, and the old ways still held sway in the way she lived her life. Gruoch cared little for Eimear's beliefs of the state of her soul and thought she had made this clear.

"God has already taken both of my mothers, my father, and my child," Gruoch said. "I do not know what is left to take."

"Do you not worry for your soul?" The pestle continued its scraping in Eimear's clever hands.

Gruoch considered Eimear's words. She still held hope that she would be reunited with her child in the next life, but to hold that hope meant accepting that Gruoch would never see Hertha again since she had not been baptized or a believer.

"To be honest," Gruoch said, surprising even herself with the truth of her words, "I have not much thought of my soul these past few weeks."

When her work was completed, Eimear followed Gruoch outside into the sunshine and handed the younger woman the small vial of herbs. As Gruoch stepped into the cooling air of the early October morning, she noticed Laoise and Fiadh, Eimear's two foster daughters, stacking freshly chopped logs into a neat pile by the side of the cottage. The two girls still lived at home with their mother, though Gruoch knew that Laoise, like herself, had been widowed young and had returned to Eimear's cottage after the death of her husband. Gruoch knew Laoise was the eldest of the two adopted daughters, though it was impossible to gauge their age accurately. Both daughters possessed a savage beauty that could not be denied. Laoise's copper hair was curly and wild, and her nervous brown eyes shifted quickly whenever Gruoch tried to meet them. Fiadh had long and pale blonde hair and striking grey eyes. She reminded Gruoch of a fairy, of one of the Folk who were said to roam the hills and valleys of their homeland.

Eimear's hair, though streaked now with grey, had been darker in her youth. Gruoch did not ask if Eimear had ever been married. Her independence and stubborn ways made it clear.

"Your daughters are lucky to have found you," Gruoch said to Eimear as they entered the yard.

"There have always been three of us," Eimear said, her tone clipped. "And so shall we always be."

Gruoch did not ask Eimear to explain herself, but a cold shiver danced its way down her spine at the words.

Gruoch met Fiadh's wolfish grey eyes as she stepped out, and she nodded once to Eimear's silver daughter. Fiadh nodded as well, giving Gruoch no more thought before returning to her task. Laoise did not look at all.

"Do not let yourself forget to take your tonic," Eimear reminded Gruoch again.

"I will not."

As she turned to leave, Gruoch heard the familiar and steady *thump* of approaching hoof beats. Eimear raised a hand to shield her eyes from the bright morning sun, and the women watched together as Ross cantered up, slowing his horse as he reached the cottage.

"My lady," he said to Gruoch before turning a wary eye to Eimear. "Would you allow me to accompany you back to the Hill? I have news of your husband."

Gruoch stepped forward quickly as Ross dismounted and gathered his mount's reins in his hand.

"Is all well? How goes the battle?"

"It is over," Ross replied. "We have won. A plot was discovered, and a traitorous lord has been put to death by your own husband's hands. The North is at peace, the heathen have been beaten back, and Moray can breathe at last."

"When will our men return?" Excitement had already begun to flow through her veins, awakening her from the slight stupor Gruoch had lived in since her husband's absence.

"I am sure they have already begun the journey back," Ross answered. "It is said that Duncan himself will travel North to reward your husband's bravery. They are saying Mac Bethad will finally be recognized as the Mormaer."

From the corner of her eye, Gruoch saw that Fiadh and Laoise had stopped working and were watching them openly, listening. Gruoch waved once to Eimear and bowed her head in thanks before walking off in the direction of the Hill, Ross walking and leading his horse next to her. As they walked, Ross filled her ear with the bloody and courageous exploits of her husband, and Gruoch concealed Eimear's delicate vial in the folds of her cape.

# FIFTEEN
# MORAY HAS NO KING

**M**ac Bethad looked weary as he rode past the gates and into the courtyard of Crown Hill, Banquo riding unsurprisingly at his side. Their tired faces and the heaving sides of their mounts made it clear that they had ridden hard and fast ahead of their company in order to breath the Hill. However, as Gruoch raced towards her husband in welcome, she saw his face light up as he broke into a smile. Banquo barked out a laugh as Mac Bethad swung his leg up and back, dismounting quickly, before catching Gruoch as she launched herself at him. Mac Bethad lifted her joyfully from her feet as they embraced in a way that was not dignified for the lord and lady of such an estate.

In Mac Bethad's arms, Gruoch could not have cared less.

She reached for her husband's face and brushed back the stubborn strands of brown hair that fell into his eyes. The skin there was red and rough from exposure to wind and rain, and dark circles were hanging under his eyes. Still, the eyes themselves shone as they took her in.

Gruoch felt herself being lowered, and her feet found the cobblestones and dirt. The people of the Hill approached, hoping to greet loved ones as well.

"Your men will arrive shortly," Banquo said aloud, addressing the crowd. "The lord Mac Bethad nearly killed his horse in his efforts to arrive before them. They will be here before nightfall." "Alane," Mac Bethad called over Gruoch's shoulder, "let the preparations be made. Tonight we shall feast and honour the living and the dead who have cleaned our shores of traitors and those who would destroy us."

Gruoch heard a bustling of movement and assumed that Alane was already springing to action, putting maids and servants to work. Banquo dismounted as well, handing his horse off to a stable boy, and walked off with Ross, who had come to greet the returning travellers. Banquo wore a strange expression as he spoke with Ross, a mixture of unease and excitement painting his dark features, half-hidden by his beard.

"Come, Gruoch," her husband said softly. "I have things to tell you."

At first, there was nothing to say. They had missed one another, and little time was spent speaking.

Gruoch and Mac Bethad lay together, still entwined, and Gruoch rested her head upon her husband's chest, listening to the steady and reassuring beating of his heart. His hands idly stroked her back and combed through her hair. The need to touch one another had not been satiated in the fires of his homecoming. Rather, Gruoch's desire to touch him had only grown. It was often thus, and she could not help but think of how she had grown from the timid and frightened girl who had lain so stiffly under Gille to this bold and amorous woman who was unabashedly in love.

"How have you been?" As he often did, Mac Bethad first broke their silence.

"I have missed you."

He laughed at the simplicity of her response, his hands still trailing along her scalp.

"You made it very clear to me. But other than your brazen longing for me," and here Gruoch slapped lightly at his arm, "How have you fared? Have you been leaving the Hill?"

She lifted her cheek from his chest and looked him in the eye, somewhat confused.

"I have," Gruoch replied. "And I did not think it would be an issue. Does it bother you that I did not pine and waste away waiting for you in our rooms?"

Mac Bethad was looking at the ceiling and did not meet her gaze.

"Have you been to visit with Eimear?"

"I have. She delivered Lulach, and she has become a friend. Does it bother you that I should meet with her?"

"No," he said, still looking away. "She only mentioned it to me earlier today, as Banquo and I rode near the cottage. She and her daughters stood by the road as though they were waiting for me. Indeed, one of her daughters waved us down as we approached."

A strange rolling sensation passed through Gruoch's stomach, unsettling her. Why would Eimear go out of her way to speak with Mac Bethad? Gruoch remembered their earlier conversation, and for a horrible moment, she wondered if her secret had been betrayed.

"I have known her my entire life. She delivered me as well when I was a bairn. She has always been an odd one and somewhat of an outsider. She seemed to *know* things, and she could accomplish things that were impossible for others." Mac Bethad's voice trailed off, and Gruoch did not push him, allowing him to find the words he sought. "She had strange news for me."

She rose to one elbow, placing her face into her hand so that she could better look at him. "Better news than what Ross brought for us? That you shall finally be recognized as Mormaer?"

"That is precisely the strange news, Gruoch. Eimear told me I had been named Mormaer before I had heard it from Ross's lips."

"She very likely overheard Ross when he told his news first to me. I was with Eimear when he rode up to the Hill."

Mac Bethad seemed not to have heard her. His eyes were filled with a strange and voracious fire, and he lifted his hands from Gruoch's back in order to jab them through the air as he spoke.

"But she said more still. She greeted me as Mormaer and said her daughter had had a vision. She bid one approach, and the girl told me I would be king." He paused a moment, collecting his thoughts. "Banquo was with me. He heard the prophecy as well."

"And what predictions were made for him?"

"The girl spoke to me alone."

As Mac Bethad's breath hitched in his passion, Gruoch's seemed to pause for a moment as she thought upon what he had said. Laoise and Fiadh had seemed to overhear her and Ross and had been watching them openly when they left. Still, why make such a prediction for her husband? Mac Bethad was a lord, but he was far removed from kingship.

"Moray has no king, my love," Gruoch said gently. "And Duncan, for all his advanced age, thrives in Alba."

"You have forgotten then. Duncan is not in Alba. He makes his way here now to celebrate our victory over the Nords."

Gruoch had forgotten this. Duncan, perhaps accompanied by his son Malcolm, was making his way to Crown Hill. The two would feast, drink, and sing songs, all the while pretending that they had not conspired with Gille to bring about the death of her father. A sudden chill passed through her, and her hand clenched, the fingernails digging themselves painfully into the soft flesh of her palm.

"How good of Duncan to come in person to celebrate the hero of Moray, who has found traitors and enemies both in Moray and afar." Gruoch's voice was bitter, and she was shocked at her vitriol. "How good of him to eat the food of the lady whose husband and father he had killed."

"Do you mourn for Gille?" Mac Bethad's voice was strangely detached and yet so obviously hurt, and Gruoch unclenched her fist to stroke the concern from his cheek.

"I have lost two men in my life who have had a hand in shaping it," she replied. "It would be wrong of me not to carry both their deaths in my heart. For all of Gille's treachery and Mael's influence, I do not believe they acted alone. You know this."

Mac Bethad had listened those first few nights after their passions were spent; they had talked together long hours into the night. Gruoch had told him of her childhood, and he had shared his. They had also spoken of darker things. Mac Bethad had shared his feelings of inadequacy and of the burden of keeping his nervous condition a secret. They spoke of the thoughts with which Mael had infected Gruoch and of her suspicion of Malcolm's role in her father's death.

"And now Duncan approaches. He will be here, within our very walls," Mac Bethad said, saying aloud the words that were careening through Gruoch's troubled mind.

"Duncan has no love for you," she told Mac Bethad. "He sees you as a pawn to be shuffled around to best suit his needs. Was he on the battlefield when you killed the Nord invaders, or was he holed away in the South, waiting and scheming should you fail and a replacement for you be needed? He had killed off one of Moray's Mormaers. What would be the trouble in replacing another?"

"Gruoch…" "And to simply bypass the Tanistry," she continued. "To forgo the traditions of your people, the very traditions your own father held so dear… Duncan has no love for Moray, for its people. We are simply a wall to protect Alba from northern threats."

"You sound like my father," Mac Bethad said finally, surprising her. "He wanted Moray to be independent, to be free. He choked on the collar he claimed Duncan had placed on him."

"So, it is true then," Gruoch breathed. "Your father wanted to rebel. He wanted Moray to be autonomous from Alba."

"He did."

"And you knew this?" Gruoch found that she was unable to restrain herself. She rose from her elbow and sat up in the bed, sweeping up a fur as she did so to wrap it around herself. "You knew your father fought for freedom, and you are willing now to live at Duncan's beck and call?"

At such words, a clear look of annoyance bloomed on her husband's face. He considered her for a moment before running a hand through his tousled hair. He sighed impatiently as though Gruoch were a petulant child doing their best to refuse a lesson.

"I hope you do not mean to suggest that I do not love my country," he began, "Or that I would dishonour my father's wishes. But Gruoch, rebellion is starving, and it is blood. It is orphaned children and mothers made widows. It cannot be for glory, for there is so little to be found in the deaths of innocents."

Gruoch's heart thrummed frantically in her chest. She let go of the fur that she had wrapped around her shoulders to keep away the chill and allowed it to slide away from her body. Mac Bethad's eyes grew darker as he took her in, and Gruoch was pleased to notice another hitch in his breathing. She sat for a moment, not speaking, allowing for the light of the candles to glow against her pale skin, on the red in her hair.

"It is precisely these innocents who need you now," she said gently, softly laying her hand once more upon his chest. "Would you let them be ruled by a king who plots to murder his loyal stewards? Would you allow my father's ghost, and the ghosts of all honest men who seek their own respite, to wander forever in the shades while his killer sups in my hall while my husband scrapes at his feet?"

"Gruoch, these things that you say, this kind of talk…."

She leaned forward then, grasping his face in her palms. Gruoch moved to straddle him quickly, pinning him in place. He groaned slightly and moved to kiss her, but she held firm and pushed him back down onto the pillow.

"If you will not do it, then I shall. Let Duncan come here. I will kill him myself if my husband cannot be man enough to do it for me."

Mac Bethad grabbed her wrists harshly, sitting up quickly and shifting her on his lap.

"What kind of decent woman says such things while her husband lies between her legs?"

"One that is no longer afraid. One who has too many spirits whispering in her ear, keeping her from her sleep. We can do this, my love. We can kill Duncan and Malcolm. We can avenge my father, and we can make Moray free."

"When you bear my sons," he growled, burying his face into Gruoch's neck, "I should hope they have their mother's mettle."

"The night you killed my husband, you asked me to help you." She struggled to speak with Mac Bethad's mouth pushing against her throat. "You said there was rot in Moray and that we would cut it out. Have you forgotten?"

He kissed her furiously, and their teeth clashed painfully. The force of his lips was crushing, bruising, yet Gruoch returned it hungrily.

"*Mo lasair*," Mac Bethad growled, his face pressed into her hair. "You shall burn us all."

Mac Bethad slept soundly that night, looking almost like a boy as his mouth fell open slightly. His exhausted body relished the opportunity to rest in their soft bed rather than on the cold shores and fields of battle, yet Gruoch could not follow suit. Her mind raced with the possibilities that had presented themselves to her, and she considered them all, thinking through each one from execution to consequence. They had never met, so Malcolm's face was a stranger's to her, and in her reverie, Gruoch's hands closed around a shadowed neck half-hidden in the darkness. She struggled to imagine throttling Duncan or slitting his throat, for when she did, her father's face came unbidden to the forefront of her mind.

If Mael and Gille's dying words could be counted on for anything, Malcolm and his father had plotted together to rid Moray of a potential firebrand in Findlaech. They had ultimately ordered that both her father and even Gille be killed in a false show of faith and support. Gruoch reflected on this ultimate cruelty, this charade of using another to fulfill one's own dark purpose, only to dispose of the puppet once the play was done. Duncan and Malcolm had needed Gille on their side, and they needed Mael to push him there. Lulach and Hertha's deaths had been mere points in a larger plot to cement Gille's allegiance to his brother and not to her.

Well, Gille and Mael were dead, and so was her father. Gruoch did not think that Duncan or Malcolm was kept awake in the night as she was, reflecting on the waste that had been laid bare. But they would be arriving soon, and they would take their rest within her battlements. They would continue to sleep soundly, knowing that as their guests, they would be protected, their safety assured by the ancient laws that dictated the responsibility of any host this far north. The land and its people could be deadly, and any guest was assured protection by these traditional customs.

All the better. They would suspect no danger.

When Mac Bethad awoke hours later, the dawn had begun to filter its red and golden light in through the windows in their room. Gruoch stretched and yawned, feigning coming awake herself as though she had not lain in wait through the long hours of the night. There was an energy that thrummed through her body that was foreign to her and granted her an unfamiliar excitement. She remembered Hertha's stories of the shield-maidens and the warrior women. Gruoch's hand may have grasped no weapon, yet she had never felt more armed.

Mac Bethad took her to himself and kissed her soundly. Gruoch responded in kind, stroking his hair gently as they embraced. She pulled herself away after a moment, though he growled and pulled to keep her near.

"There is much to do, my love," she scolded gently. "We should both rise and prepare for the day. Nothing can be left to chance."

Mac Bethad pulled away slightly, studying her face and looking deep into her green eyes.

"You have not slept," he said assuredly. "You have schemed. There is a line etched between your brows that suggests it."

Gruoch lifted a finger and touched the skin there, smoothing away the line and forcing her features to relax.

"Away, traitor," she whispered to it as she did so. "Give away no clue to my purpose. Only smiles and sunny looks today."

Mac Bethad frowned and rolled away unto his back.

"It is the only way." Gruoch kept her voice light though her anger threatened to bubble through. "We do this not for ourselves. We do this to rid Moray of its oppressors and make it free."

"I am no coward, Gruoch. I have looked men in the eye before slicing their bellies open, watching them struggle to catch the falling offal. I have walked through fields drenched in blood so that my footsteps stained the clean sand. It is the method with which I am struggling." "My love?" "This midnight sneaking, this quiet plotting. I should face Duncan myself and shout my accusations into his face. I could slit Malcolm's throat before him and make him watch as his heir bleeds out onto my floors."

Gruoch touched his face again, and though he did not flinch away from her touch, Mac Bethad did not lean into her hand as he usually did. Rather, Gruoch's hand rested coldly on his cheek, the touch seeming forced and awkward.

"If you were to challenge Duncan or Malcolm or lay a hand on either, you would invite violence upon yourself and open war. I have a plan to make it seem as though their deaths will come at the hands of another, leaving you innocent and clear and a stronger contender as a ruler for an independent Moray." "For even though they want their freedom," Mac Bethad mused, "the people will not follow one who kills he that God has ordained to lead."

"We will use their machinations against them," Gruoch whispered. "They have been clever, but their hubris blinds them. They think they are untouchable."

Mac Bethad said nothing but kissed her gently on the brow before turning from her and rising from their bed. He dressed quickly and methodically, leaving the room without glancing again in her direction.

"Come, Duncan," Gruoch whispered into the empty room. "Let the ravens scream as you enter the Hill, for they shall feast on your body ere it leaves my home again." Gruoch rose from the bed when Alane entered the room, ready to help dress and prepare her mistress for the guests they would soon welcome. She laid out Gruoch's best *léine*, one of the softest white wool, embroidered at the sleeve and collar with a golden thread in an intricate pattern. She used Gruoch's mother's pin to clasp a deep blue cloak at Gruoch's shoulder and bade the younger woman sit so she might have her hair brushed and plaited. However, after Alane had begun to braid Gruoch's red hair into a crown atop her head, Gruoch stopped her and undid the plaits. She smoothed the hair down so that it lay loose over her shoulders and down her back.

"You cannot mean to wear your hair loose and long like a maid, my lady," Alane scolded gently, sweeping it back and into her hands.

"I do," Gruoch said firmly, pushing away Alane's hands. She was right, of course, that a married woman usually wore her hair tied or plaited, but Gruoch wanted to look young and innocent. She wanted Duncan and Malcolm to see a child, a simple woman with a pretty face who bore no malice or threat. She wanted them to see the loose, flowing hair and be comforted. Suddenly, Gruoch saw herself in her mind's eye with a man kneeling before her. Her loose hair was held tightly in her hands as she wove it into a noose and secured it around the man's neck, who squirmed and pulled faintly at her hands.

"You may weave some ribbon or flowers if you must, but I want it down."

"If you insist, my lady," Alane said, though her tone made it clear she disapproved.

"Thank you, Alane. That will be all for now." Gruoch rose from her chair and smoothed the front of her tunic. "I am sure you are needed elsewhere for the necessary preparations to be made."

Gruoch smiled brightly at Alane, and though she looked displeased at leaving the long hair unbound, the housekeeper gave a slight curtsy and left the room quickly, her mind clearly working its way through the list of chores to complete before Duncan's arrival.

When Alane closed the door, a shiver of ice shot through Gruoch, and while her heart beat faster in an anxious rhythm, Gruoch did not find it was entirely unpleasant a feeling.

# COILED AND READY TO STRIKE

As Gruoch plotted to commit a murder of her own, it became clear to her that the ultimate mistake that Gille and Mael had made when they had worked together to kill Findlaech was to rush through the steps of their plan. Gille's behaviour had become erratic in the months before he left for Hibernia with his brother, whose own slippery and slick actions had been observed by those who lived at the Hill. They had allowed the mask to slip and for their deeds to become suspect. They had permitted everyone around them to watch their degradation and fall into dishonour without realizing that such a thing should be hidden away at all costs.

No one could say that she was anything but a smiling and gracious hostess when Duncan and his son rode into the yard at Crown Hill.

Gruoch thought of Hertha as they approached, remembering her words of advice when it came to disguising one's thoughts and motivations and how a woman especially must learn to present only the face that she wanted to be seen. She felt herself a serpent, beautifully dressed in bright and shiny scales yet coiled and ready to strike with poisoned fangs. All she had to do was wait for Duncan and Malcolm to step closer before Gruoch could rend their unsuspecting flesh.

Duncan was older than she had expected. He was older than her father, who had been frozen in the last memory Gruoch had of him, which was already five years old. Duncan had Bodhe's solid build, the same round and jovial face. He wore a full and bushy beard, though his skull was bare of any of the familiar red hair of his line. But though the face was similar to Bodhe's, Duncan's expression was much more solemn and grave, without the easy smile hanging on his lips. He nodded to a man beside him whom Gruoch took to be Malcolm, as the grey gelding he sat astride was easily one of the best horses in the party. Both men were well dressed in thick woollen tunics, with crimson capes draped over regal shoulders, hems embroidered with golden thread.

Mac Bethad stepped from her side and raised his arms in welcome, and Gruoch stood by, her face down as she curtsied as became a dutiful wife and lady. When Gruoch looked up, Mac Bethad and Duncan stood with their hands firmly clasped to the other's shoulders. Her husband was taller than the king, but Duncan carried himself with the confidence and ill-merited poise of a man born to privilege and who has faced too little opposition for too long a time.

"I was sorry to hear of your father's death," Duncan lamented to Mac Bethad, his voice carrying easily. "And even more pained to hear of the plot between his successor and my traitorous brother. You cannot begin to conceive of the pain I felt when I learned of their betrayal."

Mac Bethad nodded solemnly, and Gruoch noticed a subtle clenching and tick in his jaw. Duncan brought a hand and touched the top of Mac Bethad's head as he might the hair of a child upon whom he bestowed some favour. It was then that Duncan turned then and noticed her.

"This must be my niece, the fine lady of the house." Duncan swept from Mac Bethad and stepped to her, reaching for Gruoch's hands. She allowed him to take them and fought against the shudder that threatened to shake through her composure. Instead, she smiled brightly at him.

"Your Grace," she replied, bowing her head.

"What a fine welcome indeed. A beautiful woman and a gracious host. Malcolm?" Duncan turned from her to the man who had ridden beside him. The younger man's strong shoulders were carried back and proud, and his brown eyes cast themselves too slowly from Gruoch's feet to her face. Gruoch thought he must have favoured his mother, for she saw little of their fathers in his tight face. She watched as Malcolm took a small pouch from his person and handed it to his father.

"A gift, my lady. One that befits a woman of such beauty and virtue. You are a testament to your family and evidence that Bodhe's unnatural ambitions have not reached Inverness."

He pulled a pendant from the pouch, and Gruoch gasped at the diamond that had been encrusted into the silver setting. Malcolm stepped closer and lay the necklace over her head and around her throat without asking permission. The chain was long, and the pendant hung past her collarbone. From the corner of her eye, Gruoch noticed as Malcolm's gaze trailed the pendant to where it lay above her breast.

Mac Bethad spoke something to Malcolm, making the other man laugh loudly. Duncan smiled as well, offering his arm to his niece.

"Shall we walk, Gruoch? It has been an age since I last visited Crown Hill. It will be good to walk its halls once more and look upon the face of its faithful and loyal people."

She took the arm and leaned on it. "We are your servants ever, and we look forward to welcoming Your Grace into our humble midst."

*Come in, Duncan, into the viper's pit. Take in the setting sun, for I swear on the grave of my only child, it will be the last one you ever see.*

Gruoch's face was a painted and smiling mask as they walked into the Tower and accompanied their guests into the Great Hall.

Alane and her maids had been hard at work, and the room shone with their efforts. Warm fires burned in the hearths, and several torches illuminated the room. Roast pig, pies, and a collection of late vegetables heaped plates next to piles of fresh loaves of bread and cups of ale. The supper was inviting, the room was warm and well-lit, and their guests quickly made themselves at ease in the hall, sitting at the heads of the main table. Gruoch noticed that before he ate, Duncan crossed himself and prayed silently for a long moment.

*I hope his prayer sticks in his throat and chokes him*, Gruoch heard Hertha murmur into her mind.

Mac Bethad and Gruoch took their time and avoided any rushed movements. Gruoch served their wine herself, pouring it out generously into their cups. Duncan and Malcolm seemed utterly at ease and laughed when she offered a draught of wine to their guards. These men drank sparingly, and Gruoch knew they would refuse a second cup. It was no matter, for both goblets had been dosed with a sleeping mixture she had begged from Eimear in the early nights of Mac Bethad's absence.

After a few hours of raucous feasting, Gruoch excused herself, feigning fatigue and a headache. She waited outside the hall for a moment and heard Mac Bethad make some suitable excuse to leave for a moment. A roar of boisterous laughter was only more encouraged by a comment lewder than her husband tended to make within earshot of her. Within a few minutes, he joined Gruoch on the stairs and offered her his arm should they be noticed or seen by any member of the staff. To all, it must appear as though he were accompanying his ill-feeling wife to their chamber. His steps, Gruoch noticed, seemed somewhat too slow.

"Do not lose your nerve," she whispered as she held his arm. They continued their ascent up the wooden stairs, the way quiet and deserted. "We have yet to begin the real work."

Mac Bethad said nothing as they walked to their room. He opened the door for her before following her in and locking it behind them. He ran his hand through his hair in an accustomed gesture, and Gruoch said nothing as she waited for him to formulate whatever concerns were running through his mind.

Finally, the words burst forth.

"I will be cursed," he whispered.

"There is no such thing. Besides, God would not punish you for enacting justice on his behalf."

"I do not fear Duncan's God. It is the men who will curse me a king-killer. There is something unnatural in striking down an anointed leader, especially one to whom I have pledged my loyalty and my fealty."

"But he is undeserving of your loyalty!" The words were spat from her mouth, and she took a ragged breath when Gruoch saw Mac Bethad's eyes widen slightly with the force of her anger. "Duncan is a false king. He is responsible for the deaths of both of our fathers and would keep Moray under his false stewardship. The man cares nothing for our province, and his heavy taxes only prove as much. We are but a guard in the North to protect him from the heathen invaders he so fears. Without us, he would have to fight his battles himself."

"Duncan is our guest," Mac Bethad continued, "and it is our duty to protect him."

"Duncan failed first in his duty to the people of Moray when he plotted for your father to be slain as a traitor in Hibernia."

"He is my kinsman. He is your kinsman."

"He had his brother killed! At least Cain was able to wield the stone himself when he came up behind Abel and bashed in his brains."

Silence.

Then, "the people will mourn him."

"Until we heal their wounds by giving them an independent province and a king worthy of their love and support." Gruoch stepped closer but did not touch him. "Do not fear your greatness, for it is well earned. Duncan gives you nothing by naming you what you are."

Mac Bethad took her in, his hands at his sides. Neither of them moved to fill the space between their bodies, though it seemed suddenly heavy and pregnant with the implications of Gruoch's words and Mac Bethad's hesitation.

"Would you have me do this, Gruoch?" His voice was quiet, tired. "Would you have me give up the man and become the beast?"

"It is a man who does the thing he has promised," she said just as quietly, hating how her words made him flinch and hating both her bitter coldness and his moment of weakness. "No one may say more. I am no man, and I have loved a baby and nourished him from my body. I have felt as mothers do. Yet if I had the opportunity, I would have ripped the teeth from the gums of he who killed my child and bashed the man's brains upon the stones."

Another heavy silence. Finally, it was Mac Bethad who reached for her, pulling Gruoch swiftly into his arms so that she might bury her face into his shoulder. Whether he did this to comfort her or to hide from her gaze, Gruoch could not say.

"We might fail." His opposition to the plan weakened, and Gruoch knew her resolve would carry them.

She turned her face and kissed the hollow of his throat. "Screw your courage to the sticking place, and we cannot fail. I have dosed the guards with a sleeping draught. When the house awakens tomorrow and finds them bathed in Duncan and Malcolm's blood, there will be no doubt as to their killers."

Mac Bethad pulled away slightly and kissed the top of her head softly. Gruoch could feel in the way that his breath had quickened, that his decision had been made and that he would do what needed to be done.

"So be it then," he said, his voice flat. "Remember your headache tomorrow when the screams begin and the bodies are found. We all have a role to play."

"I will give no reason to doubt," she replied. Gruoch lay a hand upon his chest, feeling the solid and steady heartbeat.

Mac Bethad nodded and stepped back from her before heading towards the door. As he opened it, his voice called back softly.

"May our faces be as false as our hearts."

He was gone from the room before she could reply.

It was torturous to wait for the guests to retire and make their way to bed. Gruoch sat by the door, anxiously awaiting to hear them ascend the steps and enter their rooms. They must time the thing perfectly so that everyone would be abed and sleeping deeply enough not to be woken by the sounds of their black business.

It was Duncan that she heard first. His deep voice carried easily up the stairs, and Gruoch could make out the sounds of discontent as he scolded his guards for their sleepy countenance. She heard these words and felt relief. It would seem as though the tonic and the late hour were working together to ensure that Duncan's guards would soon be sleeping soundly enough to keep from waking at an inopportune moment.

She refused to allow herself to peek from her door, forcing herself instead to listen for the sound of his door. The iron hinges creaked and clasped loudly, and she shivered with anticipation.

Mac Bethad had still not returned to their rooms.

Gruoch counted her own breaths in the heavy silence, and after a quarter of an hour of tomb-like quiet, she finally dared to open the door. The hallway was deserted save for a solitary torch on the wall that cast a steady flicker of shadow into the passage.

She could not say what possessed her to move forward and out of the room, but Gruoch walked as though underwater, her steps slow and heavy. The rational part of her mind screamed at her to return to the safety of her room. She knew all too well that she would not be able to explain such strange midnight wanderings if someone should come across her then. It screamed all the louder when her hand grasped the solid metal of the latch, and her fingers worked and opened the door.

The hinges creaked slightly as she pushed open the door, and the sound sent a cold shiver down her spine. Her steps, however, did not hesitate and continued their methodical advancement into the darkness of the chamber. Gruoch looked down and noticed Duncan's guards sleeping soundly on the ground on either side of the door. They slept with their backs against the wall, faces slumped forward and into their chests. One let out a terrific snore, causing her to glance at the shape lying prone on the bed.

It did not stir.

The lights in the room had been extinguished, save for the fire that had recently been lit in the fireplace in preparation for Duncan. Gruoch made her way around the bed to look upon the sleeping face of her uncle, the man who had orchestrated a traitor's death for her father, his brother. Duncan's regal face sagged in his sleep, and the eyes appeared puffy in the fir light. The wrinkles seemed to sit deeper in his cheeks and forehead, and instead of a king, Gruoch saw a man made old by responsibility and duty.

Worse still, she saw her father.

It seemed as though the flickering light of the flames softened the harsh features, melting and blending them into a face that seemed nearly identical to the memory Gruoch had of her beloved father. She shook her head, trying to clear her thoughts. She had not seen Bodhe in over five years. It was perfectly reasonable that seeing Duncan had confused her and that the sight of him had infected her memory.

Still, as she looked upon his sleeping form, Gruoch was struck to the bone by the resemblance.

It felt as though she were waking from a dream when Gruoch noticed that her hands had clenched themselves into talons at her sides, as though the fingers had tensed and frozen around an invisible neck. Had she come here to choke the life from Duncan as he slept? Had her body moved and decided without her even being aware?

Gruoch forced her fingers to relax and loosen. Her hands would not be the ones to take Duncan's life from him. She knew that she could not bring herself to harm him when all she could see when she looked upon him was the sleeping form of her father. Tears stung suddenly at her eyes in her anger and frustration. Gruoch had her father's murderer before her, and there was nothing she could do.

She made her way from the room in silence, becoming one of the shadows that moved there. The hall was still empty, and Gruoch dared not linger before she made her way quickly back into her chamber.

Mac Bethad stood before the fire, looking down into the hearth. He looked up quickly as Gruoch entered, his hand tensing and bringing up a dagger he held at his side.

"Gruoch," he said with a sigh, lowering his hand. "Where were you?"

"I was looking upon Duncan." The words were flat, yet her husband winced as Gruoch spoke them. "I think I would have killed him myself had he not looked so like my father as he slept."

"We are lucky you were not seen. Malcolm has already made his way to bed. He must have just missed you."

"I don't know why, but I ...." "If we are to succeed, you cannot act so rashly. You cannot allow your womanish emotions to take control and guide you. You must be reasonable."

She felt a white rage wash through her at his words, caused by the insult he had given her and the realization that he was right. But, instead of reacting, Gruoch put her attention elsewhere, noticing a golden gleam tucked firmly into her husband's grip.

"Whose dagger do you bear?"

"Malcolm's," Mac Bethad said plainly. "He bragged of it during the night. He had it made upon being named Duncan's heir. The golden hilt had been engraved with a crown. It was too easy to take once Malcolm was in his cups." Gruoch took a step into the room and made her way to the fire, bringing up her hands to warm them. "Why do you have it?"

"We are not going to kill Malcolm."

Gruoch did not turn away from the fire. She knew that there was more to be said.

"We are going to kill Duncan with his son's dagger," Mac Bethad continued. "Malcolm wore it all night. It will be made clear that the guards, having no better motive than greed, were paid off by Malcolm to murder Duncan and clear the way to the throne."

"Then Malcolm will bear the weight of punishment, and no one will seek another suspect," she finished. "And without an heir, Alba will be thrown into chaos. They will have no time or resources to pay attention to Moray, giving us a chance to establish ourselves as an independent nation."

Mac Bethad closed his eyes, and Gruoch gently laid her hand over his as their fingers became entwined over Malcolm's dagger. Her heart leapt at this sudden improvement to their plan and her husband's ingenuity. She leaned into his arm and laid her head on his shoulder and felt Mac Bethad turn his head slightly and kiss the crown of her head.

"My heart is beating so quickly I should think you would be able to hear it," he said quietly to her.

"It is the clear and constant ringing of a bell, summoning us as agents of justice."

"It is a knell," Mac Bethad whispered. "But what it summons, I still do not know."

He turned fully then and took Gruoch by the arms. His right hand held tightly still to the dagger, and she felt its profile dig into the flesh of her upper arm. Mac Bethad leaned into her then and took her mouth, kissing her fiercely. His free hand came up to the back of Gruoch's neck, pulling her all the closer to him. His breath was warm and held the stale taste of the ale he had drunk. His tongue pushed its way past her lips, and she gave him access, allowing him to take what comfort her body could provide. Her breath came heavy and quick, matching his.

His body and lips softened then, releasing her. He looked deeply into Gruoch's eyes as though searching for an answer to some question he had not posed aloud. Whatever he found there seemed to satisfy him, for he swept away and towards the door in three swift strides.

When the door closed behind him, Gruoch felt her knees buckle, and she fell kneeling to the floor. She stayed there upon her knees before the fire, and she felt her lips move in some silent supplication.

But if she prayed, no god offered an answer.

Ross, Angus, and Banquo had often spoken of the prowess and skill Mac Bethad had shown on the battlefield. He was a feared warrior and a respected general. He had faced imposing and terrifying opponents and enemies in the coldest and murkiest fields, and though his body wore the scars of the wounds inflicted by his enemies, his hands had spilled more blood than most. According to her husband's friends and loyal soldiers, no one would dream of describing Mac Bethad as a coward.

But the man who entered their rooms that night shook with a nightmare Gruoch had not anticipated and from which she was unable to wake him.

She was still kneeling before the fire when the door opened suddenly, and she rose quickly to her feet as Mac Bethad stumbled in, holding his hands before him. Gruoch was struck by both the sight of the blood that covered them and the glint of Malcolm's dagger that was still clasped in his right hand.

"My love?" Her voice was rough, and her throat was thick with anticipation.

His eyes were frantic, casting themselves around the room as though behind each piece of furniture, an enemy lay in wait.

"The stones prate of my whereabouts."

Gruoch stepped towards him, keeping her hands open and before her as she did.

"Come to the fire, my love. Let me clean your hands."

Mac Bethad looked down at his bloody hands, bringing the dagger closer to his face.

"You marshalled me the way I was going," he whispered.

A few more steps brought her to him, and Gruoch grasped her husband gently by the forearms, careful to get no blood on her shift. She felt as though she were leading a child on unsteady and unpractised legs, and each of Mac Bethad's steps was slow and unsure.

He looked at her, catching her eyes in his frantic gaze.

"Did you hear a noise?"

"A noise, husband?"

"I heard a voice in the night, crying in the darkness. It screamed as though to wake the house!"

"Lower your voice," Gruoch whispered more harshly than she meant to. "It is you who will wake the sleepers." "Sleep no more! Mac Bethad does murder sleep!"

"Enough!" She pulled him forward and away from the door, still slightly ajar. Gruoch moved towards it and closed it quickly but quietly. Mac Bethad stood waiting like a child that does not know which way to go. She lay her hand on the small of his back and led him closer to the fire, where she bade him sit. He did so, and when he caught his weight on the floor as he settled, Gruoch saw that he had left behind scarlet prints on the boards.

She rushed to grab a bowl of water that Alane had left on the table for Gruoch's morning preparations, and she brought it to where Mac Bethad sat before the hearth. She ripped a strip from the bottom of her tunic and used it to begin washing the blood from her husband's hands.

He still held Malcolm's dagger tightly in his crimson fist.

"Why have you brought this here?" Gruoch gently pried the blade from his hands as she spoke. "It must lie with the guards as evidence of their guilt. It must be brought back."

Her husband's focus snapped back then, and his wet hand grabbed her wrist. Gruoch felt the squelch of blood and cold water on her skin and shuddered.

"I will not go back and look upon what I have done," he whispered, his focus suddenly gone. Gruoch recognized the look that was coming into his eyes. It was the same far-away stare that had taken over his features that long-ago night when Hertha, Banquo, and Gruoch had helped him through his fit.

She nodded to him, and he gently released her wrist. She glanced at the bloody prints that lingered there before helping Mac Bethad lay his head down on the floor. He did not resist her and closed his eyes tightly when he finally lay his head upon the boards. Gruoch finished wiping away the remaining blood, tearing away another strip of cloth from the bottom of her tunic to wipe away the dirty water.

She had to move quickly. The dagger had to be brought back to the guards, and Gruoch had to be back and assist Mac Bethad if a fit should overcome him, as she feared one would. His breath was shallow, and although the lids were closed, his eyes danced and moved erratically behind them.

She grabbed a fur from their bed and rolled it before placing Mac Bethad's head down gently upon a corner of it. She took the golden dagger from where it lay at his side. Her stomach turned at the sticky feeling of the hilt, drenched in blood that the fire had warmed. Gruoch rose unsteadily to her feet and forced back the bile that threatened to spill from her dry throat. Mac Bethad had done his part; it was now time for Gruoch to do hers.

Duncan's door had also been left ajar in her husband's shock and lapse of mind, and Gruoch slipped silently into the room. The smell of blood was like a punch to her gut, and she brought a hand quickly to her face to cover her mouth and nose.

Duncan lay on his bed with the covers pulled back. A blade had been taken to his throat, and it had ripped open the torso to its hips. Flashes of dark and wet innards spilled forth from the wound, and Duncan's swollen and thick tongue was slipping past the lips that had been painted with the blood that had bubbled forth. Worst was his eyes, silent and staring, perhaps with the image of Mac Bethad frozen upon them.

Mercifully and incredibly, the guards still lay in their deep sleep on either side of the door, although one had slumped entirely onto his side. A momentary fear took her. Had she given them too much sleeping potion? Had she killed them? Gruoch did not dare touch the guards for fear of waking them and placed the blade of Malcolm's dagger, which she had wiped briskly on her skirt, under the guard's nose. A slight fogging of the metal gave her evidence of life, and Gruoch could move on with her work.

Gruoch forced herself to breathe as she approached the bed, whose linens and furs were thick and heavy with the king's blood. It was easy to smear the dagger afresh, and she was not forced to touch the body. She reminded herself to move quickly, trying to hold her breath for as long as she could.

She refused to glance at the staring and horrible eyes.

Gruoch knelt then one last time at the side of the sleeping guard and placed the dagger gently into his open palm, daring to close his fingers around the hilt gently.

She stepped away and through the open door, which she closed carefully, wrapping her hand in her skirt to leave no trace of blood behind. It latched, and her work was done. Gruoch made her way back to her room, where Mac Bethad still lay on the floor before the fire, his entire body racked with violent shivers. She rushed to him and knelt at his side, taking up once more the bowl of water, whose contents had become murky and rust-brown. Still, Gruoch dipped her hands into the water, scrubbing away the signs of her guilt. The water became incarnadine as her pale hands once more became clean.

She would need to appear rested in the morning and as though she had slept away the night with an easy conscience, which would take all of her skill and attention. But before she went to her rest, Gruoch hid the bowl of dirty water under their bed to dispose of at a more opportune time and slowly and carefully helped Mac Bethad unto the mattress. His movements were jerky, and he seemed not to know where he was. Still, the fit was quieter than the one Gruoch had witnessed before, and she was able to get Mac Bethad into their bed and under the covers, where he continued to shake for a time before his body finally slipped into a desperate slumber.

*It is done, Father*, Gruoch thought to herself in the darkness. *Your killer is dead, and I remember you. If God was indeed watching our deeds tonight, he did so with a smile.*

# SEVENTEEN
# MORE FOOL HE

When Gruoch awoke the next day, it was to a grey and mercurial sky. Strong winds were whipping the dark clouds into a frenzy, and the air was heavy with the promise of rain. She lay for a moment in the stillness of her room, taking in the quiet of the chamber against the weather outside. Her head ached, and her body was stiff and sore as though she had run for miles the day before or drank too greedily of ale. Her mouth was dry, and an unpleasant coating covered her gums and the insides of her cheeks.

Mac Bethad lay awake at her side, staring silently at the ceiling. The fire had died down in the hearth, and the room was chilled. Gruoch shivered slightly in her blankets and shifted her weight towards her husband, laying her head upon his chest.

He did not reach to touch her. He allowed her touch and made no effort to move from her, but there was a tension running through his body like a current. Gruoch found little comfort or warmth as she lay her cheek against his flesh.

"The house is awake, and they will find him soon." Mac Bethad's voice was quiet, but his words still seemed to echo against the stone and wood of the bedroom walls.

"And when they do, they shall see the guard covered in Duncan's blood, and they shall spy Malcolm's dagger as well. There will be no doubt as to where the guilt lies."

Gruoch lifted her cheek from his chest and rose from the bed, shaking as the cool air hit her bare arms. She flinched slightly as her feet touched the frigid planks of the floor, but she forced herself to move quickly and efficiently. Alane would arrive shortly to help her lady dress for the day, and every pain must be born to ensure that they behaved no differently this morning than any other. Gruoch grabbed a comb and began working the teeth through the tangles in her hair, looking back to where Mac Bethad still lay prone in their bed, eyes haunted by dark circles.

"The house will soon be awake and bustling," Gruoch said gently. "We must be ready for the body to be discovered."

"Men are coming to escort Duncan and the Prince to the monastery at Saint Andrew." Mac Bethad's voice was low, but she was happy to find no waver or tremble in it. "I do not doubt they shall arrive sooner than later."

Gruoch turned her eyes to the ends of her hair, working at the remaining knots. When she felt satisfied with her work, she quickly smoothed back her hair and tied it into a tight braid. Each illusion of propriety needed to be respected and considered this morning. If she had played at the innocent girl last night, then this morning Gruoch must be the lady of the tower, the mistress far removed from any suspicion of foul play.

Alane's knock at the door caused Gruoch to jump slightly where she sat, and she cursed silently to herself. She could not afford to startle at small noises like this. Those with quiet conscience did not twitch about so.

"My lord? There are riders come for his Majesty. I've seen to their welcome, and they await you and the king in the hall."

Mac Bethad closed his eyes then, only briefly, before he swung himself quickly from the bed. He reached for his leggings and threw on his tunic before beginning to knot a perfunctory hold into his belt.

"Thank you, Alane," he answered, his voice bright in a way that did not match the exhaustion on his face. "I shall see to them presently."

"Shall I awaken the King, my lord?"

"No," the answer was not rushed and quite assured. "I will see that his men are awoken and given sufficient time to prepare their lord."

"You may enter, Alane," Gruoch called out as Mac Bethad nodded to his wife. "I am ready to dress."

Once Gruoch had been seen to by Alane, she looked every bit the magnanimous lady of Crown Hill that the crowd would need to see. Alane had pinned Gruoch's long braid into a knot at the nape of her neck and arranged it with a small golden pin. Her tunic was fresh and crisp, and Gruoch pinched at her cheeks to bring out the rose in her pale skin. She smiled at Mac Bethad as he took her arm and escorted his bride down the stairs, Alane following at a respectable distance.

A small group of men gathered, perhaps five in all, that had not been at the feast the night before. One of these was taller than the rest, with a head of thick, burnished red hair. His pale blue eyes shone in the morning light illuminating the room, but Gruoch did not miss the shallowness of his glance, how the smile around his eye did not go any deeper than that. His eyes swept the room constantly as though seeking out an invisible threat. More fool he then, to not recognize one as it swept grandly into his presence.

Gruoch was struck again as she considered Malcolm, who stood but a little way from the tall stranger. She was intrigued both by the lack of resemblance he bore to his father and the confidence with which he held himself. He had a way of looking down his hooked nose that hinted at condescension for his surroundings, but he had an easy smile like the king and a loud voice not unlike her father's.

"Mac Bethad," Malcolm boomed as his hosts swept into the hall. Mac Bethad bowed in respect to Duncan's heir while his wife curtsied prettily at his side. "The hero of Hibernia. The scourge of the heathen Norse. I thank you again, my friend, for a splendid feast and a warm hall."

"You are always welcome at the Hill," Mac Bethad said with a smile, leaving Gruoch's side in order to clasp Malcolm by the arm. "Tell me, kinsman, how long will you linger? Have you time for a hunt? Will you drink this night with us?"

Gruoch smiled sweetly at her husband as he spoke. The invitation was a perfect one and sounded most sincere. The last thing they could afford was to appear eager to empty their halls of guests.

"Mac Duff will never allow it," Malcolm replied, gesturing to the man Gruoch had noticed upon entering. Upon hearing his name, Mac Duff nodded in greeting to Mac Bethad and again in her direction. "Besides," Malcolm continued, "We must make for Saint Andrew's before we return home to Dunsinane, and Mac Duff is eager to return to Fife."

"Does your wife await your arrival?" Gruoch posed the question to Mac Duff lightly, feigning polite interest in learning about his life.

"She does," he answered in a deep and gruff voice. "She was with child when I left weeks ago. I expect she will be delivered by now." Gruoch smiled encouragingly, but Mac Duff did not attempt to continue the conversation. Instead, he sighed somewhat louder than necessary and sent a meaningful look at Malcolm. The prince laughed at his friend's impatience and clapped Mac Bethad on the back of his shoulder.

"Well then, let us wake the old man," Malcolm said, still smiling. Gruoch was shocked at his somewhat brazen address of the king. What a fool to appear so cocky and comfortable. It would only serve to further cement the appearance of his guilt when his dagger was discovered on the dosed guards.

"Allow me to escort you." Mac Bethad continued to smile at Malcolm, his face devoid of any trace of stress or tension.

"It would be my honour to wake and prepare His Majesty," Mac Duff said quickly before Malcolm could respond. Mac Bethad took this inter-jection in stride and nodded his agreement, holding out his arm in the di-rection of the stairs in an invitation to Mac Duff. They made their way to the bottom step, Mac Duff moving briskly with an air of self-importance and duty, Mac Bethad with the casual and calm air of someone benefiting from a pleasant night's slumber.

The other men in the hall paid little attention to the goings-on in the hall and were deep in conversation with one another. Though they made no real efforts to conceal their talk, it was difficult for Gruoch to make out their words from the distance at which she stood. They seemed at ease, and she was finally able to make out the subject of their talk as one man gesticulated wildly, referring to a storm that had passed through the region a few nights prior. He mimed the violence of the wind, and one of his friends chuckled at the storyteller's animated re-telling.

As her husband and Mac Duff disappeared up the staircase, Gruoch smiled at Malcolm, who wore an easy grin of his own. He gestured that she should approach, and she did so gracefully, walking with confidence and holding her head high. Gruoch curtsied again as she made her way to his side, and he waved a hand as though to interrupt her.

"No more bowing and scraping, my lady." She nodded once, though Gruoch was somewhat irritated to hear him refer to her actions as *scrap-ing*. "We are all friends here, are we not?"

"Yes, your highness." She kept the easy smile on her face though she struggled somewhat to keep the anger from building behind her eyes.

Friends indeed. Had he called her father a friend so that Bodhe would lower his guard and open the gates? Had Malcolm behaved so arrogantly before murdering him?

Had he even had the stomach to deliver the death blow himself, or had some nameless soldier carried out the prince's bloody whims?

"Yes," Malcolm repeated, his smile stretching wider on his face. There was a sudden cunning in his expression, much like that of a fox that thinks it has cornered its prey, playing with it before pouncing. *Fine*, Gruoch thought to herself. *Let Malcolm play. The rules will change swiftly enough.*

"Can I have the servants bring you some refreshment?" Gruoch posed her question lightly. "Some ale, perhaps?"

"Your father said he was my friend," Malcolm said suddenly, as though he had read her mind.

The smile that Gruoch wore suddenly ached and seemed to grow heavy on her cheeks.

"Your Highness?"

"And he was not my friend, nor my father's," Malcolm continued. "And I am glad that you have not been tainted by such treasonous blood, my lady, else I should have to put you down as well. Mac Bethad was certainly quick to believe you had no part to play in Gille's murder of our dear Mormear." He leered openly at her then. "But I suppose better man have done worse for the love of a woman."

The group of men had stopped speaking then, and from the corner of her eye, Gruoch noticed that they had turned and were watching her exchange with Malcolm carefully. There was no effort made to hide their interest in what was said. Angus stood by, his already marred face twisted even more by a deep scowl.

Gruoch erased the smile from her face and instead slipped on a mask of sorrow and humility. She cast down her eyes and allowed a deep sigh to escape her lips. When she met Malcolm's gaze once more, there was a wetness in her eyes that she hoped set them to shining.

"I loved my father as I am sure you love your own," Gruoch began, her voice demure and trembling. "It pains me that he should have proven so false when it all else, he seemed a paragon of virtue and loyalty. I can only say the same for Gille, whose disloyal heart burned me as well."

Malcolm snorted and waved a hand before his face as though her words were flies troubling him.

"Seemed. Therein lies the problem. It appears, my lady, that your family is cursed with false appearances. Any man may play at the dutiful servant. I hope that the gentleness of your sex keeps you from proving so false to your new husband."

"I seek only to serve him and to be a faithful servant to my king, your father."

Malcolm reached out a hand then, taking her chin between his fingers. Gruoch refused to make a sound at his touch, though her eyes grew wide in alarm before she could catch herself. Her eyes darted once more to the side to where Angus had stepped forward, hand gripping the hilt of a blade he wore at his side. Imperceptibly, Gruoch shook her head, and Angus froze though his hand did not leave his weapon.

Malcolm brought his face closer to hers, and his grey eyes searched her own. Whatever he found seemed to satisfy him, and he grinned again, somewhat lecherously, before releasing her gently.

"Such a fair face," he said softly. "It is a shame that you so resemble your father. His eyes grew wide as well when I had him in my grasp."

Gruoch swallowed the words that threatened to spill from her mouth, and she tried to steady her pounding heart. It was beating so hard against her chest that she was sure Malcolm would hear the frantic rhythm and mock her all the more for it. She considered her next words carefully, but she was saved from speech when a yell suddenly tore through the halls of the Hill and came tumbling down the staircase.

Malcolm's attention was torn away, and they both looked in the direction that Mac Bethad and Mac Duff had taken.

"Oh, horror!"

Gruoch could make out Mac Duff's words now, though there were new voices that mingled with the wailing and careening cries.

She heard the sound of iron swords being pulled free of scabbards, and she felt Malcolm tense at her side. Gruoch made sure to appear as shocked and confused as the others and was glad to have done so when Malcolm turned suddenly towards her, his eyes scrutinizing her in a cold and calculating manner.

"Sacrilegious murder!"

"The king! The king!"

"He has been slain! See, the guards!"

"He has killed them! Mac Bethad has killed them both!"

The voices became cacophony as they swirled and beat themselves together against the stone walls. They were quickly followed by the thundering of many feet on the staircase steps, and Mac Duff appeared first, rushing to Malcolm's side, his hands and the front of his tunic wearing the residue of dried blood.

"Some villain, your highness, has broke open the sacred temple of your father's body." Mac Duff's eyes were afire, and spittle flew from his mouth as he spoke to Malcolm.

"The king, you say?" One of the men who had accompanied them broke away from his friends and came to Mac Duff's side. "Do you mean to say His Majesty is dead?!"

"See for yourself, Lennox, if you cannot believe my words," Mac Duff spat. "Ring the alarum bell! Wake the house!"

"What do you mean by shouting such ugly and horrible words into the quiet of my home?" Gruoch's voice was shrill and anxious, and she darted her gaze wildly about the room as though seeking some explanation. She saw Mac Bethad as he finally descended the stairs and gasped at the sight of him. His tunic, clean and fresh only moments before, was now drenched in fresh blood. The crimson liquid had stained his face in a vicious splatter, and his hands had been dyed as well.

"Call for Banquo," Mac Bethad shouted to a group of huddled and shaking servants. "Bring him to me. We need the counsel of wise men in the wake of such senseless horrors."

"My lords, what has happened?" Gruoch's voice rose an octave higher.

"Take my lady from the place!" Mac Bethad's order was a roar. "This is no place for a woman. To hear said what I have seen would strike her down!"

There was a sudden and quick scuffling as servants ran to obey, and Gruoch made herself stagger, stumbling a little over her feet where she stood. Alane, who had come into the hall upon hearing the screams, reached for Gruoch and helped to steady her. As she held on to Alane, Gruoch watched as Banquo rushed into the room, hand hovering over the hilt of the sword at his side.

"The things I have been told cannot be true," he said as he approached. He took in Mac Bethad's bloodstained countenance and looked to Mac Duff, who trembled beside Malcolm. "Duff, say such things are not so."

Mac Duff ignored Banquo's words and faced Malcolm; rage evident in the etched tension of his face. "Your royal father is murdered."

"Who has done this thing?" Malcolm's voice was cold and did not waver. "Where are his guards?"

Mac Bethad strode forward at these words, his eyes full of a silent fury and accusation.

"The answer to one question lies in the answer to the other," Mac Bethad said, seething. "Lennox, Banquo, take the men and see the king's chamber. There you shall find the terrible answer to this crime."

Banquo leapt towards the staircase then, followed by the man who had moments ago been entertaining his friends with his frantic reenactments of the weather. The two men made short work of the steps, bounding their way up as though the devil himself were behind them.

Malcolm turned from Mac Duff then and faced Mac Bethad. The difference between the men was startling as Malcolm stood in his clean attire before the blood-soaked vision of the Mormaer of Moray. The prince appeared as a boy before Mac Bethad, a child facing a warrior. There was an uncomfortable tension that swept through the room, and the sudden silence that descended upon those gathered there was heavy with tension.

"Mac Duff," Malcolm said easily, "To what answer does my kinsman refer?"

Mac Bethad was spared from answering for Banquo, and Lennox burst back into the room, carried down the staircase at a dangerous pace. Lennox was white, and his hands shook. Banquo, looking just as troubled, held a familiar dagger in his hand.

"It was the guards," Lennox gasped. "Their faces were awash with the king's dried blood, and one still had this dagger on his person."

At this, Banquo threw down the blade. It clattered against the stone floor and rolled over once before coming to a stop a little way from where Malcolm stood. Gruoch watched in secret glee as his eyes became round with sudden understanding, and a growing whisper filled the hall with the incredulous words of those who watched.

"And what have these men to say for themselves," Malcolm asked.

"The traitors will lie no more," Mac Bethad said softly.

"They have been slain," Banquo explained, "Though the blood that covers them is freshly spilt."

Another pregnant pause, and then Malcolm broke the tenuous silence. "Who killed them?"

"I did." Mac Bethad stood squarely and immobile as the men took him in. He met Malcolm's eyes without flinching and with no sign of remorse. He even dared to take a step toward the prince as he spoke. Slowly, he bent and picked up Malcolm's bloodied dagger, holding it from him as though to protect himself from its foulness. "I ask you now, which of the king's loyal men could have stomached the sight of his broken body and those responsible sitting in their drunken stupor? Which man, who bears the love that I bear, would not have jumped to avenge their fallen lord?"

"It was not your place to dole out such vengeance."

"Is it a lack of courage or a lack of love that prompts such words?"

Malcolm looked for a moment as though he had been slapped, and his expression blanched at the cold fury in Mac Bethad's voice. The cunning princeling could not hide the puzzlement and fear that contaminated his face as he struggled to find the right words, as though speech had not always come easily to him. Gruoch dared a glance at the audience of men and soldiers who watched the exchange with bated breath and knew what she had to do.

"Husband," Gruoch called weakly as she allowed her knees to shake and buckle under her weight. "Help me!"

She did not know whose arms caught her as she fell, and she refused to open her eyes as her jaw slackened, and Gruoch gave every appearance of having fainted away.

"Look to the lady and get her hence from here," growled Mac Duff, and Gruoch felt nervous hands grip her arms and slide under her knees, lifting her gently. As she was carried away, it took her every strength to suppress the smile that threatened to burst upon her face as Gruoch heard her husband's next words.

"Why did you kill your father, Malcolm?"

# EIGHTEEN
# THEY CALL ON MAC BETHAD

When Gruoch left her chambers and returned to the main hall, Malcolm and Mac Duff had gone.

The trap that had been had lain for Malcolm could not have been more effective. Between the dagger brought down by Banquo, Mac Bethad's display of fierce loyalty to Duncan, and her own fainting spell, guilt regarding the king's murder had slid solidly upon Malcolm's shoulders. The guards, unable to say anything to the contrary, were quickly established as mercenaries or even simply as greedy fools, hired either way by the prince to assassinate his father during their travels.

"They say Malcolm has fled for the South, to his fortress at Dunsinane." Banquo's voice was full of spite as he stood by the fire in the main hall, emptied for their personal use. Mac Bethad sat on a wooden bench, gazing into the flames with his arms crossed before his chest. Gruoch stood behind him, listening quietly to Banquo as he recounted the latest gossip to have reached them.

"And what of the lords there?" Mac Bethad kept staring at the fire as though it could offer him the answers he sought. "Has Malcolm been welcomed back into his father's halls?"

Banquo sighed and pulled his dagger from its scabbard and inspected the blade in the light of the fire, polishing at invisible tarnish.

"If he has, the welcome will not last. Alba loved Duncan, and Malcolm's flight south has only reinforced what we suspected here. That he orchestrated his father's murder in order to ascend the throne. Albians are not blind to such treachery, even when the guilt lies with one of their own."

"And Mac Duff?" Mac Bethad's voice remained detached, cool.

"He is said to have followed Malcolm home. His own lands are not far from the fortress." Banquo completed his astute inspection of the blade he carried and then deftly put it away at the sound of approaching steps. Banquo and Gruoch turned in the direction of the entrance in time to catch sight of Ross approaching the hall, his blonde hair windswept, cheeks red from the cold weather outside. He grinned wildly as he approached, and he nodded a greeting to Banquo and dipped a knee in her direction. Mac Bethad did not turn his attention away from the fire before him.

"Greeting Mormaer," Ross called, addressing Mac Bethad first, although he still looked away. "My lady," he continued. "Ruffian."

Banquo chuckled slightly at the name-calling, walking over to Ross and clapping him soundly on the back.

"Welcome back, Ross," Banquo said. "It seems as though you are ever coming and going. It is a good thing you are yet unmarried. I can't help but think your wife should be cross with us for sending you riding all over the territory."

Ross laughed a little as though embarrassed, and Gruoch was shocked to see a hint of colour flush his cheeks beneath the blonde stubble that dusted them.

"I am happy to fulfill this duty," Ross said earnestly, keeping his eyes from Gruoch's though she smiled and tried to meet his gaze. "Especially when it allows me to bring such tidings as these."

"Please," Gruoch said, gesturing to the many empty benches. "Sit and rest a moment before you share your news. Shall I send for food? Ale?"

Ross nodded gratefully, and Gruoch walked away and towards the corridor in order to wave down a servant. Banquo had cleared the hall when the three of them had settled there earlier, preferring a quiet and unattended place in which to speak.

Gruoch spied a pair of young girls whispering and giggling with each other a few paces away, and they sobered quickly upon seeing their mistress approach. Gruoch gave each a passing glance of disapproval, even though a smile played at the corner of her lips at the sight of the maids so at ease. It had not always been so when Gille had walked these halls.

"The lord of Ross requires food and fresh ale," Gruoch called to them. "Be quick about it now."

The girls curtsied quickly and hurried off to obey, and Gruoch was pleased to hear them take up giggling after they had gone what they considered to be a safe distance from her.

She returned to the hall and found the three men there huddled in serious conversation. Mac Bethad had finally risen from his chair, though he had only approached the fire, standing before it as though it were the only way to warm his frozen body. As Gruoch made her way closer to them, she was somewhat disappointed to see Banquo shake his head ever so slightly at Ross as though to discourage him from repeating what had been shared.

"Is it so bad, my lord Banquo, that you should keep it from me?" Gruoch was unable to keep the annoyance from her voice. Perhaps her fainting performance had been *too* effective.

"It is Ross' inability to be objective and rational that I take issue with," Banquo responded. "I apologize if I offended you."

"Please," Gruoch said to Ross, ignoring Banquo. "What news?"

"The traitor prince has fled further than Alba," Ross said. "It is said he is crossing the sea and making his way to Hibernia."

This outcome they had not expected. Why would Malcolm return to the shores his father's armies had so recently bloodied?

"It seems senseless," Banquo said, giving voice to their troubled thoughts. "Though it has become clear that the fox always has a way of doubling back on his tracks and causing us to lose the sense of his direction."

"What does that mean for us?" Gruoch kept her voice low and calm.

Banquo's throat twitched with unspoken words, and though Gruoch sought Mac Bethad's eye, he had yet to turn his attention to his friends.

Ross nodded deeply at her words, considering the question.

"It means," he replied, "That Alba is left without a king and that the Counsel of Lords has assembled to name one. The people will not follow Malcolm. Duncan was beloved by the God-fearing people of this land, and they will not kneel to his murderer."

Gruoch refused to let her eyes seek out Mac Bethad once more, only to be disappointed. Instead, she forced herself to keep them trained on Ross as he spoke, her face a perfect mask of respectable curiosity.

"You have not ridden so hard to tell us this," she realized. Banquo made a strange and strangled sound in his throat, yet Gruoch kept her eyes trained on the lord of Ross.

"The people call for a protector, one who has proven himself loyal to the blood of the land." Ross paused, and his smile grew wider in his wonder. "They call on Mac Bethad to be their king."

Gruoch felt her heart leap in her chest as she took in this news, gasping slightly. She finally turned to her husband once more. As though he sensed his wife's eyes boring into the back of his head, Mac Bethad turned slowly from the fire and looked upon each of them for a moment before locking his gaze with Gruoch's. He looked on for a moment without speaking, some tenuous connection still linking them, before he addressed himself to Ross.

"No." The sound was firm and echoed in the sudden stillness of the room.

Ross' smile faltered, and he looked at Banquo as though for reassurance. Banquo said nothing and merely studied the profile of his dearest friend. It irked Gruoch for a moment that Banquo knew him in ways that she did not, that the years he had spent at Mac Bethad's side had allowed him to read her husband's moods and expressions with an ease that she did not yet possess. They all stood in silence, unsure of how to break the quiet in any meaningful way.

Banquo looked at her then and made the slightest gesture with his head in Mac Bethad's direction. Gruoch understood and felt relieved to have done so. She walked gently to her husband's side. Mac Bethad's hands were clenched at his sides, skin taught, and veins raised. Slowly, she traced down the muscular arm until she reached his hand. There, tentatively, her fingers prodded at his own until they opened themselves reluctantly, allowing Gruoch to slip her palm against his. She leaned against the arm and allowed her head to fall onto his shoulder, still saying nothing. After a moment, Mac Bethad sighed deeply as though his very soul were weary, and he allowed his cheek to rest against the top of his wife's head, against her hair. Gruoch ignored Ross's uncomfortable cough and instead set her energy to sending her every feeling, her every ounce of love for her husband through her flesh, as though it could melt from her and soak through his own, where it would be absorbed into his body.

"It is as they claimed then. Those strange women in the woods." Banquo's voice was matter-of-fact and seemed to hover in the air. Gruoch remembered then that he and Mac Bethad had been stopped by Eimear and her daughters as they returned from the last battle against the Norse invaders, that they had greeted him as Mormaer and then as King. She remembered the wild look in Mac Bethad's eyes as he had told her the tale and the laugh with which he had dismissed their words. Banquo, it seemed, had not forgotten either.

Gruoch felt Mac Bethad squeeze her fingers in his own, and she lifted her head from his shoulder. Peeking up at him as she felt Mac Bethad's cheek leave her hair, Gruoch caught sight of her husband's face in profile, and she saw the uncertainty and the shame that hung there. Whatever Duncan and Malcolm had been guilty of, Gruoch knew that what Mac Bethad had done still stung at his pride and soul. He was a fierce and brave warrior; to him, their revenge seemed cowardly and sly. Still, as she took in the planes of his face and the shine of his blue eyes, Gruoch felt her heart flutter as he looked at her and winked in the rakish and brazen way he had the first time they had met. Finally, he released her hand gently to turn and face his friends.

Ross looked on with the same expression of wonder and passion he always wore when in Mac Bethad's presence. Banquo, ever steady, seemed only thoughtful and content to wait upon the Mormaer's words before sharing any more of his own.

"I am unworthy of your praise and loyalty, Ross." Mac Bethad spoke kindly to his friend, who had the good sense to let shock show honestly where adoration had once been. "And whatever the Council may call for, I still have the sense to refuse. Moray has returned to my family's stewardship, and she is free, which is all I have ever desired. Malcolm has fled. Let his southern cousins worry about him and themselves. I have no ambition to prick me forward in this."

"No?" Banquo's question was not pointed, merely curious. "I will admit that I have never heard you yearn for a crown, but you also never been one to refuse duty or obligation when you knew it was yours to bear."

Mac Bethad sighed at his friend and brought a hand around Gruoch's shoulders, clasping her upper arm securely in his palm and pulling her against him. Though she made no sign of having noticed, Gruoch could feel the tremble and shaking of Mac Bethad's hand through her garment. Ross, once again, seemed unsettled by Mac Bethad's somewhat improper display of affection, but he did not waver. Banquo, more used to the demeanour of his dearest friend, was completely unperturbed.

"I never expected to be king," Mac Bethad continued. "I never wanted it."

"That may be so, my love," Gruoch said cautiously. "But I never expected my first husband to become a traitor or for my father to be killed for such crimes as well." She had to speak carefully. She and Mac Bethad had never spoken with Banquo about what Gille and Mael had suggested regarding Malcolm's involvement in the deaths of Findlaech and Bodhe. Such rumours needed to remain a secret for their own motive in Malcolm's downfall and Duncan's death to remain hidden.

"There has never been a king from Moray upon the Albian throne," Banquo mused. "This would be an opportunity the likes of which the North has never seen."

"Your men would follow you," Ross added eagerly. "You know this."

"You are well-loved by your people," Gruoch said gently. "Give them the king they deserve. Give them a king with the interests at heart and one who will not allow Southern customs to dictate his regency."

Mac Bethad chuckled slightly to himself, though the sound was somewhat dry.

"What is a man to do with the three of you to gang up on him," he said in a wry voice. He sighed and dropped his arm from Gruoch's shoulders. Both of his hands came to his face, where they rubbed at the stubbled cheeks before throwing themselves through the brown hair, making it stand wildly. The blue of his eyes, somewhat dimmed by the pain Gruoch knew he bore, still managed to catch the light, and there shone a twinkle that the three of them felt relieved to see.

"What do you say, Mac?" Banquo asked his question casually, though the answer he sought was anything but.

"If my father knew that I had allowed you plotters to bring me to Scone to be crowned, he would have had me whipped. Surely this kind of talk alone is enough to have him turning in his grave."

"My love?" Gruoch reached a tentative hand and touched his wrist gently as though it was only through physical touch that she could be assured of him.

"You told me once that Moray has no king," Mac Bethad mused as he patted Gruoch's hand. "Perhaps this is the moment we have been waiting for, the moment that my father dreamed of."

"Moray will be free...." Banquo breathed in a tight voice as his words trailed off into the stillness of the room.

"And Alba, leaderless, can do nothing to stop us," Gruoch finished, saying aloud what the three men had undoubtedly already concluded.

"Free," Ross repeated in a kind of dazed wonder.

"Free," Banquo said once more as though confirming it for them all.

Mac Bethad nodded at this, closing his eyes once more. Gruoch stepped to him, taking one of his hands in both of her own, while Banquo stepped to his other side and nudged him lightly in the shoulder in the way of brothers.

They stood together that morning with a certainty that promised they would always do so.

Mac Bethad's coronation ceremony had been a strange affair if only for its novelty. Though it certainly lacked the grandeur and ceremony of a Southern coronation, it still swept the countryside in a tide of hope and fraternity the likes of which even Angus could not recall. He would tell anyone who would listen that to see Findlaech's son complete his father's life's work brought a sense of peace to his heart, a kind of stillness that he believed to have been lost long ago to him, drowned in the blood and cries of fallen enemies and friends.

They had decided that Mac Bethad would be crowned to the northwest of Aberdeen, in the ruins of a circle of standing stones that put into sharp relief the majestic beauty of the Beinn Chìochan mountainscape. If he intended to rule the North as the first king of Moray, Mac Bethad understood the importance of establishing a location for his coronation that spoke both to his ties to the land and the history of its people. While Gruoch was sure that some of the good people of Moray may have preferred a church in which to host the ceremony, Gruoch saw the wisdom in choosing a location with an importance similar to Scone, where Albian kings had been crowned for generations.

It had taken just over a week of steady riding to arrive there. Gruoch was grateful for her husband's friends and their company, for once they arrived, she saw little of Mac Bethad. He spent hours in discussion with the Tanistry and the Council of Lords. He wanted to ensure that his declaration of kingship was supported by the men who had first elected to choose him as Mormaer after his father's death. And, as it ever was in the mortal affairs of kings and men, Mac Bethad and the Tanistry discussed the notion of a second, one who could lead the people should Mac Bethad be killed or rendered unable to fulfill his duties. In the proud tradition of the North, Mac Bethad insisted that power in the North still be given to a chosen ruler rather than rely on hereditary heirs alone.

"For we have all seen that even a son cannot be trusted with the life of his father," Mac Bethad was claimed to have said when he discussed such things with the Council of Lords, "and that an unbridled desire for power can turn a man's soul to darkness." Those in attendance had nodded solemnly, and while none spoke his name aloud, Malcolm had crossed their minds in an uneasy unison.

The idea of an immediate successor had been discussed during their travels, and Gruoch already knew that Mac Bethad would offer Banquo's name.

"Perhaps," he had told her with a light smile, "we will be blessed with a son great enough to be considered should the occasion arise."

Gruoch had returned his smile, though it caused her an acute pain to mirror his hope so dishonestly.

Those who could make the journey to Aberdeen and the stone circle there cheered and blessed Mac Bethad's name, reaching to touch him as he passed. Some shouts furled the name of Findlaech, and Gruoch knew Mac Bethad was pleased for the memory of his father to accompany this moment.

Though they had not expected any loyal countryman of Alba to be present at Mac Bethad's crowning since it signalled Moray's independence, a prospect that Gruoch was sure frightened many a southern villager and lord, given that this newfound statehood released Moray from financial obligation to Alba, who had also lost in its northern neighbour a crucial political tool.

Though it was far from necessary given that none expected otherwise, Angus had pointed out Mac Duff's absence from the coronation to which he and a myriad of other southern lords had been invited in a show of good faith. Rumours abounded that he had abandoned Alba for Hibernia and that he and Malcolm were working together. In his absence, a tumultuous and mercurial alliance of lords worked as a temporary rule of law in the South. Gruoch had seen enough of men to know that ambition and hunger would win out and that the Albian lords would strike at one another eventually in their desire to see themselves on Duncan's throne.

Still, the green isle seemed far, and the immediacy of her husband's coronation took precedence in Gruoch's mind. She thought of both Bod-he and Findlaech and imagined them smiling and drinking together in a hall like the one her father had built, laughing with pride at the advancement of their children.

Then Mac Bethad was made to stand before the recumbent stone, and the sacred words were spoken. If Duncan was in hell as Gruoch hoped, his ghost lacked the power to cast a pall over the moment. Mac Bethad's eyes sought hers in the crowd, blue meeting green and staying there while the prayers were chanted, and the oaths were sworn.

Although Gruoch was unsure whether they were likely to remain at Crown Hill after Mac Bethad's coronation, he announced that the court would remain in Inverness, calling it the seat of the North. Although extensive renovations would be required to make it a home fit for a king, and such expansions would not be easy or inexpensive, Gruoch was thrilled to hear the news. Crown Hill had been her home for more than five years. Her son had been born here and died here. Hertha had died here, and her ashes and soul still prowled and wove through the dark forests and misty heaths that surrounded them. Gruoch had not relished the thought of leaving their restless spirits behind and wondered if such shades would have followed her from the Hill.

*I am Queen now, Hertha*, Gruoch whispered into her heart. *What would you say to that?*

She felt a phantom tugging of her hair and smiled to herself, even as tears gathered at the corners of her eye. Gruoch allowed the wetness to saturate her lashes for a moment, taking a breath and permitting the burst of pain and love she still carried for her lost son and surrogate mother to take hold of her heart and squeeze it. Another breath and she wiped the back of one hand against her eyes, effectively clearing away from them any sign of glistening.

Mac Bethad still took the time to go out and walk among his soldiers and the people of the Hill, speaking to old men about the battles they had seen. Gruoch had even spied him chasing after a small boy, playfully taking up the child and swinging him about through the air as the child screamed with laughter. She felt a sharp sting as she watched her husband so at ease, the secret of her infertility languishing in the darkest corners of her mind.

It was not the only secret she carried.

The ease that Mac Bethad displayed in public was a false one. She knew that the guilt he still carried over Duncan's murder, deserved or not, weighed heavy upon his heart and that his mind was troubled by it. His nights were a restless twisting of limbs and pacing before the hearth. Gruoch had awoken more than once to find him standing at the window, muttering to himself in the darkness.

Now, coupled with a sense of duty and devotion for his fledgling kingdom, Gruoch worried that the stress would eat away at Mac Bethad's mind and that the lack of proper rest would snarl his mind.

She also knew that it was only a matter of time before the fits began to occur, and Gruoch considered themselves fortunate to have been alone when they first struck him.

The couple sometimes chose to dine alone in their chamber, relishing the time together that granted them a respite from the eyes of those who lived under their shared roof. That evening, Mac Bethad had been feeling unwell, and even though the air was brisk and the room quite cool, his face was flushed, and a sheen of sweat hung upon his skin. He sat bare-chested at the table across from Gruoch, pushing at the meat on his plate with a piece of hard bread. She watched him and took note of how little he ate, of the glazed look in his eyes.

Gruoch moved slowly and quietly, speaking of nothing important if only to fill the silence of the space. She commented inanely about Alane's watchful comments regarding the renovations and the constant flutter of activity at the Hill, waving a hand about the room carelessly as she expressed some point. Mac Bethad's eyes lay upon the small knife beside her plate, and Gruoch was not able to tear his attention away with her storytelling.

"My love?" she asked, her tone curious. "Have I lost you?"

"To be thus is nothing," he said suddenly, his voice clipped yet aloof. "But to be safely thus."

"Mac Bethad?"

"Chief nourisher in life's feast."

Gruoch dropped her fork into her plate and pushed her chair away from the table, prepared to rise. "My lord, are you unwell?"

Her husband's mouth opened and closed without making a sound, and his empty eyes were still focused on some point invisible to her. He looked over her shoulder with such sudden terror and ferocity that Gruoch spun in her seat to take in what he saw. When she cast her gaze behind her, Gruoch was only more afraid since she saw nothing there. A gory spectre would have been more welcome than the barren emptiness that caused her husband's eyes to widen, the whites of them traced with vibrant red veins. Still, few knew better than Gruoch the tricks a ghost could spin when a heart was heavy and open to receive them.

She turned her attention back to Mac Bethad, and her mind raced as she struggled to find the words to calm and comfort him. As she watched, Mac Bethad's right hand rose into the air, and the fingers closed and opened in spasms.

"Come," he whispered. "If you are not a product of my fevered brain, let me clutch you."

"Mac Bethad?" Gruoch's voice was low and shook.

It could not have been longer than a heartbeat before her husband slid from his chair and fell to the cold floor at Gruoch's feet. A strange guttural moan escaped him as he fell, and his limbs were struck by a sudden and violent stiffness. Foaming spittle appeared between his lips, and Gruoch forced her frozen limbs into action as she scrambled from her seat and knelt at Mac Bethad's side.

His body was taken up by the tremors that moved through it, and Gruoch struggled to keep his arms from flailing, worried that he would hurt himself. Even in this state, or perhaps because of it, Mac Bethad's strength was far beyond what she could contain, and his arms slipped from her grasp constantly and struck the legs of the table, the floor, and even her.

Gruoch was sick at the sight of his head as it tossed itself about and the way that it would suddenly lift, only to fall back and strike solidly upon the planks beneath it. The last time she had been witness to such a violent fit had been the night of her wedding to Gille all those years ago. Though there had been moments of strange otherness, or instances of small tremors, there had been nothing like this.

Worse, she was alone. There was no Banquo or Hertha to assist her now.

Although she would later think that the fit lasted only a few minutes, it felt as though hours had gone by before Gruoch finally felt her husband begin to slacken and relax in her iron grip. She let out a single, hoarse sob when his head fell back and became immobile, his blue eyes closed and ringed in purple shadows. His brow glistened with sweat, the sheen reflected in the light of torches and candles. As she ran a hand gently down his cheek, Gruoch was struck by the sharpness of his cheekbones. Had they always been thus? Or had the stress of the last few weeks taken more of a toll than she had allowed herself to notice? What she knew for certain was that these fits could not be allowed to worsen in severity or frequency, for Banquo had made it clear to her years ago that Mac Bethad's condition must be kept secret in order for his leadership to flourish. Now, with Malcolm hiding away in Hibernia amongst their enemies and Mac Bethad at the head of a newly independent country, it was all the more important than any perceived weakness be concealed.

As she took stock of the options and resources available to her, Gruoch realized very quickly that she knew to whom she could go for help. Eimear's knowledge of herbs and plants was vast, and she was a gifted healer. Hertha had respected and trusted her, which was a greater character witness than any other in terms of Gruoch's impressions of the cunning woman.

She would speak to Eimear, and Gruoch hoped the wise woman could be trusted to keep yet another secret.

It had been easy enough for Mac Bethad and Gruoch to slip away from Crown Hill the next morning under the guise of taking a ride together. Their closeness was no secret from those who lived among them at court, and they often spent time alone whenever their schedules allowed it.

Mac Bethad had still been somewhat pale as he had ordered their horses to be saddled, and the fatigue of the previous night still hung about the corners of his eyes. No one commented on his appearance. At least no one said anything to his face.

"I still don't think this wise," Mac Bethad said as the pair rode along the dirt path through the wood, making their way to Eimear's cottage. "It seems too big a risk to let another person in on the secret of my fits. Even if it is Eimear."

"She told me she was midwife to your mother," Gruoch replied, her tone light. "She has seen all there is of you. There are not many secrets left to hide from her."

Mac Bethad chuckled, and Gruoch's heart warmed at the sound.

"I suppose you are right," he admitted. "And things cannot be allowed to continue as they are."

"Eimear will help us," Gruoch said with a confidence that she tried to fool herself into feeling. "She will concoct some potion to help soothe you, to keep the fits at bay."

Mac Bethad said nothing at this, and they rode in silence through the cool woods, the pale sunlight filtering through branches crowned with dead and brittle leaves. It was in these moments, these spells of silence, that Gruoch sometimes allowed herself to imagine Lulach, older and bigger, running through the trees or perhaps even seated upon his own stout pony. She could imagine Mac Bethad teaching her son to hold a sword and how to be a leader of men. The familiar ache choked her heart for a moment, and her breath caught in her throat, and Gruoch felt the phantom squeeze of her son's tiny fingers wrapping themselves around her hand.

The small stone and thatch cottage appeared before them before Gruoch could lose herself completely in her reverie. From the corner of her eye, Gruoch noticed one of Eimear's daughters, Laoise, appear from the woods beside them. She moved silently, her copper hair blowing loose around her neck. Her lithe body glided effortlessly through the trees until she stood by silently, taking them in as Gruoch and Mac Bethad rode closer to her mother's home. Eimear herself then stepped out from the small cottage though they had made no greeting nor called out to her. Gruoch shivered slightly, feeling superstitious, and then immediately scolded herself for the foolish notions that crept quietly through the back of her mind.

Eimear nodded to them as they approached and dismounted from their horses. Laoise moved from the shadows of the trees and took the reins from them, clucking to the beasts and leading them towards a small patch of green. A quick glance around didn't reveal Fiadh, but Gruoch knew better than to assume she was out of earshot. For reasons she could not understand, Gruoch was still uneasy about why Fiadh had greeted Mac Bethad as both Mormaer and King after overhearing Gruoch's conversation with Ross.

"Your Majesty," Eimear said as Mac Bethad approached her.

"None of that," he replied tersely, though a smile sat demurely at the corner of his mouth. "You helped to guide me from my mother, Eimear. You have seen me from boy to man, and it strikes me as strange to hear you address me thus."

Eimear smiled at him, accepting the lack of formality a little too easily for Gruoch's taste. She took a deep breath and forced herself to put away the venomous suspicion that had overtaken her. It had been Gruoch's idea after all that they come to Eimear for help. She had trusted in the cunning woman for years. There was no reason for this petty irritation Gruoch felt at Eimear's familiar demeanour. Eimear was always this way; she walked with the quiet confidence of a woman who had seen the worse that the world could throw at her and who had walked victorious through its hardships.

"We need your help," Gruoch said simply. Eimear turned her gaze to Gruoch as she continued. "No one must know."

Eimear gestured to the door of the cottage, and Mac Bethad was the first to step forward. He opened it and made his way in, with Eimear following close behind. As Gruoch stepped up to the door herself, Eimear turned suddenly, barring the way.

"Not you, not this time." Her voice was calm, yet there was no softness in it. The tone left no room for interpretation.

"Where he goes, I go," Gruoch replied. "His secrets are mine."

Eimear stood in the doorway and said nothing more. Yet the message was clear: she had said that Gruoch would not be allowed to enter and would not be saying so again.

"As your queen…" "Do not finish those words," Eimear said sharply. Gruoch felt a brushing at her shoulder and turned quickly to see first Laoise, then Fiadh, slip by and enter the cottage. Their mother made a tiny and almost imperceptible movement to allow them to pass, and neither girl looked at Gruoch as they walked past. "You are queen everywhere but on my land. Here, you are a girl who still needs me to provide her with the herbs for her tea and who needs me to keep such a service to myself. You may wait here. We will send him out to you when we have done what needs to be done."

"But…" "There can only be three," Eimear said. "So it has always been, so it shall always be."

The words struck a chord within Gruoch's memory, and it seemed to her then that Eimear had said such a thing to her before.

Still.

Gruoch swallowed the rage that had been building while Eimear spoke, and she forced herself to step back and away from the door. Once Gruoch had given up enough space, Eimear closed the door and left her staring at the ancient and gnarled planks of wood that formed it.

For a moment, Gruoch felt like a young girl, untried and naive. She was angry at how quickly and efficiently Eimear had taken from her any semblance of power that she had and how little effort it had taken from Eimear for Gruoch to be cast aside in this endeavour. She knew she should be grateful for the help, and Gruoch knew that if anyone could help her husband, it was Eimear. However, her stomach was heavy with a cold feeling of dread, and she could not understand why Eimear's daughters had been permitted to participate in whatever measures would be undertaken to help Mac Bethad.

And Gruoch could not understand why she had not been invited to be a part of it.

"There are no secrets between us now," Gruoch whispered to the breeze that played gently through the tops of encroaching trees.

Her timing would need to be perfect. Gruoch knew that Eimear considered her to be a child and a malleable one at that. The older woman would not consider for a moment that Gruoch would disobey the order to remain outside and would likely not have even bothered to bar the door to prevent her from entering.

Gruoch was very much counting on this dismissal.

She waited for what seemed like a painfully long time, counting the seconds as they stumbled by as she stood alone on the stoop. Gruoch was not sure exactly what she was waiting for or how she would know when the time was right. She could only hope that her instincts, which she had not listened to or heeded quickly enough in the past, had not abandoned her.

*Now.*

The thought came unbidden and as clear to her mind as though someone had etched the idea directly into her brains. Gruoch brought a hand to the door and unclasped it quickly, pushed it open and walked brusquely into the cottage.

There was very little light in the cottage, and the only source was the flames that currently filled the stone hearth in the corner. Gruoch knew from memory that the shelves were filled with dried herbs and flowers, that there were strange charms and items displayed on tables and rudimentary shelves. She had seen them all before during previous visits. But the sight that she stumbled upon now in the flickering light of the fireplace was one Gruoch could never have expected.

Mac Bethad sat on a wooden chair before the fire, his back to her. His strong body seemed to slump weakly in his seat, though his head remained upright. Fiadh sat upon his lap, straddling Mac Bethad, whose arms encircled the woman's waist weakly. Fiadh's face was so close to Mac Bethad's that the woman's cheek and lips seemed to tickle and touch his ear as she whispered harshly words that Gruoch could not hear. Laoise sat on the floor at his side, one hand stroking brazenly upon Mac Bethad's thigh and the other upon her sister's back as though for support. Eimear stood before Mac Bethad's chair, not touching him, but the sound of her guttural whispers reached Gruoch as well to where she hovered in the door.

Gruoch's blood turned to ice as Fiadh caught her eye from her seat upon Mac Bethad, and Gruoch felt her teeth clench of their own accord as the blonde woman smiled lustfully from over Mac Bethad's shoulder. The smile did nothing to pause the continuance of strange words that spilled from Fiadh's twisting mouth and only served to set Gruoch further on edge.

She made as though to step further into the cabin, one foot taking a hesitant step towards the three women who encircled her husband. It was Eimear who caught her eye then, and the cunning woman shook her head, and the flash in Eimear's eyes was enough to halt the very breath in Gruoch's lungs.

*Three!*

Gruoch felt the word as though she had been slapped with it, and a sudden freezing pain struck her behind the eye. She was no longer aware of her body as it slowly stepped back over the threshold and into the cold morning, able to feel only the piercing agony in her head as she scrambled to leave.

Gruoch closed the door tightly as she left.

# EIGHTEEN
# THEY CALL ON MAC BETHAD

A week or so after Gruoch had taken Mac Bethad on their first excursion to Eimear's cottage, there was to be a banquet held in the king's honour.

Alane and Gruoch had been preparing the feast for days. Honestly, however, Alane managed the affair, saw to the servants, and ensured that the feast presented to the king's friends and men at arms would be worthy of the new king. Moray's first and only true king.

Gruoch had become aware of a strange yet palpable rift between herself and Mac Bethad since their visit to the cunning woman and her daughters. She had not confessed to Mac Bethad that she had spied upon him while he went into the cottage without her or that she had seen Fiadh straddle him while the three of them whispered strange chants into his ears and the still air. Gruoch had not asked any questions, and Mac Bethad had offered her no answers unprompted. All that the pair carried forth from that strange morning was a full and heavy quiet between them, one of which they were keenly aware but one they were both unwilling to break. Gruoch's reasons for keeping her silence worried at her, working their way through her mind like worms through carrion. She could not risk the possibility that the answers she might receive could be worse than the worry and the silence themselves.

To make things all the worse, the daily visits to Eimear didn't seem to be helping with Mac Bethad's fits. He still suffered lapses during which he would become confused or, worse, unresponsive, lost in his imaginings or visions. Gruoch was no fool. It was no secret that Mac Bethad kept a less-than-perfect Christian court and that, no doubt, the lack of zealots around him had protected him from vile whispers of witchcraft or demons. This lax attitude towards the Christ that Duncan had so upheld ultimately endeared Mac Bethad to Eimear. Still, Eimear was but one person and a woman at that. Gruoch knew that whatever the older woman might be capable of, her influence and power would not be enough to protect Mac Bethad if news of his illness spread through Moray and those who sought to quench the fires of hell with the blood of witches came scratching at their doors.

Eimear had hinted at such things to Gruoch the evening of Mac Bethad's supper. So Gruoch had travelled to her alone in order to confront Eimear about the lack of progress in Mac Bethad's well-being and state of mind.

Eimear was waiting for Gruoch when she arrived. The queen's hair was swept and wild about her head where the strong wind had pulled it loose from its plaits as she rode furiously. Gruoch wasn't surprised to see Eimear standing by the door, her face calm and relaxed as though the sudden appearance of a guest were not startling in the least.

As though Eimear had been expecting her.

Gruoch ignored Laoise, who stood a little way to the left, watching from the tree line with her deep and piercing eyes. She also refused to meet Fiadh's gaze, though Gruoch managed to catch a taunting and haughty grin from the corner of her eye. She dismounted quickly, tying back the reins and allowing her horse that chance to graze on the cool grass that sparsely covered the forest floor.

"Whatever you are doing, it is having no effect." The wind carried her voice towards Eimear, and Gruoch felt a twist of satisfaction when she heard how her frustration and anger effectively seasoned the words. She was no naive child of fifteen, wed to a man who kept her locked away and afraid. She was a queen, and she loved her husband. She was needed, and she had a role to play.

Gruoch now had to ensure that Eimear continued to play hers.

Eimear shook her head as she would at a petulant child's tantrum, and Gruoch felt her blood boil in response to the dismissive expression on the other woman's face. There was no movement towards the door, no sweeping arm of invitation. Instead, Eimear stood still and strong as Gruoch approached her angrily.

"There has been an effect," she said, her voice bored and uninterested. "But significant shifts take time. Sometimes change is so gradual, so subtle, that it cannot be seen so easily as by simply looking."

"Horse shit," Gruoch swore between her teeth. "The very purpose of our asking for your help was the desire, nay, the need for a noticeable effect. My husband speaks to shadows and starts from ghosts that seem to follow him everywhere. He speaks in riddles or becomes silent mid-way through a thought. The people of the Hill are whispering about him. They are watching us both, and they say nothing when I pass. Their silence is most damning of all."

Eimear crossed her arms and sighed. "You cannot be expected to understand."

"Help me then. Make me see how you and your...." Gruoch struggled to contain the vitriol that sparked her speech. "Daughters, how you are helping my husband to come out of this darkness and back towards the light. His men need him. Moray needs him."

Eimear lifted one grey eyebrow, waiting.

"I need him," Gruoch confessed, and she was enraged at herself now as she felt hot tears pricking at her eyes.

"We do not doubt your love, Gruoch." Eimear uncrossed her arms and walked towards the queen slowly. She stood an arm's length away but did not attempt to touch Gruoch, who was glad that Eimear kept her distance and her hands to herself. Gruoch knew that her body would betray her if Eimear managed to breach the final distance between them and that any show of strength would disappear at a touch. This woman had guided Gruoch's only son into the world and knew her body in ways even a husband never would. Eimear had known Hertha. She was tied intimately with Gruoch's past life, with the girl she had been before she was a queen.

Gruoch could not suffer her touch now.

"Then what do I do?" Her voice broke, and Gruoch thought furiously of Fiadh and her silver-blonde hair as she sat upon Mac Bethad's lap, leaning in and whispering into his ear. It killed her to know that Fiadh now watched her as she came apart.

"You will do what women have always done, what my daughters and I have been doing since you first came to us."

Gruoch laughed, and the sound was harsh, bitter.

"You whisper to him the things he needs to hear." Eimear's voice was gentle, but it left no room for mistake or confusion. "You need to keep his feet on the path he has undertaken and keep the shadows and ghosts from calling him away until he can no longer be found."

"There is no cure," Gruoch said suddenly, feeling her energy and anger drain away as she spoke.

"None," Eimear conceded. "Mac Bethad has always suffered these moments, these fits, since his injury as a child. You know this." Gruoch nodded. She had nothing to say.

"You must also see how stress, guilt, and uncertainty weigh his mind and unbalance it, triggering these episodes. Rather than ask how to cure them, better to ask what has happened so recently for Mac Bethad to have lost his tenuous grip on control and why he has stumbled."

Gruoch's eyes shot to Eimear's, green meeting dark grey. The old woman's expression remained neutral, but there was a spark of laughter, of challenge in those iron eyes. Gruoch forced her own expression into a mask of neutrality, the effect somewhat spoiled by the red blotches that adorned her cheeks and the shine of unshed tears in her eyes. There was no way for Eimear to know the truth about Duncan and Gruoch's involvement in his death. Mac Bethad would never...

"It is important to keep him calm," Eimear said simply. "An agitated man may say things he will later regret. It would not do for the wrong person to hear him when he does so."

Gruoch was cold then, vicious shivers coursing through her unexpectedly as though a northern wind had carried Eimear's words into her bones, turning them to ice in order to shatter them into a thousand broken shards. Gruoch trembled as her gaze left Eimear's to travel over the woman's left shoulder, back in the direction from which she had come. Hating herself, Gruoch turned slowly to look behind her. As she did, Gruoch noticed that Fiadh and Laoise had dropped any pretense at work and were looking back in the direction of the forest path.

"There is a trembling in the earth," Laoise said in a loud whisper. "I feel the rumble of hooves beneath my feet."

"Your guests are arriving," Eimear said, stepping forward now and coming to stand at Gruoch's side, still looking back in the direction of Crown Hill. "And you have work to do."

She had been dismissed.

Nodding, Gruoch walked towards her horse as though through a fog of her own. She led the jolly little pony towards a stump that seemed solid enough to bear her weight, and she mounted quickly, turning him back the way they had come.

Gruoch did not turn to watch the women enter their cottage, and she was startled at the feel of a hand at her right calf, clutching her suddenly. She gasped and looked down, ready to kick away whatever had clung to her.

It was Fiadh, standing next to the pony, her slender hand resting gently now upon Gruoch's leg. It took everything in her not to shudder at the touch or to kick the hand away.

"There are murderers and dangerous men in these woods, my Queen," Fiadh said as she moved her hand from Gruoch's calf to stroke the pony's broad neck, "And you are unarmed. Here." There was suddenly a hand once more upon her leg, but this time the hand grasped Gruoch's upper thigh, and she felt the cold strength of a dagger flush against it through her legging.

"A small knife for cutting herbs," Fiadh answered as though Gruoch had spoken. "Sometimes, I use it to cut away the weeds that choke the garden. Things must be made to give way and to make space. In a pinch, you may use it to protect yourself. That is if you doubt your god's ability to do so."

Gruoch's right hand left the reins and slowly made its way to Fiadh's, where she placed it so that the silver girl could slide her own away, leaving behind the small and wicked blade. Gruoch considered it a moment as Fiadh stepped away quietly and said nothing more as she walked back towards the cottage. The knife was small, and its wooden grip fit perfectly in Gruoch's palm. After Fiadh's words, the path through the forest seemed less bright, and the spaces untouched by filtered sunlight became more present. The night was falling quickly, and the queen would be missed.

"Your ghosts cannot protect you," Laoise called from where she now stood at Eimear's side. As the wind picked up, it turned her bronzed curls into a maelstrom, though the deep eyes bore down upon Gruoch through the tempest of locks.

Gruoch said nothing, though her blood ran cold in such a sudden and palpable way that she felt the shift in her body as though she had been lowered into freezing water.

Keeping her silence, Gruoch held the knife tightly as she gathered the reins around it and urged her pony on.

Gruoch knew the path to Eimear's cottage as well as any in Crown Hill. She had visited often and felt sure of the direction home. There was, however, no explanation she could think of that offered any comfort when Gruoch found herself backtracking and losing her way momentarily as she travelled back towards the keep. By the time she had reached the edge of the forest, night had fallen, and the route was dark.

As she left the heavy canopy of the trees, Gruoch was pleased to see that the sky was alive with starlight and that the moon itself was not hidden behind cloud cover. The pale and delicate light from these celestial bodies shone down, illuminating the fields before her. She could make out the dark silhouette of Crown Hill but a short ride away.

Gruoch heard the sound of the horse before she saw the rider, and her hand flexed suddenly around the small knife she still carried. She held her breath as her body froze, and she considered the danger she had put herself in by coming out so late in the evening unaccompanied. She had been too full of her righteous anger to think things through and recognize she was unprotected and alone. While she might be able to see her home, such sights offered no genuine or legitimate comfort or safety.

She held the reins taught and kept the pony still, and he nickered at the approaching horse. Gruoch felt the tension in her lungs relax slightly. Though her eyes had not yet identified the rider, her pony had recognized the horse as a fellow stablemate and had called out. The horse slowed to a canter as it approached, and it whinnied in response, causing her overly social mount to stamp a foreleg impatiently.

The rider slowed to a trot, and he peered in Gruoch's direction, bringing up a hand in an uncertain and cautious greeting. Then, a familiar voice called out.

"What rider is there, by the forest mouth?"

Banquo.

Gruoch sighed happily, the tense dread she had felt upon his approach melting away. She raised a hand as well, waving happily toward him.

"Here's our chief guest!"

"My lady Gruoch?"

The trotting horse was brought to a rough and sudden stop, and it shook its head in Banquo's firm grip. As he made his way closer, Gruoch recognized her husband's dear friend and smiled brightly at him.

"I am so glad to see you," she confessed, prepared for him to reproach her for her terrible judgment in riding so late. "The day slipped away from me, and I was frightened upon meeting another rider so far from the Hill."

Banquo nodded though he did not speak right away, and Gruoch was grateful once again for his silence and stillness. He allowed her the time to calm her heart and collect her thoughts before taking the conversation any further.

"Would you be opposed to my accompanying you back home?"

"Please," Gruoch said sincerely. "I am glad for this stroke of good luck and am happy to be there when my husband welcomes you back to our home."

Banquo nodded, and Gruoch clucked to her pony, nudging him with her heels. He walked on amiably, and the two mounts walked along pleasantly, and their riders laughed when the pony took a sudden step into his companion, bumping Gruoch against Banquo's leg.

The two rode amiably in easy silence, the low whinnies of the horses and the sounds of the fields around them the only breaks in the stillness of the night.

"I am glad that I came upon you," Banquo said suddenly, and Gruoch turned slightly to look at him. "There was something I had meant to bring up to you, and I was struggling to find the right time."

"Oh?" A litany of small jokes and teasing gibs came to her mind, but something in Banquo's tone kept Gruoch's tongue in check. It was now her turn to hold her tongue and allow him the space to collect his thoughts. Gruoch looked ahead as they rode, watching as the lights from the torches that adorned Crown Hill burned ever closer.

"He has gotten worse. I've noticed, and so have some of the other lords. Worried men talk. You know of what I speak."

"I do."

"Then you know that it is dangerous for Mac Bethad to let this get out of hand," Banquo continued. "If the men learn that he is prone to such moments, that they have plagued him for years, we might find our supporters cleaved in number. It was always crucial that word of his affliction not get out, and I fear that something has happened to cause his grip on his lucidity to loosen and falter." Here was the second person in the span of an evening to suggest that some singular event or occasion had caused the rupture in Mac Bethad's mind and was responsible for his declining health.

"I hear your words Banquo, and I know they come from a place of love," Gruoch began, choosing her words carefully. "But I think that Mac Bethad is simply plagued with the stress and hardship that come to any who wears a crown responsibly. Mac Bethad is King, a role he never dreamed of, and he loves his countrymen. However, their love and their welfare weigh heavy on him."

Banquo's face twisted in a tired and somewhat dry smile. "You have learned much of queen craft these past few months, Gruoch. You speak like a seasoned courtier and politician."

"My words also come from a place of love," she replied. "Banquo, there are none who love Mac as we do. None who would protect him as we do."

Banquo nodded, and though Gruoch could tell he was still unsatisfied and desired a more direct answer, he did not speak again. They rode on in a tense silence that neither could break with adequate words until Gruoch felt she might burst from the way the heavy silence echoed around her.

"We must make haste if we are to arrive before the banquet is set," she said aloud, finding a safer and easier topic to carry them the last few miles home. Gruoch stole a glance at the darkening sky above and watched as heavy clouds circled through the fading beams of the sunset. "There will be rain."

"Let it come down!"

Banquo's horse shied sharply at the unfamiliar voice that cut suddenly from the woods to the right. Banquo, distracted by his thoughts and his companion's vapid ramblings, was taken by surprise as three men burst from the trees and thickets that ran alongside. His horse reared up in alarm as the first of the men reached for the reins, pulling the animal's head down sharply. Banquo's experience as a horseman had him adjusting and settling his weight quickly, and he managed to keep himself seated. He freed a foot from his stirrup and struck at the stranger's face, catching him squarely in the jaw. The man yelled out in pain but held firmly to the reins even as Banquo tried to pull them away. Gruoch watched mutely as the beast's eyes showed white and its mouth became coated in foam. Her own mount skipped nervously, and she was forced to throw her weight back in order to keep it from taking to its legs in fear.

Banquo turned his face sharply in her direction, and the fear that darkened his features stabbed at her heart like a cold blade.

"Gruoch," he called. "Do not linger here! You must fly!"

Banquo managed to free his horse's reins from the hands of the man who had grabbed at them, and he kicked his heels mercilessly into his mount's heaving sides. The horse could only take a few strides forward before a second man, one larger than the first, took a running leap at Banquo.

It was too dark, and everything was happening too fast. Gruoch did not see what Banquo's assailant held in his large hands as he struck at her friend, but Banquo's sudden cry of pain tore through the evening air, rending the stillness of the forest with the agony it carried.

Gruoch screamed, her body finally waking enough to react with more than frozen shock. As the cry left her, the man who had leapt at Banquo turned his face towards Gruoch and took her in. She did not recognize his face, and its features melded into one another in the dizzying twilight. Only the grim determination and the set of his clenched teeth were familiar to her. She was looking upon a man preoccupied with the thought of blood and death.

She managed to tear her gaze away and find Banquo once more. He was bent over the pommel of his saddle, gripping his horse's mane in desperate fingers as he tried to stay astride. He gasped as though he could not catch his breath, his arm held tightly to his abdomen.

His eyes met her own, and Gruoch felt the sudden promise of hot tears in the misting of her vision. A blurred image of Banquo stared back at her, his groans of pain the only thing to be taken in clearly by her senses.

"Please, Gruoch," he said through gritted teeth. "He will not survive to lose us both. Fly!"

Gruoch's pony gave a panicked whinny as a man appeared at her elbow, grabbing at the reins she had dropped in her terror. She felt one of the man's hands grab at her thigh, at her waist, and her tunic. She saw the sickening excitement in the way her attacker set his mouth to a toothy grin, and as she watched his tongue split his chapped mouth and lick along the lower lip, her disgust and anger managed to break through the shock and fear.

She punched her right hand into the empty air before her, only to cock back the arm and send her elbow crashing into the man's lecherous smile. Gruoch felt soft and rotting teeth give way to the bone, and the man yelped as his hand left her tunic and cupped his broken mouth. Using the few precious seconds she had before her assailant sufficiently recovered his wits, Gruoch's hand made a mad dash for the small leather bag that hung before her saddle. She wrenched it open and thrust her hand into it. Her fingers found the wooden handle of Fiadh's small knife, and they gripped it tightly as she pulled her hand free. Her hold was clumsy, and Gruoch felt the blade slice her little finger as she struggled to right the blade. She felt and heard the intake of the man's breath next to her and knew she was out of time.

Gruoch struck without seeing, the movement guided by some kind of ancient instinct that warmed the sinews of her shaking arm. She felt the hands of murdered women, battered wives, of nameless daughters who had suffered the cruelty of violent men, and it was they that guided her strike. In her mind's eye, Gruoch saw that it was Hertha's clever fingers that covered her own over the hilt, driving the blade home. Her wild aim was true, and the wicked silver knife embedded itself in the fat and soft neck of the man at Gruoch's side.

She forced herself to meet his eyes as they looked at her in surprise and terrible wonder. He blinked only once before she tore the blade free from his throat, freeing a gush of black blood that burst upon the front of his filthy tunic.

There was a pitiful and grotesque gurgle as her attacker gripped his torn throat as though he meant to hold it together and keep his life's blood from fleeing his body. Whether it was from the rasping sounds of a man choking to death on the deluge that coursed from his broken skin or the blood's pungent stench of copper, Gruoch's pony reared up in fright. She was cast forward and barely managed to keep to her saddle as her fingers wove into the mane of the terrorized beast. Gruoch stole one final look behind her as her mount took to its legs and ran for both of their lives in the direction of the Hill's flickering torches.

The alarm was taken up quickly, and Gruoch heard the guards yelling at one another to open the gates for her and to *move! Quicker! Faster!* The heavy wooden maw was pulled open, and she rushed through, blinded by the hair being blown into her face. Gruoch threw herself from her horse as a groom rushed forward to take it in hand, and another caught her arm as she stumbled, feet ready to give way beneath her as they hit the ground. Her knees buckled so violently that Gruoch held tightly to the boy who kept her stranding. He looked terrified as the guards approached cautiously. He thankfully took his leave as Angus made his way to her.

Gruoch could have sobbed in gratitude to see the old soldier limp towards her, and she grabbed at his upper arms as his hands cradled her elbows. For a moment, she felt a little more solid as she stood supported by him. Angus' clever eyes looked over her quickly, and in the light of the torches and sconces, Gruoch became aware of the blood that coated her tunic and hands.

There was blood on Angus' sleeves where she gripped his forearms. Gruoch stared at it in wonder, forgetting herself in the stain her fingers left behind. A vision came unbidden of a night when her hands had been coated in such a way, the memory of when she had gripped a different dagger that had also been drenched in the blood of a dangerous man.

"My queen?"

"My husband," Gruoch gasped. Every lungful of air was painful. "The king. Bring me to the king."

Angus nodded, his questions bobbing unanswered in his tight throat. He waved away a few of the soldiers that had approached tentatively to where they stood. He offered her his arm, and Gruoch took it, leaning gratefully. Her legs felt as though she were wading through cold and rushing water. He led her carefully to a side entrance, far from the main doors into the tower. She shivered when they came to a stop, wrenching her arm from his in order to throw them around herself instead, casting frantic glances into dark corners. She knew nothing in the world could harm her in Angus' presence, but the stench of cold and sweaty men was suddenly overwhelming, and the firelight threw strange and violent shades onto the stone walls. In her agitated mind, each was the man she had struck, come now to avenge her mortal blow.

Angus and Gruoch made their way into the tower and into a torch-lit hall. The few guards who patrolled there hovered, unsure whether to leave their queen in such a state and return to their posts or stay and attempt some display of comfort and reassurance. They were noticeably relieved when Angus waved them away impatiently.

"Your Grace, are you hurt?" Angus took her in carefully, though he did not dare to lay a hand on Gruoch as he inspected her for wounds.

"He is dead, Angus," she said as the older man looked her over. He stopped suddenly at the words and exhaled slowly. He lifted one gnarled and weathered hand and lay it softly against her cheek. The callused palm was so familiar to her at that moment and so like the hand of her father that the tears Gruoch had managed to hold in check thus far threatened with renewed vigour to spill themselves upon her pallid cheeks.

How was it that she still had tears to shed? Her body felt like a husk, one dried and emptied by a scorching wind. When Duncan had died, it had not been at her hand. Though she carried his death within her, this nameless stranger pushed his way to the forefront. With every desperate beat of her heart, Gruoch saw the crashing froth of blood and heard the wretched rattle of death.

"And you are not." His words were simple, and his tone was soft. Gruoch closed her eyes and saw her father's great shoulders and his auburn beard and felt the first tear break free.

She opened her eyes at the sound of approaching steps, and Angus took a respectful step back as the king made his way toward them. Mac Bethad appeared in the hall, his eyes narrow and hard, with a face carved of stone. When he saw her, Gruoch saw the colour drain from his face, and she remembered her blood-slicked clothing and her red hands. Her husband broke into a few running strides before reaching her and taking her into his arms. Gruoch hid her face in his neck and threw her arms around his shoulders while he fought gently to peel her away to better take her in.

"Gruoch," he said, pulling her hands away and gently trying to take a better look at his wife. "What has happened? Are you hurt?"

Gruoch gasped and struggled to catch her breath, and Mac Bethad cupped her face in his hands, his thumb stroking her cheekbone in an effort to calm her. Angus stepped forward and whispered something indecipherable in Mac Bethad's ear. The dark blue eyes considered his friend's words carefully as he listened, and after Angus stopped speaking and took a step back, Mac Bethad nodded quickly to him. With no further hesitation, Angus bowed his head once and spun as quickly as he could manage on his lame leg before walking away with the authoritative set of a man used to taking control in a crisis. He motioned for the guards to follow, and Gruoch let out a cry of relief as she watched them move quickly into formation behind the seasoned general.

Once she was alone with her husband, Gruoch forced herself to take a deep breath. Her mind raced with a thousand words, yet there was nothing she could think of to say. Mac Bethad looked on expectantly, and she knew his patience was fraying. How could she tell him what had happened? To recall such things would be to take them from her nightmarish thoughts and settle them firmly into reality.

Gruoch's mind played back for her the terrible scene of the attack, and she saw Banquo fend off one attacker only to be struck by another. Though her eyes were open and she took in the comforting sights of home, a feeling of panic overtook her. Her chest was suddenly tighter than she could bear. Her gasps suddenly lacked air as the world around her stilled and slowed.

"I am here," Mac Bethad whispered, brushing the wild and loosened locks of hair away from Gruoch's damp brow. "I have you."

"I am a coward." Her voice trembled, and her teeth chattered desperately within her mouth. Gruoch shook her face free of Mac Bethad's gentle hands and pulled at the hair at her temples. "I did nothing but stand by and watch as they lay waste to him!"

"What are these words, love?" Mac's eyes searched hers for some explanation for her wild appearance. His words took on the tone of a man used to giving orders and being obeyed. As hard as his voice became, his hand was all the softer as it reached for hers. His fingers moved over Gruoch's and pulled them carefully from her hair. "Tell me what has happened."

"Banquo…"

"What of Banquo? Gruoch, speak plainly, for God's sake!"

She forced herself to look into the troubled blue of his eyes as she spoke. His brother had been taken from him. The least Gruoch could do was look him in the eye as she told him that she had watched it done.

"I was making my way home from Eimear's cottage, and I met with Banquo. We were riding home when we were suddenly accosted by men rushing from the woods."

There was a storm in Mac's expression then. Neither spoke, choosing instead to clutch each other desperately in the echoing hallway, where the jovial noises of feasting bounced down the stone walls and resonated in their pounding heads.

"Where is Banquo?" The dry whisper was almost too low for Gruoch to hear, and the hand at her hair suddenly tensed, sliding slowly until Mac Bethad's long fingers circled her neck. He did not tighten his grip, though a part of her that Gruoch had long thought dormant stirred and relished the idea of a long and uninterrupted sleep.

"He was struck," she said softly. "I am sorry, my love. He begged me to run, and like a coward, I did."

"Do not speak of cowardice," he hissed, eyes shining. His hand, though shaking, still did not clench. "Speak instead of these men. Did you know them? Did Banquo?"

"I have never seen them, and I cannot think why they would attack us other than to rob us. Perhaps they were desperate and saw a rich lady and her escort as a mere hurdle between them and a full purse." "Malcolm still lives," Mac Bethad spat through gritted teeth. "And I have watched that very thought turn through your mind and torture you since he left our shores. So do not speak now of desperate bandits. This is Malcolm's doing. He has sent vipers into my home to strike at me and those I love."

"You think Malcolm hired these men?"

He seethed at the question. "I have no doubt."

"But Malcolm is in Hibernia," Gruoch began, mind racing with the possibilities. "Moray and Alba believe that he killed his father and that he is a traitor. Who on our shores would do such work for him now?"

"Malcolm feels no doubt that I have ripped Moray from his grasp, and men such as he cannot bear the insult of a loss."

"The men of Moray are not loyal to him."

"Men can be bought."

"But…"

"Have you forgotten your anger? Your rage?" Mac Bethad's fury coated his voice with a thick rasp that made her blood run cold. The fierceness in his blue eyes had faded and had been replaced by the bloodshot cruelty that had adorned them on the field of battle. Gruoch saw before her the man who had struck fear in Alba's enemies and sent warriors retreating across the icy seas. "Have the months taken from you those early and vicious passions that soaked your soul in the blood of your father, your servant, and your son?"

His words stung sharper than his palm ever could.

"Tell me," he said through a broken intake of breath. Gruoch saw him shudder in revulsion as his hand dropped quickly from her face. "Tell me how you came to be covered in blood. Is it his?"

Gruoch took a step back, and Mac Bethad let her go. She found she was grateful for the space.

"It is not." The image of Banquo's arm gripping his stomach flew once again through her fevered brains. "He was still astride when he was struck. I was but a few paces away on my own horse when another man grabbed at my reins. I managed to strike him with my elbow, and then I, I took…." Gruoch steeled herself against the strength of his gaze. "I took a small knife I was carrying and buried it in the man's throat before tearing it free again."

Mac Bethad closed his eyes and turned his face from her, and Gruoch felt her heart rend itself as he did so. Bile rose into her gorge, and the room suddenly stank of panicked sweat. Her hands clenched themselves into fists at her side in an effort to keep from grabbing for him, and her every nerve burned at the look of pain that had washed over her husband.

"The first kill is one that remains with you," he said finally, "even after all those that follow had bled into one. Will you be alright?"

*Will* you be, not *are*.

"It seems like I shall ever be anything but a proper wife to you," Gruoch said. "You must have sinned greatly in some other life, my love, to deserve a wretch such as I."

Mac Bethad looked at her as though for the first time, as though Gruoch were some stranger that had fallen into his path. For a brief moment, there was no love in his gaze, only mounting incredulity and anger.

"I will not allow you to speak so about the woman I love.'

Then, as though to save himself from plummeting into grief from which he could not crawl out, Mac Bethad reached for her once more, hands open.

Gruoch ran to him, unashamed to do so.

He kissed her cheeks desperately, and her hands clutched at his arms as though for purchase. Gruoch lay her mouth against his neck, against the pulse point, and Mac Bethad jerked slightly as she did so. He pulled away, only to push his fingers into her hair and bring her lips to his. The kiss was angry and fierce, and Gruoch let him bruise her. She didn't fight him when he bit her lip and drew blood.

The salty tasted drew him back to his senses, and Mac Bethad broke the kiss and laid his forehead against hers. His chest heaved with effort, and Gruoch lay a tentative hand over his heart, feeling its rushed and frantic pounding.

"My mind is full of scorpions," she breathed.

"We will go in," Mac Bethad said, slowly squaring his shoulders and raising his head. "We will tell the lords your story and wait for Angus to return. We can only hope that he manages to arrive in time." There was a hint of hope as he spoke, and Gruoch understood the words he was too terrified to say aloud.

"I can only hope that they find his body and give us the chance to bury him with honour," she replied.

Mac Bethad nodded at her words, and Gruoch felt her heart twist as though it had been run through with her knife. They both knew that Banquo would not be found alive.

Later, when the body had been recovered and prepared, Banquo was given a hero's funeral. As he was laid to rest, Gruoch had stood at the grave and wept the tears Mac Bethad was unable to shed. And once they were alone, she cradled him to her breast as he smothered his screams and sobbed in the darkness of their bed.

# PART FOUR
## -A VILLAIN-

# TWENTY
# WHAT'S DONE
# IS DONE

G ruoch did not return to Eimear's cottage again, though Mac Bethad often did.

Whatever subtle shift Gruoch had felt in their relationship after what she had witnessed between Mac Bethad, Eimear, and her daughters had become a gulf. Gruoch felt herself scrambling precariously along an edge that seemed to crumble under her feet. There were days when things felt almost normal and easy, days that held gentle touches, smiles, and long conversations over meals. There were days when Mac Bethad could barely look at her and seemed unable to fixate or concentrate on very much at all. He would mumble and stare off into space, and she grew nervous to see that the lords were becoming more and more aware of these days and had taken to whispering among themselves. As Mac Bethad retreated further into these moments of delusion, the whisperers grew brazen, and it wasn't long before the words themselves ceased to disappear before she came into earshot. The gossipers, Gruoch realized, wanted her to hear.

This disrespect was a problem that would need to be addressed. Though it was so crucial to Mac Bethad that they were beloved of the people, it would not do for those who gossiped to forget their place.

Gruoch was still their Queen. She had not forgotten.

Mac Bethad never spoke again of Banquo, at least not on purpose. After his body had been found the night of the banquet, a call had been sent out for the men responsible for the murder. Banquo was hailed as a hero for having died defending the life of his queen, and while men such as Angus and Lennox still spoke fondly of his bravery and honour, Mac was never again able to utter the name of his closest friend.

Though there had been no intelligence to suggest that Malcolm had returned to Alba, the weight of this shadow still moved through Crown Hill, crushing out whatever meagre light Gruoch managed to kindle within her husband. Mac Bethad and Angus were convinced that Malcolm had hired the assassins that had killed Banquo, and Angus had suggested that the order could even have been made against Gruoch's life since it was no secret that she was free to travel from the Hill. As she watched Mac Bethad consider this, Gruoch felt her freedom slip from her, aching in a way familiar to how soldiers described the pain in phantom limbs.

A few weeks after Banquo had been laid to rest, Mac Bethad suffered a night terror the likes of which Gruoch had never seen from him. She awoke to the sounds of mumbling in the stillness of their chamber, and she realized quickly that he was thrashing his arms outside the furs and covers. Still hampered by the fog of sleep, Gruoch reached out to gently stroke his arm and pull him out of whatever dream had so captured him.

As soon as her hand had stroked the skin of the forearm that was held rigid and stiff above him, Mac Bethad brought his other hand like a vice to her wrist, moving so quickly that Gruoch, still half asleep, was unable to pull it away.

His eyes snapped open as he propelled himself up, and before she could register what was happening, Mac Bethad had pushed Gruoch back onto their bed as he rolled over her, one hand still clamped painfully around her wrist while the second locked itself around her throat.

"If I stand here, I see you!"

His voice was guttural in his chest, and spittle flew from his mouth as he leered down at her. Though his eyes were open, Gruoch saw no recognition there. Instead, they were clouded and dark as though he were seeing something far away and difficult to discern.

"Mac…." she managed to choke out. "Please." "What man dare, I dare. Let the earth hide you and quit my sight!"

The hand that wasn't in her husband's iron grip came to grab at the fingers around her throat, pulling desperately at the strong fingers that encircled it. It was like pulling at a tree to rend it from the earth; the roots held on desperately.

As her panic mounted, Gruoch forced herself to think. Mac Bethad, though he looked out with open eyes, was clearly in the midst of some terrible dream or, worse, one of his fits. She knew that whatever image now danced and moved before him was enough to fill his mind with terror. Had he been himself, Gruoch knew that her husband would have never raised a hand to her. This man, who pinned her down and threw daggers from his eyes, was not her husband.

Gruoch struggled to bring a hand to his face, gently cupping his stubbled cheek with her palm while she gasped for breath, fighting the instinct to claw at the clouded eyes.

"All is done," she managed to whisper. "You look but on the one who loves you."

The hand around her throat grew only tighter, and Gruoch's vision suddenly danced with black stars as a wave of nausea washed over her. Mac Bethad brought his face closer to hers as he had many times before, but instead of an intimate kiss, his lips delivered a wolfish snarl as he bared his teeth.

"Do not shake your gory locks at me! Leave me, you horrible shadow!"

Gruoch's chest burned as her lungs sought air they could not receive, and she knew that if she could not wake him, her husband would kill her before coming to his senses. Mac Bethad had only ever been a protector to her. He had given her purpose when she had given up on her life and had ignited a desire and passion of which she had never dreamed she was capable. In a way, it seemed fitting that he who had set the fire in her to burn would also be the one to snuff it out.

Though she could not turn her head, Gruoch's eyes fell past Mac Bethad's hulking form and found the room's dark corners just past him. As her vision grew feeble and unclear, Gruoch saw Hertha leaning against the hearth. She stood tall and proud as she ever did, and her hand clasped that of a small and chubby boy who stood solemnly at her side. Neither smiled as they looked at her, but Gruoch's heart swelled at the sight. Her ghosts had not forgotten her, and they would be here to take her and guide her to them when Mac Bethad finally succeeded in stopping her breath.

*It is as Fiadh said*, Gruoch thought to herself in a moment of mortal euphoria, *My ghosts cannot help me*.

She closed her eyes and felt her lips curl up into a smile.

Though her lungs gulped gratefully when the hand around her throat suddenly loosened, Gruoch felt a strange twinge in her heart as the blood began to circulate more steadily once more. The stars and spots behind her eyes faded away, and her mind became conscious of itself once more. But, when she opened her eyes, Hertha and Lulach were gone. Instead, Gruoch saw only Mac Bethad's terrified face, his expression suddenly sharp and clear in its pain as he looked down at her in fear.

"Gruoch," he said desperately. "*Mo lasair*, please. I am so sorry. Please, look at me!"

Gruoch struggled to focus on him and squinted in the dim light to sharpen the edges of his face, which still seemed dulled. As she took a few deep and painful breaths, his features came into focus, and the look of horror etched into his features was acute.

"Mac?" Gruoch's voice was hoarse, and it pained her to speak. Her throat throbbed in the sudden release of pressure, and her tongue felt clumsy in her mouth.

Mac Bethad's heavy body was suddenly no longer over her. He settled himself next to his wife on their bed and gently helped her sit up. As Gruoch managed to come up unto her elbows, Mac Bethad guided her to his chest, taking her into his arms and cradling her against him. He held her there for a moment as silent sobs wracked his body, one hand smoothing her hair. Gruoch lay her face into the crook of his neck and breathed him in, taking in the stench of his cold sweat. His skin was clammy, yet it felt flushed and fevered. Gruoch said nothing as he rocked her once, pulling her against him even tighter as though some errant wind might take her away.

Mac Bethad finally broke the heavy silence, bringing his lips against her temple as he spoke.

"This night makes me strange. My love, I could have…. I almost…."

Gruoch sighed against his throat and gently peeled herself away from his chest to better look him in the face. His arms loosened and allowed the movement, though they did not fall away. She was held in the gentle circle of his embrace as she took him in. His eyes were sunken, and there sat in them an unfamiliar glaze of pain. His gaze travelled from her eyes to her throat, only to close once more at the sight of the marks she could feel beginning to bloom there.

"What's done is done," Gruoch said to him gently. "You had gone away, but you are here now."

Mac Bethad kissed her, his mouth moving hot and hungrily against hers. What little air her lungs had managed to take in didn't feel like enough, and she struggled to breathe as his lips moved unrelentingly. They kissed her mouth before moving along her jaw and behind her ear.

However, they moved more softly as they trailed a light path down the injured throat before placing a final kiss in the small hollow between her collarbones.

"What did you see?" Gruoch asked the question gently.

Mac placed another soft kiss on the top of her breasts as he shook his head gently.

"Be innocent of such things, Gruoch," he said, his voice still trembling. "I would not burden you with such visions."

"Then let us not speak of it again," she said, closing her eyes as Mac Bethad's hands began to move.

"Let us not talk at all," he said as they fell back against the pillows.

What remained of that night was spent in a desperate effort to distract one another from the ghosts that haunted the backs of their minds, as well as the pain that harboured in Gruoch's throat and both of their hearts.

# TWENTY-ONE
# FURTHER INTO THE DARK

Ross arrived the following morning.

Mac Bethad had risen and gone before Gruoch woke, and the bed was cool where he had left the covers thrown back. She took a moment to wrap them more tightly around her body, the warm wool and fur soft and welcome on her bare skin. A shiver shot through her body despite her wrappings, and Gruoch knew that the source of the cold she felt was somewhere deep within herself and not in the bedroom that was slowly filling with morning light.

Would Mac Bethad remember his dreams from the night before? Would he tell them to her, sharing with her as he once had his every thought or worry? She had still not managed to conceive of how deep Eimear's influence had sunk or whether Fiadh's silver eyes still flashed through Mac Bethad's troubled mind.

Still, he had used his own name for her. Last night, Gruoch had been *mo lasair* once more.

She forced herself to rise from the bed and seek out her tunic and leggings. Once she was dressed and her hair was suitably coiffed and tamed, Gruoch made her way down the busy halls and the wooden stairs to the main floor as servants passed by quickly, bowing briskly in deference to her as they went about their duties. She paid them little, if any, attention.

She intended to find Mac Bethad and see if whatever bridge had been hastily erected between them the previous night still held or if the weak foundations had been torn asunder with the rising of the sun. Gruoch knew that some meetings could only take place in the cover of darkness when the promise of sleep to come offered an illusion of impermanence.

She would only know the state of her husband's mind once she had managed to track him down.

Gruoch made her way to the great hall, feeling encouraged as she approached by the echoing sound of loud male voices. Angus' rasping burr was first recognizable, quickly accompanied by the familiar tones of Ross' anxious voice. *If these two were meeting to discuss something that merited raised and worried voices*, Gruoch thought, *it is all the more likely that Mac Bethad is among his friends.* As she broached the entrance to the hall, Gruoch allowed herself the fleeting hope that Mac Bethad was indeed a participant in this discussion and not merely its subject.

"Then Mac Duff lives in disgrace."

Her husband's voice, strong and sure, welcomed her as Gruoch stepped into the hall. Then, she saw him, his back and shoulders turned to her from where he stood by the hearth. Angus stood nearby, arms crossed over his chest and face grave and troubled. Ross paced a few steps away, worrying a path into the floor. His movements were jerky and quick, accentuated all the more by the stiff stillness of Angus and the king. Another man, unknown to her, stood next to Angus. As she watched, the stranger held out a piece of correspondence to Mac Bethad, who took the paper from him slowly as though he were reluctant to touch it.

"It is as you say," the unknown man said. The dust on his clothes suggested he had been sent specifically to deliver the message Mac Bethad now held in his trembling grasp. "The traitor has fled to Hibernia to meet with the king-killer, Malcolm. There, he stirs the men of the isle with talk of your treason and false kingship. He promises rewards on Earth and in Heaven to any man who helps him win Moray back into Alba's dominion."

"He means to raise Hibernia against you," Ross spat. "Our people are tired, and they yearn for peace. The war against the Norsemen has but reached a fragile end. They will not want to pick up their swords, having only just put them down."

"They will fight to protect what is theirs," Mac Bethad said quietly, though his tone belied no weakness or give. "They will protect Moray as they have always done."

"There is talk that Siward will join with Malcolm and is amassing the men of Northumberland to march against you."

"He is loyal to Alba," Angus said thoughtfully. "No doubt it gives him little pleasure to see a new sovereign with whom to reckon."

"Malcolm is rewriting history," Mac Bethad said, his head still bent over the letter. "He is giving me credit for the murder of Gille, which I claim proudly, but also that of Duncan, to whose death which I can attest no such pride."

Her husband's dangerous words snapped her into action, and Gruoch walked briskly into the room, adorning her face with a bright and easy smile. She approached her husband and took his arm gently, nodding at the men around them as they bowed quickly at her approach.

"Such a violent start to your day, my lord?" She stroked Mac Bethad's arm gently, trying to look inconspicuous as she took in the contents of the letter he held, though it was of little use. The script was unknown to her, and Gruoch could make out nothing of the scribbles and symbols upon the page.

"Malcolm has finally declared himself against me," Mac Bethad said, folding the letter and stepping away from his wife to throw it into the flames of the hearth. Gruoch watched as the fire caught the paper and curled it onto itself, quickly becoming indistinguishable ash among the burning logs. "At least this time, he does it with words and not through assassins in the night."

They all stood silent until Angus spoke.

"Mac Duff has declared himself as well. The lords will be waiting to see how you respond to such an attack."

Gruoch looked to Ross, the man least able to hide his thoughts from his expression. She saw him wince and take a shuddering breath as though he knew the following words would come as a blow.

"And such an assault will be dealt with," Mac Bethad answered. "Ross, Angus, you will assemble a small battalion and ride south to Fife."

Angus nodded at these words, but Gruoch could see that there was a pain that suddenly crept into the lines of his face, causing his scars to stand out against the paleness of his cheeks.

"But husband," she ventured, looking from Angus' troubled face to Ross's. "What purpose does it serve you to send the men to Fife? Mac Duff is across the sea."

"He would not have taken his wife or his children," came her husband's quiet and expressionless reply. "Angus, you will give to the edge of your sword any soul in his house that trace him in his line or swear to him their loyalty. If Malcolm has been scheming to kill those I love and those loyal to me, I shall return the favour. And if Mac Duff thinks he is safe across the sea, let it be made clear that Moray, that I, will not let Banquo's murder go unpunished."

"No," Gruoch whispered.

Mac Bethad ignored her and kept his eyes trained on Angus and Ross. "When it is done, return here to me and make it known."

"Such a message would be powerful indeed," Angus began. "But the land cries out for peace. The people have born too much suffering of late. Do not add to it simply to send a message."

"I'll thank you to keep your advice to yourself until you are asked," Mac Bethad said in the same still voice. "You are dismissed."

"Your Majesty…" Ross said before a look of pure rage from Mac Bethad slowed his tongue and left him with his mouth agape.

"Mac," Angus tried again, taking a tentative step towards his king, who seemed to vibrate with a pulse of anger so vicious that the very air around him crackled with the energy. "We say only what a true friend would say. We have ever been loyal, and you know we speak the truth. If Banquo were here…."

"Banquo is dead, and his guts feed the worms of Inverness," Mac yelled, the sound guttural and raw. What disturbed Gruoch most, sending shivers of some dark and primal fear down her spine, was the look of defeat on Angus's face as he nodded. In her mind's eye, she saw a similar look of defeat and bewildered fear on Banquo's face as it had become pale and cold as he looked up at her from where he had collapsed upon his horse's neck. Gruoch closed her eyes, screwing them against the image but doing so seemed only to carve the scene more deeply into her brain until it hung like a grotesque tableau behind the living men she now watched.

Ross moved to Angus, placing a hand on the older man's shoulder. The touch seemed to awaken some clear decision in Angus, who bowed once before departing quickly, Ross at his heels. The man who had delivered the message followed them, clearly eager to be away and gone. The hall was alive with servants and maids serving plates of food and cleaning the tables and floors, but Gruoch could no longer hear their cheery talk or the sounds of their labours. None spoke. It was as though Mac Bethad's anger had sucked the air from the room, leaving them in a suspended state of suffocation as people hurried about their tasks, eager to be gone. Gruoch's ears filled with the heavy echoing silence she had not heard since her days of haunting the very halls of Crown Hill after Lulach's death.

So she stepped before Mac Bethad, not caring if the servants were watching, as she grabbed one of his hands in both of her own. She planted herself firmly in his way, unyielding. She called out her order without taking her eyes off her husband.

"Get out, all of you." Not needing to be told twice, the grateful servants scurried quickly from the hall, eager to escape their master. Once the hall had been emptied, Mac Bethad seemed to shrink. His rage evaporated. With it went his strength, and his shoulders curled in suddenly, making him appear smaller, as though he were trying to hide despite his open position.

"There is no help for it, Gruoch." Mac Bethad's voice seemed far away, and his eyes gazed out vacantly at the room before him. They would not meet hers.

"You cannot do this thing," she said, her voice barely a whisper in its harshness. "His wife and his children are innocent in this; they have committed no treason."

"You do not understand the ways of war," Mac Bethad began, still looking past her into nothing. "Malcolm has struck at my family and my most loyal friends. I shall return the favour."

One of Gruoch's hands left his, and she grabbed Mac Bethad's face, digging her nails into the sides of it. She felt herself growing stronger at the sight of his sudden weakness and surrender. She was filled with a kind of rage that had her trembling, and Gruoch was not shocked to see a drop of blood slide from beneath one of her fingers as it dug into Mac Bethad's cheek.

"There are many who would have had me join Gille's men on the pyre," Gruoch spat. "If my son had still been alive, would you have thrown him too upon the stones for his brains to spill from his head? Where is the honour in killing children?"

Mac Bethad's hand grabbed her wrist, wrenching her claws away from his marked face. He gripped her with bruising strength, and Gruoch felt the bones beneath his fingers grind together painfully. She ground her teeth together to keep from gasping at the feeling, and she refused to step back and instead swung her free hand to slap him.

He caught it easily, gripping both of her wrists and pushed her back a few paces until her back slammed against a wall. Gruoch's head knocked against the stones, and for a moment, her vision sparked and stuttered, but she shook herself into clarity.

"There are no more lines to be drawn, Gruoch, can't you see that?" Spit flew as her husband snarled his words inches from her face. "How can you speak to me of honour as though it would bring back my father or yours? The sodden line of Duncan is a canker to be cut from the Earth."

"You are the hero of your people, the saviour of Moray," Gruoch tried again, grimacing in pain as she spoke. "How can you be so small-minded that you fail to see the future you have assured for those you love? We are on the path of righteousness and justice. Do not allow yourself to fall into darkness."

"What is a little more blood on these hands? I am steeped in it so far that to try and return on my deeds would be as difficult as simply moving forward. And that is what I must do: move forward."

A single burning tear escaped despite her furious blinks, trailing quickly from her stinging eyes. Gruoch was furious with herself at this show of weakness, but the ache in her head, wrists, and heart made it nearly impossible to focus and find the right words.

"You are the one who brought me back to life," she whispered. "You found me in the dark." The hands around her wrists slackened slightly, and Gruoch took the opportunity to free herself gently. A quick glance revealed bruises that were already darkening violent jewels upon each wrist. She raised her hands slowly and lay them gently upon the face that she had scratched and cut mere moments before. Mac Bethad's expression did not soften as Gruoch cradled his head, and his eyes did not close when she lifted herself on the tips of her toes to brush a small and soft kiss on his mouth. "Please," she whispered against his lips. "Let me now bring you back. Don't step further into the dark and further from me. Do not go where I cannot allow myself to follow."

Mac Bethad's breath mingled with hers for the span of a few seconds, and Gruoch dared to hope that his silence was a sign of regret or reconsideration. There was still time to stop Angus and Ross and catch them before they left to put Mac Bethad's terrible decrees into action.

"It is not too late," she whispered into his mouth. "We can…."

"Eimear said you would lack the strength to see this through." Gruoch froze and felt Mac Bethad step back from her, his sudden absence feeling like a rush of cold air against me. "I cannot tell you how I hoped she was wrong."

*Eimear….*

"This is not a question of strength," Gruoch sputtered, shock rendering her voice small and weak. "Mac Bethad, my love, my *husband*, I have given you all I am. I have trudged through the bloody darkness at your side." She reached for the fury that had been pushed down and felt it kindle back into a blaze in her stomach. "Do not *dare* speak to me of my strength as though Eimear would have any idea as to its limits."

He said nothing. Mac Bethad made no further move to touch her, and there was no recognition in his face of their shared burdens, of the secrets that bound their souls. They had killed the man who had orchestrated the deaths of their fathers. They had found a way to each other. They had freed Moray.

*Hadn't we?*

Gruoch did not dare to ask such a question out loud.

"This is finished," Mac Bethad said as he turned and walked from her, his long stride bringing him quickly to the entrance of the hall. "I have other matters now to attend to."

As his words reached her ears, the stranger in her husband's body took his leave of Gruoch without even the most cursory of glances back in her direction.

The next few weeks seemed interminable as Gruoch waited for news of Lady Mac Duff and the fate of her family. There had been no word since Angus' departure, and she and Mac Bethad had lived in an unsteady and tenuous balance of avoidance and unavoidable cold greetings. The autumn winds were brutal, and the promise that early snows would soon fly pushed the inhabitants of Crown Hill to prepare for the inevitable arrival of winter and cold weather.

Gruoch could sense that the unease that she carried had not affected her alone. It seemed as though the pall had covered the entirety of those who lived and worked at the Hill. Mac Bethad's change in temperament had not gone unnoticed, though she could only hope that the news of his order on the lives of Mac Duff's family was yet unknown to those outside of Mac Bethad's trusted circle. She thought of Findlaech, wondering what the beloved Mormaer of Moray would have thought of his son's decisions.

Alane came to her every morning and helped Gruoch to dress, brushing and plaiting her hair. Gruoch had come to treasure these mornings with the older woman, for she emitted a sense of safety and quiet for which Gruoch longed. Though it was not the same blazing love and devotion she had felt with Hertha, Alane had become a motherly figure at a time in Gruoch's life when she thought the desire for such things was well behind her.

The housekeeper no longer scolded Gruoch for the hair that had already come loose from her braid nor for the dark circles under her eyes that betrayed her lack of sleep. The older woman would simply reach out and hold Gruoch close to her when it seemed to the queen that she was at risk of becoming a wraith once more, and her kind hands would bring Gruoch back to herself.

Gruoch remembered no mother but Hertha, and since her death, Alane had kept an eye on her, refusing to allow Gruoch to fade away from grief. She had been ever-present, even when Gruoch had done her best to ignore Alane and push her away.

One evening as Gruoch was making her way to the hall for her supper, she was stopped in her tracks by Alane before even making it so far. Alane's voice was hushed, and her cheeks were flushed with some scandal that brought alarm to her eyes. As Gruoch peered over Alane's shoulder into the hall, she saw her husband seated with a full plate before him. Mac Bethad pushed at the food before him as he ignored a man speaking from his right until the attempt at conversation was dropped, and those seated nearest the king looked at each other uneasily. Gruoch sighed once, annoyed and frustrated that Mac Bethad was still in the grips of his angered melancholy and that, worse still, the servants and nobles were finding it even harder to ignore their king's sour mood.

"Take care of yourself," Alane said briskly, dropping her hands to smooth them down the front of her tunic as she followed Gruoch's line of sight. "And look out for that man of yours. You know what it is to wander into the dark. Keep a firm hand on him; don't let him slip through your fingers."

Gruoch nodded once. "I won't."

"And mind that one," Alane's tone became harsher as her eyes danced away to take in someone else who was approaching the dining hall. "What purpose will she serve you? Surely, we have no shortage of ladies' maids." The queen turned, confused at her friend's words. As she peered over her shoulder, Gruoch felt her stomach drop.

Fiadh walked through the corridor, her pace casual and unhurried, as she made her way toward the hall. Her silver-blonde hair shone in the torchlight, and as she moved, it billowed in a graceful cloud behind her. She moved with the lithe grace of one who feared nothing, ignoring the confused and somewhat unpleasant looks from those assembled nearby. As Gruoch watched, Fiadh strode by, pausing slightly to curtsey as she passed before the queen, making her way over to a bench near where Mac Bethad sat, still refusing to eat.

Gruoch stared openly at Fiadh as she walked, and as though she felt the burn from such a stare, Fiadh lifted her gaze to the queen before offering a small smile. There was nothing demure or subservient about such an expression, and Gruoch read the challenge there plainly. She stepped away from Alane, tossing back her head and walking with an ease and confidence she did not feel as she made her way into the hall.

As she settled into her rightful place on the seat at her husband's side, Gruoch kept her back straight and her shoulders back as she smiled kindly at those who sat nearby. She nodded to a nobleman and his wife whose names she did not know, and they raised their cups in a silent toast. Fiadh sat meekly by, though Gruoch saw her fail to catch Mac Bethad's attention more than once. Gruoch forced herself to keep her eyes warm and to adorn her face with a constant smile, refusing to betray her unease by paying the girl any more attention.

After watching Mac Bethad push a piece of mutton about on his plate, Gruoch shifted slightly closer to him to speak with him without having to raise her voice.

"I am surprised to see Eimear has sent along her daughter. She makes for a generous gift, though I do not think I shall have need of more ladies' maids. Alane has never failed me yet, and I cannot think what I shall set Fiadh to do."

"Eimear thought it wise that the girl stay with us," came his curt reply. "I agreed."

"Surely she can be of more use to her aging mother," Gruoch tried.

"I have made my decision," Mac Bethad said. His tone, though formal, was not unkind. "There is no time to discuss it further."

He did not spare his wife another look before rising from the table and making his way quickly from the hall, ignoring those who stood from their benches and tables as he passed. Keeping her composure and refusing to allow the trepidation to show on her face, Gruoch smiled kindly to those who sat down, confused at the detachment from their beloved and typically boisterous king. Gruoch fought the urge to look once more at Fiadh. She did not need to see the girl's expression in order to feel her sense of victory.

*Let the girl grin and think what she would*, Gruoch thought to herself as she drank demurely from her cup. She had developed her own methods for dealing with those who would dare underestimate her.

# TWENTY-TWO
# A DANGEROUS STRANGER

When the hushed whispers spoke of the death of Mac Duff's wife in the years after it had taken place, Gruoch found the image painted was one so painfully constructed through the eyes of men that it would take every ounce of her energy to keep from tearing at her hair and screaming from the sheer ridiculousness of it all. So when Gruoch remembered how her heart had broken to know of the woman's impending death, it seems fitting that her heart should now carry a rage on the lady's behalf, that men should have not only extinguished her life but also held authorship over the story of her final moments.

Gruoch heard varying tales over the years. Some spoke of a cold and bitter wife who died angrily that her traitorous husband was not there to protect his own when the murderers broke into their home. There were terrible descriptions of walls drowned in blood, of fires extinguished by it. They spoke of halls littered with the bodies of servants and children while the soldiers who carried out Mac Bethad's orders tripped over the sheer number of them.

Or, they spoke of the slaughter of a handful of souls carried out by two or three hired assassins. They described it as though the killings were not the methodical and effortless work of a group of men used to and hardened to killing, who had learned to live with the ever-present threat of death hanging over their heads. Gruoch would laugh bitterly the first time she heard the version telling of Ross' attempts to warn the household, only to lose his nerve in the final moments before the slaughter.

History would forget that Ross and Angus rode out on that damnable day to put Mac Duff's family to the sword. It would be forgotten as well that Ross, ever the dependable solder and errand boy, was the one to report back to Mac Bethad once his orders had been carried out while Angus remained behind to see that the bodies were dealt with.

Gruoch had been walking in the courtyard as she so loved to do when Ross finally arrived with news of his mission. The days were becoming shorter, the winds bitter, and Gruoch was taking full advantage of the sun before it disappeared behind heavy grey clouds of sleet and snow. She felt the warmth of its rays permeating her body, soaking in as much of it into her bones and marrow as possible. Still, Gruoch shivered slightly beneath her fur wrap and bundled it tighter against her body, forcing herself to walk more briskly to keep warm.

When the alarm was given, and the news that riders were approaching rang out, Gruoch stepped closer to the keep as men ran forward to pull open the gates to accommodate the new arrivals.

Mac Bethad would have heard the horns and, if not, would be quickly informed that Ross had finally made his way back with news of Fife. Gruoch had seen little of her husband since their curt discussion of Fiadh's presence at Crown Hill a few days prior. Fiadh had taken up her place, taking full advantage of the distance Gruoch kept. It was not uncommon to see her walking a few paces behind Mac Bethad as he made his way down the halls of the fortress or serving him wine while he held court in the great hall.

Gruoch would have raged at this blatant intrusion into her marriage if she had not noticed more than once that her husband's eyes still found her when she entered a room and followed her whenever she left. And so, Gruoch would let the silver-haired girl play her game. She was no longer in the habit of entertaining the whims of children.

As Gruoch had anticipated, Mac Bethad threw open the main doors of the fortress as Ross and three other riders brought their horses to a halt in the courtyard, both beasts and men steaming in the cold from their apparent exertion. It was clear that the horses had been run almost to death in an effort to return quickly. The men were filthy from the road and the mud, and some still bore faded brown stains upon their tunics.

Gruoch saw Mac Bethad take in the appearance of Ross and the others, a grim understanding painting his features. As he cleared the entrance, she was not surprised to spy Fiadh standing a little way behind him. As though sensing Gruoch's gaze, Fiadh brought her wolfish blue eyes to meet it. There was something unsettling there. Gruoch had grown so used to seeing a silent challenge in the way Fiadh regarded her, but she could have sworn that there was some new meaning or intention in the way the girl looked at her now. It was as though Fiadh had something she wanted to say that she would not risk in the hearing of others.

Gruoch ignored her, pretending to have seen nothing in the way she stared and stepped instead towards Mac Bethad. She reached lightly for his arm, and he did not startle or react as she slipped it through her own, even though they had barely touched in days. She had been busy preparing their stores for winter with the servants and tenants, and Alane kept Gruoch well informed of familial situations and any other information the queen might need to preside over a smooth and efficient court. Mac Bethad had been occupied as well, spending long hours poring over maps and discussing strategy with his generals in the fortress's war room.

Gruoch felt the muscles in his forearm contract, and he gently held her closer against his side. Whatever ground was crumbling away between them, it was still not insurmountable. Though it was becoming harder to do, they had not yet forgotten the way back to one another. The king and queen could still present a united front when called to do so.

"Welcome home," Mac Bethad called out to the men, who had dismounted and passed their exhausted horses off to the stable boys who had come to fetch them. "Come in and out of the cold."

"We will see you fed, and your thirst abated," Gruoch added, smiling graciously. "Come and sit by the fire and find your rest."

Ross approached warily, tilting his head in a bow in their direction before grasping Mac Bethad's arm in greeting. Mac Bethad stepped away from Gruoch to clasp Ross's own arm. The men held their grip for a moment, communicating in that silent and physical way of males before Mac Bethad released Ross and threw an arm around his shoulders. It was a rare glimpse at the carefree and jovial leader he had once been, but the gesture seemed stale and forced, lacking the ease and authenticity it would have held before Duncan slept his final rest at Inverness.

Mirroring her husband's intentions, Gruoch offered a hand to Ross, who took it gallantly under his arm, and the three of them walked towards the entrance, servants scattering and moving aside demurely at their approach. The two men who walked with her paused at the door, allowing Gruoch to enter first, and she led them briskly and with her head high into the Great Room, its hearth already blazing and casting its heat into the cool chamber.

"Your men are not hungry?" Mac Bethad's voice was light, the question casual, but there was something there that still betrayed his displeasure. That Ross would have instructed his men to wait outside, to keep out of the following conversation, was an act tinged with shame and anger. Ross would deliver his message and his account of what had happened, but he wanted no witnesses to his guilt, even men who had helped him to carry out Mac Bethad's cruel order.

"You will find they have had little appetite since leaving Fife." Ross's voice was colder and more robust than Gruoch had ever heard it, anger flavouring it with a spice he had never before directed at his king. "The screams of children make for poor seasoning."

"Then it is done?" Gruoch's question hung heavy in the air, and Ross clenched his fists before responding.

"It is done. The traitor's family has been disposed of."

"And Angus?" Mac Bethad asked his question as though taking stock of supplies.

"He has remained to see that the Lady and their children are properly buried."

Mac Bethad smiled bitterly. "Mac Duff is lucky that my generals are so kind-hearted with traitors. It was not so long ago that enemies to the crown would have burned rather than benefit from Christian burial."

"They are not Gille," Gruoch reminded him gently. "They are not Mac Duff. Do not forget that when he abandoned you, he abandoned them as well."

"So you said before, my Queen," Ross spat at his feet, his eyes fixed firmly at Mac Bethad's feet. "It was easy to think them guilty until I heard the screams of a woman forced to watch as her children's throats were cut."

Gruoch felt her stomach flip, and the onset of nausea was so powerful and so visceral that she almost gasped for breath. She knew the pain of seeing her child dead, but to have been forced to sit back and watch the life leave his body was torture that she had been spared. Her eyes swam with hot and unbidden tears, and she blinked furiously to keep them at bay. She stole a glance at Mac Bethad, whose stoic face seemed carved in stone.

"Mac Duff fled to Malcolm's side, who sits squatting like a toad while he claims to be a king. Let them both rot in the Hibernian shit and mud and let us look to healing our fractured nation now that it has been cleansed of its festering wound."

"There is a wound indeed," Ross yelled, his voice echoing against the walls of the room. He pulled a dagger from his belt and threw it on the ground at his feet. "If only I had the courage to cut it out."

At the sound of Ross' raised voice, two guards entered the room, swords drawn. Gruoch watched in horror as they took in Ross' dagger on the floor at Mac's feet and the look of open hostility on his face. However, when they approached Ross to defend their king, Mac Bethad held up a hand, stopping them in their tracks.

"Get out," Mac Bethad said, the authority ringing clear in his words.

There was the briefest moment of hesitation as the two guards considered these words, unsure how to react. It was this pause that finally broke Mac's composure, and Gruoch watched as the mask of decorum behind which he hid his anger slipped from his face.

"I said get out!" He roared at the guards as they quickly made their way out through the doors from which they had come. Mac Bethad glared coldly at Ross, who returned the aggressive look with as much fervour as he could muster. She had never seen Ross regard Mac Bethad in such a manner. It was as though he were looking upon the face of some dangerous stranger and not upon the man he had loved like a brother and followed without question.

"Say what you have to say," Mac Bethad growled, his body tense as though ready to strike.

"I will!" Ross's voice reverberated through the hall, his words punctuated by the rage that threatened to spill forth. "If only because I think you must hear it and to prove to myself that the man to whom I have sworn my life still has a soul to guide him."

"My lord, please," Gruoch said, trying in vain to calm Ross before he said something that would trigger one of them into saying or doing something from which there could be no coming back. "Mac Bethad is still the man who has fought and bled at your side. He is still the man who avenged Findlaech and brought Moray out of Alba's oppressive shadow."

She thought bitterly then of Banquo, knowing that his absence contributed in no small way to the degradation of her husband's condition and manner. His patience and easy manner were missed, and Gruoch realized now more than ever what a tempering effect he had had on Mac Bethad's mercurial moods.

"There was a handful of guards left to watch over Mac Duff's wife and children," Ross began, his eyes aflame. "They had no reason to suspect that the High King would send his soldiers to break down their doors and destroy what or who was found within.

'Shall I describe for you the shrill piercing of a woman's scream as she is struck down by a stranger's blade? Or how I watched an old woman throw herself upon a kitchen girl before one of your soldiers pierced them both with his sword? The girl was so small that the blade was thrust clean through her back despite the woman skewered before her.

'It was so quick, yet it seemed to go on forever. We carried your orders out perfectly. We left not a groom, not a maid, not a single one of them alive. A retired warrior had chosen to post himself at the door to the lady's chambers. The man's hands trembled so with age that he could barely keep his sword aloft in front of him. I cut him down myself.

'Lady Mac Duff threw herself at me when Angus and I breached the door. She screamed at us, calling us traitors and murderers. She called for her husband and then damned him in the same breath. She'd been bathing the youngest child, a boy of maybe four, and the child stood naked and dripping on the stone floor, too terrified to make a sound. Angus covered the boy's eyes so he would not see it when I drove my dagger across his mother's throat. I tried… Every time I tried to make it as quick as possible. The boy's eyes were still covered when Angus killed him. But the blindfold fell as he fell to the ground, and his eyes had been wide open in death. I see them even now, and I know I shall carry that boy in my heart and my mind until my own death comes to cut me down."

There was silence in the hall.

"You have done what was necessary. Such things must sometimes be done," Mac Bethad said finally, and Gruoch cringed. *How can you say such things?* Her desperate thoughts clashed with the image her mind still held of a smiling man who winked at her and held her in her darkest moments. Her partner.

Ross seemed to read her mind. He stared at Mac Bethad, incredulous and unbelieving. Finally, he shook his head, his tousled and dirty blonde hair standing wildly as he ran a hand through it, exasperated.

"Such things must be done?" Ross repeated the words as though they were in a foreign tongue, strange in his mouth. "Such things should never be done! They are the actions of a man without honour, without pride! They are not the actions of a just and true king!"

"What would you know of being a king?" Mac Bethad's cool voice was alien to her, and Gruoch saw Ross recoil at the tone. They were in the presence of a dangerous stranger, and neither knew how best to proceed. "What would you know of the terrible decisions one must make? You see the crown, the glory, the beautiful queen. Yes," Mac Bethad chuckled then, the laugh dry and eerie in Gruoch's ears. "I have seen you looking at Gruoch with thoughts that carry none of the honour of which you preach." "Mac, enough." Gruoch took a tentative step towards her husband as she debated whether or not to try and lay a hand upon him and create some kind of bridge, a connection, in order to bring him back to himself.

"You have done a terrible thing for your country," Mac Bethad continued, ignoring her altogether. His dark blue eyes were trained on Ross, whose face was slowly losing its colour, the rage that had filled him ebbing away in the oncoming tide of his terror. "A terrible and necessary thing. I am not a man who closes his eyes to the deeds and endeavours of his soldiers. You have done well, and you deserve to be rewarded."

"You have not heard me then," Ross said, and his shoulders slumped, betraying his fatigue. "There is nothing you could offer me that would wipe the stain and stench of all of that blood from my hands."

"What if you could disguise the smell with a sweeter perfume? What if your hands were given something softer to hold, something to help you forget the feel of iron?"

Ross's eyes danced to Gruoch and then away so quickly that she could almost convince herself she had been mistaken in observing him. She glanced at her husband, searching his face for whatever message Ross had gleaned that had escaped her own understanding. But, instead, when she met Mac Bethad's eyes, Gruoch saw in them a pain more terrible than even that which had hung there after his father's death. She saw the resignation and defeat that rotted his handsome features, and a roll of nausea curled its way through her stomach.

"No," she whispered.

Mac Bethad tore his eyes from his wife's and took in the man who had been his friend, who had followed him so long without question or hesitation. Gruoch looked to Ross herself, hoping to see on his face an expression of horror equal to her own. She expected outrage at the idea her husband was suggesting.

What she found there chilled her to the bone. Ross's kind eyes were regarding her, and Gruoch saw his mind working, considering.

"I will not be bartered and handed out as thanks to our soldiers," she gasped, turning once more to Mac Bethad. She strode quickly to him, grabbing the front of his tunic and shaking her fists. "Look at me, damn you! Do not pretend that you cannot hear me!"

"My king…," Ross's unfinished words poisoned the air where they sat.

"I will not be a party to this." Gruoch continued to shake and pull at Mac Bethad's shaking figure, and she was too far gone to care about the tears that had begun to stream down her cheeks. "Mac, please, do not ask me to do this."

Mac Bethad still refused to meet her eyes. His gaze was trained instead unflinchingly on Ross, who still stood there, considering what he had been offered as if the prize were not a sentient being pleading for someone to hear her.

Gruoch's hands slipped from Mac Bethad's chest. Her fingers were unable to find the strength to bend and grasp at the tunic. Then, finally, her knees buckled beneath her, and she slid down before her husband, hands trailing their way down his body until they came to rest on the ground before her. Gruoch lowered her face to the cold stones on the floor, and her sobs became silent, though she felt her body shake in violent spasms as she gasped and fought to fill her lungs with air through her panic.

"Please," she whispered to Mac Bethad's feet, her humiliation complete. She was glad then that Hertha was dead and would never see Gruoch debase and lower herself like this. She would carry this shame with her for the rest of her days in a place as deep and as dark as the pits that held her memories of Gille's body on hers.

"I have destroyed the lives of too many women of late," Ross said suddenly. There was a strain to his words that suggested that he, too, struggled against the threat of an onslaught of tears. "I will not ruin hers as well."

Gruoch's eyes closed in a brief moment of respite from her panic, and relief at his words thawed the ice in her veins. Ross had refused his king's horrible offer and saved his queen from a further fatal tear to her sanity.

*I will remember*, Gruoch swore to herself. *I will remember that he refused when he could have taken what was promised. And I will remember that it was a man I love who made the offer.*

"Take your leave then," Mac Bethad said, his voice a stranger's once more. "I will call for you when I need you next."

They all knew even then that Ross would never again come to Mac Bethad's side. Gruoch was no longer sure that she could stomach it herself.

Mac Bethad followed soon after Ross made his way from the Great Hall, and he left his wife a shattered wreck on the floor.

Gruoch refused the help of the servants, who slowly and cautiously made their way back in once it was clear that the king had moved on. She swatted away their hands and the offer of arms, forcing herself to stand on her own power. When she was finally able to stand, Gruoch smoothed back her hair and ran her hands down her tunic, wiping at an invisible pain as though she were brushing away creases and dust. She watched as the servants gaped at her with wide eyes, and she ignored the whispers at her back as she forced herself to walk with her head held high. Her knees were still trembling, and so Gruoch walked slowly rather than risk faltering or stumbling in her steps.

Having finally reached the second floor, she paused for a moment outside the door to the room Mac Bethad had taken to locking himself into whenever he desired to escape her and the court. Gruoch lay her hand upon the heavy oak before resting her forehead there as well. Though she doubted that Mac Bethad would be in their apartments, there was a part of her that still longed for him and desired nothing more than for him to take her into his arms and make her forget the events that had occurred and the horrible stories that had been relayed. Her head and heart ached with a need to cleanse themselves from the black swell of blood and fear.

Instead, Gruoch forced herself away from the door to Mac Bethad's retreat, and she continued her laboured journey towards their shared rooms, though her husband rarely took his rest there anymore. He preferred, he claimed, to sleep alone since his dreams were terrible, and he had still not forgiven himself for the night he had gripped her throat as though he meant to crush it.

Gruoch's head ached with a sharp and throbbing pain behind her left eye as though some wicked spirits were digging into her brains and scrambling them with a burning iron. She pressed the heel of one hand into the offending eye socket in an attempt to smother the ache with an opposing pressure while she struggled to open the door latch with the other.

The door swung open into a room lit only by the flames in the tended fireplace. The furs and blankets had been turned down for her, and since Gruoch had heard of a young boy with a fever to whom Alane would be tending throughout the night, there was no servant to dismiss when she entered her chamber.

But her room was not empty.

"You look like hell," Fiadh said to Gruoch as the door closed behind her.

# TWENTY-THREE
# HOW VILLAINS ARE MADE

For a moment, Gruoch was a child again. She found herself trapped in the memory of helpless fear, powerlessness, and of feeling frozen within herself.

And as quickly as these feelings overcame her, so were they flushed away by a wave of violent and palpable anger.

"Get the hell out of my rooms." The words were a snarl in the quiet of the chamber.

Fiadh sighed as though she found Gruoch's appearance irritating. She allowed her grey eyes to trail from the queen's slippers and up her legs, pausing for a moment as she took in the fists clenched at her sides. It was then that a smirk broke out unto her pointed features; her iron gaze met a green one.

"I would think you would recognize a friend when you so need one." Fiadh's voice had a musical quality to it, like the soft tinkle of a bell. The lilting words caused another twist of vexation through Gruoch's guts, and her fists clenched all the harder as she imagined wrapping her fingers into the silver of that hair and pulling it from the bleeding scalp.

Eimear's daughter had certainly inherited some of her mother's otherworldly intuition for she had the sense to take her eyes from Gruoch's and to step away from the queen's hearth. She kept her eyes down and bowed slightly to Gruoch, though the latter found that the submissive gesture still smacked of insolence and mockery.

Gruoch's voice finally found her once again.

"If I have to tell you again, I shall drag you from the place myself and throw you down the stairs in the hopes that your neck breaks and they take your body back to your mother."

Fiadh straightened then and stood to her full height. Any play of submission was gone, and she looked upon Gruoch as though she was a petulant child using up the last ounce of a mother's patience.

"Where was this fire when your husband offered you to the lord of Ross?" Fiadh shot out as she glared at Gruoch, her anger clear and apparent. "All you had then were pleas and tears. Why did you not threaten to toss your husband out on his head?"

"You heard? But I had ordered all from the hall…."

"Why are you wasting your time? The traitor king has been killed, yet his son is yet alive, and his every breath is a threat to the people of Moray."

Gruoch's breath was stilled for a moment and struggled to escape her lips in the form of coherent words. If Fiadh had mentioned Duncan to her now, it was because Eimear had told her daughter what Mac Bethad and Gruoch had done. Or, worse still than that, Mac himself had told her.

"What do you want?" The words tumbled jaggedly past her dry lips and Gruoch felt the sharp and ever more familiar ache behind her left eye, the tell-tale sign of a headache that would hound her until she could find a dark and quiet place to hide away. She forced herself to look Fiadh in the eye with whatever regality she could still muster. "Do you want Mac?" Gruoch paused, forcing the promise of painful sobs back down her throat. "Take him then. I am done with him."

The words wracked Gruoch as she uttered them, and she felt the honest finality of them hit her with the pain of a dozen arrows. She felt it in her bones and in the darkest chambers of her heart. The agony of thinking that Mac Bethad was lost to her cut through Gruoch like a heated blade, severing the few fragile strands that still held her together. In that instant, she was a ghost once more, and she felt the invisible weight of Lulach's tiny hand sliding into her own.

"I am done," Gruoch said again in a vain attempt to convince herself that it was true.

The room was quiet as Fiadh considered the words. Gruoch turned from her unwanted guest then, exhausted and craving her bed. She walked towards her mattress, to the furs and covers beneath which she planned to bury herself until she wasted away. She could not take her own life for fear that it would keep her from Lulach forever, but Gruoch would not stop death from coming to claim her. Once she was finally rid of Fiadh, when the wolf girl was tired of torturing Gruoch with her games and her threats, the queen would bar the door and never open it again. She was half-dead already. A week without water or food would surely finish the task.

Let Mac Bethad find her when the servants complained of the stench of death creeping beneath the door. Let him do with her body what he would while her soul flew towards the furthest North, towards freedom and her child.

"We have work still to do."

Gruoch ignored Fiadh's voice and continued her thudding steps in the direction of the bed. Fiadh moved quickly, stepping between Gruoch and her destination and grabbing her painfully around the upper arm. Nails dug into flesh even through the wool of Gruoch's tunic, though even the anger in Fiadh's grip could do little to reawaken Gruoch's resigned flesh.

The lack of reaction angered Fiadh even further, and she forcefully shook the arm she held. The haze in which Gruoch found herself lifted only when she felt the sharp sting of a palm as it connected with her cheek.

Gruoch's teeth knocked together, and there was a pitched buzzing in her ear as her eyes struggled to refocus. She brought a hand to the injured cheek and felt it already warm and tender. Fiadh considered her for a moment, taking in the clarity slowly creeping back into her green eyes before she released Gruoch's arm and struck her on the other cheek.

Gruoch felt her chapped lip split under the assault, and the taste of copper leaked onto her tongue. Her senses had returned to her then, and she felt her skin come alive in a wash of stinging needles. She brought a hand to her bloodied mouth and rubbed away the liquid traces of Fiadh's assault.

"Touch me again, and I will break your hand."

"Stop making promises you don't intend to keep."

"What do you know of anything?" Gruoch spat. "When will you stop speaking in riddles and just leave me to my misery?"

"When I have done with you! When you keep your end of the bargain!"

"What bargain?!" Gruoch was tired and done with this conversation, but the lingering taste of blood and the residual hurt in her cheek kept her grounded and focused. Fiadh had known what to do to keep Gruoch from disappearing. "I owe you nothing, yet you have come to take everything from me. I have already told you that you are welcome to it!"

Fiadh's clever hand snapped towards Gruoch's face once again, but this time she caught hold of the wrist before the hit could land, and she felt a shudder of satisfaction as Fiadh grimaced quickly in pain before taking control of her features once more.

"I told you that you would not touch me again."

Fiadh nodded, and Gruoch released the other woman's wrist. Fiadh brought it quickly to her side. Gruoch noticed the pains she took to avoid bumping it against her hip.

"My mother gave you back your life so that you would help us, not so that you would waste it by snivelling and hiding away in your bedroom like some heartsick maiden." Fiadh's voice was still a melody though the timbre of it was now much colder, and it had lost the warmth of its earlier music. Shocked, Gruoch considered the words. Of everything she could have possibly expected, these were the last words she had thought to hear.

"Your mother thinks she holds some kind of favour from me?"

"You would have died like a stuck pig, you and the bairn both, had my mother not guided you both towards your lives."

"She performed the duties she was hired and entrusted to do," Gruoch said. "If Gille had even suspected that she had not done all within her power to save his wife and son, he would have had her burned in our yard as a witch."

Fiadh snorted in derision at the words, and she took a step back and away from Gruoch. The queen's eyes followed her guest as she made her way slowly back toward the hearth. As she moved towards the table, Fiadh pulled away one of the wooden chairs and placed it near the fire. She returned and grabbed the second, placing it so that it sat facing the first. She lowered herself into the farthest chair and motioned to Gruoch that she should join her.

Gruoch could have laughed at the ridiculousness of being invited to sit on her own furniture, of Fiadh welcoming her to make herself comfortable in her own rooms. Perhaps most impressed by the brazen courage of it all, Gruoch was intrigued enough to move away from the bed and to take Fiadh up on the offer of her own chair. So Gruoch sat, back straight and hands folded in her lap. They sat in strangely companionable silence as they watched the fire as it snapped cheerily within the fireplace. Fiadh seemed to be in no rush to continue speaking as she sat across, sitting very still in her seat, watching as a log was consumed and slowly turned to embers upon its edges.

Finally, she spoke.

"It is good that you see your first husband for what he was," Fiadh said quietly. She kept her eyes on the burning log in the flames, and Gruoch took the time to study her. In the light of the fireplace, she was able to make out the delicate lines at the corners of Fiadh's eyes, as well as the gentle crease between her brows. Not some supernatural wood sprite then, despite her silver colouring. Just a woman.

And, like Gruoch, she was tired.

And she was angry.

"My mother saw you for what you are, for what your handmaid had raised you to be. You were a perfect opportunity and the missing piece we had been waiting to use. Gille was Duncan's man, and Duncan was a blight upon the land. He had been too long in the South and had forgotten the Old Ways and the Old People who had cared for Moray long before the Nazarene monks stepped foot on our island."

"God has always been here, Fiadh," Gruoch replied, feeling a fatigue that hung in her bones. She had not expected to argue theology and lacked the intention and energy to do so.

"Your God is not all gods, yet all the gods are one," Fiadh said, further fuelling Gruoch's frustration. "The Old People knew this, and Duncan had forgotten it and them. The lands were dying under his rule, and the knowledge we had kept faithfully for hundreds and hundreds of years was fading from the world and from memory."

"I swear that if you do not make your point soon, I shall fade away as well."

"There are foolish Christians, and then there are dangerous ones," Fiadh explained, though Gruoch still could not fathom what she meant. "Gille and Duncan were fools, easily guided and manipulated by hypocritical dogma and small-minded beliefs. Malcolm," she paused for a moment as though to make sure Gruoch was paying attention. "Malcolm is a dangerous Christian. He would use the Christ not as a tool for proselytizing and conquest but as a motive for murdering and clearing away those who still held fast to the Old Ways of our ancient mothers."

"You didn't need such theatrics to tell me what I already knew." Gruoch closed her eyes and saw Gille's head severed from his body. The image of it rolling a few feet away after the swing of the sword and the look of terror that still seemed to hang in the empty eyes burst forward from a dark and neglected space in her mind. "You didn't need to bring me here to tell me that Malcolm is dangerous."

"Then you understand why you cannot abandon Mac Bethad." Gruoch opened her eyes and found Fiadh staring at her, leaning forward slightly in her chair as though to facilitate understanding or to force a connection between them. One of her hands clasped the side of her seat so harshly that her knuckles were white.

"You would rather Mac Bethad than Malcolm," Gruoch said aloud. As she spoke, the obvious truth of it struck Gruoch, and she saw the truth of what Fiadh spoke in her frantic expression. Whether or not Gruoch believed her words, it was clear to her that Eimear's daughter believed the things she said.

"Mac Bethad is a good man who has not forgotten his familial ties to the land he protects. He has not turned his back on the spirits and gods who have watched him since his birth and who have protected him on the field. He will not allow the Christians to push us into the darkness. He will not allow the world to forget us."

"Mac Bethad is no longer the man he was," Gruoch said quietly. "He has done something for the love of me that has broken him."

"He did not only kill Duncan for you," Fiadh said, and Gruoch shuddered as she heard the words spoken aloud. These were things that still echoed in her mind and through her blackest dreams, and they had begun to bleed out during her husband's waking nightmares. To hear them so matter-of-fact from an outsider caused a painful tightening of her chest. "He killed Duncan because he knew it was his destiny to save Moray. His love for you merely stoked the fire within him and gave him the strength he had not yet found."

"Whatever he was, it is lost now." Gruoch heard the tremor in her voice, and she suppressed it, forcing it back down her throat. She took a breath and began anew. "None of us are as we were. Love has made villains of us both."

"This is how villains are made, Gruoch. In the wake of a so-called hero's poor decisions." Fiadh released her strenuous grip on the chair, and she reached her hand towards Gruoch tentatively. The queen felt her body release some of its tension as she reached out her own hand to touch the extended fingers before clasping the hand in her own. "Malcolm is not the hero that this land or its people need. History must not be allowed to make that mistake. You must not allow him to make you the villain of your story."

"What do you want from me?" The question was a whisper. "Tell it to me plain."

Without releasing Gruoch's hand, Fiadh slowly lifted herself from her seat and came to her knees before the other woman. Fiadh brought her brow to their clasped hands, and Gruoch felt the cold sweat upon the other woman's flesh as it touched hers.

"There is always a need for strong women when men play at greatness. Stay with Mac Bethad. Guide him and keep him from stepping too far from the path of sanity. We cannot allow him to lose the support of his men and let Moray fall back into Malcolm's venomous grasp."

Gruoch considered Fiadh for a moment, watching the firelight dance on the back of the silver-blonde head. Whether it was the clammy feel of a forehead against her hand or how small Fiadh suddenly appeared as she knelt before her, Gruoch could not tell, but she suddenly saw the wolf-girl as she was. She was just a girl made older by the world. She was not some mystical force to be reckoned with, not some powerful siren seeking to seduce Gruoch's husband and take her place.

She was just another woman who was frightened to lose whatever power she still clung to. Gruoch pulled herself from her chair and knelt as well, laying her cheek upon the crown of the silver head. She stroked the delicate strands, weaving them amongst the burnt red of her own, watching as the two became molten plaits in the flow of the flames.

Fiadh was not the powerful one.

It was her.

"He has lost his way," Fiadh said as though acknowledging Gruoch's silent thoughts. "You must set him back on the path."

"Tell me what you need me to do," Gruoch said. The words were uttered from the place inside of her that still carried the love of a shield maiden and the pride of a father.

# TWENTY-FOUR
# FEVERED DREAMS

Fiadh had argued that the easiest way to give Mac Bethad his strength was to make it appear as though Gruoch had lost all her own. Gruoch had considered this and seen the truth in such things, but to return to that meek and naive child that slunk about behind Gille was an idea she could no longer stomach. What was more, Gruoch had explained to a frustrated Fiadh, Mac Bethad had never loved her for her weakness. If she was to reawaken the man Moray had chosen as a leader, she could never do so demurely.

"He thinks that his suffering is his alone, that the guilt he feels is his alone," Gruoch had mused, saying aloud the thoughts that had plagued her since Duncan's death. "Perhaps the best way to remind him of who he was is to make it clear that he is not alone in his thoughts."

The women understood that they needed Mac Bethad to inspire in his remaining men the kind of love he once evoked in them and that the easiest way to bring about such opportunities would be by reminding him of the man he had once been. There was no man, whether friend or foe, who could deny that Mac Bethad was a brave and tireless warrior who lived his life in service of his land and of his beloved father. They needed to create chances for Mac Bethad's loyalty and heart to shine through the heavy and dank fog that now cloaked his every step. Though invisible to those around him, the miasma that surrounded Mac Bethad was palpable and kept him isolated and untouchable. He was alone even when in a hall full of raucous soldiers and friends. Though none could see what darkness hung about him, the despair held his men at bay, and none dared approach their king.

The sleepwalking was Fiadh's idea. She thought it was the perfect way for them to reintroduce among those still loyal to the king that the true traitor was Malcolm. They hoped to achieve this by one of the most effective means available to them: gossip.

"The easiest way to ensure that everyone in the keep knows a secret is to first call it a secret," Fiadh told Gruoch, trying to convince the hesitant queen to go along with her plan. Gruoch was still unsure. She did not believe so strongly in her skills as an actor, and Fiadh had already underlined the importance of selling a convincing narrative.

"You can do this, Gruoch," she said as they pored over the details and the hints to drop one more time. "After all, you'll only be speaking the truth."

They knew that is was essential that they move quickly before too much ill-will could accumulate and spill out from Crown Hill into the neighbouring settlements. Mac Bethad would need every available man if Malcolm and MacDuff were to be kept away from Moray. And so it was that the conditions were ideal, and the first steps of their plan were put into action.

Gruoch and Fiadh sat together in the queen's room as Gruoch brushed out her hair. It lay heavy and long against her back, and the burnished amber shone in the soft light of the fire. The tunic she had chosen was thin, and her legs were bare and exposed to the cool night air that swept through the fortress. She shivered, both from the cold and from the feeling of dreadful anticipation that she felt at the onset of this latest scheme, this newest play. Though Gruoch understood her role and the importance of playing it well, the lie still sat uneasily within her breast. She had spent so long building herself up to be strong that it seemed alien and foreign to her now to act as though she had forgotten herself in her grief and womanish fears. Fiadh noticed Gruoch's frustrations and warned her against letting them show.

"We need to give the men something else to talk about," Fiadh repeated, her nerves all the more apparent as she regarded Gruoch critically, searching as if for some minute sign of imperfection. "We need to control the direction of this story and make the true villain all the more obvious."

"You needn't keep speaking as though I don't understand," Gruoch said sharply, annoyed with the inspections and nerve-wracking rambling. "Let us have done with this. I am cold, and I am tired already."

Fiadh nodded and made her way briskly to the door. She would ensure that there would be witnesses to Gruoch's excursion and fan their concerns sufficiently in order to encourage them to share them with others. Hopefully, sooner rather than later, all those living within these walls would have heard of their queen's frightening and mysterious excursions in the night and repeat the terrible things she whispered to herself in her sleep.

More importantly, Mac Bethad would hear of them as well.

As she gripped the handle and pushed open the door, Fiadh nodded to Gruoch once more. The queen returned the gesture and watched the wolf-girl slip silently from the room into the dark corridor.

Gruoch waited a moment before taking up a torch that had been left by the fireplace, lighting it by placing the end gently into the crackling flames. It took quickly, and she brought the torch away, making her way slowly and steadily toward the door. Gruoch opened it wide, her torch held out in front of her, and she stepped out. She left the door ajar and made her way into the dark corridor. Her bare feet burned from the chill, but she kept her expression vacant, her stare wide and empty. She could take no risk that an observer might come upon her suddenly and catch her in a wakeful and attentive state. Gruoch allowed her eyes to glaze over and for her face to slacken.

Her steps were slow and methodical in their feigned randomness and disarray. She ran a hand along the wall of the corridor as she went, the rough feeling of the stone keeping her grounded.

The first time she spoke in the echo of the silent hall, her voice croaked and caught in her throat. Gruoch forced out the words, choking on them, as her voice untangled itself and her staged whisper became smoother.

"One: two: why, then. It is time to act!"

Fiadh and Gruoch had discussed what seemingly nonsensical phrases she might throw out and had picked out tiny seeds of truth to plant amongst their deception. Gruoch had resigned herself to let the hearers make of her speech what they would, so long as the necessary details were remembered in the retelling.

"Fie, my lord, a soldier and yet so afraid?"

Step.

Step.

Step.

Then, suddenly, the tell-tale creaking of an opening door. A cough, and then nothing.

"Who would have thought the old man had so much of the darkness in him?"

A shuffle and rustling of clothes and the soft padding of feet into the hallway. Gruoch forced her gaze to remain fixed ahead of her as she walked, the palm that glided along the wall her only indication of space and direction.

"My love, why do you fear who knows it?"

Gruoch winced despite her efforts at neutrality. This latest phrase was perhaps too on the nose. She kept her tongue for a moment and chose to pause, halting her steps and bringing the torch close to her face as though she were studying something in the distance. She took the momentary pause as an opportunity to collect herself and plan her next move.

Gruoch pulled her hand from the wall then and rubbed it vigorously against her hip. Her palm brushed against the thin fabric of the tunic, and she winced inwardly at the feel of its hem sliding further up her thighs as the material bunched in her hand. Whatever a witness might think of her words, it was her hope that her slovenly appearance would sway them to pity. Here was the Queen of Moray, so tortured by concern and love for her war-hero husband that she wandered the halls of her home, clad only in her sleeping shift, hair unbound and feet bare.

*There*. She made out the unmistakable sound of someone walking behind her and a whisper harshly cut short by a second listener, urging the first to silence.

"The thane of Fife has a wife," Gruoch spoke roughly into the dark. "Yet where is he now?" She kept her hand at her side, rubbing at her hip as though to wipe some terrible and repulsive matter from her flesh. "Will his hands never be clean?"

The sound of yet another door opening and a fresh lurching of her heart.

"Malcolm," she growled, the sound a guttural and primal utterance. "What, yet another spot? I tell you again, my father is buried and cannot come out from his grave."

More furious whispers. It was Fiadh's turn to act now. Gruoch couldn't go on and keep up this semblance of disturbed sleep. She needed her accomplice to come to her, to wake her from her fevered dreams, and escort her back to bed.

As though Gruoch's thoughts had summoned her, Fiadh stepped out from a shadow and gripped the queen suddenly by the elbow. The hand that held the torch aloft startled and sent the light of the fire dancing violently across Gruoch's face. She kept her gaze out of focus, staring off into the distance just over her shoulder. Fiadh played her part to perfection and brought a soft hand to Gruoch's cheek.

"My queen?" Her voice was all concern and innocence. "My queen, are you well?"

Gruoch gasped suddenly as though breaking through the surface of some dark water, desperate for breath. She allowed her eyes to focus and cast them about before allowing them to settle on Fiadh's face. She licked her lips, looking slowly about herself.

"Come," Fiadh said gently. "Give me your hand."

"What's done cannot be undone," Gruoch said to her, and a look of surprised alarm danced across the other woman's features. Gruoch was not meant to speak now; she was to allow herself to be guided silently back to her chamber. "Malcolm has steeped Moray in blood. Malcolm has cast the children of Alba into darkness."

Gruoch sighed deeply and allowed her expression to become once more a mask of disorientation. Fiadh placed a hand gently behind her shoulders and guided Gruoch back in the direction of her chambers. As she passed a servant who stood watching her as she went, gaping wide-eyed, Gruoch's heart twisted in pleasure at the sound of frantic prayer.

After the third night of sleepwalking, Mac Bethad called for a healer to come to Crown Hill and attend to his wife, and Fiadh was assigned as her personal handmaiden and caretaker. Gruoch waited, hoping against her better judgment that Mac Bethad would come to her to see for himself what troubled his wife and caused her to wander the halls in the dead of night.

He did not come.

When they were not speaking of the queen's strange and pitiful afflictions, the people of the keep spoke of the treachery of Malcolm's deeds in renewed and fervent whispers as though his very name had become sacrilege before the holy altar of Mac Bethad's destined kingship.

And as Fiadh worked to ensure a future for the Old Religions and its place in the North, Gruoch worked instead to ensure her own.

# PART FIVE
## -A MYTH-

# TWENTY-FIVE
# SOMETHING WICKED

The rains were torrential the day Gruoch learned that Malcolm had landed once more upon Alba's shores.

November had been cruel. The rains had barely abated over the past few weeks, and the sun had been an elusive stranger. The weak rays were insufficient and so scarce that the earth was flooded, and the roads were washed out. Travel had become even more difficult and precarious, and the heavy storm clouds choked out the light, casting Moray into darkness growing near impossible to bear.

The tempers of those living at Crown Hill matched the mercurial weather. Gruoch heard the servants snapping at one another, and she found her patience to be wearing thin. The sounds of their squabbling drove her mad, and she found no quiet corner, even in the enormous keep, that could offer a reprieve from the bickering and snide remarks.

What irritated her the most was the constant presence of Fiadh a mere few feet away and a healer who often trailed after her, keeping a watchful eye on his queen. Mac Bethad had summoned him after the first of Gruoch's nocturnal walkabouts, and she knew that this stranger had followed her through the halls at Fiadh's side as they kept up their ploy.

Five times Gruoch had feigned sleepwalking, moving through the halls, sometimes silently and sometimes brusquely in order to show no pattern or premeditation.

Even though Fiadh grumbled that a sleepwalker would have no fear of the dark, Gruoch found herself unable to travel the midnight halls without a torch or lit candle in her hand. She had never been a superstitious woman and firmly believed that once dead, the bodies of the departed remained wherever they had been laid. Gruoch had no doubts in the finality of death and the promise of the hereafter yet she still found herself staring into shadows and had found grim mockeries of Banquo's face in dark corners.

She told no one that the dark had begun to stare back.

Gruoch made sure to make a convincing show for the healer's benefit, and Fiadh did her part as well, doting on her queen as Gruoch travelled through the castle while it slept. Fiadh assured her that the healer was taking note of her words and that the servants and the inhabitants of the keep had begun sharing with one another the disturbing ramblings in hushed tones.

"More importantly," Fiadh explained, "they speak with renewed vigour of Malcolm's treachery and Mac Bethad's righteous cause."

Gruoch did not dare tell Fiadh that she cared little for how the people regarded her husband. He had shown her the degradation of his person that day when he had offered her to Ross as some sort of reward for having killed Lady Macduff and her children. Whoever he had been when he had kissed her in the depths of her despair or when he had saved her from the mob that had taken Crown Hill, he was no longer that man. Gruoch had forced herself to accept that the bronze-haired rogue whose blue eyes had shone with laughter had died in some quiet and unknown moment. Worse still, it had occurred without her noticing.

"Of course," Gruoch told Fiadh rather than reveal her own secret plans. "Just tell me what I have to do."

Gruoch nodded as Fiadh whispered her continued machinations, only half-listening. It was only more of the same. She wanted Gruoch to continue the sleep-walking charade, to be attentive to Mac Bethad, and to continue to cast their desired illusion over the people of Moray: that Mac Bethad was still the hero who had saved them from the Nords, that he was still the honourable son of their former Mormaer.

As the two women roamed the halls of the keep to remain in the eye and minds of those who lived amongst them and who were charged with their defence, Gruoch took the opportunity to consider the floor plan, to learn where every door led, and to observe which corners and rooms were quiet and unused. She looked upon the halls and rooms of her home not as a welcoming place of safety, but as a trap she knew she would soon be forced to flee. It was only a matter of time before a quick escape would be a matter of life and death. Let Fiadh continue scheming on behalf of her mother and their Old Religion. Just as Gruoch had survived when those around her had been slain, so would she survive Malcolm's inevitable arrival.

Whether Mac Bethad would live was up to him.

Gruoch knew that she could no longer bear the weight of another's life upon her shoulders. Keeping herself alive would be challenging enough. And in the clearest moments of honesty, when the stillness of the night afforded the opportunity to reflect openly within herself, she could admit that the man that she had loved from girlhood was long dead. She was a widow in her heart if not in name.

As expected, Ross did not return to Crown Hill under Mac Bethad's orders. There had been other losses as well. A few soldiers and lesser lords that had followed Mac Bethad into battle for years deserted him after the massacre of Macduff's family. Though their desertion hit Mac

Bethad's pride harder than it did the strength of his forces, Gruoch knew that the blow had still landed heavily against his heart. He no longer walked among them or took any meals in the hall, preferring to shut himself away.

Angus had left the slaughter in Fife and disappeared. As much as Gruoch missed him, she hoped vehemently to never again lay eyes on him if it meant seeing him march against Crown Hill or, worse, dead and cold in the sea of mud outside the ramparts.

Less than a fortnight after news of Malcolm's arrival had reached them, Fiadh made her way into Gruoch's rooms to rouse her from her sleep. She burst into the room without knocking, making her way briskly to the window.

"Something wicked has come," she announced as she dealt with the wooden shutter. She unclasped it, allowing both a faint, grey stream of sunlight and a cold wind into the chamber. "The wicked thing is she that comes daily to waken me and nightly to summon me to my prowling," Gruoch groaned as she turned away from the light.

Fiadh scowled; her sharp face painted in irritation. This outward demonstration of frustration was nothing new to Gruoch. Fiadh considered herself a righteous warrior with a cause to fight for and a reason to continue regardless of how the world was crumbling around her. Gruoch was struggling to find the desire to even rise from her bed.

She had lost.

Malcolm was still alive, and his every breath was a dagger in her heart and a wound on the memory of her father. Duncan lay cold and withered in the earth, but his son lived still. Her vengeance seemed doomed to remain ever incomplete and just out of reach of her grasping hands.

"They say Malcolm and Macduff have settled in Fife, and from there, they plot to overthrow your husband."

"Let them," Gruoch said tonelessly. "I am tired, Fiadh. So very tired."

"You do not have the right to be too tired to do what is needed," she replied, brusquely pulling the covers away from Gruoch as she came around the bed. "We will all sleep when we are dead, but death comes not for us this day."

Gruoch rose slowly to her elbows and lifted herself to a seated position, bracing her back against the wall behind the bed.

"All I wanted was to avenge my family," she began as Fiadh tossed a pair of clean leggings next to her. "Lulach and Hertha. And my father. Mael is dead, and so are Gille and Duncan. There has been so much death already, yet Lulach is still not here. Hertha haunts my every move, and my father rots in the earth under a traitorous charge. I thought that taking from Malcolm all that he held dear would ease this ache, but all I have achieved is the ruination of my husband."

"You give yourself too much credit, Gruoch." Fiadh stopped and stood before the bed, arms crossed and eyes afire. "Mac Bethad is hardly ruined. All he needs is a guiding hand to bring him back to the path."

Gruoch picked up the leggings and threw them at Fiadh. She hissed in indignation as they fell into a limp pile at her feet. Gruoch smiled at her irritation.

"Then you can lead him," she said, still grinning. "Do not think that your desire to do so is not plain to me. We have tried your ploys and sleepwalking plots, and while the remaining men keep a tenuous loyalty to Mac, it is not enough. We are all in need of more certain advice."

Fiadh grew still at Gruoch's words, and the queen watched a serious contemplation dance across the girl's features. Clever silver eyes took Gruoch in, considering some silent question before reaching a resolution.

"Go to your husband," Fiadh began, bending to pick up the discarded hose. She tossed it once more to Gruoch, who caught it deftly. "See what comfort you can give each other in times such as these and mention me not. I have preparations to attend to."

"Preparations?"

"Spend the day with him," Fiadh repeated, more confidently still. "Return alone to your chamber tonight, and I will meet you here. You will have your certainty then."

When Gruoch finally brought herself to seek him out, she was surprised that Mac Bethad was difficult to find. She had sought him out first in Gille's old rooms, the ones Mac Bethad had been using in his desire to avoid even her, but the cold and cluttered room had been empty. A servant who could not bring himself to look her in the eye when pressed had informed Gruoch that Mac Bethad had made his way to the hall. Surprised, Gruoch had excused the servant, who rushed away gratefully.

As she made her way into the Great Hall, Gruoch spied her husband easily enough. He had brought a rough wooden chair away from a table and placed it near the fire, and his studious eyes considered the dancing flames within the hearth. His face was cast into a warm light which set his blue eyes to shining, and for a moment, it was easy for Gruoch to see him once more as she had those years ago when she had been but a child, and he had ridden like a storm into her life.

The hall was empty save a few soldiers breaking their fast and the servants who waited silently upon them, serving up bowls of steaming porridge. A heaviness hung over the room, and those who found themselves under its protruding shadow seemed just as tired as she felt. She was amazed once more that Mac Bethad's condition had such a heavy effect on those who sheltered within his walls.

A few soldiers bowed their heads and called out formal greetings as she approached, though the fatigue behind their formal words made Gruoch feel all the more dismal. Still, she smiled warmly at those who addressed her and walked with her head high. Mac Bethad, having been alerted to her presence, did not turn to face Gruoch as she approached. He remained concentrated on the flames, though he hunched further forward and clasped his hands tightly before him, elbows resting precariously on his knees.

"Your Majesty?" Gruoch curtsied as she spoke, and she watched as Mac Bethad winced at her words and the detached greeting. There were shadows beneath his eyes that hinted at a sleepless night, and the nails she could see had been bitten to the quick. A knuckle or two were raw and bloodied, giving silent witness to his condition. Gruoch felt her heart as it constricted for the briefest of moments in pain before her mind stepped in, quickly replacing any sympathy or love with images of her at Mac Bethad's feet as he offered her to his friend.

*Do not allow yourself to forget*, she reminded herself. *His pain or regret can not mend the tears he has ripped into your soul.*

"You slept well?" His question was perfunctory and formal. The distance in his words blasted her with a bitter chill, but Gruoch forced herself to welcome the detachment. Her every instinct screamed that they were living in a borrowed moment and that things could not long continue as they were. Malcolm would make his move, and they would either beat him back or fall under his sword.

Either way, Gruoch did not plan on being present when the final move was made.

"Like the dead," she replied, relishing the fresh wince that constricted her husband's face.

He sat in silence for a moment longer, and she stood by, offering no pleasantries or comforting talk that might fill the awkward quiet. She was tired of taking on the weight of keeping others at ease. It was easy to keep her shoulders back and her head high when she was not burdened with caring whether or not everyone and everything around her was fine. There was a clear and resounding comfort in finally choosing to play this game as though she intended to win, no longer a peon to be sacrificed as part of a larger strategy.

"There are things that I must tell you," Mac Bethad said finally, rising from his chair and turning to face her. Gruoch was struck by how pale his face appeared and how prominent the dark shadows under his eyes seemed now that he faced her properly. "But I do not want to do it here."

"I stand by your leisure, my Lord." Gruoch kept her voice clipped with the reverence of a servant.

"That's enough," Mac Bethad rebuked, though his voice was still soft. "Meet me in my chambers in an hour."

Gruoch did not move as he walked by her, though her eyes closed of their own volition as Mac Bethad's fingers brushed her own as he passed.

# TWENTY-SIX
# A SHARPER KIND OF ASSURANCE

"Thank you for coming." Mac's voice greeted her as Gruoch slipped through the door to his rooms, as warm as the sunlight that gleamed through the windows. She nodded as she entered and took a quick look around the room. Gruoch hesitated as she moved into the room, surprised at the figure that had taken up Mac Bethad's typical place before the fire.

Angus leaned against the stones of the hearth, arms crossed stiffly over his chest. His weight was shifted off of his injured leg, and it seemed as though there was more grey in his hair than when he had last been at Crown Hill. There was exhaustion painted upon his weathered face that mirrored the fatigue clear in her own expression. Gruoch's heart twisted with a sudden joy when she saw Angus' eyes light up as she walked in. His unexpected appearance filled her with an unbidden and dangerous hope. She had never expected to see him again after the slaughter of Lady Macduff and her children. Gruoch dared look over to Mac Bethad, who stood a few paces away at a table, pouring ale into three goblets.

She hesitated for only a moment before making her way briskly to where Angus stood. He pushed off from the stones behind him as she moved, and he gripped her by the forearms in greeting. There was a smile in his eyes as they took each other in, and Gruoch felt a sincere smile cross her lips, though the light feeling that warmed her was fleetingly alien to her.

"It is good to see you," Angus said gruffly.

"I am so glad to see you again," Gruoch replied. Throwing decorum to the wind, she pulled her arms from Angus' grasp and threw them around his neck. She buried her face into his chest, taking in the comforting smell of wind and dust that seemed to permeate from him. She was struck once more by familial memories, and it was easy to pretend that it was her father whom she held tightly in her arms.

Angus was a dear friend, and Gruoch had missed him.

"There now," Angus said in his stiff manner as he pulled back from her embrace, though Gruoch could tell he was pleased. "Enough of that."

She stepped back and allowed her arms to fall to her sides. Both turned towards Mac as he approached, a goblet in each outstretched hand. Angus took the first, and Gruoch took the second, and they waited as Mac Bethad turned back towards the table to take the third goblet. He lifted it and cleared his throat.

"To Moray," he said simply.

"To Moray," Angus echoed. Gruoch kept her silence but brought the goblet to her lips, drinking deeply.

She choked down the drink. She had still never developed a taste for ale.

"I am glad you are both here," Mac said as he set his goblet on the table next to him. He considered Angus and Gruoch as he stood, and only the constant shifting of his weight betrayed his nerves. "There are things I must say to you and amends I must strive to make."

Gruoch scoffed, and Angus caught her eye. Amends? Whatever Mac Bethad felt he had to say, she wasn't sure she had the stomach to listen.

"Angus," Mac began as his friend inhaled deeply, as though steeling himself. "Whatever anger you harbour against me, I hope your love of Moray will be enough to blunt it. You must know that Malcolm marches against me and that Macduff will no doubt be at his heel." Angus nodded. The seasoned soldier belonged to a network more established and loyal than Gruoch could ever guess. Doubtlessly, he would have heard of Malcolm's arrival before the news had even reached Inverness.

"He comes to challenge my kingship and my power from Alba," Mac continued. "And he believes that he will be welcome to it."

This lucidity, this bold directness, was unexpected.

"I will lay down my life before I allow him to cause Moray any more suffering."

Angus looked sharply at Mac Bethad as though he were trying to find a lie in his old friend's expression. Gruoch searched it herself, weighing the tired glaze in his eyes against the significance of his words. Was Mac Bethad truly willing to awaken at last to avoid bowing at Malcolm's feet?

"I don't believe you," Gruoch said, breaking the silence. "We have done so much to afford you the crown you wear, and for days, weeks, you have been like a wraith in your own home. You have harmed us and your own legacy irrevocably."

Mac Bethad smiled bitterly and nodded. "It is precisely this harm which motivates me now."

"You would have harmed me," she continued, "when you swore to cherish and protect me. What good are your words now?"

"Gruoch," Angus began, walking tentatively towards her. "Let him say his peace."

"If Alba will take him back, let them have a cursed king," Mac Bethad said. "But Moray is free and will remain so as long as there is breath in my body."

The stillness of the two men made her all the more anxious, and Gruoch couldn't help a few paces upon the worn floorboards.

"We are too far North," she began. One step. Two more. "Would you allow Malcolm to move his forces towards Inverness? Towards the people your father gave his life to protect."

"I will not."

"And yet," another three paces, her steps falling heavier than they had. "And yet you tell us that you do not plan on challenging Malcolm's presence in Alba. Are we to believe that you will not concede these lands to that snake once he decides he won't accept a halved kingdom?"

"There will be no concession," Mac Bethad said, his voice stronger than it had been, its edges sharper. "I will not contest Malcolm's desire to take back the title to his cursed land. I never wanted it. All I have ever wanted was a free and independent Moray, and I will tell Malcolm as such. I will bury Findlaech's ghost and the whispers of conspiracy that haunt his memory."

"Would that I could forget my own dead so easily," Gruoch snarled.

"Because I love you, I will forgive you for saying such a thing," Mac Bethad whispered. His voice remained low, and he didn't need to shout for Gruoch's mouth to close on an unspoken retort. "But only once."

Gruoch looked back at him with dry eyes.

Mac Bethad took a deep breath and ran a hand through his greasy hair, sending it tumbling in familiar waves. "I will remain in the North," he continued, "and Malcolm will accept that his power will not cross my border."

"Or?" Angus remained calmest of all, and Gruoch could see the wheels of his mind turning swiftly as he considered Mac Bethad's words. She knew that Angus was already steps ahead, deciphering the next steps and attempting to see the game to its conclusion.

"Or I will kill him," Mac Bethad said simply. "The men are still loyal to me, and I had friends, once, who might return under the right conditions."

"Malcolm will never agree," Gruoch interjected. "You have insulted him, and he is further incited by Macduff's desire for vengeance. He will fight to be named king in Alba, and if he does, he will not rest until Moray is once again within his grip."

"Alba's lords still fight amongst one another to see who will be king," Mac Bethad continued. "Malcolm will not receive a warm reception from them."

"The men will never follow a man who killed his father and his king," Angus agreed, and Gruoch forced herself to keep her eyes away. "Much less one who plotted to kill the Mormaer as well."

"What of my father's men?" Gruoch caught Angus' eye once more. "Are there any left alive? They will not fight for Malcolm if they know the truth of my father's death."

"Most are dead," Angus answered slowly. "But not all. There remain some yet who would ride under your father's name."

Gruoch felt the words fly from her before she could smother them back.

"So, Malcolm is allowed to return to Alba and retake his power? Do we curse the memory of our fathers so deeply that we will allow their murderer to walk unfettered upon this land?"

"All Findlaech desired was to see Moray freed from Duncan's clutches," Angus said after a long silence. Mac Bethad looked down, unable to meet their eyes. "So it is, and so we will ensure it remains."

"And Bodhe?"

"Your father loved you, Gruoch," Mac Bethad said, his voice somewhat hoarse and thick. "He would not want your life to be given over to this endless search for vengeance. And Lulach…" His voice trailed off as Gruoch hissed through her clenched teeth. "Lulach would want you to live a true life, for both your sakes."

"Do not presume to tell me what my son would want."

"There are entirely too many presumptions and not enough solid plans," Angus said gently, stepping towards Gruoch and placing a caring hand behind her shoulder. He remained there as she struggled to calm her pounding heart and control her frantic breath. As though he felt her pulse begin to slow, Angus removed his hand and stepped towards Mac Bethad without looking back. "What do you propose?"

"You will help me then?" Mac Bethad's voice was tinged in hope, and as Gruoch looked at him, it seemed as though a shadow had lifted from behind his eyes. She could almost see the spark that had lit a rebellion and stoked a similar fire within her.

Angus and Gruoch said nothing. It was impossible to think clearly in the midst of Mac Bethad's simmering excitement. Was this really the man who had made Ross the cruellest of offers on her behalf? Was this the man who had ordered his friends to slaughter an innocent woman and her children?

Mac Bethad had shown himself capable of the direst cruelty and a tyrannical desire for vengeance that shook Gruoch to her core. Yet he was also the one who had saved her from the mob who had cheered at her husband's execution, who had held her when she had lost herself in Lulach and Hertha's deaths, who had winked at her in her father's hall.

This inexplicable shifting of moods was as dangerous as anything Mac Bethad had proven himself capable of. Could this man order the slaughter of a woman and her children only to speak of treaties and peace in the next breath?

Gruoch screwed her eyes shut. Would things truly change if Malcolm accepted Mac's terms and let them remain in Moray unmolested?

Could they?

Gruoch could see in Angus' eyes that he was willing to forget Mac's descent into a seemingly temporary madness and that the love he bore for Findlaech's son would carry him through.

As for her, knowledge born of love would no longer be sufficient.

She would require a sharper kind of assurance.

"Take off your mantle and hose and come sit closer to the fire."

Shivering, Gruoch did as Fiadh asked. The sharp air bit at the exposed flesh of her bare legs, and though her tunic was warm and strongly woven, it did little to relieve the chill that clung to her.

"We should bare ourselves entirely," Fiadh said, almost sneering as she watched Gruoch tremble in the cold. "Yet it would not do to have your chattering teeth distract the spirits."

Gruoch moved closer to the hearth and knelt before a large clay bowl that sat in the shadow of the flames. It was filled almost to the brim with clean, still water. Fiadh was kneeling on the opposite side, watching Gruoch closely as she settled into place.

"You must be careful what you say and speak only the truth," she said. Her voice was a harsh whisper that seemed only to amplify the wails of the thrashing winds outside. "Whatever you think you see, tell me."

"Me?" Gruoch raised a brow.

"You," Fiadh replied. "These are your questions, and you must ask them yourself. If you are honest and your desires strong, you will receive your answer. But first…"

Fiadh reached for a small vial on the floor beside her. She pulled the stopper and placed it gently at her side before taking a small sip of whatever was inside. As she drew her mouth away, Fiadh licked her lips as though to catch any errant drop. She breathed deeply in, once, before handing the vial to Gruoch.

"Carefully," Fiadh said as Gruoch reached to take the vial from her. "Do not spill any of it and be sure to take only the smallest of tastes upon your tongue."

Gruoch steeled herself, watching Fiadh carefully for any sign of betrayal or trick. Fiadh's face remained impassive and blank, and Gruoch forced herself to lift the drink to her own lips and taste it.

It was bitter and sweet all at once, and Gruoch felt her tongue begin to numb as soon as the liquid touched her. She blinked once as her vision clouded slightly, and she forced herself to breathe deeply as Fiadh had done as she felt her chest tighten slightly.

"It eliminates the distractions that deafen you to what is beyond the veil," Fiadh said as Gruoch handed the vial back. Once it was properly capped once again, Fiadh placed the vial upon her lap. "But too much will slow the senses so that your heart will forget to beat, and you will be lost to the painless sleep."

Gruoch forced her heavy body to take another breath.

Quickly, Fiadh darted a clever hand into the glowing embers of the fireplace and pulled out a piece of broiled wood. Gruoch winced at the sight of her fingers pinching it, yet Fiadh didn't react to the heat of the object she held. She moved brusquely and with purpose. Reaching carefully over the bowl to avoid disturbing its contents, Fiadh drew a nimble circle that enclosed the two women. Gruoch watched as the piece of charcoal left behind a grimy and dusty line and said nothing. Her work complete, Fiadh sat back across from Gruoch. With the end of her index finger, she smudged a crescent upon her brow with the dust that remained.

"What is it that you do?" Gruoch asked quietly, her eyes never leaving the black mark on Fiadh's face.

"A deed without a name," the other woman whispered back. "And now, ask what you will ask. You need only speak, and the water will answer."

"The water?"

Fiadh dropped Gruoch's gaze and looked steadily into the still contents of the bowl. Gruoch felt only a moment of hesitation before allowing her own eyes to take in the surface of the water.

"Tell me then," Gruoch said in a voice more breath than words. "Hear my speech and tell me my thoughts."

*Look into the water.*

Eimear's voice.

*Look, eldr.*

Hertha's.

*Look and see.*

It was Fiadh's voice then, echoing frantically through the channels of her mind.

And so Gruoch looked. She bent forward slightly, placing a hand on either side of the bowl.

At first, there was nothing to see but the flickering of the flames upon the stillness of the surface. Then, in a movement too subtle for Gruoch to be sure she had seen it at all, a ripple broke at the centre of the bowl. The tiny, gentle wave glided across the surface before disappearing at the rim and breaking against the clay. As Gruoch peered into the ripples, she saw her own red hair and green eyes reflected back at her. As she watched the water ripple and flow in the light of the fire, her hair faded and became cropped, and her face became wider. As Gruoch looked on, the eyes in her reflection darkened to black and a purple, swollen tongue fell from her open mouth. She felt her heart pound a tenser rhythm in her chest, yet she could not pull her eyes away as her reflection seemed to back away. She could still make no sound when she saw the necklace of ragged flesh at the base of her throat and the black shadow that began there.

When the face spoke, it was Bodhe's voice that she heard in her head.

*Daughter*, Bodhe said through her taunt and chapped lips. Beware. *Beware the lords who come from Fife. Beware the lord who lost a wife; beware the lord who'd take your life.*

"Father, please stay." Gruoch croaked, struggling to speak. Her mouth fought against her, tightening and clenching her jaw.

"You may ask, but It will not be commanded." Fiadh's rough voice sounded just as pained. "Keep your eye on the water."

Gruoch understood that to try and do anything else would be futile.

So, she watched as her own face floated further away into the black water, only to disappear within the rings of a fresh and final ripple. The water remained still a moment longer until a delicate whirl began in the centre of the surface. The swirling water began to move faster, and as Gruoch watched the spinning waves, she saw once more a familiar sight.

Her son.

He was wrapped in a blanket, and his tiny features were as they had been at his birth, and he shook his fists in the fury of all newborns, and though he opened his mouth to scream, there was no uttered sound from the water.

Instead, it rocked through Gruoch's mind. Though the shriek was piercing, Gruoch was unable to close her eyes or bring her hands to cover her ears. She remained stiff as she leaned slightly over the water, and Hertha's voice filled her head once more.

*Be bloody and resolute and laugh to scorn the power of men, for none of woman born shall harm Mac Bethad.*

Gruoch tried to lift a sluggish hand from the bowl, suddenly struck with the desire to reach into the water and pull her son out and back to her body. Again, Fiadh's voice brought her back to herself and kept her still.

"Do not take your hands from the bowl."

And so Gruoch obeyed though her heart screamed in agony as the image of her son faded from the water and from her sight. Her hands clenched themselves more tightly in their grip. Gruoch felt her body tip slightly, bringing her face ever closer to the surface of the water. As she did, she felt a sudden fresh breeze caress her cheek and assail her senses with the scent of leaves and dirt. Looking deeply into the bowl, Gruoch noticed a small, dark shape rise from the suddenly murky depths. As it rose and broke the surface, she realized it was nothing more than a small twig adorned with a single leaf.

When Gruoch heard the next voice, she did not immediately recognize it as her own.

*Be proud yet take no more care of those who fret where conspirers are. Mac Bethad shall be vanquished only when the woods move against him.*

"This cannot be," Gruoch whispered. "My heart throbs to know. Shall Malcolm then live and rule?"

*Seek no more*, her own voice rebuked.

"Tell me!"

As the roar of her voice broke through the trance and the quiet, Gruoch felt her hands lift the bowl above her head. She took in the look of abject terror on Fiadh's face before throwing down her hands and sending the bowl crashing into the stone hearth.

The flames sizzled for only a moment before they were extinguished. As the women watched, dark and thick smoke rose from the ruined logs, twisting and dancing in strong tendrils.

"What have you done," Fiadh whispered.

Gruoch rose to her feet and held out her hands. She watched as the smoke curled towards her and wrapped itself gently around her hands and wrists. There was a comforting warmth in the feel of the smoke, and Gruoch felt somewhat eased, though her heart ached with the burning of her unanswered question.

"Will Malcolm kill us all?"

The smoke continued to climb, and Gruoch closed her eyes and welcomed its embrace. When she felt it reach her face and touch her lip, she breathed it in and felt it travel through her every limb and rush beneath her flesh.

As she felt the smoke fill her mind, Gruoch gave herself over and truly allowed herself to See.

# TWENTY-SEVEN
# THE WOODS MARCH
# AGAINST HIM

Gruoch's ghosts no longer contained themselves within the shadows.

Now, as though the scrying had awoken something primal and powerful deep within her, Gruoch found her dead to be of some matter much more substantial than they had been in the recent past. When Lulach reached for her hand now, Gruoch could feel the cold of his small and delicate fingers, could make out the tiny bones there. When Hertha's eyes blazed towards her, Gruoch did not shrink, even when her foster mother's hands brushed through her long, red hair as they had done in life.

Duncan often ascended the wooden stairs, only to disappear as he entered the room where his body had been slain. He had looked at Gruoch only once, his throat adorned with a circlet of dark, dried blood. He had ignored her since.

Fiadh knew without needing to ask that Gruoch had awoken something, that she had managed to reach into the darkness and grab something tangible and real, and that this power had been torn and ripped away. That Gruoch had hidden it within herself.

Fiadh's silver eyes would tremble when the queen looked at her.

*Be still, wolf-girl,* Gruoch would say in the place between their minds, knowing that Fiadh could hear her when the girl would wince and recoil. *It is not yet your time to be so afraid.*

Malcolm had refused Mac Bethad's offer of peace.

Rumours had reached Crown Hill even before the official news had arrived by rider. Although Mac Bethad had made good on his promise to extend a truce to Duncan's eldest son, which would have seen Moray remain a loyal yet independent ally of Alba, Malcolm had refused. Either through intimidation or a convincing show of nationalism, he had managed to convince those who had been so distraught at his supposed involvement in Duncan's death to put aside their horror and rage and gather instead under a conquering banner. The holes in his soldiers' ranks had been filled with the arrival of hired Hibernians, who remembered their utter defeat and destruction at Mac Bethad's hands and were eager to achieve vengeance.

It seemed to Gruoch as though the promise of blood split was ever a sufficient motivator for men who claimed at broken hearts, as though any insult could be forgotten in the possibility of glory. If Malcolm had indeed succeeded in convincing his followers that Mac Bethad was somehow responsible for Duncan's death, as Gruoch assumed he must have done, then it would be a mighty rallying cry as they marched north to retake Moray from the so-called tyrannous grip of a king-killer.

It would take at least a fortnight for Malcolm and his armies to march to Inverness, and the inhabitants of the Hill knew there was little time to waste. Alane had been busy seeing to the stores of food and supplies kept within the walls of the keep, and Angus had overseen the significant wave of farmers and tenants who had left behind their homes and settlements to seek shelter.

Mac Bethad welcomed any who arrived.

"Crown Hill is theirs," he would say to any who grumbled and questioned the wisdom of letting in so many more mouths to feed before what could be a lengthy siege. "Moray is theirs. What is there to protect or fight for if not them?"

Gruoch watched it all, ever aware of Fiadh's constant supervision. Still, there was little that could surprise or catch her unaware. Gruoch was attuned to the very heartbeat of the Hill and every pulse of life within it. It had taken opening her eyes and ears to the world of the dead for her to truly become one of the living. Now, there was no secret that was not whispered to her and nothing that could not be relayed by a pair of dry, blue lips or a scratching, halting exhale. Her spirits kept her apprised of it all, and Gruoch no longer troubled herself with the ramifications of such an unholy communion. She knew she would be a fool to turn her back on the dead who served and protected her more loyally than anyone ever had in life.

She reminded herself of this often when Mac Bethad sought out her gaze or when he would walk by, close enough to brush her arm or for her to catch the scent of him. She raged against her body and heart when she felt them respond to his proximity, steeling her mind tighter to retain her focus. Her husband may have found his way back to his countrymen, but she was still unable to see in his face the man he had been before his cruel offer to Ross.

Gruoch could no longer afford to be the kind of woman who allowed herself to be hurt by the men who ruled over her life. The deaths of Lulach and Hertha were sharp reminders of this. Since she had no intention of joining their shades beyond the veil yet, Gruoch could not afford to trust her safety to anyone but herself.

She reminded herself of this once more when word from Ross arrived.

The woman who had approached her in the courtyard appeared like any of the other refugees who had travelled to Crown Hill in anticipation of

Malcolm's approach. She wore the rough-spun clothes of a peasant and had the worn and weathered hands of one who had spent their life toiling to survive on the harsh mountainsides of Moray. Still, her movements had been quick, and her voice clear when she had gripped Gruoch's arm suddenly as the queen had made her way through the small crowd of newcomers, offering aid or warm words of encouragement.

Gruoch showed no shock or surprise on her face as she became aware of the hand that gripped her upper arm so tightly. She knew that any show of alarm would alert the guards and soldiers who patrolled the yard and those charged with keeping her safe. The slender fingers that she spied at her sleeve belonged to another woman, and the sudden shift in Gruoch's stomach hinted at something yet to come.

Gruoch turned gently and casually, a soft smile upon her lips, and faced the woman who had reached out to her. There were deep shadows beneath the other woman's eyes, and the skin upon her cheeks was red and chapped from travel. Yet, though she appeared exhausted, there was a desperation in her gaze that Gruoch noticed immediately.

"My lady," the stranger whispered roughly, "I have been asked to deliver a message for your ears alone."

"Come," Gruoch said aloud, still smiling kindly as she motioned that the woman should walk with her. "I can provide you with the supplies you seek."

The woman followed silently and allowed herself to be shepherded to a quieter corner of the yard. When Gruoch noticed her guards look in her direction and begin to follow, she shook her head slightly. Though they frowned, the two men obeyed, staying where they were and keeping their eyes trained upon her.

"There is little time," Gruoch said as she turned her back to the guards and began to look through a small pile of tunics and shawls that had been placed by to be distributed to any of the needier arrivals. "Tell me what you have come here to say."

The woman reached out and touched one of the tunics, following Gruoch's lead.

"You have a friend who wished to warn you," she said, her voice husky from dust and thirst. "He says you must do everything in your power to escape from Crown Hill before Malcolm arrives and that your husband will never succeed in fighting off Alba's forces. Their numbers are far greater than your husband anticipates, and they only continue to swell."

"Who is this friend?" Gruoch unfolded a tunic and held it against the other woman's body as though to guess the fit.

"I did not know his name, and he did not give it. He said only that he had the blood of one innocent woman on his hands and could not stomach the thought of more."

*Ross*. Gruoch felt the prickling of certainty in her hands as her mind conjured the name.

"He marched with Prince Malcolm into my village, and most of the men joined his movement. They are saying devils have taken Mac Bethad and that he had turned his back on God. They say he slaughtered the rightful king who was a guest in his home at the time." Gruoch said nothing, knowing that the woman would say all without needing to be pressed. It was as though her message were something she needed to purge from herself, and the need to do so made her speak desperately. "They are saying God will pardon any Morayan who takes up Malcolm's cause and those who do not will be killed alongside the false king and cast into the pits of Hell."

Gruoch nodded and handed the woman the tunic she held in her hands. The newcomer took it gratefully and inhaled deeply, words spent.

Gruoch's smile tightened as she led the other woman back to the group and motioned for a servant to bring over a flagon of water. Gruoch locked eyes with the woman who had brought her the message and nodded once, swiftly.

"Make sure these travellers are well taken care of," Gruoch said to the servants who stood looking on. "They are our brothers and sisters, and they have risked much to make their way here to stand by their king."

The woman melted into the group, and Gruoch did not look back as she swept away from them and made her way back into the tower.

When Malcolm's army arrived at Crown Hill, the forest marched as well.

Gruoch heard the cries and the piercing sound of the horns as they blared out at first sight of approaching soldiers. Small wooden towers had been built behind the walls that encircled Crown Hill, allowing soldiers or guards to see over the walls and spy on approaching forces or travellers. As Malcolm's forces moved closer to the Hill, the cry was taken up, and all those who sheltered there were taken, some more strongly than others, with the paralyzing certainty of approaching danger.

Gruoch had been walking through the yard at Angus' side when the enemy was first spotted, and she faltered in her step when the shouts of alarms assailed her. Angus reached out and steadied her, gripping her firmly and gently by the elbow as she breathed deeply and steeled her nerves. When he was sure she was alright, Angus turned quickly and addressed one of the men on the raised platforms.

"How many?"

Though the question was simple, the watchman struggled with his answer. He swallowed nervously before attempting a response.

"I do not know, my lord," he said weakly.

"I do not need an exact count, man," Angus barked back. "An approximation, at least!"

"I could no sooner count the trees of the wood," the watchman shot back, his eyes growing wider as he spoke. "Though it appears as though this is what you ask of me!"

"Speak plain!" Angus' voice held no pity or patience, and Gruoch watched as his hand shot to his side and touched the hilt of his sword.

"I see riders," the man continued, his words wary. "I know foot soldiers must accompany them, and yet I have no way to assess their numbers. They have hidden themselves, my lord."

Though Gruoch knew his old injuries still plagued him, she watched as Angus stomped towards the wooden platform and gripped the ladder there before hauling himself up the rungs and joining the guards there. The watchman who had been addressed stepped back and lowered his head in shame as his commanding officer took his place on the platform and looked out over the wall and towards the approaching army.

Angus looked on for a moment before turning harshly to the watchmen at his side and growling out an order Gruoch could not make out. The one who had spoken to them descended quickly from the platform and ran towards one of the soldiers' barracks nearby.

Angus followed though he was not able to do so as quickly. When he reached the bottom of the ladder, Gruoch approached him quickly, and her movements were hastened by the look of concern on her friend's face.

"What is it?" Gruoch observed Angus as he spat out a desperate and angry bark of laughter.

"The sly bastard has hidden his men," he said bitterly. "They have caught down branches or boughs from the forest and are having them carried before the first ranks. Though the line is wide, there is no way to tell how deep the army swells."

"Mac Bethad needs to be told." Angus nodded at her words. "Aye," he affirmed, "he does. And you need to make yourself scarce. The men will ride out to meet them to avoid a siege. With so many coming to seek shelter here, we haven't the resources to survive more than a few weeks, assuming the enemy does not simply take the Hill before starvation is a concern."

"I thought us safe here," Gruoch questioned.

"Safer than most," Angus said gruffly, "But Crown Hill was nay built with the intention of defending itself against Albian troops." He paused momentarily and seemed to remember to whom he was speaking. "You should be in the Tower with the other women."

"Angus," Gruoch called out as he turned to hurry away, "Can we win?"

Angus did not turn back as he marched quickly towards the barracks, his only answer a sharp and direct movement of his arm in the direction of the tower.

The yard was suddenly thrumming with violent and frantic energy, and though the dismissal was hard to stomach, Gruoch knew that Angus was right. Horses were being brought out, and weapons were being distributed and thrown into the hands of crowding soldiers, and Gruoch risked being crushed by the throng if she did not move from the place. She rushed towards the Tower's main doors, where Alane waited impatiently for her. The older woman's face was lined with worry and concern, and she let out a tense breath as she spied Gruoch approaching.

"There you are!" Alane shouted over the din of hooves and feet. "I had lost sight of you when the alarm was raised."

"I was with Angus," Gruoch offered, the words sounding pathetic as she heard them.

"Your husband was looking for you," Alane continued as the two made their way into the tower. "Did you see him as well?"

Gruoch shook her head and felt angry with herself at the twisting of her heart. Mac Bethad had sought her out, knowing he might be killed, wanting to see or speak with her one final time. What would it do to her mind if his body were broken on the field of battle?

What would it do to her heart?

Malcolm would never allow her to live. Gruoch knew too much, and she was sure she was just as suspect in Duncan's death as her husband was. She was certain that Malcolm could orchestrate some way to be rid of her, and Gruoch was just as sure that she would do everything within her power to rob him of the satisfaction.

She had heeded Ross' warning. She would not be trapped again in a snare of Malcolm's making.

*More than Ross' warning*, Hertha's voice reminded Gruoch, whispering from the shadowy place in her mind. *You know well the danger the forest poses. The woods march against him.*

Mac Bethad would lose, and Gruoch would be left once more to the mercy of a cruel man.

"I did not see him," Gruoch said to Alane, who had looked upon Gruoch's silent dialogue with a look of distant fear as though she struggled to understand whatever quiet thoughts could possibly keep the queen from providing her with a quicker answer. "I will watch from my window."

"Of course," Alane replied as the two made their way to the staircase and began to ascend the steps.

"Alane," Gruoch said sharply, "I do not require your assistance. Surely there are men who will need healing or assistance in the hours to come, and your talents will be most welcomed." Alane slowed at these words, and Gruoch continued to make her way steadily to the next floor and did not turn back as she called out a final instruction to Alane.

"Send Fiadh to my room. Now."

Gruoch heard the older woman scurry away to do as she was asked and closed her eyes, taken for a moment in the grip of a pain that nearly took her breath away. There would be no way to thank Alane properly for all she had done, no final embrace or words of friendship.

If Gruoch was seen again by anyone at Crown Hill, it would only be a ghost they saw.

# TWENTY-EIGHT
# THE QUEEN
# IS DEAD

"You summoned me?"

Fiadh did not bother to knock as she made her way into Gruoch's room, closing the door quickly behind her as she entered. Gruoch turned from the window where she stood, gazing out towards the battlefield. Malcolm's forces had halted less than a kilometre from Crown Hill and lay in wait for Mac Bethad and his men to join them in the field. There was a stagnant stillness in the evening air, as though the very world around them had grown thirsty for the taste of men's blood and was eager to gorge itself on the feast to come.

As Fiadh entered, Gruoch motioned to the two wine goblets that sat on her table. Gruoch lifted the cup nearest her and took a sip of her drink, allowing the liquid to wash away some of the thickness that had crept into her throat. Fiadh gave a defiant toss of her head, sending her blonde hair back over her shoulder, though she accepted the silent invitation and reached for the other wine goblet.

"I have need of you," Gruoch said as Fiadh took a long swallow, "and there is little time to lose."

"You don't seem overly confident in your man's abilities," Fiadh remarked, licking away traces of the drink from her lips like a cat lapping at cream. Her voice was too casual as she posed her next thoughts to Gruoch. "Is there something you know that I should know as well?"

"Has the world grown silent to you, Fiadh?" Gruoch matched the other woman's easy tone. "Do the spirits no longer answer your questions?"

Fiadh said nothing and chose instead to cross her arms tightly as she waited for Gruoch to make her point. Gruoch sighed and placed her unfinished drink once more upon the table before making her way to Fiadh, coming to a standstill an arm's reach from her guest. Gently, as though handling some skittish animal, Gruoch brought her hands to rest upon each of Fiadh's shoulders. She looked deeply into the sharp eyes that looked back before testing a weak smile.

"You are the only one who knows me now," Gruoch said, honest emotion choking her voice. "You have been open with me, and you have introduced me to parts of myself that I would never have discovered. Whatever else has passed between us, you are my friend, and I do not wish you to come to harm."

Fiadh lifted one pale eyebrow quizzically as she took in Gruoch's words, sifting through them as though to find some concealed lie amongst the kindness and consideration. As Fiadh cast a pointed look towards the hands that still lay on her shoulders, Gruoch lifted them away and clasped them together instead in a tight fist at her stomach.

"One successful look into the scrying bowl does not make you a Seer, my queen," Fiadh said as her delicate chin rose somewhat higher at her words. "What makes you think there is any danger from which I require your protection? What help can you hope to offer me against the bite of Malcolm's blade?"

"A little bit of feminine trickery," Gruoch replied, turning from Fiadh and walking towards her bed, where she had lain out a beautiful woven tunic of soft wool. A warm mantle dyed with saffron lay at its side.

"Clothes?" Fiadh snorted the word derisively though she stepped closer to Gruoch as though to inspect the piece. "You think the Albians will hesitate to run us through if it should mean destroying your beautiful tunic?"

"I do not believe that Malcolm means to kill me," Gruoch said, ignoring the bite in Fiadh's voice. "I am still his kinswoman and his father's niece. I will likely be granted some protection, though I cannot say as much for any woman or lady's maid Malcolm's soldiers come across."

"Speak plainly."

"If you wear my clothes," Gruoch explained, "They will think you some noblewoman and are less likely to hurt you for fear of offending some great house or potential ally. However, dressed as you are, you will likely be treated as any other spoil of the coming battle."

Fiadh reached out and fingered the tunic gently. She carefully considered Gruoch's words as she looked over the garment and spoke without turning away.

"You are sure then," she said, "That we will lose?"

"I will not take the chance," Gruoch replied honestly.

Fiadh was silent a moment longer before she finally nodded to Gruoch, who lifted the tunic from her bed. Fiadh removed her simple tunic before reaching out for the one Gruoch held. The latter handed it over quickly, helping Fiadh slide it down over her head and smoothing the sleeves. Gruoch bent to pick up Fiadh's discarded tunic and balled it into her hands.

"I did not think you cared," Fiadh said in the stillness of the chamber. "I thought you hated me."

Gruoch said nothing, choosing instead to hold her peace. Fiadh smoothed down the front of her borrowed tunic and then ran a hand over her hair, smoothing away a few pieces that had been mussed when she had pulled it on. Fiadh blinked heavily as she looked around the room, and she squinted at Gruoch as though the other woman had become harder to see.

Still, Gruoch said nothing.

"What have you given me," Fiadh whispered as her knees buckled, and she reached to catch herself on the edge of the bed.

Gruoch kept her silence as she watched Fiadh stumble and remained still as the silver wolf-girl collapsed unto the floor at her feet. The queen remained this way as she watched Fiadh's chest rise and fall gently with the pace of her breath, observing the way the eyelids fluttered slightly before coming to a close. The eyes did not move behind their lids, and save for her steady breathing, Fiadh was still.

Gruoch had dosed her heavily and knew that Fiadh would remain asleep for hours. Eimear's tinctures were effective and reliable, and Gruoch would need the next few hours to put the final stages of her plan into motion.

First, she peeled away her own tunic and hose and hid both beneath her pillow. Gruoch shook out Fiadh's tunic, which she still held balled in her hands, and pulled the garment over her head, pleased at the added wrinkles in the fabric. She knelt at Fiadh's side and lifted the hem of the tunic enough to catch the waistband of the girl's hose and pulled it away, peeling the leggings down and free. She moved steadily, and her heart beat out the rhythm of a battle within her chest, pushing her forward and steeling her resolve. She pulled Fiadh's leggings, still warm from their owner's flesh, unto her own legs.

Satisfied with the fit and appearance of her borrowed clothes, Gruoch turned quickly towards the fireplace, where the charred wood from the previous night's fire remained. She reached for the ashen log, crumbling pieces between her fingers and into her palms. She ran her hands down her tunic, effectively soiling the sides of it in an effort to conceal the still considerable quality of the material. Next, she brought her fingers to her face, smudging her cheeks and chin slightly before wiping the worst of it away on the backs of her hands. She could only hope she appeared as a servant might, one who looked lowly and unimportant enough to avoid detection.

She reached once more into the hearth and sullied her hands afresh before running her fingers and palms through and over her long auburn hair. She twisted the strands and snarled them, darkening her hair past what she hoped was any recognizable shade. She rose and made her way to her small chest, finding there the small silver knife that Fiadh herself had once gifted her the night of Banquo's murder. She held the blade in her right hand and slowly held out a lock of hair in her left. Gruoch took a long and shaky breath before bringing the edge of the blade to her hair and cutting it free. When she released it, the strip of shorn hair fell just below her chin, and Gruoch opened her hand, watching as a piece nearly as long as her forearm glided gently to the floor.

Having found her resolve with the first piece, Gruoch made short work of the rest of her hair, cutting it to a jagged length no fashionable woman would wear. She ran her dirty hands through what was left of her mane one more time before taking in Fiadh's prostrate body, which still lay where she had fallen.

She moved to her fireplace and placed new logs into the hearth. Though it took her a few tries, thanks to the slight shaking of her hands, Gruoch finally managed to create a spark, and she coaxed the tiny flame, watching it kindle the wood and gather strength. Once she was sure the log was burning sufficiently, Gruoch grabbed one of her larger candles and lit it carefully. She placed it in a holder by the window and dared to take another look out onto the field of battle.

As though the flame from her candle had been the awaited spark, Gruoch watched as a line of riders and foot soldiers burst forth from the gates of Crown Hill, rushing towards the disguised lines of Malcolm's men. When the first clash of metal swam within the screams of dying men, Gruoch made her way from the window and knelt at Fiadh's side. She could only listen and wait; outside, the world chose her fate without her.

Fiadh had begun to stir before the battle was decided, and Gruoch helped her gently to her feet. Fiadh's steps were unsteady as she rose, and she held on tightly and desperately to Gruoch's arm, much like a child trying to wrestle itself from the throws of some encompassing nightmare. Gruoch knew that Fiadh would likely feel nauseated and weak from the strength of the sleeping draught, much like Duncan's guards had been as they had awoken at the end of Mac Bethad's sword, and the girl was submissive and easily handled.

Gruoch walked her patiently towards the window, cooing gentle words of encouragement as she did so. Fiadh obeyed meekly as her eyes struggled to focus, and her feet sought a surer purchase beneath her. It was easy to lead and hold her there while Gruoch watched the final waves of Mac Bethad's soldiers and riders abandon the field and retreat in the direction of Crown Hill. The sound of thunder that accompanied their movements had grown softer and weaker than the storming torrent that had followed them out to battle, hinting at how devastating the blow to their numbers had been. They were on borrowed time now, Gruoch knew. It was as Angus had said: they could not hope to survive a siege. The only choice left was to choose how one would die.

Gruoch had already decided how it would end for her.

As she watched the gates open to receive the oncoming slew of soldiers, Gruoch reached for the candle she kept close by, the one she had been keeping close by for weeks. The one she had been seen carrying as she feigned to sleepwalk through the halls of the tower.

How sad it was that the queen had shown such turmoil, they had whispered. How terrible that she had lost her strength. She had become so pitiful that few would be surprised when she chose to take her own life.

Gruoch had already encountered the smell of burning flesh and hair once in her life, and the odour had remained burned into the nightmarish recesses of her mind, accompanied by the sight of Gille's head rolling free from his body and the sound of men's bodies breaking upon the stones and hard-packed earth of the courtyard.

Still, as Fiadh's hair quickly caught the flame from the end of Gruoch's candle, as her eyes widened in fear and desperation as the fire blazed hungrily on her clothes and licked at her flesh, Gruoch felt her guilt stab like a frozen knife in her guts. She welcomed the pain in her hands when she reached out roughly to push Fiadh's shoulders, sending the girl tumbling back blindly out of the window. It seemed as though an eternity had passed as Gruoch kept her eyes locked with Fiadh's while the girl fell through open air as though through water; the world around them suddenly slow and heavy. She looked on as Fiadh's body, engulfed in flame, finally broke through the surface tension of whatever mad dream held her in Gruoch's gaze and shattered upon the ground below.

Gruoch gathered every tear, every ounce of pain, every broken dream and every bit of her bitterness as she screamed into the evening air like an animal being run through with a spear. Her voice carried through the yard and down every hall of the tower as those who heard crossed themselves with fear as though in the presence of some fiendish demon.

"The queen!" Gruoch screamed. "The queen is dead!"

# TWENTY-NINE
# YOU ARE
# NO GHOST

Those brave enough to enter her chambers would do so soon, and Gruoch knew she would have to move quickly. Her moment to act was now, and there could be no looking back. When she slipped from her rooms for the last time, the sounds of terrible cries and panicked screams drifted up from outside, where Fiadh's body lay littered upon the hard ground.

The hall was blessedly deserted, though the cries and moans of wounded men and terrified women eddied its way up the staircase, bounding along the rough stones as though upon the wings of some biting wind. Gruoch kept her head down and slumped her shoulders forward, tucking herself within the folds of her dirty tunic as much as possible while masking her face and hair with her mantle as best as she could. The first sound of footsteps on the stairs scratched its way into her ears. The rank smell of sweat and fear soon followed on the heel of a desperate servant making his way toward her abandoned chamber. He had, no doubt, been sent to the queen's room to see if anyone lingered there, to find anyone who had seen or spoken to the queen before she had launched herself to her death.

The bare-faced boy blew past Gruoch in his rush to reach the queen's quarters, and she breathed a soft sigh of relief at both the success of her disguise and her ability to melt herself away into the shadows that danced in the flickering torchlight.

Two other servants ran up the stairs and by Gruoch, neither one sparing her more than the most cursory of perfunctory glances. The threat of Malcolm's army had never been more tangible than now, with Mac Bethad's troops already cast back into shameful retreat behind the Hill's walls. It would only be a matter of time before the Albian army made its way through the walls and into the heart of Crown Hill. And just like a rat that could escape a trap when put under sufficient stress, Gruoch intended to do whatever was necessary to ensure she did not die within the tower's walls.

She would not give Malcolm the satisfaction of killing the last member of her family. Hopefully, the news of the queen's suicide and the burnt condition of Fiadh's body would convince them all that Gruoch had jumped to her death rather than beg at Malcolm's feet. They were still wailing and calling out her name, and as she descended the final steps into the Great Hall, Gruoch caught sight of Alane standing silently by the hearth where the shape of a woman's body lay hidden beneath a roughly spun blanket. The housekeeper said nothing while she stood vigil at what she believed to be Gruoch's side, stroking the linen softly as tears streamed down her cheeks, catching the spark of the firelight.

Gruoch felt her heart twist at the sight of Alane's pain and the confirmation that Alane's love and affection had been true. The fight to survive had rendered her gifted at deceit and presenting a false face to the world. Still, as she looked upon the grief and suffering etched into every line of Alane's eyes, Gruoch knew she bore witness to a visceral and sincere sadness.

*May you be safe, my friend*, Gruoch thought desperately to herself. *And may any listening spirit bear witness to my plea and watch over you, keeping you from harm.*

She watched as Hertha's hand clapped lightly unto Alane's shoulder, though the crying woman gave no sign that she felt the weight.

Keeping herself masked as well as she could with her mantle, Gruoch walked further into the hall, keeping her gaze down and making every effort to avoid detection. Most of the people gathered there were too distracted by their own fears and concerns to pay her much attention, and Gruoch could slide through the crowd easily enough. The dirt and ash on her clothes and skin repelled those she walked by, causing them to step unconsciously away from the filthy woman who slipped past.

There would be guards at the gate, her most apparent means of escape. It would be impossible to convince the guards to open them for her and allow her to leave, much less try and steal through them unawares. Gruoch risked lifting her face slightly to take in the walls surrounding Crown Hill. They were too tall for her to scale, and no doubt sentries would have been posted to patrol them. Ross had likely risked much to send her his warning, but it seemed his efforts might have been in vain. It was all well and good to know she had to escape, but Gruoch was as trapped as any other.

*Then if I am to die, I will die knowing that my end is imminent. I will not die running like some cornered beast.*

If she were destined to die at Malcolm's hands, she would look him in the eye as he ran her through. She would not blink her fear and grant him any further satisfaction. She felt a moment's pause when she remembered Fiadh and the girl's wasted death before the thought was swept away. There was no more guilt, no more fear.

Just this interminable waiting.

Gruoch did not startle when Lulach slipped his small hand into her own, and she smiled at the cool touch of the spirit's grip. She closed her eyes and pictured her son once more as he had been in life, memory and dreams crisping the blurred edges of the image. Lulach had become a memory founded upon touch and smell rather than a reliable vision. He was the sound of a laugh, the grip of tiny fingers, the smell of a baby's hair.

She smiled as she held the tiny hand and allowed herself to follow when it tugged.

"The gates!"

The yell that tore through the heavy evening air was hoarse as it was shrill, the final sounds rising into a desperate shriek. A chorus of cries and alarms carried the initial scream further into the yard until Gruoch was awash in a growing cacophony of panic and rushing feet. She opened her eyes and watched as people began to push and shove each other in a fruitless attempt to *move! Make space!* Those too weak or old to support such brusque movements were thrown to the ground and trampled.

With a strange and detached coolness, Gruoch remarked upon the sight of such terror and her own collected observance. Not so long ago, there had been a time when she too would have been frozen and imprisoned by her fear; now, she was accustomed to such horror. She had become it herself. It would no longer spur her into action.

There was a terrible and profound thudding at the gates. Gruoch turned to look in their direction and saw the wooden doors shaking as though they had been struck violently from the other side. Then, after a moment, the great sound of wood on wood was heard once more, and the gates trembled in response.

*They have a ram,* Gruoch thought in strange amazement. *And the doors will not hold.*

The men and soldiers gathered there had realized the same thing, and they rushed forward, bearing their swords before them as they stood through the steady pulse of the ram against the gates, watching the proud doors splinter and break under the constant crushing pressure.

*Move. Do not stay here.*

Hertha's warning was stern, and Gruoch felt the desire to obey, even as her body remained frozen in wretched fascination. It seemed to her that her body had been seduced by the promise of its demise and the death that it had stayed off longer than she would have ever thought possible. She saw herself as the ghost she had been, hair filthy and eyes haunted as she stalked the tower halls after Lulach and Hertha had died. Perhaps she had died then, and these moments since had been nothing more than a lucid nightmare.

Perhaps it could be good to rest.

"Come away from there," said a gruff voice as her elbow was gripped by a vice-like hand, and she was pulled back. "If you've any sense to you, you'll take to your feet and run once those gates are busted through."

Gruoch looked for the source of the voice and caught only the briefest glimpse of Angus' face as he rushed past her to join the men. Although he had not recognized her, the weathered veteran had taken a moment to warn a foolish woman to save herself, to do what she could to escape the violence that would no doubt befall her at the hands of the conquering forces. Yet Gruoch could yell out no word of thanks or friendship as she watched the old man who had been both confidant and protector, who had been as a father to her.

She hoped his death would be swift and that he would feel little pain when Death finally reached for him.

"You should do as he says," said a voice behind her and at the sound, a thrill of feeling sparked beneath her skin as though she had been licked by a flame. "You should hide."

Mac Bethad's voice was low as one hand gripped her shoulder; his sword firmly tucked in the other. "Only death awaits you if you stay out in the open."

Gruoch moved as once possessed, and she did not speak of her own volition when she opened her mouth to address him.

"Those already dead have little to fear at such times, my lord."

The body next to her became still, and Gruoch heard the sharp intake of a suspended breath.

"What did you say?"

Gruoch's body continued to move without her, and her face raised itself to take in Mac Bethad's look of utter desperation. His eyes were dry and bore no evidence of tears, yet a shadow hung behind them, a darkness that suggested whatever light had once burned there had finally been extinguished.

"I am not afraid," Gruoch said again as she looked deeply into the blue of his gaze.

"Gruoch," Mac Bethad whispered, and his fingers pushed down harder where they rested upon her shoulder, the tips digging themselves into her flesh.

"Mac Bethad," she said simply.

"I knew you could not be dead."

"I am," she affirmed as his eyebrow rose questioningly. "I am but a shadow now."

"They told me you had thrown yourself from your window." The hand on her shoulder came away and cupped her cheek at these words. Its touch was imbued with wonder like that of a child daring to touch the paper wing of a butterfly. He stroked the skin softly as though afraid the illusion might be swept away by his touch. Then, as though he could not help himself from doing so, Mac Bethad brought his forehead to her own, leaning down and into her. "I knew it was not true. I knew it *could* not be true."

"Your wife is dead," Gruoch said once more. "I am but a ghost. You should not cling so…." "If my wife is truly dead, then so am I. Let us haunt this place together."

Gruoch closed her eyes and leaned into him. "You are no ghost."

"Who am I then?" His desperate question threw her back to a night that seemed an eternity away. Gruoch brought her hand to his own, where it still rested against her cheek, where it had been when he had first posed her such a query.

"Mine," she said as her eyes swam with tears. The words were as true now as they had been the night they were wed.

"I have always been yours," he whispered in a guttural voice.

As she heard the shatter of the gates echo through the courtyard, Gruoch felt herself being pulled tightly against her husband, his arm encircling her waist. He spun her deftly so that she stood behind him, hidden by a broad shoulder. Together, they watched as the gates gave way, and Malcolm's army poured through the opening like a blade slicing through soft flesh.

There was a brief moment of shocked silence before the cries began anew, punctuated by the sound of iron, of breaking bones, and bodies hitting the dirt.

Gruoch wiped the back of her filthy hand against her eyes, wiping away the moisture. She would be dry-eyed when she faced her death. She would grant Malcolm not one tear more.

She felt Mac Bethad's indecision, his hesitation. She could feel his thoughts churn and collide as he contemplated his next move. She peered around his shoulders, watching as Albian soldiers and riders poured in through the gaping wound that had been the gates only moments before.

As the soldiers moved forward, Gruoch could not help but keep a sharp eye out for Malcolm and was disappointed when she did not spy him amongst the first wave of invaders.

"Just because you don't see him yet, do not fool yourself in thinking that Malcolm would miss the opportunity to sweep in at the final moment and take some of the glory for himself," Mac Bethad spat as though he were reading her mind. "Come. You cannot be here."

His mind set, he turned his back on the broken gates, the swell of his enemies, and the sounds of his men dying. There was no debating with him now; Gruoch felt herself being swept along, away from the gates. She risked a glance at his face and noted the tight set of his jaw and the emptiness in his gaze. She knew it killed him to walk away from the fighting, to do anything other than rush headlong into battle and stand at the sides of his men. Instead, he had chosen to bring her clear of the danger. He had chosen her.

After she had already chosen to leave him.

Here was another one of her carefully laid plans, fallen into ruins.

"There is another way, a tunnel," Mac Bethad said curtly as he led her away. "An escape route that was planned should the Hill ever successfully be taken or attacked. The Mormaer before my father had it built."

"Mac…"

"You will go through the tunnel," he continued, "and get away from here. You will keep going until you reach the woods. Then, you will hide there until it is safe, however long that may take."

Their steps were hurried yet sure as Mac Bethad guided them further into the courtyard, past the outbuildings and where the emergency shelters had been erected. They moved past where the livestock was stabled by the huts where grain and other dry crops were stored.

It was almost quiet in this far-removed corner. It was a space Gruoch had seldom explored, even in her ghostly wanderings. The ground was uneven here, the terrain broken and steepled by stone and ancient roots. Gruoch found her breath had become somewhat laboured in the effort to maintain the fierce pace Mac Bethad set over the trickier ground. Still, his hand on her back was a firm and constant pressure. It guided her ever forward, ever faster.

Gruoch walked with her hands extended to keep her balance as they rushed towards the far reaches of the wall. As they approached, her eyes roamed the small space, seeking the escape Mac Bethad had assured her was near.

"There," he said in response to her silent question. "Do you see where the rocks have been piled along the base of the wall?"

As he spoke, Gruoch spied the few large rocks that had lay not far from them. They seemed ordinary to her, which she supposed was an intentional design, and though she saw the stones to which he referred, Gruoch still saw no sign of an exit. Mac Bethad led her to the small mound where his hand finally left her back, and he fell to his knees, using his hands to pull the stones away. They tumbled slowly though his movements were rushed and furious, and the strain of the work shone in the flush of his face. Without needing to be told, Gruoch fell at his side and began pulling away at the stones that lay before them. Her fingers scrambled for purchase, and her arms ached with the effort, but a small and dark opening in the ground revealed itself after a few moments of desperate work.

Gruoch stopped pulling away the stones and took in the sight of the tunnel's entrance, its narrow mouth sending a shiver of close dread down her spine. If she forced herself, she would manage to crawl through.

Mac Bethad would never fit. It was clear that the tunnel would not permit the breadth of him, and as Gruoch took him in, she was only reaffirmed in her knowledge that Mac Bethad had not abandoned his men to save her. He had merely delayed his part. He would see her to this tunnel and ensure she escaped Crown Hill, but he had no intention of leaving it himself.

All of the things which Gruoch wished to say, words that she needed to tell him, flooded her mind and coated her tongue, which, despite everything, remained still and stuck within her dry mouth.

"The tunnel is long, and it is dark. You will need to crawl." Mac Bethad spoke with the cadence of one who had spent himself running, the words coming in halted yet hurried jumps. He did not meet her eye. "You will smell fresh air when you come to the end of it and find yourself safely enough away and close to the forest edge, as I have said."

In her silence, Gruoch reached for his hand, the fingers bloodied and raw from the rough work of pulling away the stones. Her skin was tender and bruised, but the familiar touch of him was like a calming balm, cooling her. Mac Bethad looked at the hand that now covered his own before glancing at her face.

When she finally caught sight of the deep blue of those eyes, she found that her voice had returned to her.

"What has become of us?" Gruoch's question was a whisper, and she dared speak no louder. "We could not have been meant for this."

Mac Bethad's gaze held her own as he considered her question, turning it over in his mind and mouth before giving his answer.

"It seems as though fate has spoken to us in a double sense," he said in a tone of heartbreaking simplicity. "We were so sure that we were right, so ready to believe our cause just. It is clear to me now that history will remember us differently. We will not be the ones to tell our tale."

"I have every reason to hate you for what you did," Gruoch whispered, "and I do. Yet I find myself unwilling to go and leave you to die."

"You are not leaving me to die," Mac Bethad said fiercely as he reached out a hand and gripped the back of her neck, thumb resting on her jaw as he took her in. "You are leaving so that you may live for us both."

Mac Bethad, the seasoned warrior that he was, would have been aware of his surroundings and would have been attuned to every sound or movement that could spell danger. He had survived dozens of bloodied battles and had split more enemy blood than most men ever would. His feats were legendary, and his talents were brutal.

As it had before, his love for her blinded him to danger.

"Rise, you dog. I want to look upon your face when I cleave your life from your wretched form."

They both froze at the sound of a voice, one gutted by anger and by despair. Mac Bethad rose slowly to his feet though he did not turn away from Gruoch until she had masked herself once more with her mantle and crouched ever closer to the displaced pile of rock. Her eyes shot to the newcomer as Mac Bethad remained before his wife in a vain attempt to shield her from view.

It was not Malcolm who had found them.

*Beware the lord who lost a wife; beware the lord who'd take your life.*
Macduff.

"Turn and face me," Macduff called out. There was a moment of silence in which none of the players moved until Macduff called out once more, his face a twisted grimace of rage. "Turn!"

Mac Bethad did as Macduff asked and stepped in slow, controlled movements, keeping himself at all times before Gruoch. He remained between her and the man whose life he had destroyed.

"I will not fight you, Duff," Mac Bethad called back, his voice steady. "My soul is already too charged with your blood."

"Not mine," Macduff shot back. "Not mine! My wife's! My children's! Their blood stains your hands and rots away at your soul. That is, if a demon such as you is even in possession of such a thing."

"There is little in my life that I regret as deeply as that decision made out of pride and cowardice. But I tell you now: If you approach me further, I will kill you where you stand."

"They say your wife took her own life when we beat your pathetic troops back from the field," Macduff hurled back. "I was disappointed to hear it. I looked forward to ripping her throat out and drowning you in her blood, knowing that you could not save her. I wanted you to know the pain and the dishonour of a wife's murder at your hands!"

Gruoch tore her eyes away for a moment and considered once more the tunnel that lay before her. She knew it was only due to his concentrated thirst for vengeance and some blessed circumstance that Macduff had not yet noticed it or even made to move toward them. However, she knew with just as much certainty that such luck was not meant to last indefinitely. If she were going to try and escape, she would have to move soon and quickly.

Though they did not touch, she could sense the tenseness in Mac Bethad's body and could see how his legs trembled not in fear but in desperation for her to be gone. The time was upon them, and Gruoch knew what she had to do, yet when faced with the sudden ending of it all, with the unflinching truth that when she crawled into the tunnel, she would never see Mac Bethad again, she found herself unable to make the first move.

"Fight me!" Macduff's cry was as anguished as ever, and he took a wretched step towards Mac Bethad, even as one knee seemed to buckle as he did. "Fight me or yield! Either way, I will take your life and appease my wife's ghost by condemning your spirit to the pits of Hell!"

"Curse your words and curse your anger," Mac Bethad said in a calm tone that did not seem to match the ferocity of his words. "I do not wish to fight with you, but I will kill you where you stand if you do not retreat from this place and run back to your master's heel."

It was the calmness, Gruoch thought later, that betrayed Mac Bethad. His refusal to rush at Macduff and end it without the need for talk or threats. He was delaying what both men knew was bound to happen, acting as though he were trying to buy time.

It was at that moment that Macduff finally looked at Gruoch. Perhaps her disguise would have been sufficient enough to fool Macduff into believing she was a mere servant hiding from the fighting had Mac Bethad not betrayed them both with a sharp intake of breath and a defensive step forward. Sudden understanding shone wildly through Macduff's eyes as he realized who knelt in the dirt behind the man he had come to kill.

"So, the fiendish queen yet lives," he growled. "Truly, God has blessed me this day and set his favour upon my purpose."

"You will not live to touch her."

"I will kill you both, and the world will know you for the abhorred tyrants that you are."

He struck so quickly that Gruoch almost failed to see him move. The thundering strike of iron upon iron as Macduff's blade met Mac Bethad's struck Gruoch into movement and sent her scrambling backwards. Macduff's sword danced madly, striking twisted blows towards Mac Bethad that the latter struggled to parry and block. The lord of Fife moved as though he felt no pain or fatigue, as though he were fuelled by some deep source of manic energy that no sane or mortal man could match.

Gruoch watched as Mac Bethad struggled to control the movement of their fight, desperately manoeuvring so that he might keep himself between his wife and the man overcome with the need to destroy her. Mac Bethad struck Macduff squarely upon the upper arm, and the latter cried out in pain. The thin chain mail he wore protected the limb from being gashed open, but the sword's edge still managed to mangle Macduff's light armour.

The strike sent an unmistakable wave of pain through Macduff, whose grip on his sword loosened just enough for Mac Bethad to knock it from his hand and deliver a vicious punch to his opponent's jaw. Gruoch watched as Macduff's eyes widened in shock as the blow landed, and he shook his head dizzily as though to clear it. Then, sensing his chance, Mac Bethad tightened his grip upon the hilt of his sword, and with a scream that carried more pain and horror than Gruoch had allowed herself to consider, he pierced through the space between himself and his enemy, goring the blade into Macduff's stomach.

The other man let out a gasp as the metal ran him through, and his hands rushed to the wound when Mac Bethad pulled his blade free. The layers of thin mail and tunics could not withstand the ferocity of Mac Bethad's arm, and Macduff could only watch in chilled fascination as his hands became flooded with the dark purple and crimson that streamed despite the tight clench of his fingers. Gruoch watched as Macduff fell to his knees, still grasping at the source of all the blood in a feeble attempt to staunch it.

"I suppose I am the rarer monster," Mac Bethad exhaled as he watched Macduff fall before him. He kept his grip on his sword as he took in his fallen adversary one final time before turning on his heel and returning to Gruoch's side.

"I will not yield," he promised her as Gruoch reached out to touch the hilt of his sword. "I will not kiss the ground at Malcolm's feet. I will not do our fathers nor you the dishonour."

"Macduff's threats will not come to pass," she said suddenly, the blazing truth of her words warming her belly and setting her resolve. "I will not allow it. I will not allow history to turn you into the monster and make Malcolm the avenging saint."

"I believe you," Mac Bethad replied with a dry and humourless chuckle. It was a false sound, and though he looked at her with the same fire and intensity that had consumed her in easier times, Gruoch found that his voice could not match it. She knew that in his mind's eye, Mac Bethad already saw himself weaving his sword toward Malcolm and understood how he longed to be at the sides of his men. He had loved her as best he knew how and had afforded her this final chance at her life.

This was where her part in his story would end.

"I love you," she said. "And you are mine."

He reached for her then, and she moved willingly, their lips coming together in one desperate and final embrace that held all the painful memories of what had gone and the promise of wasted opportunity. She breathed him in, committing every sense to memory, inscribing the smell and feel of him into every beat of her heart.

She felt the spirits pulling at her shoulders then and drew back from her husband in time to watch the blade of a small dagger burst from his neck.

Mac Bethad's eyes bulged, and his tongue shot out from his gaping mouth. Blood blossomed at the corners of his mouth, and crimson spittle foamed upon his lips. Blue eyes became locked with green, and a quick movement at her wrist shared all the information that she needed. Her husband released his hold on his sword.

When Mac Bethad crumpled forward, Gruoch was ready, and Macduff's drenched face was revealed. His mouth curled into some heretical smile of false victory, and she reached for the sword her husband had dropped. As she lifted the blade and drew back her arm, Gruoch slipped the weapon from under cover of her husband's body, thrust it forward and up, and slid it back into the wound her husband had left in Macduff's torso.

Though Mac Bethad's weight was significant, Gruoch felt suddenly supported by hands pushing up against her back and hips. She heard Hertha scream as the blade found purchase within Macduff's guts and felt Fiadh's laughter ripple from her lips as she brought another hand to the hilt and twisted the iron, ripping more flesh. She heaved one final time, and Macduff fell backwards into the dust and dirt.

He did not rise again.

Gruoch managed to unclench her hand though it ached as she did, and Mac Bethad's sword fell into the blood and dust. The hands of Hertha and Fiadh and of countless other nameless souls that had held her in an impossible embrace under Macduff's assault left her, slowly peeling away in an ebbing tide of numbness. She was left alone and shaking, covered in sweat and the blood of two men.

Without help, Gruoch could not support Mac Bethad's weight, and she twisted slightly, pushing it gently to the side so that she might move from under it. She caught his head deftly in her hands as the body slid down, and Gruoch could not suppress the deep sob that tore from her lips at the sight of his face.

There was no light in those mischievous eyes now and no darkness either. They had become void of anything that belonged to Mac Bethad, emptied of any breath of his spirit.

She was the last of them now. Hertha, Lulach, Bodhe, Gille, Findlaech, Banquo, and now even Mac Bethad had moved on, leaving her behind with only herself for comfort and strength. Gruoch screwed her eyes shut and refused to allow any further noise to escape her. Her husband had died so that she might live, and she had made him a promise.

She would honour her dead.

When Gruoch finally pulled herself from the darkness of the tunnel to the stillness of a forest cloaked in night, she allowed herself to recognize the gesture for what it was.

*Rebirth.*

She was not surprised when, even in the darkness, her feet led her of their own volition to Eimear's cottage. She knew the cunning woman would be waiting for her in the darkness of her open door. Gruoch found her there, illuminated only by the faint light that filtered from the sky through the canopy of trees.

Gruoch fell to her knees at Eimear's feet.

"There must always be three," Gruoch croaked as she reached for Eimear's hand with fingers made thick and heavy with the blood of an enemy and that of a husband. "That is what you said, that there would always be three."

Eimear took Gruoch's hands in her own and helped the younger woman to her feet. Gruoch felt as her hands lifted and raised until warm breath kissed them. She looked at Eimear, still shrouded in shadow and crowned by the pale moonlight. The cunning woman nodded and pulled Gruoch into the cottage.

"You are welcome here, sister."

# THIRTY
# A WOMAN OF FATE

*I* *must tell you that most of what you know of me is a lie.*

*True, some of this fabrication is of my own doing, my blood and sweat bringing together the threads of the tapestry of my life. Nevertheless, I have allowed my deeds and my choices to become narrative and evolve into lore. It is the natural progression of any story.*

*Eimear never told me that she forgave me for the death of her foster daughter. Rather, it was accepted as an inevitable part of both our stories. We never mentioned the silver-haired wolf girl again, though her clever eyes and wicked smile follow me still through darkened corners and in my dreams. I am an old woman now, the oldest of the three, and my sisters do not know the names of Eimear or Laoise.*

*The women came when they were needed so that the circle might remain unbroken. They have supported me through these years as only sisters, mothers, or daughters can. We have been all to and for one another.*

*Malcolm took Crown Hill the day I escaped and slew most of those he found inside. Though bribed with a promise of lands and a title, Angus refused to recognize Malcolm's authority in Moray and was killed brutally for it. I have heard that Ross, the constant sufferer, was the one who ensured that Angus was appropriately buried rather than left to the elements. Moreover, Ross reminded the prince that the burly soldier had helped him bury Macduff's slain family. Macduff who, as legend would later recount, had been cut from his mother's womb. Another breeched boy and a woman who had not been as lucky as I.*

*Those who agreed to swear fealty were pardoned and taken in by Malcolm's armies, though Moray would never forget their betrayal and cowardice. Such men found no welcome in their ancestral homeland and left it to seek new lives further south.*

*As is often the case, there was no story to tell me of Alane's fate or that of the other women I had known at Crown Hill. Their lives, once extinguished, served no other purpose in the narrative of the men who held all the power. Alane had served a tyrant and a traitor; I could only hope that her death had been swift and that she had not suffered. I sometimes called out for her spirit and sought her near the ground of the keep, but if her ghost still haunted the home she had so cherished, it would not raise itself for me.*

*Facts became fluid, and stories became more important than truth. Mac Bethad became a greedy and ambitious lordling playing at kingship, and I became his wretched queen, bullying him into action with cold deeds and colder words. But, I will admit, some aspects of these depictions please me. I am glad history has not perverted me into some weak and demure victim. On the contrary, I am pleased they remember me with voices hushed in awe and spiced with reverent fear.*

*I have looked to see if the tale of Moray and the people who sought to protect her would ever become so twisted as to become merely a fictitious, romanticized version of the events in my life. Though the scrying bowl gives me no satisfactory answer, it has shown me a sea of faces that reflect pieces of my pain and learning. Girls and women by the hundreds of thousands or in such numbers that I cannot conceive, know my name and know me for what I am and what I was. See themselves in me and my story.*

*A girl.*

*A mother.*

*A queen.*

*A villain.*

*I am become myth, and such armour suits me.*

*I carry it now as I wait for the one who will come forward when she is needed and when the world must be reminded that true power lies not in brute force but in the minds and hearts of those who carry the flame and use it to nurture their spirit.*

*Mo lasair.*

*Let us go forth, and may we tell our own stories.*

# ACKNOWLEDGEMENTS

As always, thank you first and foremost to you, the person who chose to pick up this book and give it a chance. Thank you for assuming it might not be terrible and for making it this far, at least.

Another shout-out to my wine (and book) club ladies who have always cheered me on and been the best bunch of girls to get sloshed with on a Friday night and talk politics, community, and what books we love. When are we writing that collection of short (autobiographical) stories?

Thanks to Becka for once again being a rallying point for support and kind words. I appreciate your taking the time to answer my unending questions! I hope your heart and head feel better when this finally comes out.

And to one of the few real Instagram friends that I've managed to find, a big thank you to Courtnee Turner Hoyle for reading both of my stories and giving me such beautiful feedback and support. She is a wonderfully gifted storyteller; everyone should take a moment to look up her work. You won't regret it. And Courtnee, if ever you find yourself in Canada, I hope you stop by for a cup of tea.

Thank you to my wonderful friend Michelle, who knew of the first ending and fixed it. You were absolutely right.

To my maman and my dad, who always encouraged me to put myself out there and to try things, even when I was too afraid to consider doing so. Thank you for being my first fan club and support system.

And to Drew: thank you for letting me talk about plot holes and pick your brains. Maybe someday you'll even read this one ;)

# AFTERWORD

Let me begin by reminding you, gentle reader, that this is, above
and foremost, a story, and what I have tried to create is not a faithful
and factual recreation of historical events but rather an exploration of
a character whose identity has been lost to history in the wake of *that
Scottish Play*. If you are disappointed that my depiction of Gruoch
was far from strictly historical, might I suggest taking a look at Susan
Fraser King's *Lady Macbeth*, which contains a much more historically
accurate retelling of the historical figure.

I have been a lover of Shakespeare's plays, and particularly his
characters, for over two decades, and I have often wondered at one of
the most famous women in his collection.

Lady Macbeth.

I wondered at this woman who is often described as cruel, ambitious, guilty, manipulative, and, well, a bitch. It is difficult to experience Shakespeare outside of the male gaze for which it was written.
It seemed unfair to reduce such a powerful and lasting figure to a few
simple and misogynistic ideas.

Any historian would take one look at my story and have no diffi-
culty pointing out the anachronisms and blatant fabrications in regard
to the locations mentioned and used. Forres would have been home
to the historical Duncan's castle, which is situated in Moray. Also,
Crown Hill, Mac Bethad's castle in Inverness, was not built until 1057
before being replaced by a stone fortress. I allowed myself to play fast
and loose with the history and locations in order for this story to be

better formatted as a novel and not an exhaustive and factual piece of non-fiction.

One of the more considerable liberties I have taken is with the geography and political division of 11th-century Scotland. While the area was divided along clan lines into six regions, each governed by a mormaer or petty king, I chose instead to simplify the notion into two kingdoms, Moray and Alba. Shakespeare has already proven that taking away certain details can make the central conflict all the more heartbreaking. Was it necessary to explore the complex and challenging regional aspects of the area at the time, or was it more important to establish a nationalistic conflict between two warring powers, one in dominion over the other? The central question and conflict at play in my story are that of identity, loyalty, and perspective. *The Tragedy of Macbeth* has already shown how effective a simple duality can be: honour or dishonour? Ambition or subservience? Life or death? Better, I thought, to simplify things at the risk of insulting historians to concentrate instead on the human conflict at the core of the story.

To me, it seemed infinitely more interesting to ponder *why* Gruoch was so insistent upon Duncan's death and Macbeth's kingship. Did she simply desire power and a crown for herself? To what avail? For a creator of such complex and rich characters, Shakespeare had let me down here. Though Lady Macbeth is granted a certain character development and arc when she demonstrates her guilt while sleep-walking and when it is suggested that she took her own life, it seems too neat and tidy to be satisfactory. It seemed like Shakespeare was being too obvious and pointed with his message of ***follow the natural order of things and be loyal first and foremost to God and Country, or bad things will happen to you as they should and as you deserve.*** *Macbeth* is far and away one of my favourite plays to experience and teach, and I am always pleased when a student questions me about the characters' motivations. Macbeth himself says that there is no reason to kill Duncan as he is a good and just king, his guest, and his kinsman.

Thanks to the tireless work of historians and academics, we know that Duncan was not exactly the wise and benevolent king he was made out to be by the Bard. We also know that the historical Macbeth was a competent and beloved ruler who led his people successfully for over a decade.

All this to say, please do not "@ me" as the kids say, regarding anachronisms or historical inaccuracies in this novel. It is not a history book or an exploration of fact. It is imagination, and it is fan fiction at its very heart. The map at the very beginning is the first of many creative liberties taken in this story.

Novels are not successful mediums for stories if they do not follow certain formulas or build themselves upon certain blocks. I was beyond lucky to participate in a Zoom call in the summer of 2021 with Sofia Segovia, the incredible author of *The Murmur of Bees, Tears of Amber,* and other incredible novels. She clued me to this very important idea as she discussed her own liberties taken with the history of characters that appeared in her retelling of a family desperately trying to survive World War II in Prussia and Germany.

Still, I did conduct quite a bit of research into the historical figures of Gruoch, Mac Bethad, and Gille in order to adorn my story with facts and historical accoutrements that I felt only served to make my own story richer. Sometimes, the best things come from real life, and who am I to turn my nose up at the fact that Mac Bethad killed Gruoch's first husband or that he seemed to genuinely care and love her?

Sadly, there is very little information other than lineage to be found about Gruoch herself, as is the case for many infamous women of history. They serve as accessories in the glory and tales of men. Again, as Sofia so eloquently put it during that memorable call, women rule during times of peace and history only cares for war.

So, to wrap up this apology/rant/explanation, I hope you found in Gruoch something that you could relate to, something that spoke to you regardless of gender identity or societal expectation. We have all been loved, wronged, wounded, and hungry for justice or balance in our lives. Yet these feelings do not define us so much as the constant digging in of our heels, the frantic pulling up of ourselves, the desperate kicking to remain afloat. Gruoch played a game, and she played it well, but she was, above all things, a woman who struggled to make sense of a life that afforded her few choices.

May we all keep treading water a little longer. The shore is in sight.


All my love,
Christine

# ABOUT THE AUTHOR

Christine has been obsessed with stories, particularly myths and fantastical histories since she was a child. As retreating into fantasy and make-believe has remained a perfectly legitimate coping mechanism as she journeyed into adulthood, she figured she might as well share some of her better imaginings with the world. She lives in Southwestern Ontario with her family, who has thus far been patient with her escape into the world of her stories.

Mostly.

# ALSO BY C.H. FOLAN
## WRITTEN AS "CHRISTINE FOLAN"

*"The spirits in Christine Folan's novel are certainly hair-raising, but her stark, unflinching portrait of family members becoming completely unrecognizable to one another is the most frightening thing of all." - Michelle Hogmire, book review editor*

There are things that wait in the dark. The century-old farmhouse was meant to be a haven for Anna Pall and her daughters, seventeen-year-old Nina and ten-year-old Sam. It was meant to be a fresh start following her bitter divorce from her unfaithful husband and an opportunity for Anna to rebuild and strengthen her fractured bonds with her girls. Instead, the terrifying and violent events that occurred there ended up splashed on the pages of tabloids and newspapers, following Nina into her reclusive adulthood. Anna, Nina, and Sam are subject to the darkness in their new home, one that feeds on the pain and fears provided by the Pall women. The shades that hide in this darkness will test the delicate fragments of the family's sanity and leave at least one body in its wake.

# IF YOU ENJOYED THIS BOOK…

**Please consider leaving a rating or review if you can. They mean so much to indie authors and go a long way in helping new readers find our work.**

## But mostly, thank YOU for your support!

**Come hang out with me on social media**
Instagram: @c.h.folanbooks
Tiktok: @c.h.folanbooks

**Find the unofficial "The Queen is Dead" playlist on Spotify.**
https://tinyurl.com/The-Queen-Is-Dead-Spotify